FIRSTBORN

By

Bruce Tiven

PublishAmerica
Baltimore

First printing

ISBN: 1-59286-489-9
PUBLISHED BY
PUBLISHAMERICA BOOK PUBLISHERS
www.publishamerica.com
Baltimore

Printed in the United States of America

Dedication

This book is dedicated to my wife, who didn't laugh at me when I said I was going to sit down and write it. It represents thousands of hours of work, many of which would have otherwise been spent with her.

Acknowledgement

I would like to thank some of the people who, knowingly or unknowingly, helped me to persevere in my effort to get this book published. My wife, Mary, my children, Hillary, Sara, Josh, and Ben, whose enthusiasm provided the initial springboard. Annie Evola, Judi Gorman, Ron McGory, Seth Malek, Joyce LeBaron, Jim Busby, and Ann Vellone who convinced me that enthusiastic response wasn't limited to family. And Ken Clark, who made me promise not to be discouraged by the onslaught of rejections and promised me that someone would eventually pay attention. A special thanks to Mary Chapman, whose editing made the story more enjoyable to read.

Chapter 1

The woman knew the time had come to give birth. There had been a gentle flushing of what seemed like water from her body, and she had begun to feel mild contractions. The man was by her side ready to help in any way.

This was new to both of them. They had seen the start of new life many times among the creatures. They had watched the lioness lay on her side and, with little effort, bear three little cubs. Some of the creatures had birthed standing. All the newborns had been covered in what appeared to be some type of coating. They were prepared with warm water. She felt the contractions growing more powerful, but there was only the mildest discomfort. She decided to lay down, it seemed more comfortable.

It had taken nine cycles of the moon. Now they knew. Time had varied so much among the creatures.

The strength of the contractions grew, but she felt nothing that she would consider to be pain. And then she could feel the child moving from her womb, through the birth canal. Another contraction and another and the child was out. The man gently scooped up the little life and brought it to the arms of its mother. The child didn't make a sound, but it was alert, looking into the eyes of the woman. She looked the child over carefully, a beautiful little boy. Both the man and the woman smiled. Their first child and he was perfect.

Chapter 2

The boardroom of Comtec International was perhaps one of the most elegant rooms of its kind in the world. Everything was the best money could buy. The décor was deep mahogany and rich Italian leather, completely in contrast to the "glitziness" of everything else about the company.

Comtec International was a leader in the communications industry, specializing in the design of hardware that could keep up with the never ending new demands being made. People needed to communicate faster and clearer. No matter how fast it could be done today, tomorrow it needed to be faster. Comtec was a primary provider of communications satellites, and last year they had grossed over seven billion dollars.

The President and Chairman of the Board of Comtec was Adam Adamson. He was an unusual man, to say the least. He had come to Comtec only eight years earlier. He had an impressive resume that indicated that he, at one time or another, had headed up no fewer than five major corporations. Interestingly, he never stayed more than five to seven years at any of them. More interesting than that was what he seemed to accomplish at each of his previous positions. The statistics were quite remarkable. Each time he came to a corporation his entry was as the president and chairman of the board. Not one of his past positions listed on his resume showed a lower entry level. Without fail every corporation he went to work for prospered beyond their wildest expectations. And each time he left, it seemed to be simply due to a desire on his part to move on to something else.

Now, Adam Adamson sat in this boardroom rich with mahogany and leather. The boardroom table was over thirty feet long. Its top was black polished marble, over two inches thick. Around the table sat twenty-four men and women who made up the management of Comtec. They were all capable and hard working people dedicated to their jobs. Some had been with Comtec before this new president, some were hired after his arrival. All were in awe of him.

He was obviously brilliant. He seemed to reason on matters at lightening speed, but he was not intolerant of everyone else taking longer to reach the same conclusions. He had made changes in the way the company was run. He encouraged everyone to use their imagination. He challenged his employees to try new things, even if there was a chance of failure. He taught them not to be afraid of failure, but to recognize it as a valuable learning tool. And he assured them that there would be no penalty for failure. There would only be a penalty for failing to try new things.

He had spent much of his first few years working with the research and development people, and almost overnight he had helped them overcome major problems that they were having in their development of new technology. Somehow things just seemed to go more smoothly when he was spending time with the engineers and scientists. He had a knack for getting more out of them than they had ever been able to produce before. He helped them reason in new directions, and in the last six years Comtec had patented several designs and technological procedures that not only put them at the top of the game in producing satellites, but was earning them almost a billion dollars a year in royalties from other manufacturers.

This was the weekly meeting where they would sit together and discuss various projects. Problems, solutions, successes, and failures were all discussed with no sense of fear. Everyone agreed that the typical cutthroat atmosphere of most corporations was gone almost immediately after Adam came on board. No one missed it.

As the corporate sales had gone up so had the profits. And Comtec was very quick to share the wealth. The average salaries of the management team had tripled in the last eight years, as had the average salary of the non-management employees. Benefits had improved as well. Vacations were increased, profit sharing plans were instituted that were unmatched in the industry (or in any industry for that matter). It had become a commonly repeated phrase that if you came to work for Comtec, stayed twenty years and took advantage of their profit sharing plan, you would be a millionaire even if your job was in the janitorial department. If you were management or research it only took ten years.

Of course Adam had only been there eight years, but no one at Comtec could even imagine leaving. There was not a single unhappy employee. Even Juan Hernandez considered himself the luckiest man on earth. He was discovered by Adam on a trip to New York to meet with a company they were considering as a supplier for certain electronic parts. He could close his eyes and remember the day as if it were yesterday, even though it had been almost seven years ago.

Chapter 3

He had been doing the landscaping work at Nextronic for about ten years. They had a beautiful ten-story glass building in a high tech industrial park in upstate New York. Juan Hernandez was a hard working man who took pride in what he did, and he did it well.

The Nextronic property always looked a cut above every other building in the industrial park. Not that any of them looked bad, but Nextronic always looked a little better. The grass was greener, thicker, and free of weeds. The shrubs were always perfectly trimmed. The flowers were beautiful, and there were flowers in bloom from very early spring until late fall. It was obvious to everyone that Nextronic had something extra. They had Juan Hernandez.

As the limousine pulled into the Nextronic driveway, Adam could not help but notice the landscaping. He had just started to discuss a new building project with his people back home. He intended to build what would be a small campus consisting of several buildings. There would be spacious park-like grounds for the employees to enjoy, and he knew that it would take a landscaping team to create and maintain what he had in mind. As he stepped out of the car at the entrance to the building he spoke quietly to the driver, asking him to find out who oversaw the landscaping. He told the driver that he would like to talk with whomever was in charge of their landscaping before he left.

His meeting with Nextronic lasted twenty minutes. His meeting with Juan lasted three hours. He had found the people at Nextronic to be all he had hoped for. They had a top quality product and were willing to offer very competitive pricing. Adam quickly recognized the quality of their product, and he let them know that they were Comtec's new supplier. For Nextronic it meant an additional ten million in sales annually. The management of Nextronic would have given Adam anything he asked for, so when he asked them to give their gardener the afternoon off they didn't hesitate. But as the limousine pulled out with Juan Hernandez in the back seat with Adam Adamson, the president and CEO of Comtec, they certainly scratched their heads.

It was a full stretch limousine that allowed Juan Hernandez to sit across from Adam. Juan remembered how surreal it all seemed, him in his dirty work clothes sitting with a man he didn't know, dressed in what Juan supposed was a suit costing several thousand dollars. He remembered thinking it was strange that the limo had pulled away from Nextronic without a word being spoken to the driver. He wondered how the man knew where to go. Of course, he also wondered where he was going and why. But what stood out in his memory the most was how this obviously wealthy man made him feel instantly comfortable.

Adam had immediately reached out his hand and he had done it with such confidence that Juan was compelled to reach out and shake it. He didn't even stop to think that his hands were dirty from the work he had been doing. He knew that this man didn't care that his hands were dirty.

"Hi. My name is Adam Adamson. What's yours?"

"Juan Hernandez."

"Nice to meet you, Mr. Hernandez. Would it be all right with you if I call you Juan?"

Juan was not used to receiving this degree of courtesy. "Sure," he replied.

"That's great. Please call me Adam." Juan nodded.

"How about a cold drink? I have water, club soda or iced tea."

At first Juan said, "No, thank you," but Adam pressed on the basis of it being a hot afternoon. Juan accepted a glass of ice water.

"Juan, I have to tell you that I am very impressed with your work at Nextronic."

Juan felt a little sense of excitement. Surely this very successful man didn't invite him for a ride in his limousine just to compliment him on his work.

"Thank you, Adam. I do enjoy my work."

"Tell me about yourself, Juan. Are you married? Do you have any children?"

For almost two hours they drove and talked. Juan found this man unusually easy to talk to. And he was sincerely interested in what Juan had to say. He sensed an intelligence in the man's thinking and reasoning that he had never seen before. He found Adam to be immensely likable.

They talked about Juan's family, his children, his hopes for his children to have much more than he ever had. His oldest son was a very bright seventh grader, and Juan hoped that one day he would go to college.

Adam told Juan a little about Comtec. He explained in a basic sense what it was that Comtec did. They developed communications satellites. Business was very good. They were about to undertake a massive building program and the end result was going to be a beautiful campus for all of the employees at Comtec. He emphasized the word beautiful and told Juan that this was where he came in — the "beautiful" part. He asked if Juan would consider moving his family out to California. He told him about the area around Comtec.

Juan considered the offer for several minutes with neither man speaking. "Of course, I will have to discuss it with my wife and children."

Adam nodded. "Of course."

"I imagine it would be expensive to move all the way across the country."

Adam smiled. Juan was no fool. "Comtec will take care of all your expenses to relocate. We'll provide the financing for any home you find that you like. You'll start as head groundskeeper at an annual salary of one hundred thousand dollars."

Juan became dizzy. His head started to spin. It reminded him of the one time as a high school student that he had gone out with some friends and gotten drunk. The spinning he had experienced then he was experiencing now. He tried desperately to keep control of himself. He wanted to laugh and yet at the same time he wanted to cry. He knew this man was not someone who was just toying with him. This man, in just a few hours, had managed to present him with a change in life he thought he could only dream of.

Juan had always been a religious man. He believed in God and prayed to God all the time. He never really expected God to answer him. He never really expected God to do something for him.

He finally looked Adam in the face, tears welling up in the corners of his eyes. As he spoke one escaped from his left eye and ran down his cheek. Juan made no effort to hide it or wipe it away.

"It would be an honor to work for you, Adam."

Adam smiled and extended his hand for a second time. Juan grabbed it with both of his.

"I was hoping you would say that, Juan. I'm very pleased."

They spoke briefly about how soon Juan could make the move. He explained his desire to give Nextronic a two-week notice. Adam respected the man even more. Juan explained that he rented an apartment so there was no concern with having to sell a house. He would lose his security deposit, but under the circumstances, who cared?

Adam took down his address and explained that he would have the company send out a check for five thousand dollars as soon as he got back. That was to cover the cost of getting his family and belongings out to the West Coast. Adam offered to have Juan's wife come out a little sooner so that one of his assistants could help her do some shopping for a house. He gave Juan one of his business cards after writing on the back of the card one of his direct lines and his home phone number. He assured Juan that it would be all right to call him at any time if he had any trouble.

As mysteriously as the driver had known where to go, he knew when to pull back into the Nextronic driveway. The limo stopped, the two men shook hands one more time. Adam spoke first, "I'll see you on the West Coast."

Juan just didn't know what to say. "Thank you" seemed so inadequate. "You certainly will, sir."

"Hey, what's this 'sir' business? It's Adam." He was smiling.

"You certainly will, Adam." Juan managed to say.

What he wanted to say was, "You certainly will, Lord." He wanted to fall to his knees and kiss the man's hand as he had seen people do with the Pope. Juan had never understood why people did that. He always thought it was ridiculous. Now suddenly he saw it all so clearly.

The limo had stopped. Juan opened the door and got out, blinking at the bright sunlight. He wondered if it had been this bright a few hours ago, or if his vision was suddenly different. He didn't really know, but he did know that he had to get home as quickly as he could.

Quite a few of the Nextronic employees had seen the limo pull back in. They had seen the gardener climb out and they were very curious as to what that was all about. They would have to wait. Tomorrow would be soon enough. The rest of this day belonged to Juan, his family and God. Juan told himself there would be a lot of thanking going on tonight.

Chapter 4

The meeting broke up shortly before lunch like it did almost every week. Everyone went off to their various responsibilities and Adam went to his office. It was only a short walk from the boardroom to the executive suite, which included a large sitting room with a beautiful custom made desk centered on the back wall of the room. An attractive woman in her middle thirties sat at the desk working diligently.

To the right of her desk was a door that led into the office of Nancy Drummond who was Adam's personal secretary. She had been the personal secretary of Edward Keaton who was the president of Comtec when Adam Adamson arrived on the scene. Sharply to the right, on the wall that ran perpendicular to the wall behind Nancy Drummond's desk, was the door that led into Adam's office. To the left of Nancy's desk was the door that led into the office of another woman who was now Edward Keaton's personal secretary. To the sharp left was the door into Edward Keaton's office. Mr. Keaton was presently the senior vice president of Comtec. He came back into his office from the meeting just a few minutes after Adam.

Most people in Edward Keaton's position would have been resentful. But then, who could begin to understand Edward Keaton's position? When he thought about it he just chuckled to himself.

He had handed over the company to Adam Adamson almost eight years ago and he had never regretted it for a minute. He believed he had made more money in the last seven years than he would have ever made if Adam hadn't appeared on the scene. It wasn't that Comtec had been doing badly. Quite the contrary, Comtec was a growing company even then. They had gone public a year earlier. They had plenty of cash, and their research and development people were on the verge of some real breakthroughs. They had several contracts in progress and it seemed that the communication age was just dawning. Edward Keaton thought he was sitting on top of the world then. He just chuckled to himself. How could he have ever known what was to happen?

Chapter 5

He could remember distinctly that it was a miserable, rainy day when his phone rang that Friday afternoon. It was his secretary. "Mr. Joshua Mitchell from Sonatec Systems."

Joshua Mitchell was the president of Sonatec. Sonatec was a huge player in the manufacture of radar and sonar systems, and they did a lot of work for the government. Josh was one of those people who often played golf with the Joint Chiefs of Staff, and he had played golf with the President of the United States twice.

Edward had met him at a very exclusive seminar for chief executives about ten years ago, and they hit it off instantly. Josh was a very fun guy given his position. He had a wicked sense of humor, but he didn't make jokes at the expense of others. He was actually quite considerate of others, which was not a common trait among highly successful executives.

Edward picked up the phone. "Hello, Josh, it's nice to hear from you."

"Hello, Ed, how's everything in sunny California?"

"Sunny." Edward would like to have said something very clever and funny, but he wasn't a quick wit and he knew it. He didn't want to sound like he was trying too hard.

"Say, Ed, I'd like to ask a rather large personal favor."

The words "large" and "personal" together in the request for a favor made Ed nervous.

"I'm always willing to listen." Edward felt that was a safe reply.

"I have a friend who is coming out to California next week and I think you may find him quite interesting. I wonder if you would take a little time to meet with him?"

Edward felt a sense of relief, this didn't seem like a difficult favor to grant. "As a favor to you I would be happy to meet with him, Josh, but tell me, what exactly am I meeting with him to discuss?"

"Ed, I know this is going to sound a little mysterious, but I think it would be best if I just ask you to trust me, and give him a little of your time."

"OK, Josh, I'll be happy to, but I must say, you really have my curiosity working overtime now. Can't you give me at least a clue as to what it's about?"

There was a small, but obvious hesitation. "Actually, Ed, I don't really know. I'm just doing a favor for someone I've come to admire and trust. He actually asked me to give you a call. His name is Adam Adamson."

"Unusual name." Edward caught himself verbalizing what he was thinking.

"Well, he's a most unusual man, but I think you'll be glad you spoke with him."

"And he's coming out next week, what day?"

"He said he would like to meet with you at about ten in the morning on Tuesday."

Edward looked at his day timer for that day, the morning was open. "Tell him I could see him at eleven." Always good to create the impression that you're busy. Let him know I'm doing him a favor, he thought.

"I'll let him know, Ed. Thanks a lot."

They talked for a few more minutes exchanging little bits about how good business was for both of them, and what they thought the future trends would be. They talked about family, and they talked about golf. No, Josh said, he hadn't played golf with the President since they talked last. And then the conversation was over. Edward figured the guy probably sold some product that he might be able to use. Well, he thought, if he has something half decent and it will seem like a favor to Josh, I'll give him a break. With that thought, Edward put the whole conversation out of his mind. Tuesday would come soon enough.

His phone rang on Tuesday morning at ten fifty-eight. Nancy Drummond, always the professional, announced that a Mr. Adamson was here for his eleven o'clock appointment. Edward hung up the phone, got up from his desk and walked out into the sitting room to greet his mystery guest.

Adam Adamson was an impressive looking man. Edward couldn't put his finger on what it was that was so impressive at the time, but later, when he thought about it, when he really analyzed it, he realized that what made the man so interesting was simply his appearance. He seemed to be perfect. Edward realized that he was not only a very attractive man, but that his dark hair was cut very neatly with every hair in place. His teeth were gleaming white and perfect. He could have been in a toothpaste commercial and they would not have had to retouch the video. His skin was lightly tanned, and he seemed very young. But then as they spoke, Edward reevaluated his age, deciding he was probably quite a bit older than he looked. He was dressed in a dark gray suit, impeccably tailored. He wore a crisp white shirt with a beautiful, patterned tie that complemented the suit perfectly. Even his shoes were so shiny that at first Edward thought they were patent leather. Adam carried a slim, expensive looking briefcase. Edward Keaton was not a small man; he stood six feet three inches and weighed about two twenty-five. He guessed Adam to be an inch or two shorter and probably twenty pounds lighter.

Edward reached out his hand as he approached his guest. "Hello, Mr. Adamson, I'm Edward Keaton. Please come on in." He motioned toward the door to his office. Adam stepped in front of him and entered, with Edward right behind him.

The office was spacious, and there was a sitting area with a small couch and two large stuffed chairs facing each other. Between them was a coffee table with a striking arrangement of fresh flowers. Nancy changed them every three days or so.

Edward motioned Adam toward a chair and they both sat facing each other. Edward looked at him for a moment trying to size him up. He found himself thinking this was no sales rep plying a product.

Edward spoke first, "Adam, can I offer you something to drink? Water, coffee?"

"Nothing, thank you."

Edward's curiosity had waited long enough. "So, Adam, I guess we have a mutual friend in Joshua Mitchell."

"Yes we do. I've known Josh for quite some time. Did a little consulting work for him about ten years ago. I really appreciated his calling you, and I very much appreciate your taking the time from your busy schedule to meet with me."

Edward almost felt guilty for pushing the meeting back an hour.

Adam continued, "Let me get right to the point, Mr. Keaton."

Edward interrupted, "Please call me Ed."

Adam went on. "All right, thank you, Ed. I have a proposition for you. The only thing I ask of you before I present it is that you give me your word that you will hear me out completely, no matter how crazy it might sound to you."

Edward nodded and held out his arms with palms outstretched as if to signal "the floor's all yours."

Adam looked him in the eyes for about ten seconds. Edward thought it to be a negotiating ploy, but what were they negotiating? Then Adam spoke softly, but confidently, "Ed, I would like to take over here at Comtec. I would like to become president and CEO."

Edward didn't know if he should laugh or throw him out, but he quickly remembered his promise to hear him out. Adam had said no matter how crazy it might have sounded and it sounded extremely crazy. Edward had promised him he would listen. He didn't promise he would remain silent throughout.

"That does sound pretty crazy, Adam."

Adam laughed softly, "I'm sure it does, but let me explain."

Over the next three hours he explained to Edward that he was already a financially secure individual. He had stopped working for the money a long time ago. As a matter of fact, he would ask no salary. He had set up a charitable foundation some years back and he would expect a percentage of the increased profits to be donated to that organization with no questions asked. He was willing to put twenty million dollars into an escrow account that could only be released by a new executive committee that would be formed. It would consist of himself as the president and CEO, Edward as the senior vice president, and a man named Philip Benson, who at that time was the vice president of Comtec.

The twenty million would be released back to Adam after the first year. If Edward and Philip Benson were not confident in Adam's leadership by that time, Adam would resign.

Adam produced a resume of corporations that he had worked for in the past twenty years, all as the president and CEO. The list was impressive. All were corporations whose market positions in their particular fields improved tremendously while Adamson was on board. Several of the names on the list were corporations that Edward knew of personally. One was a company in which he had owned stock. He remembered making a lot of money with that stock and he now realized that it was over the four-year period that Adam had been at the helm. He remembered doing so well, that at the end of the four years he sold the stock and pocketed a bundle. His recollection was that the company was still growing quite well.

Adam explained that his intention was not to eliminate Edward in any way, but that Adam could only use his talents for the best interests of Comtec if he had absolute authority. He assured Edward that he had no intention of laying people off or merging with another company.

Edward discussed the fact that there were stockholders and they would have a say in a decision like this. Comtec stock was selling on the market for about two hundred dollars a share. Adam offered to pay two hundred and fifty dollars to any stockholder who was hesitant. Edward found himself thinking about how old Adam looked, compared to his resume that went back twenty years. It didn't seem to jibe.

When Adam had laid the entire offer out for Edward's consideration it almost seemed too good to be true. It was what Edward had long come to recognize as a "win-win" situation. He would have to swallow his pride and be willing to take second chair to Adamson, but the long-term financial gain seemed irresistible. He wondered if this was some type of scam, but then he thought about the twenty million dollar escrow account. If Adamson could afford to do that, what would he need a scam for?

Within the following two weeks Edward had arranged for Adam to meet with the entire board of directors, and separately with the upper management teams. In the end, all agreed that there was no reason not to give Adam the opportunity he was asking for. Seemingly, his entire motivation was simply the challenge of seeing what he could do to improve Comtec's position in the market and to bring some money into this charitable organization that he had established years ago.

Everyone agreed that he was a very likable individual. He had the same comforting affect on everybody he met. The last challenge would be the stockholders, although Edward thought that having the entire board of directors in agreement was going to make it a lot easier.

Of course, Adam's offer of fifty dollars over the market price for each share of stock for any stockholder who wanted out would also likely be grease on the wheel of progress. Edward did not anticipate a major problem and, in fact, he didn't have one.

The stockholders listened intently to his presentation. There were some questions, mostly related to Adam's qualifications. When Edward rattled off the statistics on the last three corporations that Adam had been involved with, such as gross sales and net worth before his presence, versus gross sales and net worth and stock value increase after his tenure as president, the stockholders were in a state of euphoria. They couldn't get the motion onto the floor fast enough. There were no takers on the offer to sell the stock at fifty dollars over the market value.

The transition went more smoothly than Edward had anticipated. The more he got to know Adam, the more he was in awe of him. He recognized an intelligence that was both beyond and different from anyone he had ever met. Adam had a way of presenting information, never making you feel less intelligent because you didn't know what he knew. The man seemed to have no ego, and he was genuinely kind and concerned about everyone around him.

Edward prided himself on being a very considerate employer and his employees would have agreed. But Adam was different. Very, very different. He seemed to command some extraordinary loyalty from everyone. Perhaps it was the fact that interesting things started to happen as soon as Adam was in charge.

He had spent much of the first several months just hanging around the research team. Picking their brains, eating lunch with them, talking with them constantly. Adam was not afraid to delegate responsibility to others. He delegated, made sure the person understood what was expected of them, and then would occasionally follow up to be sure that everything was going well.

Those to whom responsibility was designated didn't feel that Adam expected more than they could do. Much of the major decision making he left up to Edward. He had commented to Edward that he was doing a great job before he came along and he was confident that he would continue to do a great job. He had increased Edward's salary by thirty percent immediately, as he had done with all of the top management.

As everything ran smoothly, Adam wandered around in research and development. Was he extracting, or, was he actually implanting information? One day Edward had lunch with one of the engineers he had hired ten years ago. He made the observation that Adam asked amazing questions. He felt that Adam wasn't so much looking for answers as he was steering the thinking of the person he was talking to. The engineer said that after a day with Adam asking him hundreds of questions he found himself thinking in directions he would never have gone before. He was amazed that in seven weeks of having Adam around, he had been able to solve two major problems in a new manufacturing process they were trying to develop. Research had been stumped for eight months.

Chapter 6

The Aegis building in downtown Los Angeles was not one of the tallest or newest buildings in the skyline, but it was beautiful, eleven stories with each floor consisting of approximately 35,000 square feet.

There were twenty-four tenants in the building, mostly law firms and architects. The International Multicultural Assistance, or IMA, occupied the tenth and eleventh floors. They were a quiet little non-profit organization. There was little ever said about them. They were never in the news, although they spent many millions of dollars each year providing financial assistance to a wide variety of organizations and individuals.

Tim Groff was the director of IMA. His common line when he would explain what he did was to say that the director is what you call the president when it's a non-profit organization. People didn't really understand, but it seemed to satisfy them.

Actually, Tim didn't discuss his employment much, because what he did was give away money and when you told people that, they tended to want to know where and how to get in line. Only his closest friends really understood what he did and they knew that their friendship required they put his employment out of their minds.

Tim had, on several occasions, explained that he could not access one cent of IMA's money for himself. They had very strict rules and they were carefully audited. There was no monkey business. To some degree what he said was true. There were strict rules — but they were Adam Adamson's rules. They were audited — but they were Adam's auditors.

The part about not accessing one cent for himself *was* absolutely true. Of course, his annual salary was more than he could spend, so it really didn't matter.

Tim Groff first met Adam when he was in the accounting department of a corporation that Adam had run fourteen years before. He was a hard worker and he was honest. He had been aware of some questionable practices within this particular company, but was afraid to bring the matter to the attention of his supervisor. He wasn't sure how many people were in on what was going on, and he had no idea who was responsible. It bothered him, yet he didn't want to lose his job.

Shortly after Adam had taken over, he made the rounds to each department and talked briefly with each employee as he always did. He eventually got around to Tim's office and just walked in one day. Tim remembered how he had poked his head in his doorway like some underling afraid to be a bother. When Tim looked up and saw him he was a little startled, and when Adam asked him if he had a few minutes to talk, he was taken aback by the immediate feeling that he could have said no, he didn't have time right then, and Adam would have said, "OK, I'll see you another time." Of course he didn't say that, he immediately said, "sure," and Adam came in and sat down.

They talked for about twenty minutes and Tim came away with the same feeling everyone always had after they talked to Adam. Tim hadn't revealed anything to him during their conversation, but he did go to him two days later, and, in the privacy of Adam's office, laid out the entire matter. They discussed who Tim suspected was involved and how he thought the matter could be handled. Of course, Tim mentioned that he hoped no one would lose their jobs. Adam assured him that he would try to not have that happen. Adam also expressed appreciation for his honesty, and the trust he showed in coming to him.

Tim remembered the one thousand-dollar bonus that was in his next paycheck. And the activity that had so troubled him just seemed to stop. No one lost their job, and Tim never noticed any attitude from anyone. However Adam had handled the matter it was obvious to Tim that his name had not come up, and he was glad.

It was a year and a half later that Adam called him and asked him to come to his office. He explained that he was forming a non-profit charitable organization and he wanted Tim to become its director.

As an accountant he had been making a little more that sixty thousand dollars a year. Adam offered him two hundred and fifty thousand dollars a year to start. He explained that Tim was going to be overseeing a large amount of cash and he had to be scrupulously honest.

Adam explained that the initial funding for the organization was coming from a donation that he himself would make. He made Tim swear that much of what he was going to tell him would never be repeated. Tim had no problem agreeing.

Adam told him that he had come into money some years earlier. He didn't go into great detail, but he did tell Tim his money was all in numbered Swiss bank accounts. Adam commented that it was one of the best things about the Swiss. He also told Tim that he actually held a Swiss citizenship.

His initial donation to this organization was going to be fifty million dollars and he would be very involved in how the money was invested. He told Tim his arrangement with the company was that in lieu of salary, fifteen percent of the increase in profits since his taking over would be donated to this new organization. The first payment was going to be due in the next several months, and was going to be an additional eleven million dollars. He intended to invest quite a bit of that money in stock in the company, as Adam was quite certain developments that were almost completed would have a major affect on the value of the stock. In the next year or so he expected to yield an additional five million.

So in short order, this new charitable organization would have at its disposal close to sixty-six million dollars, perhaps more.

That was twelve years ago. They had moved into the eleventh floor office in the Aegis building. The office was 5,000 square feet. Tim started with three file girls and two investigators.

Today IMA occupied all of the tenth and eleventh floors and they had seventy employees. They gave away between eighty and a hundred million dollars each year. At the moment their bank accounts and investment accounts totaled almost a billion dollars. Their entire capital supply was Adam Adamson's money from corporations in lieu of his salary, along with the profit from investments they made. Tim ran IMA much the way he had learned from watching Adam. Everyone was well paid, although Adam usually was consulted on pay raises. Everyone was treated like family.

One rule was that no one employed by IMA could solicit funds for anyone they were related to, or even knew, personally. On rare occasions a case involving someone who worked there was considered, and even acted on; but it had to be handled by someone other than the person who knew them.

Tim remembered the first and only time an IRS auditor came in the door. He had been hoping it would happen because IMA was run spotlessly. There was not a misappropriation of even one penny. *Everything* was done by the book.

It was a common business philosophy to always leave a little something not done perfectly so that there would be something for an IRS auditor to find. That way the IRS could justify their existence. The theory was they would stay until they found *something*, no matter how long it took, but Adam Adamson didn't care. One of his rules was everything was exactly right. Tim laughed to himself as he recalled the poor IRS auditor pouring over records for days. The days turned into weeks. When he was finally done, he thanked Tim for his hospitality and congratulated him on having the first audit in his years with IRS where he could not find a single, even minor, violation. The IRS had never been back.

Tim would meet with Adam once a month to discuss IMA. Occasionally,

Adam would give him the name of an individual or an organization to check out. That usually meant that Adam expected IMA to make a donation to that individual or organization.

IMA never made political donations to individuals or organizations. They got involved in such things as relief in disaster situations. IMA might donate money to help a city rebuild; or they might donate to individuals who lost their homes, or small businesses that suffered serious damage that weren't insured. IMA would latch onto stories about people who needed medical treatment, but couldn't afford it. Such people often received an unsolicited check in the mail from IMA. Donations were also made to dog pounds that were underfunded, or to a town to increase police services, where services lacked.

The checks always came in the mail with a brief note explaining what the money was for. Nothing was ever said to explain what IMA was. Truth was, most people who got money in the mail with no strings attached didn't care what the organization was. They were just happy to get the money. Tim was proud that in their twelve years he wasn't aware of one time that they had been taken. Their investigators were very careful and thorough.

There was a penthouse above the eleventh floor of the Aegis building where Adam lived. It was 3,000 square feet, and very luxurious. There was a separate elevator from the lobby that went directly to the penthouse. There was also a separate elevator that went from the penthouse to the eleventh floor office of IMA.

On the eleventh floor there was also an apartment were Gus Stoltz lived. Gus was Adam's personal driver.

Adam's limo was garaged under the building. When Adam traveled, Gus drove. If they flew, Gus always traveled with Adam. He was a cross between a driver and a bodyguard, although Adam had never been threatened in all the time anyone had known him.

When they flew, they rented a limo from the airport. On occasion, they went places where you couldn't get a limo, and that was all right with Adam. It actually made for some funny stories. Gus driving around in some little rental car that was all they could get. Gus was always ready to go. Rumor had it that Gus had been with Adam the longest. As far back as anyone knew Adam, Gus had been his driver. Rumor had it Adam didn't even have a driver's license.

Chapter 7

Nancy Drummond looked up just in time to catch a glimpse of Adam as he walked through the sitting room into his office. She smiled to herself. She had been happy as Edward Keaton's secretary. There was none of the funny stuff she heard about from some of her friends who worked as secretaries for other companies. They were always talking about harassment from this one or that one, but she had never dealt with anything like it. She didn't know of any other secretary in the company who had, for that matter. So when Mr. Adamson had become the new president, and asked her to work as his secretary, she had been hesitant. But in fact, eight years later, she enjoyed working for Mr. Adamson even more than she had for Mr. Keaton. He was kind and respectful, as Edward had been, but when he spoke to her it seemed like he was talking to someone he loved. Oh, she knew that he didn't have any special feelings for her, but he always had a special tone in his voice. It was just different. She thought the world of him.

Four years earlier her husband had gotten sick. They had been married for twenty years. When Adam found out that her husband's illness was serious, he met with Nancy and several of the secretarial supervisors. He arranged for other secretaries in the company to be able to cover for her at a moment's notice. He told Nancy to take whatever time she needed, whenever she needed it. She wasn't to worry, others would cover. And she wasn't to worry about her paycheck either, it would not be affected. Whatever time she needed would not come out of personal days, or sick time, or vacation time. He also told Nancy that while he didn't want to stick his nose into her personal business, he wanted her to know he and everything he had was at her disposal if she needed *anything*. He further told her if she wanted to seek other medical help he would cover the cost. If she wanted to take her husband somewhere, he would fly them wherever they needed to go. She could remember him looking into her eyes. She had felt so attached to him. She didn't think anyone had ever looked at her with such a look of understanding, as if he were able to not only read her mind, but her heart as well. He told her that all he did, his work and his accumulation of assets was for situations like this. It was to be able to do things for other people. She remembered him saying "what good does it do to have all the money in the world if you can't help other people with it?" She had wanted to throw her arms around him and never let go, but, of course, she didn't.

It was a difficult time for her emotionally. She loved her husband and she was afraid of losing him. She did feel some kind of attachment to Adam, she couldn't help herself. It wasn't that she loved him, although she *had* tried to determine how close they were in age. She couldn't put her finger on how old he was. She would have guessed that he was in his early forties, but based on his past employment history it seemed that he would be in his mid to late fifties, though that seemed impossible. If you dressed him in jeans and a sweater, she thought, he would look in his early thirties. So, it was anyone's guess.

She once called one of the girls in personnel and asked if she knew how old Adam was. She didn't. Nancy hinted around that she should take a peek in his personnel file. There wasn't one. Adam wasn't married, and no one had ever seen him with a woman, so there was talk that perhaps he was gay. But some of the employees who spent a lot of time with Adam shot that theory down because they felt that they would have picked up on it. After all, no one had seen him with a male companion either. And he certainly had never said or done anything that even hinted at being inappropriate with them. Come to think of it, Nancy couldn't recall him doing anything that could be considered inappropriate. In the eight years he had been at Comtec no one had ever seen him lose his temper. No one had ever heard him utter a single curse word. He had, on occasion, a glass of wine or two when out to dinner with some of his management team. He didn't smoke and didn't allow employees to smoke in his presence or anywhere on Comtec property. It was a well published company policy that any involvement with illegal drugs would be grounds for immediate termination of employment.

All in all, Nancy had taken about three months off during her husband's illness. It had been a long battle that lasted two years, but in the end her husband died peacefully at home. Nancy had been alone for two years and she was just getting used to it. She was glad that she enjoyed her job as much as she did. It kept her going. She never had any children. She and her husband always planned to do that later, after they had gotten established financially. By the time they felt they were at that point, they decided it was too late.

When she looked at herself in the mirror she thought that she still looked pretty good for forty-four years old. Some of her work mates had recently encouraged her to go out with them. They would say things like "why should you be alone for the rest of your life?" or "you're still a young woman." And, while she appreciated their concern and their comments about her youthful appearance, she knew that her heart wouldn't be in it. She couldn't imagine dating again, and she certainly wasn't about to start with brief meaningless sexual encounters. That wasn't her style.

She and her husband had been in love their entire marriage. She could not imagine having a physical relationship with someone she didn't love, she could not imagine ever falling in love again, so she kindly turned down the invitations to go out.

She remembered a brief conversation with Adam one day, about a year earlier. It was shortly after her first invitation to go out with some of the girls. She had mentioned to him that she had taken up reading, but that it was hard to find a decent book to read. He surprised her by making a comment about reading the Bible. There had never been any indication that he was a particularly religious person. He had no religious affiliation that she was aware of, but he had said something about the Bible being a very interesting book to read, full of wisdom and comfort. That was the entire comment, but it motivated Nancy to go out and buy a modern English Bible and start to read it at home. It had taken her a while to get used to it, but she had kept up, and a lot of it she *did* find interesting, although most of it she didn't understand. She had been reading a little bit most nights, and she was just about all the way through the Old Testament. She had already decided that if she didn't find any of it particularly comforting she would ask Adam where the comforting part was, but not until she had read the book cover to cover.

Chapter 8

It was a typical California day. The sun was bright and the sky was dark blue. The temperature hovered around the eighty-degree mark. Gus moved the limo out of the garage and over to the back of the building next to the loading dock. There was an outside faucet and drain there, and once in awhile Gus liked to wash and wax the car himself. He knew he didn't have to do it. Adam had told him a long time ago that it wasn't in his "job description." Gus remembered laughing at that. What exactly was his "job description?" He supposed it would officially be "chauffeur," but he knew that over the years he had become the person that Adam trusted the most. Perhaps "friend" would be a more accurate job description.

He was waxing the car because he enjoyed doing it. He liked to see the shiny finished product. Much of his time was spent waiting around, and most days Adam worked in the building, so Gus' responsibility consisted of driving him in and driving him home. Adam was usually in by eight in the morning and he would work until five or six.

Gus had a small space in the basement of the Comtec building that was like a mini apartment. He thought of it as his personal motel room. It gave him some place to himself while he was at Comtec.

He had a computer in the room along with numerous books. Gus was an avid reader. Mostly non-fiction. Gus had acquired a taste for learning and he didn't limit himself to any particular field. He had computer programs designed to teach, and he had used the computer to teach himself French and Japanese. He had chosen French first because he thought it was a romantic language. After he mastered French, his next choice was Japanese, because he thought that one day he could find himself in Japan with Adam, considering that Comtec dealt with several major component suppliers from Japan.

That hadn't happened yet, but today there were three top management people visiting from a Japanese firm that desired to become a supplier to Comtec. They spoke fluent English, but they had the habit of commenting briefly to one another in Japanese. It was mildly rude, but they either didn't understand it to be so, or they didn't care. Adam had arranged to have dinner with them tonight, as they were to return to Japan early tomorrow morning. The visit had gone well and they were under the impression that future orders from Comtec were imminent.

Gus brought the limo around to the front entrance at five thirty sharp, as instructed. There was a window that partitioned off the driver from the rest of the passenger compartment, but circumstances rarely merited using it. Adam and Gus often talked when they were driving alone. Adam told Gus that he wanted the window down tonight and he wanted Gus to pay careful attention to comments in Japanese spoken between the three guests. At the end of the evening Adam wanted to know exactly what was said.

As they drove in toward the city, the conversation was light. They talked about the beautiful weather and the number of golf courses in the area. They expressed regret that the length of their visit hadn't allowed them to get in a round. One of them, Adam knew him as Whey, explained that getting a tee time in Japan was like getting a dentist appointment in the U.S. It typically took about six weeks. In Japan he said, if you were sick and couldn't keep a tee time, you would sell it to someone even on a very short notice. No tee time went unfilled in Japan.

As he said this, one of the other men muttered something in Japanese to the third one and they both chuckled quietly. As the limo glided down the highway they passed a large billboard advertising a high-class strip club. There was a picture of a beautiful woman very well endowed and scantily dressed. Another brief blurb of Japanese passed between them and this time all three were involved. They didn't laugh, but they were all smiling at some inside joke. Adam acted as though he didn't even notice.

Dinner went well and the limo pulled up to the hotel just outside the airport at about eight-thirty to drop them off. They would be heading out very early in the morning for their flight home. As the limo headed for the Aegis building, Adam and Gus talked.

Adam was curious about the Japanese banter. Gus explained that the remark during the golf conversation was basically translated "this one doesn't know a putter from a driver."

Adam laughed, considering how many rounds of golf he had played over the years. The second comment was in reference to the strip club billboard. They were thinking that maybe Adam would take them there after dinner. Adam smiled. Men were the same no matter where they came from.

Adam rattled off a sentence in Japanese. He had perfect recall. Gus translated "that still leaves us an extra 12%." Adam made a note to draft a letter to Whey tomorrow to the affect that Comtec would like to buy their product … but they were about fifteen percent too high.

Adam looked at the back of Gus' head. Gus was a very large black man. His head was shaved, and it looked like it was polished to a high gloss finish.

He was the only man alive that Adam trusted enough to confide in. No one knew Adam as well as Gus. There had been others, but they were gone. Gus and Adam had been together for a long time.

Chapter 9

They pulled into the garage under the Aegis building at nine o'clock. Gus maneuvered the limo into their reserved space. It was twice as long as a typical space to accommodate the stretch. They walked up the stairs from the garage to the main lobby. As they walked they discussed the next morning's schedule and agreed on seven o'clock. In the lobby, Adam inserted his key in the control switch of the last elevator on the wall. It would take him to the penthouse. Gus pushed the button for any of the other elevators that would take him to the eleventh floor.

Gus stepped out into the corridor on the eleventh floor. The lighting was low at night. A computerized system turned off half of the corridor lights between seven in the evening and seven in the morning. Gus turned left and walked to the end of the corridor. The last door on the left was the door to his apartment. He unlocked the door and stepped in.

His apartment was very comfortable. The living room was furnished with large furniture. An oversized couch and two chairs. The room was finished in earth tones, browns, beiges, and dark greens. There was a series of shelves at one end of the room and on the shelves was stereo equipment. It was very high quality equipment with large speakers, one on each side. Gus liked to listen to music. He often chuckled at the size of the speakers because he never listened to the music very loudly. He actually preferred to listen on headphones. He was primarily a fan of jazz and classical, with a little affection for the blues.

In a corner was a desk with a computer. This was how Gus really liked to spend his spare time. There was no TV in the living room. Gus didn't watch much TV. There was one in the bedroom where he would usually watch the late news. Sometimes if there was a special on that had to do with the Bible, he would watch. Not that he was a big fan of the Bible, but his association with Adam had given him a very different view of it and he enjoyed asking Adam questions about the accuracy of the "Bible" shows that were on TV. Adam knew everything there was to know about the Bible.

Gus had eaten in the restaurant with Adam and the three Japanese men. He took a quick shower and sat down at the computer. He was working on Russian. He wasn't sure why, but he felt that Russia held out some interesting business opportunities in the future. He thought that Adam may someday make a move to Russia, and it would be helpful if he was fluent in the language. Gus and Adam had been in quite a few places together. Gus sat back in his chair and closed his eyes for a moment and thought about his first meeting with Adam.

It was in Boston, Massachusetts, in nineteen fifty-seven. Gus was twenty-four years old. He had just started working in the shipping department of a company called Avionics. They designed and manufactured airplane interiors. Toward the end of his second week of employment, Adam happened to come through the receiving area and, noticing a new employee, stopped to say hello. He introduced himself only by name and was impressed with Gus' openness. He recognized qualities in Gus that told him he could be put to better use than working in the shipping and receiving department. About three months later, Adam reappeared in the receiving area. Gus was sitting at a small desk finishing some paperwork. Adam had been getting monthly reports on Gus' progress confirming his assessment that Gus was a hard worker. Gus was surprised to see Adam again; by now he had learned that he was the president of the company. He stood up quickly, extending his hand. "Mr. Adamson, it's nice to see you."

Adam shook his hand and motioned for him to sit down. "You too, Gus, how's everything going?"

"Great thanks."

"Say, Gus, I was wondering if you would consider a job change at Avionics?"

This took Gus by surprise. "A job change?" he said, looking at Adam with a look of confusion.

"You know, Gus, we've gotten some terrific contracts in the last year and we've got big shots coming in from all over the place on a regular basis now. We've decided to invest in our own limousine to pick them up at the airport, and take them back. We're going to need a driver, and I want someone who has a good head on his shoulders and who I can trust. I think you're the man."

Gus thought for a moment. "You're sure it's not just because I'm a Negro?"

Adam smiled, "Gus we have twelve people in maintenance, five of them are 'colored.' We have nine people in our purchasing department, three of them are 'colored.' I'm talking to you first because this is an important responsibility. It's not just a shuttle service for our customers. I'm going to use the limo for my personal transportation. You would become my personal driver, which means we're going to spend a lot of time together. It will require someone I can trust, and you're my first choice."

"Why me?" Gus asked.

"I'm not sure how to answer that, Gus. I knew the first time I met you that you had potential. I just feel that I can trust you, and the more you get to know me, the more you will understand why that is so important."

Gus was taking this all in. He was surprised because after that initial brief conversation three months earlier he didn't think that Adam even knew he existed.

Adam spoke again, "Gus, your personnel file says that you're single, is that still the case?"

Gus nodded.

"Right now you're making about two hundred and ten dollars a week. This new position would represent a two hundred dollar a week increase in pay."

Gus almost fell out of his chair.

"Also, there is a small guest house behind my house that would be available for you as living quarters if you would be interested. There would be no cost to you for the guest house. Electricity and heat are included. You'll have to pay for your own phone."

Now, Gus' mind was reeling. He was being offered an immediate doubling of his pay and free housing at the same time. He was presently living in a room in his sister's house. She was married and had three kids so it was cramped. Lately there had been friction between them, because his sister really needed the room, but she didn't have the heart to kick her little brother out. Of course, his contributing to the household came in handy though.

Gus realized that he was sitting there for a long time in a daydream and Adam had stopped talking. He looked up at Adam, who had sat down on the corner of his desk.

"If I don't like it can I get this job back in shipping and receiving?"

Adam laughed out loud and then he looked down at Gus. "I knew there was something special about you. Who else, after hearing my offer, would be careful to hedge his bet like that?" As he said this, he reached out and put his hand on Gus' shoulder. "If you don't like the job, Gus, not only can you come back into shipping and receiving, but you can keep the pay increase."

How could Gus say no. "OK, Mr. Adamson, I'll give it a go."

Adam looked at him and smiled, "It's Adam, Gus."

"OK, *Adam*," Gus said, and they shook hands again.

Gus remembered going the next day with Adam to the local Cadillac dealer to order the car. He remembered the look on the salesman's face when he saw him with Adam. In those days, there probably weren't a lot of black men going into Cadillac dealerships. Not even in Boston. But they settled down with the sales manager and made all the choices that were available at the time. The car would be black of course. They decided on dark red leather interior. Yes, a window partition was available between the driver's seat and the passenger compartment. They added it in.

The car was delivered to Avionics about seven weeks later. It was beautiful. Adam had a garage built behind the building to house the limo. The garage was three cars wide and one and a half times as deep as the limo required.

There was a drain in the floor, which allowed for washing the car even in the winter. Adam explained to Gus that the car was to be washed and clean at all times. He told Gus to use any of the men from the maintenance department to take care of it. He made sure that Gus understood that washing, waxing, or cleaning the interior of the car was not part of his job description. If he chose to do it himself that was his business, but he did not have to do it. Gus thought back on the wisdom of that edict all those years ago. It enabled him to wash and wax that car and never feel bad about it. He never felt that he was doing something that was "beneath" him. He knew that he could have someone else do it any time he wanted to. Occasionally he did.

Gus moved into the "guest house" the same week the car arrived. Now, that he was going to be driving Adam to work and home again, it all made sense. The first time Gus walked into the guest house he looked around and started to laugh. It was a beautiful two-bedroom home. The living room had a large stone fireplace. A triple wide window looked out at an in-ground pool that was between the guest house and the main house. There was a twenty-foot strip of lawn between the pool and the guest house. The kitchen was large enough to accommodate a table and chairs, which were already there. Actually, the house was fully furnished, and everything was exquisite. Even down to the silverware and dishes, it was all there.

Gus remembered the first trip to the grocery store. He felt a little strange pulling into the parking lot with the limo, but he had no choice. Gus didn't own a car. He had almost always come to work on the bus. On occasion he had driven his brother-in-law's car to work, but that was only rarely, when his brother-in-law was gone for a few days out to sea. His brother-in-law worked for a shipbuilder, and would occasionally go out on sea trials for a couple of days. His sister didn't drive, so Gus would take his brother-in-law to work when he was going out and then he could use the car.

After a few weeks he mentioned to Adam that he felt funny going to the store in the limo. Three days later there was a new Chevrolet in the driveway when he got home. It was a 1957, aqua and white Belair. Gus smiled as he remembered the car. What would it be worth today? Probably ten times what it cost new, maybe more. Adam told him it was to use for anything personal, so he didn't have to take the limo. Gus was shocked to find that the car was registered in his name. Adam told him it was a little "bonus."

In 1966 Adam made a move to Digitronics Corp. in New York. Gus came with him He was now Adam's personal assistant and driver. That was his official job description. Of course, no one questioned it. Whatever Adam wanted was fine with them.

Digitronics purchased a home for Adam about eighteen miles outside of New York City. It was surprisingly similar to the house in Boston. There was also a guest house, but this time it was a converted barn. It was two stories, and absolutely beautiful. Gus thought it looked like something right out of Homes and Gardens Magazine. Little did he know that the magazine had actually done an article on the house two years earlier.

There was no pool, but there was a tennis court, and adjoining the property was a private golf course. It was at that time that Adam decided to take up golf. Gus had convinced him he needed a hobby. Gus called it a mental diversion.

Gus was now thirty-three years old, and he had been with Adam for nine years. Adam had already confided in him about many things and Gus had long understood what Adam meant when he had said, so long ago, that he needed someone he could trust. He believed everything that Adam told him, even when so much of it was unbelievable.

He listened to Adam about certain foods to stay away from and he took supplements that Adam suggested he take. He took some things that Adam gave him without asking what they were. They didn't taste bad and they didn't make him sick so he figured it couldn't do any harm. And he felt great. He was nine years older, but he didn't feel it, and he didn't think he looked it either. As a matter of fact, the last time he had gotten together with his family, which was around the holidays in 1965, they remarked about the fact that he didn't look a day older than when he moved out of the house in Boston in 1957. Maybe it was the good life.

Adam insisted that Gus accompany him to the golf course to join. Gus tried to explain that it might not be a good idea to bring a black man along to a private golf course in Westchester, New York. The Digitronics limo was a 1966 Rolls Royce stretch. It was dark blue. Adam joked that he would say that Gus was simply the chauffeur. Gus had been with Adam long enough to find that very funny, so off they went.

They pulled up to the clubhouse of the Westchester Estates Country Club. The building was impeccable. They walked in, and were told that they would need to speak to the manager of the golf club. His name was Arnold Christianson and his office was on the second floor of the building.

Arnold Christianson looked a little annoyed at Gus' presence, but he put forth an effort to be professional. He shook Adam's hand and when Adam introduced Gus as his personal assistant he shook Gus' hand as well, and he invited them both to come into his office.

Adam explained that he was the new president and CEO of Digitronics Corp., which seemed to impress Mr. Christianson. His demeanor changed. He seemed to be much more interested. Adam explained that he had never played golf, but was desirous of learning. Mr. Christianson assured him that they had a wonderful teaching pro who would be able to help him develop a solid basic foundation in the game. He also mentioned that his fees were quite reasonable.

Christianson explained that membership was awarded by committee, and that the committee met every other week. The initial membership fee was eight thousand dollars, with an annual membership fee of four thousand dollars starting the second year. Members had unlimited use of the course. There was a beautiful dining room downstairs as well as a lounge. The dining room served elegant dinners every night. Each member was required to spend a minimum of one hundred dollars per month in the dining room. He explained that the amount was billed each month whether spent or not.

Adam had nothing to gauge these costs against, so he sat quietly and took it all in. Members could have guests with them at any time. The fee for guests was thirty dollars per guest, which would also be billed to the member. No cash passed hands at the club.

Suddenly Arnold Christianson took a hushed tone as he spoke, "There are some club guidelines regarding guests who are allowed to play." He looked very secretive.

"And just what are those guidelines, Mr. Christianson?" Adam asked also in a hushed tone.

"Well, ah, perhaps we might discuss this issue at another time?" He made the slightest eye movement toward Gus.

Adam didn't want to intentionally embarrass Gus or Mr. Christianson for that matter, so he agreed that this could be discussed later. He spent about three minutes filling out the membership form, and he and Gus left the clubhouse to take a look around. Gus didn't play golf either, so they didn't really know what they were looking at, but it all looked very nice.

Two weeks later Adam received a letter from the country club. They were happy to inform him that his membership had been accepted. It was a typed letter signed by Arnold Christianson. There was a hand written PS telling him that he had spoken to the pro and he looked forward to meeting Adam at his earliest convenience. Also in the envelope was a sheet of paper that explained certain rules. Included was the need to patronize the dining room and or the lounge. There was also a sheet of paper explaining the guidelines for guests. The bottom line was that they didn't want any guests on the course whose faces weren't white. Really white. It seemed that darkly tanned probably meant Italian and they were not welcomed either. Also Mr. Christianson's name was more telltale than Adam appreciated. They didn't want Jews playing on their golf course either. Adam suspected as much when he came to the question on the application that asked about religious affiliation. Adam had answered by writing in "Christian — no particular affiliation."

So this meant that Gus couldn't play golf with him, and he didn't like that idea. He made a series of phone calls, which led to several dozen additional phone calls over the next several weeks. Nine weeks after Adam had been accepted as a member of the Westchester Estates Country Club, he was the new owner of the club. Only he and Gus and the directors of the club knew it. Even Arnold Christianson remained as the manager.

Adam's investigation had established that he was actually very good at his job. The club was well run and did well financially. The membership fee was immediately reduced by fifteen hundred dollars a year. Those members who had recently paid dues had checks cut back to them. Arnold Christianson was given a modest raise. The board of directors had their membership fees waived as long as they served on the board. All of these benefits seemed pretty good, even if it did mean a "loosening" of certain policies.

The club now accepted members based solely on their financial ability to pay for the membership. The color of their skin or their religious persuasion was no longer taken into account. Adam and Gus learned how to play golf and they actually became pretty good at it. Adam got better and better. After three years Adam was better than the pro, but he refused to enter into tournaments. He played just for fun and he preferred to play with Gus. Gus got to be a seven handicap. Adam eventually shot about eight under par on average, but only when he was playing alone with Gus. Someone told him he should be on the pro tour. Adam laughed.

Chapter 10

The boy remembered how it used to be when they lived in the beautiful place. Often in the afternoon he would go for a walk with his father. It would always be slightly breezy on those walks, and they would walk close to the river. His father would tell him to sit by the river and watch the animals quietly for a short while. He loved the animals. Some would stop and let the boy pet them. Others would lick him as they came to the river for water. He had no fear of the animals and they had no fear of him.

Watching his father walk a little further up the river, he saw him stop and talk to another man. The boy never saw where the man came from, and he never saw where he went when he and his father were done talking. And, the man looked funny. He had something on his body that covered him. It was very strange to the boy. He, his mother, and father had nothing on their bodies. What was the purpose of such covering he would wonder.

Now, he and his mother and father had something on their bodies, too. Skins from animals. When he asked why, he was told that he would understand when he got older. And they no longer lived where it was most beautiful. He watched his father work hard to make food grow from the earth so they could eat. It was very different. He never took walks with his father to the river anymore. He never saw the other man his father had spoken to.

Several years later, his father took him on a walk. It was long, and it was difficult for him because he was so little. His father would pick him up and carry him part of the way. He remembered walking with his father up a long, gently sloping field. When they got to the top of the slope his father stopped. In the distance the boy could see what appeared to be a wall of stones. On the other side of the wall, beautiful trees were visible. He recognized it. It was where they used to live. There was an opening in the wall and there were two men standing there, one on each side of the opening. They looked a lot like the man that his father used to talk to by the river, but they were bigger. Between them there seemed to be a large ball of fire that just floated by itself above the ground. Nothing around it caught fire. The two men never seemed to move a muscle in all the time they watched them. The boy was amazed at the sight, and confused that the beautiful place was so close that they could walk to it. Why didn't they go back and live there? He turned to ask his father, but the words were caught in his throat when he saw his father, who was sitting near him, crying. He walked to his father concerned, for he had never seen him cry before. His father took him in his arms and hugged him. As he cried with his lips so close to the boy's ear, he whispered softly, "Forgive me my son, please forgive me."

Chapter 11

Adam changed into sweat shorts and a tee shirt and went into the kitchen to get a large glass of ice water. Most nights, he got home earlier, around six. Elizabeth was usually there when he got home, but tonight it was already after nine. He took the water into his living room, setting the glass down on a table. The living room, like the rest of the apartment, was elegant. There was no clutter. Each piece of furniture complemented every other piece.

He sat in the chair next to the table where he had placed the water. He reached to a smaller table on the other side of the chair for the remote control. When he touched a button, classical music started to play quietly from speakers on the other side of the room.

On the table next to his water were the LA Times, the New York Times, the Wall Street Journal and the Washington Post. He would read the LA Times and the Washington Post first, because they were lighter reading. Then he would read the New York Times thoroughly, and finally, he would read the Wall Street Journal, committing the entire newspaper to memory. He usually started a little earlier, but tonight, due to the dinner with his Japanese guests, he would breeze through the two Times a little more quickly. He would be in bed by 1:30. That would give him four and a half hours sleep. Over the years he found that four and a half to five hours worked best for him. On business trips where there might be a long day here and there, he had found that a fifteen-minute "cat nap" was equivalent to two hours sleep for anyone else.

He was finished with his reading a little after 1:00. He came out of the bathroom and sat down on the edge of his bed, glancing briefly at the clock on the night table. It was 1:08. He closed his eyes and, in a low undertone, he began to pray. When he finished he looked at the clock again. It was 1:24. "Too much," he thought. It would soon be time to start thinking about a life shift. What would he do with Gus? Could he take him with him? He would have to think about it.

He and Gus had been together now for over forty years. He had confided in Gus and he trusted him with his life. He had taken Gus with him every time he made a change in his employment and Gus understood everything. He knew why Adam had to move on after so many years in one place. But a life shift was different and he didn't know if Gus could handle it. He would discuss it with him soon.

He had met Gus shortly after his last life shift, and that was almost fifty years ago. He would miss Gus terribly. If he left Gus behind he would leave him with financial resources so that Gus could do whatever he wanted for the rest of his life.

A life shift would also mean closing down IMA because he could not continue to be involved and deposit funds. Left on its own, with funds on hand, he had no way of knowing if it would continue to operate the same way. He would have to think about it. Perhaps he would talk to Tim Groff about creating an organizational charter that would ensure a steady course. He would also discuss it with his attorneys. At the moment IMA had assets in excess of a billion dollars.

Adam's net worth between deposits in several Swiss banks and properties owned throughout the world was over eighty billion dollars. He was one of the wealthiest men in the world, but with most of the money in numbered Swiss accounts his wealth was a well guarded secret. The beauty of the Swiss accounts was that everything was done with access codes. A life shift had no affect on his Swiss accounts. No new paperwork to create, no concern about identity. Only the account numbers and pin numbers mattered.

Properties that he owned were a little different. Papers had to change hands if someone with a different name was suddenly the new owner. It was a lot of work, but some of the property that Adam owned was truly priceless by today's standards. How many times had he done this? How many times had he created an entire network of new paper? Too many times to think about. New technology since his last life shift would likely make the process easier. As Adam thought about these things, he drifted off to sleep.

Chapter 12

Elizabeth was his housekeeper and cook. She would usually be there when he got home, and she would have some delectable meal ready for him. She knew what he liked and she knew that he preferred his evening meal to be light. He tended to eat a good breakfast and a good lunch, so he eased off on the dinner.

She was in her late fifties. Her husband had died almost ten years earlier. She had been a cook and housekeeper for several well-to-do families in the area, and they had all been good people, but Adam was special as far as she was concerned. She did all shopping for him, not just food. If towels were looking a little old, she bought new ones. If she dropped some dish, or felt she needed some new cooking utensil, she bought them. Adam had opened a checking account for the household, and put her name on the account. She could write her own checks. He trusted her completely. She had the little checkbook, and wondered if he realized how that made her feel. She made sure the things he liked were in the house. He was big on orange juice and he loved apples. Actually, he loved most vegetables. He would eat a plate of raw vegetables like other men would eat potato chips. He favored fish over beef, but would only eat small portions of either with a meal. He didn't keep any beer or liquor in the house, and at first she thought he might have been a recovering alcoholic. She quickly figured out that he simply didn't prefer to have it around.

He was somewhat of a neat freak. Sometimes Elizabeth would laugh at the thought of her being the "housekeeper." What was there to keep? He made his own bed, except on Mondays, when he would leave it unmade because she was going to change the sheets. If he used any dishes after she left in the early evening, he would always put them in the dishwasher. She had never seen the kitchen floor dirty. Even the bathroom somehow managed to stay clean. Sometimes she wondered if he had someone else coming in to clean up before she showed up, but she knew that wasn't the case. She would send his laundry out and put the clean laundry away when it came back. She would make sure that his dress shirts were hung in the closet, just the way he liked them. All the whites together, all the light blues, and so on.

He used one room in the penthouse as a study, and told Elizabeth he would prefer she not go into that room. He assumed responsibility for keeping it cleaned. Once, Elizabeth had poked her head into the room just to look around. Adam didn't keep the door locked, so she reasoned that it was all right to just take a peek. Two walls of the room were shelves full of books from floor to ceiling. Elizabeth thought she recognized a set of some type of encyclopedia, because there was a series of books that all looked the same. On another shelf there was another series of books that looked similar, but she noticed the last couple of books on the right looked newer, and the last few on the left looked very old. All the books in between seemed to gradually look older or newer, depending on which side you were looking from. There was a desk at one end of the room that seemed out of place. It looked to be a hundred years old, and it was quite large. In fact, to Elizabeth it looked massive. The top was like a large table, but it was thick, she guessed a foot thick. The legs were round and huge. There was a computer on the desk, and it was dwarfed by the size of the desk. There was a small elegant leather chair in the corner of the room where the bookshelves met. A smaller table was next to the chair, and on the table was a lamp. There were several books on the table, and the top one was opened upside down as if Adam had stopped reading in the middle of something, and was intending to get back to it.

She didn't look for long because she felt as though she was betraying his trust just looking in the room.

Elizabeth loved working for Adam. He was very generous with her and she appreciated it. She had several younger girl friends who were quite attractive, and she would have loved to fix him up on a date with any one of them. She mentioned it to him once in a very casual way, and he had seemed amused by her concern for his companionship. He assured her that he was not lonely, nor looking for a companion. She wondered if he might be gay, but there was no indication of that, in any way. He certainly had a manly way about him, and he was rarely seen in the company of men either. Unless he was with employees in a work related situation he was never with anyone except Gus, and Elizabeth knew for sure Gus wasn't gay. Recently, while vacuuming the apartment one morning, the elevator door from the eleventh floor IMA office to the penthouse opened and there was an attractive young woman who seemed lost. Elizabeth guessed her to be in her early forties. The young woman explained that she had spent the evening with Gus and that he had told her about the penthouse apartment where his boss lived. She was curious, so she thought she would come up and take a peek. Gus had explained that the housekeeper would be there. Elizabeth was impressed that the girl had the courage to walk into the IMA office and push the button on the elevator that was in their lobby, and she was surprised that no one in the office had stopped her. But impressed or not, she wasn't about to give this stranger a tour of Adam's apartment. She explained that she would not be able to let her off the elevator, and after a quick glance around, the woman apologized and pushed the button that would take her back to the eleventh floor.

Elizabeth shook her head at today's youth. She thought it would be best to tell Adam what had happened. Adam left hours ago, which meant Gus also had left hours ago. Gus must have left this woman in his apartment. Something about that seemed risky to Elizabeth.

Elizabeth went to the lobby every afternoon to get Adam's mail. She thought that for a man so important, he didn't get a lot of mail. It seemed he didn't have any family. Of course, there was always junk mail, but other than that he only got magazines he subscribed to. "Biblical and Archeological Review" was one she always expected, and he also had a subscription to "The Watchtower," although she didn't understand why anyone would want to read *that* magazine. She had looked at one once. She thought some of the things in that magazine were sacrilegious! The one she looked at said that the trinity was a false teaching, and that Jesus Christ was not God. That was enough for her. She had thrown the magazine away, and promised herself that she would never look at it again. But much to her dismay, Adam subscribed to the magazine. So twice each month, she would carry it up to his apartment.

Early in the afternoon Elizabeth went out to do some food shopping. She used the elevator, taking her directly to the lobby. In the lobby that elevator could only be accessed with a key, and Elizabeth had her own key. She enjoyed the three-block walk to the little market where she did food shopping. She had her little two-wheeled cart, pulling it along behind her. She stepped out onto the street, surprised by the brightness of the sun and the dark blue color of the sky. It was a beautiful day. Elizabeth turned and began to walk to the market, taking no notice of the young man watching her from across the street.

Chapter 13

Philip Dreason had been in and out of trouble his entire adult life. He was forty-seven, and he had spent seventeen years, eight months of those in a reformatory, or in prison. Everything he had ever been involved in would fall into the petty crime category. He was proud of the fact that he had never killed anyone. The cops were always keeping an eye on him, as he was an ex-con and he couldn't really afford to relocate. Besides, all his buddies were here, and they were just like him. They didn't want to work, and they had no particular skills, but they wanted to live the good life.

One of his friends, Lewis, bought a lottery ticket every week. It was the type where you had to get all five numbers right plus the special number to win millions. Lewis insisted that someday he was going to win, and then he wouldn't have to keep getting involved with all their schemes. Lewis really liked using the word "schemes." He would exaggerate it as he said it. "Oh, boy," he would say, "here comes another one of your scheeemes." He would draw it out. He had been doing it for so long that it automatically made everyone laugh. They knew he was going to say it whenever there was a new idea put on the table, and they were constantly coming up with a variety of ideas to beat people out of money.

One of the guys in Philip's group was Lester Berkman. Lester was Jewish, which was a little unusual for someone who was a petty thief and hung out with a gang of petty thieves. Lester's brother worked in a large bank in LA, and happened to mention at a family dinner one night that there was a new scam that had been discovered involving ATM machines. The way Lester's brother explained it was that someone could go to a bank and open an account with a phony ID and a phony social security number. Once they had an account with a balance of over four hundred dollars they could use their ATM card to steal money. They would go to an ATM, and request whatever the maximum amount was, say, for example, four hundred dollars. When the machine would spit out the four hundred it would be twenty $20 bills. What the person would do is reach into the middle of the money and take all the bills out of the middle leaving only one or two bills at each side. The ATM was not capable of detecting that some of the money had been taken, so the machine would think the money was untouched. After a minute or so the machine would take the money back in and electronically void the transaction. The person would get three hundred twenty dollars and it wouldn't be deducted from their account. Lester's brother said that it had the security people in the bank very concerned. Lester had a hard time sitting there and finishing dinner with the family.

He couldn't wait to get with Philip and the boys. This would be the first real great idea that he brought to the table.

They all listened to him relate the story. Even Lewis admitted it was one of the best schemes he had heard in a long time. Ken was another one of the gang, and he tended to be the detail man. When others would come up with ideas, he was the one who would consider all the details. If they still thought the plan could work, he would be the one to work it all out. They all appreciated Ken's talents. He was responsible for the success of most of their ideas.

They liked Lester's story. Ken said they would need to open a bank account in a phony name. He explained that, while the plan would probably work, all the transactions that are canceled are still going to show up on the computers in the ATM machines. Eventually someone would put it all together, and they would realize a lot of money was missing. It was important that the account number didn't lead to anyone in the group, or their families, or even their neighborhood.

Another member of the group, Todd, had the solution. He had visited a cousin at Minnesota State University six months earlier. One of the guys in his cousin's dorm looked so much like him, it was a little spooky. Even he could see the resemblance. One night he had the opportunity to sneak into his room and steal his wallet. He took two others at the same time just so it wouldn't seem too obvious that it was him. He still had all of the ID's that were in the wallet, including a driver's license from New Jersey.

He brought the license in the next day to show everyone, and they were all amazed. The picture on the license looked just like Todd. To make it even better, he had a social security card, a library card, a student ID card, and a credit card all with the same name. Everyone agreed this would work.

They had pooled together five hundred dollars. Todd went into a local bank branch and opened an account. He practiced writing the signature on the license and ID card, and he had it down pretty well. He explained to the customer service person in the bank that he had just moved out to California from New Jersey, and was looking for work. It took him fifteen minutes to open an account. He was told that the ATM card would come in the mail within the week. He gave them a post office box, explaining that he was staying with some friends. A week later, the card was in the box.

That night they took their trial run. Ken gave Todd a hat with a fairly large brim and a pair of sunglasses with lightly tinted lenses. He explained that ATMs all had cameras, and they didn't want any pictures to show Todd's face. He pressed the importance of keeping the brim low on his face. The sun glasses would cause a reflection, so there would be no good pictures of his eyes, but the lenses were light enough that he would have no trouble seeing. They reviewed the process several times. Todd approached the first ATM while everyone else waited in the car. It was close to eleven. They had already stopped at another ATM, but Ken told him to just do a "balance inquiry" at that machine. The slip showed a five hundred dollar balance. Now, Todd stood in front of the ATM, feeling a little nervous. He swiped his card and put it in his pocket. The screen read: "English or Spanish?" English. Then it read: "Please enter your PIN." Todd entered his number. Various dollar amounts appeared on the screen, four hundred being the largest. He touched it. The machine made a few noises and started a whirring sound. A slot opened and a pile of bills came halfway out. At first Todd stared at it, and then he did as they had practiced with pieces of paper. He reached in and took the bills out of the middle of the wad, leaving two on each, the top and bottom. He gently wiggled the rest out and waited. While he waited he folded what he had, putting it in his pocket. The machine didn't do anything. He looked around to check that no one was coming. Suddenly the machine started to beep. "BEEP — BEEP — BEEP." It was loud, and Todd was worried it might draw attention, but as he looked around there was still no one in sight. While the ATM was beeping, the screen flashed: "PLEASE REMOVE CASH." The machine beeped for what seemed like an hour, but was actually forty-five seconds. Then it sucked the remaining money back in. The screen read: "transaction canceled." Todd ran back to the car and jumped in and they drove away. Ken was driving, and was very careful to obey the traffic laws. He didn't want them getting caught because they did something stupid with the car.

As they drove down the street Todd pulled the money out and counted it. There was three hundred twenty dollars. It worked perfectly. They all started to laugh except Ken who said it was too soon to laugh. They all stopped laughing and he explained that they needed to stop at another ATM and check the balance in the account. They all appreciated how smart he was. They stopped a few minutes later, and Todd got out and did another balance inquiry. He grinned as he looked at the receipt, still showing a balance of five hundred dollars. While he was there, he figured he might as well give it another shot. Minutes later he was back in the car with another three hundred twenty dollars. Now they all laughed.

Ken figured that they didn't want to do the same thing at the same ATM, because that might alarm the bank too soon. They decided it would be best to make the rounds to different branches even if it meant staying up all night. By the time they called it quits that first night, they had over twelve thousand dollars. At the end of a week they had over one hundred thousand dollars, and they hadn't been to the same ATM twice. They decided they would keep up the same routine, working the ATMs each night, trying not to hit the same ones. They would go to different smaller outlying towns, sometimes two different towns in a single night. After two and a half weeks they had over two hundred and fifty thousand dollars.

At the last ATM they tried, the screen read: "INVALID CARD." Todd ran back to the car and told Ken what the screen said. Ken said the party was over. The banks had realized what was going on, and they had zeroed in on the account. They drove back to Philip's apartment, which was their central meeting place. They put the ATM card in an ashtray and lit it, watching it melt into a blob of plastic.

Lewis suddenly remembered the five hundred dollars in the bank account. How were they going to get their five hundred dollars back? Philip took the pile of money they had gotten that night and laid it on the table. He got up and left the room for a minute and came back with a cardboard box from a case of Budweiser beer. He opened the box and dumped its contents onto the table. A little over two hundred and fifty thousand dollars was on the table, except for what spilled onto the floor. The five men stared at it. They each looked at one another and realized how funny Lewis' concern over five hundred dollars was. They laughed hysterically.

What to do with the money became a more complicated problem than they had anticipated. If they had gotten ten thousand dollars, they could have each taken two thousand, and that would have been that. But split five ways the money came to almost fifty thousand a piece, and they all agreed that if any one of them suddenly had fifty thousand dollars it would draw immediate suspicion. They felt quite sure that the scheme was not going to lead back to them in any way, but it would probably hit the papers, and if it did, and they suddenly had money, even the cops could put that together.

They decided to each take a thousand dollars for now, and leave the rest in the box in Philip's apartment until they decided what to do with it. For a bunch of thieves they trusted each other pretty much, and they especially trusted Philip to hold the money. Of course, they made it a point to say that should the money somehow disappear, they would be obligated to kill Philip, but even that no one took seriously.

The money had been in Philip's apartment for almost a month when he chose to grace his family with his presence for dinner one evening. His mother tried to keep family communication open, but Philip's father had a real poor attitude toward him. His father was a hard working man who provided as best he could for his family. Philip's sister was a "good girl," his father would say. Sure, Philip thought, a thirty-eight year old single "good girl." Philip and his sister Sally got along fine, but they were different in so many ways, and lived very different lives.

She recently had gotten a job in the secretarial pool at Comtec. At dinner she talked about Comtec, and how they paid such a higher hourly wage than any other company around. She talked about Adam Adamson, and the stories surrounding him. How he was some kind of whiz in big business, and how every company he worked for made a lot more money, and how he would just up and leave one day and go to work somewhere else. There was a rumor that he also oversaw some type of charity that gives away money. She went on and on.

Philip started to pay attention when she started talking about her brief visit to Adam's penthouse. Philip's parents no longer worried about what their daughter did or who she did it with, and Sally wasn't embarrassed about spending the night with Gus, or admitting it to her parents. She told the whole story about going into the office of IMA on the eleventh floor, which was where Gus' apartment was, and just getting onto the elevator in their lobby. She talked about the housekeeper who was there, and how she wasn't allowed to get off to look around, but that the place looked pretty fancy just from what she could see.

Her parents listened with interest. To them it sounded a little adventurous. Philip listened intently. To him it sounded like an opportunity.

By the time Philip left his parent's house that night he had carefully pulled from his sister everything he thought he could without raising her suspicions. He knew that the penthouse was in the Aegis building, and that it was above the eleventh floor. Gus told Sally that there was an elevator inside the IMA offices that led to the penthouse, and that there was another elevator going directly from the lobby to the penthouse, but it required a key in the lobby to access it.

Philip first approached Ken with this information because he thought Ken would be able to foresee all the obstacles. If this was impossible, he would rather not bring it up to everyone. He and Ken agreed that it would be interesting to get into the penthouse, and that it would likely yield money or jewelry or both.

Ken thought the first challenge would be getting another person up the elevator at IMA. He had no idea if Philip's sister just happened to be extremely lucky, or if the attention paid to the elevator was lax. They would have to find out. His second concern was a potential security system in the penthouse. If there was one, it could be silent. They would have to think about that. Finally, there was the housekeeper. There was no way that they wanted to get into a situation where they had to deal with her. In all of their schemes over the years, they had never dealt with a victim face to face. They had never hurt anyone, or even threatened anyone, and they were not about to start now. Ken thought that overall the situation had merit. He told Philip to give him a couple of days to think about it.

Two days later they all sat around the table in Philip's apartment and laid out the "scheeeme." Ken had given it a lot of thought, and he felt he had all the bases covered. First, he reasoned that the Aegis building was in the middle of the business district and it was full of law firms and architects. All the people who came in and out of that building were going to look like professional people. Only one person would look different, Ken reasoned, the housekeeper. Todd's assignment was to watch the building for the next several days, figure out who the housekeeper was and try to determine if there was a routine to what she did. He was to make notes about when she went in, and when she came out. Where she went to shop, and how long she took.

Lewis was going to find a sandwich shop somewhere in the vicinity of the Aegis building. He was going to go into the shop and make notes on a half dozen of their most popular lunch specials, including prices. They would make up a sheet as if it were from the sandwich shop, with the phone number. It would look like he was soliciting lunch business. No one would suspect that the real reason for coming into the office of IMA was to see how easy, or difficult, it was to get to the elevator. Ken explained to Lewis that he needed to go in and look around in a way that didn't alarm anyone. If they asked him who he was, then he would pull out the sheet and give it to them, leaving immediately.

Ken was going to check out the lobby at the Aegis building to see what he could regarding the elevator that went to the penthouse. Lester was going to the library research department to see what he could find out about Adam Adamson. In one week they would meet again and figure out what the plan would be.

Chapter 14

They named him Hacaliah. His father told him that it meant "wait for God." It eventually became obvious that his mother and father were getting older. They started changing in their appearance, losing their stamina. He realized there was a notable change in them around his seven hundredth year.

They had long ago explained to him that after he was born they had done something that alienated them from God, who, they explained, had been their father. He had many brothers and sisters, and as he got old enough to take notice of things he realized that his mother and father didn't have the same little "button" on their stomachs that he and all his brothers and sisters had. His parents explained that it was because God was their father.

His mother died when he was seven hundred and eighty. His father died when he was nine hundred and twenty-six years old. He had settled in a village not far from where he lived most of his life. Every hundred years or so, he would venture back to the area where he first lived with his parents. He would go to the beautiful place to look. Each time he went the same two men were always there, standing at each side of the gate. They never moved, and the ball of fire was always there. It had been almost ninety-five years since he had traveled there. It was a four-day journey from where he now lived. Most of his visits to the beautiful place had resulted in his looking from the same distant slope that he had visited with his father so long ago.

But the last time he decided to venture a little closer. After all, he reasoned, the men never moved and they never acknowledged his presence. He had walked much closer than he had ever been. He could see the faces of the men clearly. They had beards. He got close enough to realize that the ball of flame wasn't a ball at all. It was what seemed to be a blade of a sword on fire, spinning all by itself. No one was holding it. He found the men frightening, for as he got closer, he realized how large they were. He estimated that he would only have come up to their chest and he was not short among his fellow men. He was a stone's throw from the men, and although he was frightened, something pushed him to keep moving closer. He got close enough to feel the heat of the sword blade that continued to turn. He knew the men had to see him, but they made no indication they were aware of him. He realized that if he continued to walk toward the sword it would probably kill him, so he backed away. He could still see the overgrown remnants of what had once been a beautiful place. No one who hadn't seen it before would be able to tell that it had been anything special. Only the men standing guard would have indicated something unique about the area.

The world had become an increasingly violent place, and Hacaliah found it more and more difficult to be peaceable. His father had impressed upon him the importance of being peaceable, and so far he had kept his promise to never harm anyone. He knew that he was different because his parents aged and died, while he continued to look the same as he had at thirty years old. He had moved several villages away to avoid the scrutiny of his family, because they, too, aged and he would possibly be the target of their frustrations.

It was time, he thought, to go back to the see the beautiful place. He wasn't sure why he traveled back there every so often, but something moved him to do so. He felt some kind of connection to that place. After more than three days travel, he found himself walking up the same slope he had walked over a thousand years ago with his father. He could close his eyes and bring to his memory that day, as though it had been only yesterday. He reached the top of the slope and looked down to the stone wall he had seen so many times before.

His heart leapt as though he had been hit hard in the chest. Were his eyes playing tricks on him or was there a third man standing in front of the sword? He was smaller. A shocking recollection flashed into Hacaliah's memory. It was the same man his father used to talk to by the river when they lived in the beautiful place. Yes, he was only a little boy then, but he was sure it was the same man. For a moment he was frozen, but then he broke into a run down the slope toward the wall. He didn't know exactly what he felt, but it was like finding an old lost friend. He had no fear of this man like he had of the other two. He stopped at a stone's throw away. He looked at the man, and was quite sure the man was looking at him. He did look like the man his father used to talk to. The clothing he wore was the same. He stared, not knowing what to do.

Suddenly the man spoke to him, "Hacaliah, do not fear, come here to me." The man seemed to speak effortlessly, not yelling. At the distance between them, Hacaliah should not have been able to hear him clearly, but he could. Hacaliah walked forward, somehow sensing he need not fear this man, coming close enough to reach out and touch the man, but he did not do so. He looked into the man's eyes and saw kindness and wisdom. The man's appearance was perfect. His skin appeared to be as a baby's skin. The man waited while he was examined.

Hacaliah spoke first, "How do you know my name?"

The man smiled, "I know you well Hacaliah. I have watched you all your life."

Hacaliah was confused. "I don't understand."

"I know you don't, come sit and we'll talk." The man gestured to one side and as Hacaliah looked toward where he gestured there was a table and two chairs that hadn't been there before. On the table was bread, fruit and water.

Hacaliah and the man talked for hours. The man explained that he was a messenger from God. His name was Gabriel. No, he was not the angel that his father used to talk to by the river. That was a different angel who no longer had God's favor.

Gabriel talked with Hacaliah about things beyond the imagination of most people, things that related to the existence of humans, and the far-reaching purpose of God. For the first time, Hacaliah had a clear understanding of why he and his parents had suddenly left the beautiful place when he was little, and why he alone, among humans, had not aged. His father had explained things to him as best he could. He had impressed on Hacaliah the importance of not taking a wife, and not having children. It was possible that any offspring, like Hacaliah, might not age and eventually it could draw attention to him and his offspring. Now, this man from God helped him to understand that his father had been correct. Hacaliah's offspring would have been born without the inherited imperfection that his parents had passed on to all other humans.

Gabriel explained that he would always need to be careful that people around him did not realize that he did not grow older. It would require his regularly relocating throughout his life. It would mean having little to do with others. Hacaliah would have to be a loner.

The last thing the man told Hacaliah was that he had a relative who lived two villages away from him. His name was Noah and he had found favor in God's eyes. Hacaliah was to travel to that village, find Noah, and bring him back to this place. Gabriel explained that he had information for Noah that was of the utmost importance. He would expect Hacaliah to return with Noah in seven days.

Chapter 15

Adam sat at his desk and found himself mentally preoccupied with the thought of making his next life shift. It meant a new start in a different part of the world. This would not simply be a relocation to a different state with a different job. It would be time to change his identity, and the part of the earth he lived on. His method had become to make these life shifts every fifty years. It removed him from the area where he knew people from a time when it would be obvious that he had not aged as those around him.

Fifty years on the other side of the planet would assure him that everyone who might recognize him would be gone, just as would now be the case when he moved to Europe. He wasn't sure where he would go.

He owned a magnificent castle in England, and a large country home in Spain. The English castle sat on top of a hill in the town of Winterton by the Sea. From the top floor you could see the North Sea. It was one of Adam's favorite places. His country home in Spain was outside the city of Valencia on the coast of the Mediterranean Sea. Adam loved the sea and this home had eight hundred feet of Mediterranean beach. Both of these properties would need to be transferred to his new identity, which he hadn't decided on yet.

He thought about IMA and Tim Groff. The amount of charitable work this organization had done since it began was quite amazing, and he hated the thought of simply shutting it down. Besides, there was the complication of almost a billion dollars on deposit. What would be done with that? Adam was waiting for a call back from his attorney on that question. He also had personal funds in a few local banks that would have to be transferred out. He thought most of it could go to the Swiss accounts, but some he would keep available for his immediate use, and some he wanted to have available for Gus. He hadn't said anything to Gus, but he knew he would have to soon. Even if Gus elected to stay, Adam felt safe letting him know what was going on. After all, Gus knew as much as anybody Adam had confided in.

He would also have to let the board at Comtec know that he was leaving, but first he had to set everything up.

Chapter 16

Gus hung up the phone in his little office in the basement of Comtec. He had arranged to meet Sally for dinner at Antonio's, an Italian restaurant just a few blocks from the Aegis.

Gus really enjoyed her company. He had developed relationships with various women over the years although he could hardly be considered a "womanizer." Gus thought back to when he first met Adam in 1957. That was forty-three years ago, and he could think of only ten women with whom he had developed a relationship that went beyond an occasional dinner. None of them had lasted more than several months. Gus was a likable and generous person. He did very well working for Adam. He had always been a saver, and Adam had provided him with living quarters ever since Boston, so Gus had saved quite a bit. It had grown and compounded to where Gus had close to two million dollars between his bank account and his investment portfolio. On occasion Gus had sent money to his sister in Massachusetts. He had only talked to her a few times since moving away, and it seemed like everything was fine at her end, but it made him feel better to send a little extra money to her just in case.

His generosity was equally evident when he dated. When Gus took women out to dinner it was always to the finest places. He would buy little gifts for them and if the relationship was really going anywhere he would buy very nice and expensive gifts. He had seen Sally three times. This was to be their fourth date, and he really liked being with her.

She had told him about her family. That her father was a laborer for a large contractor, but he was getting close to retirement and Sally worried about him. She was afraid that he didn't really have the financial ability to retire. He never made a lot of money, and he had raised two kids. She told Gus about her brother Philip, describing him as a loser. She told him about his "gang of thieves" he spent his days with. Gus listened with interest, which was something she liked about him.

Gus called Antonio's and made reservations for eight o'clock. Adam's schedule didn't call for anything special today so he was sure that he would be home by six-thirty. He figured a quick shower and change and he could be out by seven-fifteen. It was a twenty-minute walk to Antonio's, and Gus liked to get there a few minutes early. It allowed him to sit at the bar, have a drink, and watch all the beautiful people. Antonio's was a very popular spot.

The rest of the day was routine, and Gus got a call from Adam telling him that he would be leaving in ten minutes. That was Gus' signal to get himself ready to go, so he shut down his computer. Russian was a more difficult language than he had anticipated.

It seemed that the typical rules of grammar did not apply, as if the language lacked any logic to it. Eight minutes after Adam's call, Gus was in the limo at the back entrance to the building. Adam exited a minute later, and climbed in. Gus pulled away without a word. The limo was a Mercedes 600 SEL V-12. Gus loved it. He could barely hear the motor. They drove along quietly, neither man speaking. Gus had long felt that he could talk to Adam at any time. He didn't have to wait for some right time. He and Adam were really friends, far beyond any employer employee relationship. He sensed something on Adam's mind. He had been a little quiet this morning, too.

He decided to bring it up. "Anything wrong, boss?"

Adam looked at him in the rear view mirror. "What makes you ask that, Gus?"

Gus looked back at him through the mirror. "You seem a little quiet. I don't know, maybe a little lost in thought."

Adam smiled faintly, "You know me too well, my old friend."

"Anything you want to talk about?"

"Yes, but not tonight. I'm working on a few things. When I have all the details and can answer questions that you're going to have, then I'll sit down and we'll talk."

"Sounds serious."

"I suppose it is."

Adam said no more and Gus knew that it must really be serious. Gus had moved with Adam five times. He understood Adam's need to move and he had always been willing to go with him. That was why he never got serious with any woman. He didn't feel that he would be able to take a wife with him, moving often, without some reasonable explanation. He wasn't about to reveal to anyone things that Adam had told him in confidence. Gus forced himself not to think about what Adam may have planned for the future.

He started thinking about dinner with Sally tonight. He would walk to the restaurant in hopes that they could take a nice walk back to his apartment. The last time they had really hit it off together, and she had stayed the night. He was upset with her for going up to the penthouse, but she had apologized profusely. Of course, Gus had been deeply embarrassed when Adam discussed it with him. Adam had been quite surprised when his housekeeper related the story to him. He had never considered that there could be a security concern, but the incident had made him wonder if he should put a key on the IMA elevator to limit access.

The limo pulled into the Aegis garage at about ten minutes to six. Traffic had been a little lighter than usual. Adam and Gus took the stairs, as always, to the lobby. Adam inserted his key into the last elevator on the wall, briefly discussed the morning's schedule and said good night, disappearing into the elevator. Gus stepped into the elevator in front of him, and it took him non-stop to the eleventh floor. He thought about the advantage to being in the building at that time of day, and how he almost never had to stop on his way to the eleventh floor. During the normal business day it could take three minutes to get the elevator, and get to the eleventh floor, even though there were four full-service elevators.

About an hour later Gus stepped out of the main entrance of the Aegis building and headed south toward Antonio's. It was a beautiful evening for a walk, and Gus whistled as he walked. He really liked Sally and he was looking forward to seeing her. He wasn't going to think about what Adam wanted to talk about. He was going to put it out of his mind, at least for this evening.

Chapter 17

Philip looked at his buddies sitting around his kitchen table. Lester, Todd, Lewis and Ken. All eyes were on Ken. He had a folder in front of him like a secret file that an FBI agent might have, and he had a little smile on his face that said he had it all figured out. Everyone was anxious to hear what he had to say.

Philip was impatient. "C'mon, Ken, let's hear it." They all chimed in with comments urging Ken to start talking.

Ken opened the folder in front of him. "OK, OK, here it is. I think we can do this." They were hanging on his every word.

"The old lady housekeeper seems to go out just about every day at one in the afternoon. She walks to Mickey's Market over on the Boulevard. It's a few blocks. She never buys a lot and it always fits in a small pull cart she has. But, she's a slow walker, so she's usually gone for an hour. Lewis checked out the elevator on the eleventh floor inside those offices. The receptionist apparently goes to lunch at one o'clock, so the phones are being answered by other people. No one really watches the front office, and they have nothing on the front door that makes noise when someone walks in, so we should be able to walk in undetected a few minutes after one. If the housekeeper goes out like she usually does, that works out perfectly."

"But how many of us can go tramping through their office without them noticing?" Lewis asked.

"Not to worry," Ken answered, "we only need one to do that. See, the elevator from the lobby to the penthouse is key operated, but I'm betting that the elevator from the penthouse down to the lobby isn't. That would be too inconvenient. Lewis, you go back in with another sandwich sheet just in case they see you. If it's clear, get on the elevator and go up to the penthouse."

To the others he said, "He'll have to get off the elevator in the penthouse and get on the one that goes down to the lobby. He'll come down to the lobby where we'll be waiting. When he gets to the lobby, we'll know that we're in. But then we're going to let him go back up by himself for a few minutes. We'll have walkie-talkies so that we can talk back and forth from the lobby to the penthouse. We'll have to buy real good ones."

"Why is he going back up by himself?" Todd asked.

Ken was expecting the question. "Because we don't know if the place is alarmed. If it is and the cops get a call, we'll see them come in. They're not going to have a key to the penthouse elevator so they'll go to the eleventh floor. If we see them do that, we call Lewis, and he comes down the lobby elevator, and we're gone."

Everyone nodded their approval. This was Ken's specialty, thinking of everything.

Ken continued, "Now, if everything seems clear, Lewis comes back down, and me and Philip will go up. Lester, you and Todd are going to keep a look out for anything suspicious, and you'll have the walkie-talkie. If you see anything at all that doesn't look right you let us know."

Lester spoke, "What if the housekeeper comes back sooner than we expect? Suppose she comes back while you guys are up there?"

"Good question," Ken said. "There has to be a stairway out of the penthouse somewhere. Construction codes won't let a place like that be totally dependent on elevators. One of the first things we'll do is find the stairs, so that if you call us to say the housekeeper is coming, we can leave by the stairway."

Everyone was impressed that Ken had even covered that base.

Philip spoke up, "What exactly are we going to do up there?"

"That's the one unknown," Ken admitted. "We have no way of knowing what's up there. I have figured this much. We have to be very careful not to mess anything up, or touch anything if we don't have to. If we have to leave in a hurry, we don't want anyone to know we were there. We're going to be wearing rubber gloves so we don't have to worry about leaving fingerprints. We may find that there's really nothing there, but I'm thinking there may be some cash lying around, or some jewelry. I'll tell you this, we're not taking anything big. No TVs or stereos or computers. We don't need that stuff, and it's more trouble than it's worth."

Everyone nodded in agreement. Ken seemed to remember something. "By the way Lester, what did you find out about our man in the library?"

Lester didn't have a file, but he pulled a little notebook out of his pocket and flipped open the top cover like a detective making notes in an investigation. It seemed a little humorous, but he had a serious look on his face.

"Well, he's sort of a strange dude. The New York Times and the Wall Street Journal both have extensive research programs on the top corporate executives all over the world. They tell you all kinds of stuff. If they're married, how many kids they have, where they went to school, what education they received, and what their employment history is. They usually have a picture too, although they're usually older pictures. But this guy is a mystery. The earliest information they had on him was back in the late fifties when he worked for a company in Boston. He was the top man there, and they made a fortune in the time he was there. That company's business tripled. Then he jumped to a company in New York, then to Washington State, then one in Philadelphia, then one in Texas, then out here to California. Every place he went it was the same story. Business went through the roof, and then bam, he was off to someplace else. But what's really weird is that they had absolutely nothing on him before that first job in Boston. It was like he didn't exist before that. No education, no birth date, no marriage information, no picture, no nothing. They did say that it was estimated that he's worth millions because he worked for all these companies without getting paid. They all made contributions to a charity he owns."

Lewis chimed in, "You can't own a charity."

Lester continued, "Hey, what do I know? OK, so he doesn't own it, but he's the head of it. Maybe he takes money from them somehow, I don't know."

They sat quietly for a moment, contemplating his being worth millions.

"Well," said Ken, "we'll soon find out."

They agreed that they would give it a shot in a few days. Ken explained that he and Philip were going to have to go out and buy suits and get haircuts.

Everyone seemed shocked. Todd spoke first, "What's that all about?"

Ken looked directly at him as though he was the only one interested in the answer. "Look, we're going into the lobby of the Aegis, possibly to hang around a little, and then eventually to get onto the elevator that goes to this guy's penthouse. You think we can do that looking like we look, without drawing a little attention to ourselves?"

Todd felt a little foolish. "Well, I didn't think about it."

"No, you didn't." Ken had a little hint of annoyance in his voice. He wasn't really upset, but he saw this as an opportunity to squash anyone's questioning him in the future. "We're also going to carry attaché cases which we'll use to carry out whatever we take."

Chapter 18

Adam worked on a list of things he would do in preparation for his next move. There were the properties in England, Spain, and Venezuela. There was an apartment in New York City. He would put the transfer of these properties in the works right away. He would have his attorneys handle everything so that he would not have to worry about forging any legal papers. He had decided to move back to England initially.

There was a new electronics group that had formed a few years earlier. They were in a field of research that dovetailed with Comtec. He would probably make them his first visit. He would have to assume a new identity, and he had been thinking for days about a new name. He had chosen Adam Adamson as a play on words when he came to the United States. He wanted to keep the word game going when he made this move and he had been trying to decide on what name to use. He had finally landed on the name Abel Cain, which were the names of his brothers so long ago. He daydreamed for a few minutes about his brothers. He always marveled at the human memory and how it was similar to words chiseled deeply into granite. No amount of years could wear the memories away. It was hard to believe that it had been over six thousand years ago. It was one of the Bible's accounts that Adam had found seriously lacking in detail. Yes, Cain had, in fact, killed his brother Abel. But there was so much more to it. Cain had really been a good brother, and a good man. He had worked hard in the fields and he loved the land. His crops were prosperous. But Cain had also traveled with his father back to the beautiful place. Cain had seen the men standing at the gate preventing entrance. His father had explained what happened, and why life was so much more difficult. Cain had come to hate his father for what he had lost. No, his brother had not possessed some deep spiritual appreciation for God, he was simply a man who realized what gift had been lost, and he resented his father and mother for it. He was miserable to them, and did little or nothing to help them. Even food that he gave to them was given begrudgingly. Shortly after killing his brother, Cain took one of their sisters, Hela was her name, and left. Adam never saw him again.

So now when he made this life shift he would call himself Abel Cain. Yes, some would joke about it, but he wouldn't mind it any more than the occasional comment he received about the name Adam Adamson.

He was going to meet with his attorneys tomorrow to discuss IMA. He had to admit that he hadn't thought the process through to this point when he had instituted IMA. He had hoped that it wouldn't have been necessary to dissolve it, but some of his calculations were a little off, and now it seemed that it might be necessary. He was to meet with Roy Hazelton and a couple of his associates in the morning. They had been working for a few weeks on some type of charter that would allow the organization to continue to function without him. That really was his preference. He was afraid that dissolving it would bring much more attention to him than would his removing himself from it. Besides, it really did a lot of good each year. The donations were so varied, from giving to individuals, towns, police departments, even on occasion to State police groups. Everyone who knew about IMA loved them. Shortly after an FBI agent had been shot through his bulletproof vest by some hi-tech bullet, IMA had purchased the newest vest available for the FBI and several other agencies whose budgets had been drastically cut. IMA had spent twenty-nine million dollars on vests that year. They were so well liked that there had never been an audit on their books since the first time an IRS auditor had been there, in their third year of existence.

Adam decided that some time tomorrow he had to talk with Gus about his decision. He had to give Gus the opportunity to stay here without him, and he had to make sure that Gus felt free to do whatever he wanted. Gus wasn't getting any younger. They had been together since 1957 when Gus was twenty-four. Now, Gus looked forty-seven, but he was sixty-seven. Adam had to wonder how long Gus would be able to keep up with him. He figured if Gus worked out, and stuck with the nutritional diet that he had worked out for him, he could probably live to a hundred and ten. He could work with Adam, including driving, probably until he was eighty or so. After that Adam would have to start being concerned with his reflexes. He knew that Gus had been investing wisely over the years, and he thought that he probably had a nice nest egg put away, but Adam intended to leave him in a financial situation that would allow him to do anything he wanted for the rest of his life. He had about fifteen million dollars on deposit in various local banks, and he was going to transfer five million of it to an account in Gus' name. He had mixed feelings about Gus' coming with him. He had come to love Gus over the years. He trusted him completely, and Gus had been a good and loyal friend. He would miss him terribly.

Chapter 19

Dinner at Antonio's was always a treat. Gus had earned a reputation as a very good tipper, and the result was he was treated like their biggest celebrity when he walked in the door. Gus loved to eat, and although he usually stuck to the regimen that Adam had written down for him decades earlier, he did occasionally go out and feast on a sumptuous meal. Since he had been living at the Aegis, Gus had been coming to Antonio's on the average of once every few weeks. Over the last eight years that added up to over one hundred and fifty visits. Gus usually dined alone, but sometimes he had a woman with him. He was always polite, and he was very generous with his tips. It was common for him to leave a twenty-dollar tip on a fifty-dollar tab. When he had someone with him, the bill averaged between a hundred and a hundred thirty dollars. He would then leave a fifty-dollar tip for the waiter.

Tonight was no exception. The food and the service was the best it could be. The waiter, who had waited on Gus many times before, was practically falling all over him. The hostess brought him his usual drink moments after seating them, and took a drink order for Sally, which was on the table within two minutes. Gus and Sally engaged in light talk through the meal. She talked about how much she liked working at Comtec. She asked Gus about Adam, and how he had met him. She asked him what he was like. Gus loved talking about Adam because he was such a good and interesting person, but Gus was always careful not to say anything that could create a problem.

Sally mentioned that her brother Philip had called her a few nights earlier. It had seemed strange to her, because he never called her. It wasn't that she didn't like to talk to him, but they had nothing in common. She told Gus he had made small talk for a while, and then slipped in a few questions about Adam.

Gus was surprised. "What kind of questions?"

"Oh, I don't know." Sally was surprised that Gus seemed so interested.

Gus pushed a little. "Really, Sally, what kind of questions? I'd like to know."

It made her stop and think back. She looked up at the ceiling, really trying to remember. "Oh, I know one thing, he asked if Adam worked every day or stayed home some days."

"What did you tell him?"

She looked at Gus with a surprised expression. "What do you think I told him? I don't have any idea. I've only seen the man once, and that was when he was walking down the hall."

Gus had a concerned tone in his voice. "Why do you suppose he would want to know that?"

"With my stupid brother, who knows what goes through that head of his? He asked me if you carried a gun!" She chuckled at the stupidity of that question, but Gus didn't laugh. These questions were raising red flags in Gus' brain. He decided that taking Sally back to his place tonight could be a bad idea, but he didn't want to alarm her. She could see that he had not taken her brother's inquiry as lightly as she had.

"Gus, what's the matter? Do you think there's something to worry about?"

Gus looked at her, knowing the need to cut the night short, but still with a desire to take her home. "Sally, I don't know your brother. You tell me, should I be worried about these questions coming out of the blue from your brother, who you tell me is a small time hoodlum who hangs out with a group of other hoodlums?"

Sally thought about it for a moment. "You know, Gus, I didn't really take him seriously, because I never have. But now that you put it that way, I think it would probably be a mistake to just laugh him off. I believe he and his friends are capable of anything."

Gus looked at her. "I appreciate your honesty, Sally. It's one of the things I like about you. I'll mention it to Adam. He'll know what to do, and I'll be sure to tell him that you mentioned it out of concern."

"Thanks, Gus, that's real nice of you." Sally realized that their evening was going to end, and she didn't want Gus to feel bad about it. She said she was a little tired, and that it would probably be best if she grabbed a cab home. Gus agreed. He paid the bill and they stepped out onto the sidewalk. They embraced and kissed and then she looked up into his eyes. "Thanks for a great evening, I'll see you tomorrow."

Gus hailed the next cab, and as she got in, Gus opened the front door of the cab, gave the driver a twenty-dollar bill and gave him the address. The driver recognized the address as a fare that would be about eight dollars. He looked at Gus to see what Gus wanted to do, and Gus told him to keep the change and get the lady home quickly and safely. The driver thanked him and off they went. Gus crossed the street and hailed the next cab. As he got in, he told the driver to take him to the Aegis building and to step on it. He looked at his watch. It was only nine-thirty. Adam would still be up.

It was barely a five-minute ride to the Aegis. Gus rode up the elevator to the eleventh floor. He went to his apartment and called upstairs to Adam. It was very rare that Gus would call Adam at night, or that he would go up to the penthouse uninvited. Adam would often ask him up, and they would chat. Sometimes Adam was in a mood to reminisce and when he did, the stories were amazing. He had related to Gus experiences from the seventeen, and eighteen hundreds, and from what history called the dark ages. Adam could even shed light on those dark ages.

Adam answered the phone on the second ring. Gus simply said that he needed to talk to him, and Adam told him to come right up. Gus went down the hall to the IMA entrance and let himself in. He didn't bother to turn on the lights; there was enough light shining through the door from the hallway to dimly light the office. He stepped to the elevator and pushed the button. The door opened immediately. The trip to the next level took only a few seconds. Adam was sitting on the couch reading the Wall Street Journal. The New York Times and the LA Times were on the table in front of the couch. Adam got up and greeted Gus like he hadn't seen him in days.

"What can I get you to drink?" That question always made Gus laugh. He knew that his choices in Adam's penthouse were orange juice or water.

"Ice water would be great," he said it with a slightly mocking tone.

"One ice water coming right up," Adam said as he walked into the kitchen. He came out with a glass full of ice cubes in one hand and a bottle of water in the other, which he was pouring as he walked. He handed it to Gus, and they both sat down. Adam was thinking that Gus wanted to talk about their conversation earlier. "So, what's on your mind, Gus?"

Gus sighed deeply, "Adam, I'm a little worried about something and I think we need to discuss it."

Adam looked at him with total attention. It was something that Gus had become used to. When you talked to most people, they glanced at you now and then, but Adam looked at you almost unblinkingly. You had the feeling he was looking through you. It was just Adam's level of concentration, and Gus knew it. Adam continued to look at him. Gus had made a statement, Adam had accepted it, and there was nothing for Adam to say, so he was listening, ready for whatever it was Gus had on his mind.

Gus explained the whole conversation with Sally at the restaurant regarding her brother, his questions, and his reputation. Adam asked a question here and there, but he listened carefully to everything Gus said. He asked Gus questions that forced Gus to analyze his own thinking and fears. When Gus had explained it fully, Adam asked him what he thought they should do. Gus said he didn't know, but he was confident that he, Adam, would know what to do.

Adam thought out loud for Gus' benefit. "Well, what could Sally's brother have in mind? Is he thinking he's going to kidnap me? His question about you carrying a gun is pretty wild. Is he planning to rob me? He'll be pretty disappointed."

Adam never carried more than a few dollars on him, and he kept very little cash in the apartment. There was a wall safe in his study behind a picture. It had been there when he bought the penthouse. There was probably twenty-five thousand dollars in it. Even a professional thief would have a very hard time getting into it.

"If he's going to break into the penthouse that will be quite a trick. And what's here to steal?" He was still thinking aloud. "I have very little of value, unless they're going to steal the refrigerator or the stereo or the furniture. I don't have much in the way of jewelry."

They finally decided that there wasn't anything they could do that Adam would consider reasonable. Sure, he could hire a guard around the clock to stay in the penthouse, but he just didn't see the sense of it. He was sure it was nothing to be concerned about, and he felt if they did try something, it would be of no consequence.

Gus went back to his apartment and called Sally. He thanked her for telling him about her brother and his questions, and asked her to be sure and let him know if there were any new questions. She assured Gus that he would be the first to know.

Chapter 20

They had been working on the large boat for almost fifty years. Noah's wife had been working along with them right from the beginning. She was a good woman who was supportive of her husband. Her name was Mala. Noah had been almost five hundred and fifty years old when Hacaliah had come looking for him. He was a large and powerful man. His reputation was as a fair and good man, and there were few of them around at that time. His wife was similar in age, and they had two sons, and a daughter.

Noah looked over at Hacaliah who was working with his eldest son, Shem. He thought back to his first meeting with him. When Hacaliah found him and introduced himself, Noah greeted him as a relative. He invited Hacaliah into his home. Hacaliah explained the need for them to leave the next day and journey to the beautiful place, three days journey away. Noah said that he had heard stories of such a place, but he had never spoken to anyone who had actually seen it. He was quite intrigued by the stories that his newfound relative was telling him, and he was ready to go the next morning with complete faith in the truthfulness of what Hacaliah had told him. He found the story about the men standing guard and the other man suddenly appearing, fascinating. And the part about the table of food, why, that was simply impossible to imagine. He couldn't wait to get started.

They had arrived at the beautiful place at the end of the seventh day. When they reached the top of the slope Hacaliah stopped. He wanted Noah to experience the effect of looking down on the place from that vantage point. Noah stopped beside him, and Hacaliah pointed. Noah followed his outstretched finger and gazed down on this most unbelievable sight. The two men were standing on each side of the gate just as he had been told, the burning sword was there, too. Noah didn't know what to say. He gazed for several minutes, taking it all in. But there was no third man. He looked at Hacaliah, and saw he was not concerned. The man had told him to be back in seven days and he was back in seven days. The man would be there.

They started down the slope in silence. When they got to within two stones' throw of the gate, the flaming sword, that was spinning in between the two men, stopped. Noah and Hacaliah stopped. In its stopped position the two men could see how large the sword was. Hacaliah estimated it to be longer than he was tall. It had stopped with the blade pointing up toward the sky. Suddenly, the man that had spoken with Hacaliah came out through the gate from within the walled area. He was smiling, which put both men at ease, and he walked forward and met the two where they had stopped. He greeted them both by name.

They stayed with the man for three days as he explained to them all that God had in store for the earth in the near future. Noah was to build a large boat, an "ark" the man called it. He gave them specific instructions on its length, width, and height. He made it clear that they could not change any of the three dimensions. The height, width, and length would make the vessel stable in the water when the rains began. He gave detailed instructions regarding the interior of the large boat. There would be three levels. The top would be completely enclosed with a roof extending over the sides of the boat. This would allow the rain to run off, and not sink or flood the vessel. There would be a door in the side of the boat at the top level. A ramp of some type would have to be constructed. There would also be ramps from the top level to the second level, and to the third level, as well. In the lower two levels, hundreds of pens, varying in size would be constructed. The top level would be where Noah, his family, and Hacaliah would live. The type of wood they were to use was specified. They were to use the gopher tree. The boat was to be pegged and coated with pitch. Noah and Hacaliah listened patiently and carefully as all of this was explained. Noah felt as though the man was not only explaining everything to him, but somehow imprinting it deeply into his mind as well. It seemed to Noah that though he had been listening to instructions for hours, he could recall everything he had been told.

When the man was finished with the instructions for the building of the ark, he asked if there were any questions. Noah asked if the boat was to be built near the water so that it could be pushed into the sea. To his surprise, the man told him that it would not be necessary to build near the sea. Noah then asked the question that had been most on his mind. What was the purpose of this large vessel? The man looked back and forth at the men before him. He sighed a great sigh, and explained that God had become displeased with the conditions of mankind on the earth. They listened in a stupor, as he told them of God's intention to destroy all of mankind except Noah, his family, Hacaliah, and some of the beasts of the earth. The only surviving land animals and birds would be the ones that were with Noah and his family on this large vessel.

There was going to occur an earth-wide flood that would destroy every living land creature not on that vessel. That was why it was so important to make it exactly the size specified. There would be a need for food storage for all the animals, as well as for the people. Noah told the man that he had a wife, two sons, and a daughter. His two sons were married, so he had two daughters-in-law. Along with Hacaliah, that would make a total of eight people. The man said there would be adequate room for all, and that if others should desire to be on the boat with them it would be acceptable. There were to be several barrels that would allow for storage of water. The man explained where on the top level the barrels would be placed and how they would create a small hole in the roof with a gutter that would allow rainwater to fall into the barrel. If one barrel got full, they were to move it out of the way and put an empty one in its place. If the barrels were all full, they could put a cover over the hole, so the rain would not come in.

The man explained there would only be enough room on the boat for two of each species of animal. A male and female of each would be required, so they may regenerate their numbers after the flood. Noah inquired as to what would happen to all the vegetation, if the entire surface of the earth was to be covered in water, especially salt water. He was told the vast majority of vegetation would be destroyed, because it would be under water for a long time. But after the floodwaters receded, vegetation would grow again rapidly. Within twenty years the earth would be covered with flora and fauna. As for the concern about the salt water harming the earth, the man explained that the rain would fall and the springs underneath the earth would overflow with fresh water. The result would be a dilution of seawater where it would not cause permanent damage to the soil. After the floodwater receded, it would take a thousand years for the sea to return to its natural saline level.

There were other questions that were patiently and completely answered. After a full three days, Noah and Hacaliah returned to Noah's home. He lived away from the closest village, and after explaining everything in detail to his family, they began the work.

That was fifty years ago. Now, Noah looked over to the bow of the great boat where Hacaliah and his son, Shem, were applying the final coat of pitch. This had been an overwhelming task, but somehow they had managed to accomplish what they thought would be impossible.

There was quite a bit of attention for the first few years from the people nearby. Some would come to watch out of curiosity. Some would make unkind remarks about the foolishness of building such a large vessel nowhere near water. Noah and his family were ridiculed. On occasion, there were some who would actually help, but they would never stay for more than a day or two. Noah was not afraid to tell them what he had been told about the earth being destroyed, but no one seemed to take him seriously. Now, all these years later the curiosity had long ended. No one came to see what they were doing anymore.

The boat was enormous. It took almost three stones' throw to reach from one end to the other. They were nearing completion of the building of the boat, and they had started gathering animals into pens outside. All creatures on earth were docile. There was no fear between the creatures and man, and the gathering of them was simple. The women had been gathering the animals for nearly a month. They had all the creatures that Noah had been told to bring. They stored various grains for themselves, and other foods that would last for some time. They stored hay and other vegetation that could serve as food for the animals also.

When the ark was completed, Noah, his family, and Hacaliah rested for several days. They had worked for so long they had forgotten what it was like to stop. They wondered what to do next. It was now the morning of the third day of resting from the building work. Noah came out from his house, and in the distance, standing by the great vessel was the same man that had given him the instructions all those years earlier. He looked no different. Noah walked out to meet him, and as he approached the man turned to him. He looked pleased.

"Noah, you have done just as you were instructed. Everything looks like it is ready."

"It is."

"Good. This day you shall begin to move all the creatures into the ark. Get your family and all of your supplies in, as well. In seven days from this day, the great deluge will begin. Your family and all the creatures should be settled in before that day arrives.

Noah, Hacaliah and Noah's family worked diligently over the next four days to accomplish all they had been instructed. On the morning of the fifth day, they all climbed up the ramp for the last time. All the creatures they gathered were in their pens. All the food for the animals, as well as for them, was stored. Noah estimated that there was enough for slightly more than three months.

At the top of the ramp Noah and Mala stopped and looked around. They were saddened at the prospect of all the destruction about to take place. It was true that the world around them had become brutal, but there were a few good people that they knew. They had implored these few to join them, but they were not men of faith. They hadn't seen the man who appeared from nowhere, or eaten the food that would appear with no preparation. They had not heard the instructions regarding the building of the great boat.

And the animals. There were so many creatures that would die. They were peaceful and innocent. It saddened them to think that only the creatures they had taken with them would survive.

Noah's son, Shem, appeared in the doorway with a large wooden mallet. Noah and Mala stepped inside and made room at the top of the ramp for him. He swung the mallet down hard at a peg that had held the ramp fast to the side of the great vessel. He did the same on the other side and the ramp stood in its place, free from the boat. They had decided to stay on the great ship, but to leave the ramp in case they needed to get to the ground for some reason, or in case anyone they had spoken to changed their mind and joined them. They had not seen anyone else in a year, so they knew there was little chance of that happening. There was also the desire to get as much fresh air as possible into the boat, and the open hatchway helped. Noah knew that once the deluge began the hatchway would have to be closed.

Their first night staying on the boat was the beginning of a difficult adjustment. The living quarters were not so bad, but the animals were also adjusting to something very different for them, and they were noisy all night. They were not used to being in pens inside, and they were not used to having the other creatures around. The noise was continuous, and no one got much sleep.

On the sixth day, the sky looked noticeably different. There was always a haze, but this day the sky was much darker, more like it looked as the day turned into night. Noah knew that something different was about to happen. When he and Hacaliah had spoken to the man all those years ago, the man had explained that it was going to rain. They had not known what that meant, because they had never seen it. Most days started off with a very heavy mist, and that was how all the plant life on the earth was watered. Water had never fallen from the sky, not even lightly. The man explained that along with this rain, the underground water springs of the earth would also erupt. It was difficult for Noah to fight the feeling of anxiety. He was six hundred years old, and he wasn't sure how he felt about seeing something for the first time.

Mid-morning of the seventh day everyone was edgy. The noise level from the creatures had been less the second night, but it was still difficult to get a good night's rest. Noah, his wife, and family along with Hacaliah all stood at the hatchway looking out at a sky, as they had never seen it. There was an ominous darkness. A thick textured look they had never seen erupted, and the wind picked up.

Suddenly, there appeared the stain of large water drops on the top platform of the ramp. Just a few first, then more, and more. So, this is what rain looks like, Noah thought. His sons rushed to the large ropes they had attached on the inside corner of each large door that swung out to create the hatchway. They pulled the great doors in, and they swung closed, fitting together in the middle so no light showed through. There was a large hasp in the middle of the two doors that they put an equally large peg through. There were also two pegs midway back on each door, one at the top, and one at the bottom. These pegs were hammered in to make the two doors tightly closed. No water could come in. The hatchway was high above what would be the water line, so the hatchway did not have to be watertight.

Above the living area for the people was a loft that could be reached by climbing a ladder. Standing in the loft, Noah could reach up and touch the roof of the boat. There was a small window on each of the four sides, and each window had a panel much like a miniature door that could be opened or closed. They climbed into the loft and opened the windows to watch. It was raining hard now. The sound of the rain hitting the roof of the boat was like no sound they had ever heard. They kept watching the roof for any signs of leaking water. There were none. Soon, the rain was so hard that they couldn't see the house that had been their home for so long. As they looked down to the ground closest to the boat, they could see water forming on the ground like a pond. Noah sobbed. He could not help himself. If there had been any question in his mind as to the reality of this moment, it was now gone. He had devoted the past fifty years to one objective, saving his family and himself. He looked over to Hacaliah, who also had tears in his eyes. It was a cruel race of mankind that was about to be destroyed, but it was impossible to not feel compassion for them. Noah wondered what would have happened had this man not sought him out. What if this man had ignored the instructions given to him all those years ago? What if he had never ventured back to that place where he had lived as a little boy? Noah realized that he and his family owed their lives to this man.

The tremendous noise of the rain upset the animals. It took half a day to calm them. Eventually, the sound became similar to no sound at all. It was difficult to speak over the noise, so conversation was kept to a minimum.

After six days of steady rain, they looked out the windows toward the ground. It looked like the boat was sitting in a lake. They could see some nearby trees, and it now looked like the water was several feet up on the trees. On the tenth day, about midday, something that Noah had feared the most happened. Someone started beating on the side of the great boat from outside. They were yelling to Noah to open the door, and let them in. Noah and the family were amazed that anyone could have reached them. The last time they looked outside, the water had risen above the trunk line of the trees, leaving only branches visible. Noah had expected the boat to start floating, but that had not yet happened. Now, there was someone outside.

They must have had a small boat to get to them. One of the instructions given by the man just before they entered the boat was not to open the door once it had been closed. The man had been very specific about this. He had repeated it to Noah, and asked him if he understood clearly. Now Noah wondered if the man had foreseen this happening. The person never said who he was, so Noah assumed it wasn't someone he knew, but rather someone who had heard that they were building the boat. After nine days of rain, it must have occurred to this man that there was a good reason for building the boat. The man had not been out there long when they felt the great vessel lift off its shoring and begin to float. There were some groaning sounds from the wood shifting as the great vessel floated free, and in minutes the boat was quite a distance from the ramp and the sound of the poor soul who had desperately tried to save himself.

Noah's daughter's name was Maalana. She was a lovely woman who had been born to Noah and Mala shortly before they started working on the boat. By the time she was thirty, she had made it known that she was attracted to Hacaliah. This came as no surprise to anyone. After all, Hacaliah was a very handsome man. He was also the only man that Maalana knew, aside from her own brothers. Hacaliah had explained to her that he was not able to take a wife for himself, although he could not explain why to her. He assured her that had he been able to do so, she would have been his choice. She seemed to accept his explanation at the time, and the subject had never come up again. But now, in the limited and small confines of the great vessel, Maalana's feeling for Hacaliah manifested itself again. One night, long after everyone had retired to sleep, Hacaliah sensed that someone was very close to him. He opened his eyes and struggled to see in the darkness. He felt someone lower them self next to him on his sleeping mat. He was mildly startled, but he didn't feel threatened. He spoke softly so as not to awaken anyone, "Who is it?"

He heard a whispered reply, "Hacaliah, it is I Maalana." As she whispered, she moved closer so that her body was touching his.

"Maalana, what are you doing?" he whispered emphatically, trying to achieve a tone that was difficult when one was whispering.

"Hacaliah," she said, as her hand touched his face, caressing his cheek, "you know I have always had affection for you, and lately that affection has become a burning desire to be your wife. Please, Hacaliah, allow me to lie with you this night as your wife."

Now Hacaliah felt a sense of panic, "Maalana, you know I have great affection for you, too. You are like a sister to me. Please understand that I cannot take a wife for myself. You ask of me something I cannot do."

"But Hacaliah, have you no desire to enjoy the pleasures of a wife or to have children?"

"Maalana, I desire both those things. I am a man and I see your beauty. You are very desirable. You must believe that my unwillingness to make you my wife is not from lack of desire. I simply cannot do so."

"Is it some type of oath you are under?" she asked.

"In a way it is, my dear sister." He was desperately trying to diffuse the situation.

"Hacaliah, I'm sorry for my forwardness."

"I understand, Maalana; you know that like a dear sister I have great love for you."

"I do know that Hacaliah, and I thank you for it." She kissed him gently on the cheek, and rose quietly and went back to her own sleeping area. Hacaliah stared out at the darkness. He wondered what it would be like to hold a woman in his arms in passion. To touch her flesh. And then he told himself that this would be something he would be able to do some day far into the future, but not now. Some day the opportunity would be there. But right now, having a wife and bearing children would only bring death to him and to his children. He knew this, and it was a reality he had long ago learned to accept.

The rain lasted for forty days. After twenty days they had been unable to see anything but water. There were no trees, no mountains, just water. One morning, when they awoke they realized they didn't hear the sound of the rain. They rushed up to the loft, and opened the windows. The sight amazed them. As far as the eye could see, in every direction, there was only water. The sky was still a little gray and hazy, but the rain had stopped. They were happy. Perhaps they would not have to spend too much more time in the boat.

Everything was working out well. The animals had gotten used to being in their pens, and to each other. Caring for them was a full time chore. Cleaning up after them, hauling bucket after bucket of dung up to the loft to throw out the window, was a full time job. Noah estimated that they had enough food for another two months.

The next day brought with it a sight never before seen by any living creature on earth. The sky was deep blue. The sun was a bright light that could not be looked at directly. For the entirety of human history, the sky had always been hazy, and the sun had been a dominant bright light. It was not so bright that you couldn't look at it, so this was different and wondrous. They could not stop looking out the windows. The bright sunlight shining on the water was also quite beautiful, and one day while watching out the window, they saw a school of the Great Sea creatures jumping out of the water and shooting huge flumes of water into the air through the holes in the tops of their heads. It was a marvelous sight to behold.

Some days the sea would be a little rougher, with swells that would rock the great boat noticeably. Other days, the sea would be so calm that it seemed they were not moving at all. At night, the sky was even more amazing to see. Stars were clearly visible. The sky was a sharp black color that was as unknown to them as the daytime blue sky. The moon was now also clearly visible for the first time. It was surprising how much light it produced when it was full.

They estimated they had been in the boat for over two months. There was enough food for one more month, and the water supply was getting low. It had been twenty days since the rain stopped. An empty storage barrel was in position under the hole that had been part of the original instructions. The protective flap was off. That night, while everyone slept, it rained. When they awoke in the morning the barrel that had been empty was nearly full. They moved it, and put another barrel in position. The next night it rained again, and that barrel was also filled. That night the rain made enough noise to waken Japheth. He saw that the barrel was just about full, and he moved it, putting an empty one in its place. It, too, was filled before the rain stopped. It continued like this throughout their time in the great ark. There would always be rain when they needed water.

After almost three months in the ark, the food ran out. Noah knew there would be some solution to this problem, although he didn't know what it would be. He felt that the water supply was purposely being kept up, and somehow food would also be provided. What choice did they have? There was nothing around them but water. They ate the last of their food the night of the ninety-third day. Noah thought there was enough hay for the animals for another week. When they awoke the next morning they went to the window, and saw something that looked very different. There were small deck areas in the front and rear of the boat. The windows were just large enough to allow a person to climb out onto the deck. From there, a man could climb up onto the roof of the living quarters.

The front and rear deck of the ark was covered in something that looked like wet bread. Noah held the legs of his son Shem and hung him out the window allowing him to scoop some of the stuff into his hand. They pulled him back in, and everyone examined it. It didn't smell bad. It felt like bread that had gotten wet. Noah took a small amount onto his finger and tasted it. It didn't taste bad at all. It tasted like a very sweet bread. Everyone tried little tastes, and they all agreed that it was something that could be eaten.

They stuck Shem out the window again, this time with a large pot. He scooped the stuff into the pot until it was full. He noticed the roof of the living quarters was also covered with the stuff. He estimated that there was much more than they could ever eat. They all ate until they were completely satisfied. As the day went on, there were no ill effects from the stuff, and they decided that it was fine to eat. They even noticed that after eating their fill in the morning that they weren't hungry for the rest of the day. A few hours after they had gathered the stuff, there was none left to be seen on the deck of the boat. It seemed that whatever had been on the boat evaporated.

The next morning the stuff was back. Again, Shem climbed out the window with a large pot, which he filled very quickly. He handed the pot in to Noah, who passed him a second pot. In all, Shem filled four large pots with the stuff. They ate their fill, and left a large pot full of the sweet bread on a shelf for later. When they went back to the pot much later in the day they were surprised to find that the stuff inside had become putrid. There was no question that it could not be eaten. Mala washed the pot out several times with water drawn up from the sea.

The next morning they took how much they thought they would eat. There was still some left over, and Hacaliah asked for the pot with the remaining stuff. He took it and climbed down to the next level where there were many smaller creatures in pens. He first approached a pen with monkeys. They looked at him eagerly anticipating food. Hacaliah scooped a little of the stuff out of the pot and held it up to the monkey. The creature studied it for a while and finally reached its hand through the wooden bars of the pen and took some of the stuff from Hacaliah's hand. The monkey sniffed it, and then quickly tasted it. He seemed to like it, for he quickly licked his hand clean, and reached back and took more from Hacaliah. Hacaliah didn't wait to watch the monkey any longer. He moved down the row and stopped at a pen containing sheep. Here, too, he held some out on his hand. One of the sheep started to lick his hand, continuing till every morsel of the stuff was off his fingers. Hacaliah continued down the row to a pen containing a pair of lions. Like most of the creatures on the boat, the lions had been eating straw, and the straw was soon to run out. Hacaliah offered some of the mysterious stuff to the lion. Like the sheep the lion licked the stuff off of Hacaliah's hand until his fingers were clean. Hacaliah continued down the row, and offered some to an ostrich. It ate the stuff immediately. He climbed down to the lowest level where there were very large and heavy animals. He offered the stuff to a cow that was in the first pen, then to a zebra, a rhinoceros, and finally to an elephant. All ate the stuff happily.

Hacaliah went back up to the living quarters and explained that every animal had eaten the stuff. It was obvious that this stuff was a gift from God to allow them to survive for how ever long they would be in this great boat. And that would allow them to survive far beyond the limit of the food supply they had put on to the boat. They had not been given any idea as to how long they would be on the boat, and now Hacaliah and Noah understood why. It hadn't made any difference how much food they brought. Provisions would be made for them beyond that food supply. And so it was that every morning there would be this stuff on the deck and roof. Each morning Shem and Japheth would climb out and gather up all of the stuff on both decks and the roof. This is how they would feed the creatures, as well as themselves.

They had been on the boat for more than eight months, when one day they felt the bottom of the boat bump against something. The boat continued to float freely, but this told them that the waters were receding. There were now objects that Noah surmised were mountaintops just under the surface of the water. One morning, after over ten months they opened the window, so Shem and Japheth could climb out, and they were surprised by what they saw. What appeared to be many small islands had popped up out of the sea. They realized they were floating above some mountain range, and these were the tops of the mountains that were now visible. They were very excited. Soon, they would be able to walk on land again. They floated around in this vicinity for weeks, noticing the water level dropping, as the tops of the mountains grew larger.

Three weeks after the mountains had begun to appear, it happened. The boat hit something under the water very early in the morning before anyone had awakened. The impact awakened everyone, as well as all the animals on the boat. The boat had stopped floating. It seemed to be upright. Noah, Hacaliah, and Noah's sons climbed down to the lowest level to see if there was any water coming into the boat. They had only the earliest light of day, and little of that found its way all the way down the opening to the lowest level, but they could not see or hear any water coming in. The great boat never moved from its landing place. As the waters receded they saw they were wedged into a crook in the side of a mountain. There was quite a bit of the mountain above them, but much more seemed to be below.

They stayed in the great boat as the waters continued to recede. Two weeks after the boat became lodged on the side of the mountain, there was no water left to be seen. The ground looked like it would not support anything walking on it. Hacaliah and Noah suspected that a human would sink out of sight in the mud. They waited. After they had been in the boat for more than a year, the ground appeared to have dried out. Noah decided it was time to open the doors to the hatchway. His son's took up the large mallet that had last been used to drive the pegs in that held the doors tightly shut. Now, this same mallet pounded those pegs back out of their positions, and the great doors swung open, one to the left, one to the right. The boat had lodged into the side of the mountain so that the ground was almost the same height as the hatchway. There was a distance of the height of a man between the boat and the land. Japheth took the mallet and pounded out the hinge pegs on one of the great doors, while Shem held the rope that was used to draw the door closed. When the final hinge peg was out, the great door started to fall away from the boat, but Japheth pulled the rope and thus the door toward him until it was inside the boat. They laid it down flat and it reached from the edge of the boat to the dry land. Noah, Hacaliah, and all of Noah's family stepped out of the boat on to dry land for the first time in over a year. The ground felt firm, and there was small green vegetation already growing up from the ground. They were situated at a point on the mountainside where the land sloped gently downward. They looked down into a valley below. There were several other mountains nearby. They released most of the animals immediately after coming out of the ark. Those few that would be beneficial for them as they built a new place to live were kept. The second door had to be laid down on top of the first to support the weight of the larger creatures.

All on the boat had realized that had the boat been facing the other way when it lodged in place, they would not have been able to get the doors open. They would have had to climb out the window, climb to the ground, and cut a hole in the side of the boat. They were very glad it hadn't happened that way.

The cows, horses, and elephants were especially beneficial for getting heavy work done. Some of these creatures had been helpful in building the ark in the first place. Over a period of several months they utilized much of the lumber from the great boat to build several buildings that would serve as a home for them and the creatures that were kept. After a year, they had developed a small farm using seed that Noah had stored on the boat. They were growing food for themselves, and the vegetation of the earth had been recovering rapidly. Their animals were also multiplying at a surprising rate. In the first year off the boat, Mala and both Shem and Japheth's wives became pregnant. All gave birth to sons. Noah and Mala named their son Ham. Japheth's first son was named Gomer, and Shem's first son was called Elam. For the next twenty years, many sons and daughters were born to the three couples. Maalana waited patiently while the sons of her brothers grew old enough to marry. She knew that only then would she be able to have a husband and children. It was the eighteenth year after they had stepped onto dry land when Maalana was married to Elam, Shem's first son. He was seventeen, and she was fifty-two. He looked seventeen, and she looked to be in her late twenties.

After fifty years their homestead had developed into a small community. After one hundred years there were several thousand people living in, and around the community that had been established. One hundred and fifty years after they stepped off the boat, their community had grown large. Four or five thousand people had moved away yet there were nearly five thousand still living in the community.

It was about this time that Hacaliah decided it was time for him to move, also. It was noticeable that people born after the flood had much shorter life spans. By the time they were two hundred years old, they were showing signs of aging.

Hacaliah knew that it wouldn't be long before it was obvious to others that he was not growing older like they were. He had become a farmer also, and had done very well for himself. Many had been willing to work for him on his farm, and he had a reputation for being very fair, kind, and generous. Over the years he had acquired many cattle, sheep, and horses. He used the many wagons and farm utensils he had invented to make tilling the soil easier. He now took four of his wagons, and loaded them with food and various material needs that he thought would help him get re-established. Six of his best workers approached him when they heard of his decision, and requested that they be allowed to go with him. They expressed a willingness to take their families wherever he went.

And so, one hundred and fifty years after they had come out of the great boat, Hacaliah left Noah and the community that had built up around them. He took his four wagons, each pulled by two horses. He took two additional horses tied behind each wagon, along with various cattle and sheep. The six other families came with him in three wagons filled with their belongings. Hacaliah headed west down through the valley.

Many who had come back through the area spoke of a "Great Sea" off to the west and Hacaliah felt that he was ready to live closer to the sea. They traveled for three days, continuing toward the setting of the sun for as long as there was daylight. On the fourth day, Hacaliah suddenly sensed a familiarity to the area, although as he looked around nothing in particular seemed familiar. As they moved forward he tried to remember what it was that was vaguely familiar to him. Then he realized they had been climbing a long sloping field, which reminded him of his travels to the beautiful place where he had lived as a young child. The place he had visited with his father, and that he himself had visited many times. He looked around again to try to connect other landmarks, but he couldn't. The flood had changed so much of the terrain. As they reached the top of the long sloping meadow, Hacaliah's heart jumped. There, in the valley below, was the unmistakable stone wall with the opening to the beautiful place!

There were no longer men standing there to guard it, no longer anything inside to guard. But it was the place where he and Noah had stayed for three days over a hundred and fifty years ago, as the man gave them instructions to build the great boat. He stopped at the top of the hill, and looked down for several minutes. Everyone traveling with him stopped behind him, waiting. They had no idea why he stopped. They assumed he was deciding which way to go. Hacaliah thought about the memories from so long ago. He estimated it had been almost eighteen hundred and thirty years ago that he had been born on the other side of those walls. He marveled at his ability to draw up memories, as though they happened just a few days ago. He could still remember sitting by the river as a little child while his father spoke with a man, much like he and Noah had spoken to a man one hundred and fifty years ago. He decided there was no reason to go down to the wall, or into that place that was his first home. The guards were gone, so there was no longer anything special inside those walls. He headed south around the walled area, and continued west toward the Great Sea he knew was ahead of him somewhere.

Chapter 21

Adam was sitting in the conference room at Comtec reading a document that had been prepared by his attorney Roy Hazelton. Hazelton was the senior partner of Hazelton, Hunter, and Fath, one of the more prestigious law firms in town. He first met Adam when Adam had come to the West Coast. He had arranged to transfer Adam's finances from New York to California, and he set up the original twenty million dollar escrow account that was part of the Comtec deal. He had been very impressed the first time he met Adam, but he was even more impressed when he transferred his funds from several different financial institutions and found they totaled almost seventy million dollars.

Adam also had Hazelton handle the sale of the golf course. He had owned it for twenty-four years. Golf had become very popular over those years, and the golf course had been greatly improved, well run, and well maintained. Adam cleared a twelve million dollar profit. He gave it all to IMA. He didn't keep a penny for himself. That impressed Hazelton the most. A few years later, Adam had transferred most of his fortune to several accounts in Swiss banks. He thought Adam might still have ten or more million locally.

When he had gotten the call from Adam regarding a change in the way IMA was run, he had wondered if Adam knew of something he hadn't shared with anyone. Roy thought that Adam might be ill. He had long wondered his age, because he looked too young for his resume when they had met eight years ago. He didn't look much older now. Roy figured that Adam was one of those rich people whose weakness was a desire to look young forever. He figured Adam must have had plastic surgery to maintain his youthful appearance. The only problem with that theory was he had not been aware of Adam being in the hospital at any time. Come to think of it, he couldn't remember Adam ever having a cold, or even taking a vacation. Whatever the case, he had long ago learned not to question anything Adam requested.

After handling all of Adam's initial West Coast business, he did his own research on the man. He knew quite well what happened every time Adam got involved with a company. Roy had called his broker, and asked him to buy every share of Comtec he could get his hands on. The broker called him the next day to say that he could find only a few hundred shares. Hazelton asked him to offer two hundred and fifty dollars a share, which brought protest from the broker because the market value was only two hundred. Hazelton patiently explained to the broker that in this particular instance, he didn't want to be second-guessed, and he was paying the broker to do what he asked. Two days later the broker called and told him that at fifty dollars over the market price, he could purchase twelve thousand shares. Roy checked his account balances, pooled several of them along with the firm's pension fund, and scraped up the three million required to make the purchase. Thinking back he remembered not losing a night's sleep over it. That was how confident he felt after checking Adam out. That stock had split twice, and two years ago, the total value of Comtec stock owned by Hazelton, Hunter, and Fath was close to nine million, six hundred thousand dollars. Roy had sold off some of his personal stock, just to have some cash back in his accounts. He personally had three million back in the bank, and another three million remaining in Comtec stock.

Now, he wished he knew what was going on. If Adam was going to be out of the picture he would have to consider what to do with all the Comtec stock.

Roy Hazelton had two junior partners with him. They were both experts in the structure and charters of non-profit organizations. They had put together an excellent plan to ensure IMA would continue to operate in the same manner that it had, even without Adam Adamson. The charter called for an executive committee consisting of nine individuals. There would be a chairman of this executive committee. The vice chairman would also be the president of IMA. The position would be filled initially by Mr. Groff. Seven other senior IMA officers would make up the rest of the committee. Each year, there would be an election to determine who would be the chairman of the committee, and who would be the president of IMA. All members of the committee would be required to vote. There could be no abstentions. In the event that someone was unable to be present, due to grave illness or death, the elections would take place without them, and the committee would have to continue voting, until a majority won. The finances of IMA would be overseen by this committee, but the president would have the overall responsibility to invest the money. IMA presently had investments totaling almost one billion dollars. Invested properly, this would enable them to donate one hundred million dollars a year, indefinitely.

The document Adam was reading at the moment was this new structure. It probably could have been summed up in twenty pages, but Hazelton, Hunter, and Fath was going to earn its money. The legal terms added to impress inflated the document to fifty pages. The document was put together with the help of the most up-to-date desktop publishing, and it was beautifully bound in leather. Hazelton and his two juniors each had an unbound copy. Roy had them along in case there was a question he was unable to answer, although he had read the document thoroughly, and had spent three hours with the two juniors going over every detail. He wanted to appear to be completely informed, and able to handle any question.

He had hoped to go through the document with Adam paragraph by paragraph, but Adam had opened the document and, while looking at the first page, held up the first finger of his right hand in a gesture that said: "hold on a minute." He then started leafing through the pages at the rate of one every fifteen to twenty seconds. Roy thought he was simply skimming. No one could read through all the legal terminology that quickly. He considered this to be a waste of time, because they would have to go over it anyway. But it was Adam, and so he sat there with his two junior partners doing what he hated most in the world, waiting.

Adam closed the book and laid it gently down on the table. He looked at Roy Hazelton for about ten seconds. For the last two of those seconds, Hazelton had a fleeting thought that something in the document was terribly wrong. Then Adam smiled. He commended Roy for a job well done. He had four minor changes he wanted to see, and he proceeded to rattle them off; page, paragraph, and the wording as it was, and how he wanted it changed. Roy Hazelton was shocked, as were the two men with him. Adam asked them to make the changes and have the corrected document back the next day. He would sign it, appoint the first chairman himself, and have all the necessary people sign it. With that he stood up, shook hands all around, thanked them again, and left the room. Within seconds there was a young woman at the door of the conference room to show the men out.

Adam returned to his office and checked his calendar. He had blocked out two hours for lunch. He and Gus were going to a little restaurant they both liked for lunch. Someone once recommended it to Gus, and he had tried it. He was so impressed by the service and the food that he mentioned it to Adam, and one day on the way back from a meeting they stopped there. Adam agreed that it was quite nice. The tables weren't right on top of one another. You could have a conversation without others so close they could hear everything you said. To ensure a quiet opportunity to talk, Adam had asked Gus to make the reservation for one-thirty. The lunch crowd would be pretty much gone. They would have the dining room practically to themselves.

Chapter 22

Elizabeth left the penthouse at one o'clock, as she did almost every day. She stepped out into the bright sunlight in front of the Aegis building. She looked around at the people walking every which way, and thought about how busy and hurried everyone looked. She was glad that she wasn't in a hurry. She turned left toward the market, and strolled leisurely down the sidewalk, her little cart in tow.

When she reached the corner, Lewis crossed the street and entered the Aegis. He was dressed like someone who worked in a sandwich shop. Ken and Philip crossed the street and entered the Aegis three minutes later. They were wearing their new suits, and sporting their new business haircuts. They actually had a good laugh with the whole crew earlier in the day when they got together. They had been able to buy suits that fit, right off the rack. It was great. They bought the jackets and pants separately so there was no wait for any tailoring. They were ready much sooner than they expected, so they decided to go for it instead of waiting another day or two.

Lewis had with him a sheet of the day's specials. They really were the specials from the sandwich shop around the corner, so if he had to hand it out to cover himself there wouldn't be a problem. If they called and ordered lunch, the sandwich shop might wonder how they were getting the phone order, but Lewis wasn't worried about that. He pushed the elevator button, and one of the elevators opened almost immediately. He stepped in and pushed eleven. The door closed and the elevator took him to the eleventh floor. When he got off, he turned to the IMA entrance. He had done this before.

He opened the door slowly and walked in. He was wearing sneakers, to minimize the noise of his footsteps. He looked around and saw there was no one in the reception area. His heart started beating a bit harder. He stepped over to the elevator, and pushed the button, continuing to look into the reception area. The door opened immediately and he stepped in, his heart pounding. He could feel it in his head. The door closed while he was looking at the buttons. He saw that there were only three buttons. One was marked "up" one was marked "down," and the third was an emergency button. He pushed the up button, and within five seconds the door opened into the penthouse.

Lewis was really nervous. He looked around to be sure that there was no one there. The door started to close, hit him in the shoulder, and opened again. He stepped out into the penthouse. He didn't want the elevator to start buzzing because the door couldn't close. The door closed behind him. He took a careful look around. It was the nicest place he had ever been in. He started to walk through the living room, looking for the kitchen. He needed to find the stairway. He had taken only a few steps, when he remembered the walkie-talkie. He reached into his jacket pocket, pulled it out, and turned it on. It squawked for a second. He half whispered in to the thing, "Ken … are you there?"

Ken's voice came back clearly, "I'm here Lewis, everything OK?"

"Yeah, so far all's clear. I'm gonna check out the kitchen and make sure I know where the stairs are. Everything OK down in the lobby?"

"So far, everything looks normal."

"OK, I'll check out the stairs and then I'll be down."

"OK."

Lewis walked into what appeared to be the kitchen, and it was. It was beautiful. He thought it looked like it was from a magazine, or something. He walked to the back of the kitchen, and there was an alcove on the left. Sure enough, there was a doorway with a peephole. He looked out the peephole, and saw a stairway. He tried the doorknob, and it turned from the inside. He was all set if he needed it. He went back in to the living room and pushed the button for the other elevator. It took close to fifteen seconds for the door to open, he stepped in and pushed the down button. The door opened in the lobby, Ken and Philip were standing right there. They all looked at each other.

Lewis spoke first, "Everything OK?"

Ken nodded. "Go back up and wait. We'll give it five minutes to make sure no cops are on their way."

Lewis nodded, pushed the up button, and the door closed.

Ken and Philip talked to one another, trying to give the impression they were just a couple of lawyers waiting for an elevator, or waiting for someone. Everyone who came through the lobby seemed to be in a hurry to get in or out, and no one paid any attention to the two.

After a little more than five minutes, Ken spoke into his walkie-talkie and told Lewis to come down. The plan was that Lewis would come down, Ken and Philip would go up, and Lewis would go across the street to keep an eye out for cops or anything suspicious. A few seconds later the elevator door opened, Lewis stepped out, and Ken and Philip stepped in. No one else in the lobby noticed anything. Lewis stepped out onto the street and walked across the street to watch. He felt a tremendous sense of relief. He figured whatever happened now, it wouldn't be him that got caught.

Todd was following the housekeeper with another walkie-talkie so he could communicate when she got near the building, if he had to. Lester was around the corner in a parked car.

The elevator opened into the penthouse, and Ken and Philip stepped out. The door closed behind them, and Ken listened to see if it was returning to the lobby automatically. It didn't. They looked around for a few seconds before moving. It was quite a place. Neither of them had been in a place that looked like this before. They each had a wide briefcase. They had decided larger ones would hold more. They started to look around more carefully. Ken reminded Philip not to disturb anything, if it could be helped. It was to their advantage if their presence went undetected for some period of time.

They carefully looked behind each hanging picture. The living room revealed nothing. There was no furniture in the living room that had drawers or cupboards. There were shelves with things on them, but nothing of any particular value. Ken estimated that the stereo equipment was worth thousands, but he wasn't about to start lugging that stuff around. They moved into the bedroom, which also revealed nothing worth considering. He thought that for someone worth as much as this guy was, he sure didn't spend his money on anything for his apartment. Ken opened the closet door. Philip wasn't watching him, but he heard him whistle, which caused him to look over.

"Hey," Ken called out, "check this out."

Philip walked over to the closet and looked in. Hanging there were a dozen suits. All dark blue or dark gray with slight variations of subtle stripes. Ken took one out and looked at it.

"Must cost a couple thousand," he said more to himself than to Philip.

Philip gave him a little nudge with his elbow. "Maybe it's your size. Try it on, you can leave yours in its place." They both laughed at the thought.

They had spent less than two hundred bucks apiece on their suits. The thought of leaving one of them hanging in this closet was funny. Next to the suits, there were shirts. White, and light blue, two-dozen, all perfectly pressed and hanging facing the same direction. "This guy is an organization freak," was Philip's comment.

Ken agreed. "Look at the shoes."

On a rack to one side of the closet were easily ten pairs of shoes. All shined, some black, some burgundy, some tan. There were even a couple of pairs of sneakers or running shoes.

Ken asked himself what it was, exactly, that he had hoped to find! They were sitting on almost a quarter of a million dollars back in Philip's apartment from the last deal. What did they need? Why were they taking this risk? He looked over at Philip.

"What are we doing this for? We've got a box full of money sitting at your place."

Philip looked back at him. "It's the adventure, my man, the adventure!" He grinned a wide grin, to make his point.

"Yeah, well I'm not sure I need this kind of adventure. This seemed like a great idea, but now that I'm here, I'm thinking this is stupid."

"Well, you might be right, but we are here, we're in it now, so we might as well have a good look around."

Ken didn't disagree. "But let's be real careful about not messing anything up. If we walk out of here with nothing, I don't want to leave any sign that we were here." Philip didn't answer, and Ken took his silence as agreement.

They moved out of the main bedroom and found a second bedroom that appeared to be a guest room. It had a bed, a night table, and chair. Everything was very high quality and the room was beautiful, but you could tell no one used the room. The closet was empty. The next room was a library, obviously used as a study. There was a computer on the table. Both men remarked on the table. It was massive and unmistakably old. Ken walked to the shelves, and started to look at the books. There was nothing he was familiar with, although he wasn't much of a reader. He noticed there were quite a few different Bibles. Some looked to be very old and they were large. Others looked newer, and they were much smaller. There was a section of shelves with books that looked different. There was nothing written on the outside edge to tell what the book was. Some looked old. Actually, as Ken looked, he realized that they went from looking very old at one end to progressively looking newer at the other end of the shelf. And they didn't all look exactly the same. The oldest seemed to be leather bound, and after a few of the books they were made of some other material. He had no idea what it was. He pulled one of the newer looking ones out, and opened it somewhere in the middle. It was some kind of journal.

The book was filled with lined pages, and there were entries written in black ink. The writing was very neat and legible. He looked at the first entry on the left hand page. It was several lines down. The lines above must have been from an entry on the previous page. The entry Ken looked at was dated "June 4,1896." He didn't take the time to read the entry. He flipped back about halfway between where he had opened and the beginning of the book. The first entry on the page was dated "January 12, 1890." Ken wasn't quite sure what he was looking at. He went to the first page of the book and looked at the first entry. It was dated "September 21, 1879." Ken's heart started to beat a little faster. He slid the book back into its place, and pulled out the first one on the shelf. The oldest one. It was bound in leather. He opened it to the first page. The writing looked the same, but it was a different language. He couldn't tell what it was, although it seemed to use the same letters as the entries in English. The first entry was 01-08-1612. Ken's head started to spin. He was trying to understand what he was looking at, but his initial thoughts defied all logic. He quickly looked at other entry dates. The last entry in the first book was 07-12-1701.

Ken slid the book back in to its place, and took out the last book on the shelf, the newest. The first entry date in that book was "February 3, 1958." The writing seemed to be the same, but now it was back to English. He read a little of this first entry:

> Today I spoke with Gus Stoltz in the shipping department about working as my driver. I know that this man can be trusted. I sense in him a higher standard of honor than is typical in men today. I believe him to be trustworthy.

Ken flipped quickly to the last page in the book. It was still blank. He fanned back through the pages, looking for the last entry. He found it a third of the way back into the book. It was dated only the day before, "August 16, 2000."

> Tomorrow I will discuss my next life shift with Gus. I sense that it is imperative that I make this shift in the very near future. I hope Gus will come with me, but I expect that he will not be willing to do so.

Ken slid the book back onto the shelf. He had to tell himself to calm down, because he wanted to scream. He didn't want to say something that would scare Philip, and he didn't really know what to say. What was he thinking? What was he seeing? The writing all looked similar. He would think at first glance that the writing had all been done by one person, but the entries spanned from 1612 to 2000. It couldn't be one man! Or could it? Ken suddenly remembered Lester's comment after his research. He had said that there was no history on Adam before the late fifties. Lester's words had been something like: "It was as if he didn't exist before the late fifties." He remembered that the Wall Street Journal web site had no information on his birth date, or the origin of his birth. Ken sat down in the chair that was near the shelves. He put his elbows on his knees and his head in his hands, deep in thought. Philip looked over at him and thought it was a little strange that he would be sitting like that.

"Ken, you OK?" Ken nodded. "What's the matter?"

Ken shook his head slightly from side to side. It was his attempt at sign language to say: "Don't ask me, this is way too complicated, and way too fantastic, and you won't understand it because I don't even understand it." But of course Philip wasn't able to understand all that in the gesture, so he pressed.

"What's the matter, Ken? You're sitting there like you got a headache or something." As he was speaking he was looking behind one of the pictures on the study wall. As he pulled on it, it swung away from the wall on a hinge, and revealed a wall safe.

"Well, looky here, what have we got?" This distracted Ken momentarily, and he looked up to see the safe. He got up and walked over to take a closer look.

"Forget it," he said quietly to Philip. "This baby is top quality. We'll knock ourselves out, and we'll never get into it."

Philip looked at him. "But, Ken," and as he spoke he reached out and put one hand on the handle, "suppose it isn't even locked." And as he said "locked" he tried to swing the handle to the side. It didn't budge because it was locked. He looked at Ken, and Ken looked at him. Ken's look said: "I could have told you it was locked." Philip's look said: "you were right." He swung the picture back against the wall.

Ken walked back over to the shelf. He slid one of the books out from the older looking books, and put it on the table. He then moved over to the newest book, and pushed against the entire row, shifting the books and closing up the space where he had removed the book. He stepped back and decided that everything looked pretty much the same. He opened his briefcase, put the journal in and closed the briefcase. Philip watched all of this.

"What the heck are you doing?"

Ken didn't even look at him as he closed the case. "Taking something that I think might be worth a fortune."

Philip looked puzzled. "An old book?"

Ken had too many things going through his head to stop and explain anything to Philip. "I'll explain it later. Let's just get out of here." He headed toward the elevator, and Philip knew not to argue. He had agreed that the whole idea was probably stupid so he didn't see any reason to keep looking around, and he could tell something was really bothering Ken. If he wanted to leave he was going to get no argument. Ken pushed the elevator button and the door opened immediately. They stepped in, the door shut, and in seconds it opened into the lobby. They walked out of the building onto the sidewalk.

Philip saw Lewis across the street. They crossed the street, and the three of them walked around the corner to the car. Lester started the car as they got in. He noticed Todd wasn't with them.

"Where's Todd?" he asked.

Lewis answered him, "He's still following the old lady. Swing down toward the market, if he's not on his way back, he'll be outside the market somewhere."

They had only been in the penthouse about twenty minutes, and they figured she took almost an hour to make the trip to the market and back. They pulled up to the market and sure enough Todd was standing outside reading a newspaper. He saw them and immediately walked over and got into the car. He looked all excited. "Well, how'd we make out?"

Philip spoke, "It was a bust."

Todd looked confused. "What do you mean a bust?"

Philip spoke up again, "I mean we didn't take anything. But Ken took some old book.

Todd and Lewis were in the back seat with Philip and had been looking at him while he spoke. Now all three of them looked at Ken in the front seat.

Todd spoke up, "Ken, what's with the old book? There wasn't anything better worth taking in this zillionaire's apartment?"

Ken didn't turn around as he spoke, "Look, guys, what do you think we should have taken? We're sitting on a quarter of a million bucks in cash, and we don't even know what to do with it. Should we have stolen some jewelry that was maybe worth a few hundred or even a few thousand dollars? What would be the point? I took something that I have a feeling will be worth a small fortune."

Todd considered himself the back seat spokesman. "Some old book?"

"It's not an old book, it's a journal."

"OK, excuse me, a journal. Who's going to pay a fortune for a journal?"

Ken smiled as he thought about the answer to that question. "Adam Adamson," he said quietly as he patted the briefcase on his lap.

Chapter 23

Christine Girasoli had been up since five o'clock in the morning. It was now a little after one o'clock in the afternoon, and she was in the bathroom putting the finishing touches on her hair and make-up. Her husband Carl was in the den, all dressed and ready to go. He was catching a little golf on the golf channel. Some tournament in Japan where he hardly recognized any names. He was trying not to think about how uncomfortable the next couple of hours might be. He told himself that it might turn out to be fine, but he knew that it probably wouldn't. He also knew that his wife was having an anxiety attack about this whole thing, and it was up to him to keep his cool. He looked at his watch. It was ten minutes after one. They had to leave in the next ten minutes to be on time, and God knew that they didn't want to be late. Harris Pearson could never tolerate anyone being late!

Harris Pearson was Christine's father. Her mother, Mildred was a wonderful woman who always looked for the good in things. No matter what it was, she somehow found a positive slant to it. She was a devoutly religious woman, and Carl remembered the story about a time when the conversation at the dinner table had once come around to the devil. Someone at the table challenged Christine's mother to say something positive about him. She thought for a minute and then said, "Well, he's very good at his job." Of course everyone broke out in hysterics over that, including Mildred herself. Harris Pearson was almost the direct opposite of Mildred. He was a sour man who rarely found pleasure in anything, and displayed a feeling of pleasure even less often. He was very intelligent and had a relative sense of fairness. Those were probably his only two good qualities.

Harris Pearson was a WASP in the truest sense of the word. White Anglo Saxon Protestant. He prided himself on being able to track his predecessors directly back to the Mayflower. He was Massachusetts born and bred, and he didn't like people who were not of the same stock. That certainly included Italians, who in Pearson's eyes were all hoodlums or bums. When Christine had announced that she was in love with a man named Carl Girasoli and was going to marry him, her father flew into a tirade. She had never heard or seen her father act like that before. She had always been "Daddy's little girl," and this marked a stark change in their relationship. He hadn't gone to their wedding, although Mildred was there. There was a generous check as a wedding present and it did have Harris Pearson's signature on it, but he never acknowledged in any way that he approved of the marriage, or her husband.

Shortly after they were married, they moved to California where Carl was working as a story editor and writer for a television studio. It was a wonderful job. He did very well financially, providing an elegant home for his wife and children. They had some of the most interesting friends from the entertainment world. They had been married for twenty-five years, and their children were throwing an anniversary party for them on Saturday night, and it was going to be a real bash. Their son, Carl, Jr., had contacted Mildred about the party, and asked them to please come to it. He had even offered to send them the tickets, although the cost of flying out to California was of no concern to the Pearsons. Harris had made millions. The problem now was two-fold. First, Harris was a stubborn old codger in his early eighties. In spite of the fact that his daughter had been happily married for twenty-five years, and had two wonderful children, he was still angry she had married an Italian. Second, he was sickly. He had already had two heart attacks, and he suffered from emphysema. On top of that, he had broken his hip a year ago and was still in a wheel chair. When Mildred discussed the trip with her husband, he said no. But Mildred had detected that it was a half-hearted no. Harris Pearson was an old sick man. He knew that he would not live a lot longer, and perhaps it was time to see his daughter before it was too late. Mildred pushed him just a little, and he gave in.

It was decided that Mildred and Harris would stay in a hotel in town. It was a beautiful new hotel, and it would be much easier to accommodate Harris's wheelchair. They were going to meet for lunch at a lovely little restaurant just a half block from the hotel. The weather was delightful, and Mildred welcomed the walk. Harris's wheelchair was electric, and he still had all his wits about him so he would be able to negotiate to the restaurant with no trouble. Besides, Harris hadn't talked to his daughter or her husband in twenty-five years. Suddenly staying in their home as guests was just out of the question. It would have been far too awkward.

Christine came into the den and found her husband sitting on the couch watching golf on TV. He looked up at her, and he could see that she was ready to go. He thought to himself that she was ready to go, in more ways than one. He knew she was ready to snap from the anxiety of having to face her father. He had already assured her that it didn't matter to him how her father acted, but he knew she was worried the old man would make a scene.

He pushed the button on the remote to turn off the TV, and sprung to his feet in a mocking hurry to get going. He smiled, and she shook her head. She knew she had to calm down. She was hoping that things would go well, and they would be able to clear up twenty-five years of Harris Pearson's being a stubborn, hurtful man. She wanted everything out of the way so the anniversary party could be free of any underlying resentments. Carl tried to help her see that her expectations were a little unrealistic, but it was an emotional issue, and he didn't want to upset his wife any more than she was.

They got into the car at fifteen minutes after one. Carl thought it should work out just right. It would take about a half hour to get to the restaurant, and ten minutes to find a parking place. They should be a few minutes early. Certainly Harris Pearson would be pleased.

Chapter 24

Adam and Gus arrived for lunch precisely at one-thirty. They were shown to a table toward the back of the main dining room. There were several other tables in the room, with people still eating lunch, but no party was within three tables of Adam and Gus so they were free to talk privately. They ordered lunch and made very brief small talk about the day. Adam knew he had to lay his cards on the table.

"Gus, you know that you've come to be the most trusted person in my life, I consider you to be my only real friend in the world."

Gus wasn't sure how to reply. "Adam, I don't know what to say, you know all these years I've been with you have been the best years of my life. Tell me, boss, what's going on?"

"Well, Gus, you understand why I make a move to a different part of the country every so many years?"

Gus nodded.

"And you understand I avoid any real social life, so that I don't start running into people I haven't seen in years?"

Again Gus nodded. He had understood all this for a long time.

"Well, Gus, every so often, depending on the world around me, I have to make a major move. I call it a life shift. I don't simply move to a different part of the country, I relocate to a different part of the world, and assume a completely different identity."

Gus thought about that for a moment. "And you're telling me this because you're going to make this, this life shift?"

Adam suddenly looked a little weary, Gus had never seen this look before. "Yes, my friend, I'm afraid I am."

Gus thought again for a few moments. "What about me, Adam? What do you want me to do? Should I go with you, or do you not want me to go? I have no idea what you expect."

"I don't expect anything, Gus. What you do has to be your decision. I would love to have you make this move with me, I can arrange for a new identity for you, too, but you have to do what you want to do. A life shift would mean leaving all traces of Gus Stoltz behind. You haven't had much contact with your family in the last decade, so I don't think anyone is going to be looking for you. But, Gus, I want you to know that if you decide to stay,

I'll be leaving two million dollars in a bank account in your name. You won't have to worry about money for the rest of your life."

Gus looked at him for a long time. He looked deep into those wise eyes, and he knew Adam was being sincere in his kindness. He started to laugh. He kept it under control because he was in a restaurant, but he laughed out loud. It was infectious, and Adam started to laugh, although he wasn't sure what it was he was laughing at.

He looked a little puzzled, even though he was laughing. "What?" he said to Gus. "What's so funny?"

Gus got himself under control. "Boss, I've been with you over forty years. I haven't worried about money since the day I moved into the old guest house in Massachusetts. There has hardly been anything come along in those forty years that you let me pay for myself. I've been putting my money into the stock market for forty years. Last time I checked my portfolio was worth a little over two million."

Adam laughed, but this time he knew why he was laughing.

They talked at length about what was involved in a life shift. Adam explained how he transferred key real estate holdings to his new identity. It appeared that he was selling the properties. He had different agents handling each one, and none of them knew about the other holdings, so there was no suspicion. The bulk of his fortune was in three different Swiss bank accounts and they were strictly numbered accounts. None of the three banks even knew him by name. As long as he knew the right numbers, it didn't matter who he was.

They talked about Comtec and how Edward Keaton would revert back to the presidency. Adam was confident he would continue to do things in a similar vein to Adam's. They talked about IMA, and the new charter.

They were so engrossed in their conversation that neither of them noticed the party that sat just two tables away. They didn't see the old man in the wheelchair or his wife. They took no notice when the younger woman and her husband came in. They hadn't seen the teary greetings, or the young woman bend down to hug the old man in the chair.

But suddenly the conversation lapsed for a moment and Adam looked over in the direction of that other table. At that same moment Harris Pearson happened to glance back over toward Adam. Harris Pearson stared for a long moment at Adam. It took Adam a minute to register the face. It had been a long time since he had seen it. Pearson seemed confused. He looked over at the large black man sitting across the table from Adam. Gus saw Adam's expression change dramatically, and he looked to see what had caused it. When Pearson saw Gus' face and then glanced back at Adam he reacted as if he had seen a ghost. His eyes grew wide with fear. His breathing became labored and very fast. Everyone at his table thought he was choking on something. They started to react, but the old man waved them off. He tried to speak, but he couldn't. Something was obviously scaring the old man out of his wits, but the family had no idea what it was. The old man's breathing was out of control, and Mildred became hysterical. She started yelling for someone to call 911. The old man was desperately trying to speak, but he couldn't get the words out, he couldn't catch his breath. His frustration from his inability to speak and the lack of oxygen finally triggered a massive heart attack and the old man slumped over in the chair.

Gus didn't recognize the old man and he turned to Adam. "Boss, what should we do?"

Adam looked at Gus with a very serious look on his face. "Gus, do absolutely nothing. Try to act like nothing has happened."

"Boss, who is that old man?" Gus knew that Adam recognized him from somewhere.

Adam didn't want to get Gus any more excited than he was. "Gus, I'll explain it in a few minutes."

Within three minutes or so, two paramedics came wheeling in the front door of the restaurant. They realized immediately that the old man was in cardiac arrest and they started CPR. After a few minutes of working on him and giving him an injection, he seemed to be stabilized and they wheeled him out on the gurney they had wheeled in. Mildred went with him in the ambulance, and the younger couple said they would follow in their car.

Adam and Gus left a minute later. When they got in the limo, Gus wasn't sure what to do. "Boss, what was that all about, who was that old guy?"

Adam was trying to think the situation through. "That old guy was Harris Pearson!"

Now, Gus understood the dilemma. "Harris Pearson from Avionics in Massachusetts?"

"The one in the same," Adam replied with noticeable concern in his voice.

Gus was speaking more to himself than to Adam. "Man, no wonder he went nuts when he saw us. We should be looking about as old as him. I know I don't look anywhere near that old, and you don't look any different than you did back then. No wonder he freaked out!"

"Well, Gus, it's not just his freaking out. First of all, I certainly don't want the old man to die on my account. Secondly, Harris Pearson had very powerful connections with the military. If he pulls out of this, you know he's going to be talking to anyone he can get to listen to him."

"Boss," Gus was trying to calm the whole situation down, "we don't know if old Harris can even talk. He must be well into his eighties."

"I don't know, Gus, I got the impression that he would be able to talk under more normal circumstances. This is going to force me to make my move sooner."

Gus didn't know what to do or say. "Boss, whatever you do, I'm going with you. I got no reason to stay here. What do you want me to do now, do we head back to Comtec, or do we go home?"

Adam was relieved to hear that Gus was willing to go with him. "Let's head back to Comtec for right now."

Adam sat back in the seat and thought about how quickly he could put everything together. He figured that he had three days before Harris would recover enough to be able to talk to someone about what he saw. It might take him a little while to convince anyone that he wasn't just a crazy old coot, but he would likely be discussing it with important people within four or five days. Adam knew he had to be non-existent in five days.

Harris Pearson was the vice president and comptroller at Avionics when Adam took over as president in 1956. At that time Pearson was in his early forties. He was a difficult man to get along with, and he was one of the few men in Adam's experience who was resistant to his leadership. Pearson was a real "skinflint," who watched every penny like it might be his personal last. He didn't like Adam's way of rewarding the efforts of the employees with higher wages. Adam had found him to be extremely diligent and honest, however, so he worked with him patiently, and as Pearson saw the overall income and the profit of the company increasing he started to come around. It was only a year after he started with Avionics that Adam had purchased the first Avionics limo, and moved Gus up from the shipping and receiving department. Pearson had not been too happy about that decision, especially when Adam told him to almost double Gus' pay.

By the time Adam left Avionics nine years later Pearson had come to respect his every decision. Avionics had more than tripled their gross sales and their net profit. They had gone public on the New York Stock exchange, and in five years their stock value had almost tripled. Harris Pearson had already become a wealthy man, and he was sorry to see Adam leave. That was in 1966. Poor Harris couldn't handle seeing Adam thirty-four years later still looking exactly as he had the day he left.

When they got back to the office Adam phoned Roy Hazelton. Roy was on the line in less than a minute. "Hi, Adam, what's up?"

Adam didn't want to have to go into an explanation, so he was a little abrupt. "Roy, something has come up that has altered my time schedule a little. I just want to make sure that you'll be here first thing in the morning with the new charter documents."

Roy was only concerned about pleasing Adam. "Yes, sir. We'll be there at nine, unless you need us to be there earlier."

"No, nine will do just fine, thanks." Adam hung up.

Adam went across the reception area of the executive offices to Edward Keaton's office. His secretary smiled and greeted him as if she hadn't seen him in weeks, even though she saw him come back in just a few minutes earlier. Adam looked at her, and she knew he meant serious business. "Is he in?" She nodded.

Adam knocked on the open doorway, and went in. Edward was working at his desk. He got up and walked over to Adam. "Adam, come in, come in. Sit down. To what do I owe this unexpected visit?"

Adam spent the next twenty minutes explaining as little as he thought he could get away with, as to why he would be leaving. He would call a board meeting for tomorrow morning, at which time he would inform the board and recommend that Edward be reappointed as the president and CEO.

Edward looked at Adam for a moment. "You know you are a strange bird, Adam."

Adam wasn't sure what he meant, but he could tell that it was said in a light-hearted way. "What do you mean?"

"Well, eight years ago you came waltzing in here, announced that you wanted to be the president and CEO. I looked at you like you were crazy, but you convinced me that you were serious. I took it to the board, and everyone agreed that you could have the job. Now, here you are telling me that in three days you're gone, and I can have the job back, just like that!"

"Well," Adam spoke calmly now, "Edward, I'm only offering you the job of president because I happen to think you're the best man for the job."

Edward was sincerely grateful. "Thank you, Adam. Coming from you that means a lot. You know I've never regretted making that decision eight years ago. You've been the best thing that ever happened to Comtec. Just look at our growth, look at our market value!"

Adam was embarrassed. "Thank you, Edward. It's been a real pleasure to work here."

Edward's expression changed. He had a more serious question. "Just out of curiosity, what are we going to do about Gus?" Keaton was already thinking like the president. He didn't want to keep Gus around at the salary Gus was paid.

Adam put his mind at ease. "He's going with me, so you won't have to worry about him."

Adam stood up to leave, and Edward extended his hand. Adam took it. He thought he saw a little moisture well up in Keaton's eyes. All Keaton could say was, "Thank you, Adam, for everything."

Adam walked out of Edward's office, and stopped at the door to Nancy Drummond's office. She was sitting at her desk working. She looked up, "Good afternoon, Mr. Adamson."

"Good afternoon, Nancy. Please let the entire board know that there will be a mandatory meeting tomorrow morning at ten o'clock. If anyone says they have other appointments, tell them to cancel them. There will be no acceptable excuse for not being there."

Nancy looked slightly alarmed. "Right away, Mr. Adamson." She picked up the phone and started dialing extensions immediately. Adam went back to his own office. He called Tim Groff at IMA, and asked him to come to Comtec the next morning at nine. Tim agreed to be there. He checked with the agents handling the transfer of real estate in different countries. Three had completed the paperwork, and one promised everything would be final within the next two days. Adam explained it had to be done in two days, and the agent reassured him that it would be. He called a well-known moving company that specialized in overseas shipping, and made an appointment to meet movers at the penthouse in two days. He explained that he wouldn't need to meet first to discuss the scope of the move. No, he didn't need to know the cost in advance, he would write out a check on the spot that day. Yes, he already knew the address in England where everything was going. He hung up the phone, sat back in his chair, and thought for a moment about leaving. He would have to leave something special for Elizabeth. She had been such a good housekeeper. He called Nancy at her desk and asked her to call the travel agency Comtec used to arrange all the company travel. He wanted two first-class tickets to London for Friday morning, for Gus and himself. That gave him three days to pull it all together.

Chapter 25

Mildred Pearson sat in the waiting room with her daughter and son-in-law. The doctors had been working on him for over an hour, and she was apprehensive. She found herself thinking about what she would do if he died. She did love him, in spite of his constant crankiness. But over the last few years it had become very difficult to take care of him. She was no spring chicken herself, and she was tired. They could well afford to have around-the-clock care for him. They could afford to have full-time servants for that matter, but Harris wouldn't hear of it. He had only agreed three years earlier to pay for a cleaning woman twice a week, and even then it was only because he couldn't lug the vacuum cleaner up the stairs. He had suggested they buy a second vacuum and keep it upstairs permanently. It was one of the few times that Mildred really got mad at him, and he had agreed to the house cleaner.

She felt guilty for thinking that her life would be much more enjoyable if he died. They had millions of dollars in the bank. The house they owned, they had purchased in 1954. It was a wonderful old Victorian in a neighborhood that had maintained a high quality all these years. She guessed that the house was worth well over three hundred thousand dollars. Christine was her only daughter, and she had a wonderful life out here in California. The weather was beautiful most of the time, and Mildred thought she would love to live out here and spend some time with her daughter before she died. She would be seventy-three in a month. She was spry for her age, but she knew that she was at the point in her life where there could be a turn for the worse.

The door to the waiting area opened, and a doctor dressed in scrubs walked in. Mildred thought about how young he looked. He introduced himself quickly, and got right to the point. Harris was stabilized, but he had suffered a major heart attack. They were moving him up to ICU where he would have to stay for at least three or four days, during which time they would evaluate his condition more fully. All he could say was that he anticipated a reasonably full recovery.

Christine and Carl looked at each other knowing they were going to have to deal with this, and their party. The party was Saturday night, and if her father stayed in ICU for four days, that would mean he could come out on

Saturday. She didn't know if she should feel sad or mad. She asked the doctor if they could see him. The doctor explained that he was heavily medicated, and it would be best to wait until the next morning.

Christine and Carl invited Mildred to stay at their house with them for as long as it took for Harris to be released. They would worry about what to do with Harris when the time came. Mildred said she would really like that.

Chapter 26

He had journeyed with two of his best men for almost a week. They worked their way east, then north, along the coast of the Great Sea. They now stood on the top of a low mountain, and looked down on the city of Jerusalem. Simon had not been to this city in over two thousand years. When he left this area it was called Salem. He had moved down to the Great Sea after leaving Noah and settled in what eventually became the city of Sidon. It was a beautiful area right on the coast of the Great Sea. Simon lived there for almost a hundred years before moving south, and settling in a remote area in the hills, between the Great Sea and the salt sea. Shortly after settling in this area, he had met Abraham, a man of great faith. Abraham stayed with him for several days, resting with a small band of men after fighting against the armies of a man named Kudor, who claimed to be the king of the land of Elam. One of Noah's grandsons was named Elam, and had first developed the region. Simon had known him well. Now he was returning to this place that had become a large city. It was the time of the Passover celebrated by the Jews, and it was said that this man, Jesus, who was able to cure the ill and raise the dead, would be here. Simon had heard much in the past few years about this man who claimed to be the Son of God. Simon had paid little attention to the stories until he heard about his raising several people from the dead. That had gotten his attention. This one spoke of other things that interested Simon, such as the kingdom of God, and people living forever. When Simon heard these things, he knew he had to meet this man face to face. He needed to see this "Son of God." And so, he had come to Jerusalem. It was likely the worst time to be here. Jews from distant lands came here for the Passover. The streets were crowded far beyond normal. The shops and open markets were full of people, and the crowds tended to be somewhat unruly. There was serious division among the people regarding respect for the authority of the Romans, who controlled all of Judea, and the authority of the religious leaders of the Jews. One of the consequences was that many had little respect for either. It was a difficult environment, if you were a peaceable person.

Simon and his two companions eased their way through the crowds. Their horses were walking behind them. Horses were not common in this region, as most people used donkeys, and these were exceptionally beautiful horses.

Simon raised them on his farm in an area known as Cyrene, just south of the Great Sea. Many people turned and looked at them as they walked with these rarely seen animals. The people seemed to see the horses as a symbol of wealth and power, and as they noticed them, got out of the way. Simon saw this, and wondered if the horses were also going to attract an element in Jerusalem he would not want to deal with. It was said that a large number of thieves prospered in Jerusalem, and that they were not beyond doing serious harm to individuals, if it was required to steal their possessions. This was one of the reasons Simon brought two men with him. They were young, quite tall, and very strong. He hoped that would intimidate the thieves enough to keep them away. They made their way through several streets. Simon was looking for the house of a leather tanner named Mark. This tanner's uncle worked for Simon. When he had heard that Simon was going to Jerusalem, he insisted Simon would be welcome in the home of his nephew. The uncle had written a letter to his nephew, asking him to extend to Simon and his two companions the hospitality he would extend to his uncle. Simon carried the letter with him. He followed the uncles' directions, and eventually came to the house the uncle had described. It was a good-sized house, and Simon was happy to see a walled-in yard. Perhaps their horses would not be stolen after all.

Simon knocked at the door, and in a few moments it opened. A woman stood in the doorway. She looked at the three men, trying to recognize any of them. When she was sure she did not, she spoke, "Who do you seek?"

Simon replied kindly, "We seek the tanner named Mark. Is this his home?"

The woman nodded. "It is. Please come in."

Simon hesitated, turned, and looked at the two men with him. "Wait here with the horses." He turned back to the woman and stepped into the house.

The woman closed the door behind him. She looked at him as she spoke, "Please wait here, and I will tell my husband that there is someone here to see him." Simon nodded and she walked away.

Minutes later, her husband appeared. His wife did not return with him. He was a handsome man who Simon guessed was in his early forties. He seemed to be humble in his demeanor, perhaps the wife had mentioned the horses. "I am Mark. How may I be of service to you?"

Simon reached into the sash of his coat, and brought out the parchment that contained the uncle's letter. "My name is Simon from the district of Cyrenaica and the city of Cyrene. Your Uncle Tobias, the brother of your mother, is the man who trains my horses in Cyrene. He has sent you this letter."

The man took the parchment from Simon, and opened it slowly. Few people received letters, and this could well have been Mark's first. He was going to savor the moment. He read the letter silently, with a smile on his face. When he finished, he looked at Simon. "My uncle is a good man and he speaks very highly of you, Simon of Cyrene. You and your companions are welcome in my home for as long as you like."

"Thank you, Mark. Your kindness will be appreciated. May we bring our horses into the yard for protection?"

"Of course." Mark gestured for Simon to follow him, and they exited the house from a side door that led into a spacious yard. On one side of the yard, Simon noticed the hides of several animals stretched out on some type of line. There was also a good-sized barn at the back of the yard. They walked over to the gate and opened it. Simon stepped into the street, and looked to the right, where his two companions were still standing.

"Jason, Quartus," Simon called out, and they turned and saw him standing only a few yards away.

They immediately walked with the horses into the yard, and Mark closed the gate behind them. Mark called out a name, and in a moment a young boy darted out from the barn. Simon thought he might be fifteen. Mark waited until the boy was standing directly in front of him. "Stephanus, take these horses into the barn. Brush them, secure them in the large pen, and feed them for our guests."

The boy bowed ever so slightly, in respect. "Yes, Father." He turned to the three men, took the reins of the horses, and walked them into the barn. Simon could hear him talking to the horses as he walked.

It was late in the day, and soon the men were sitting and sharing a meal together. Along with Simon and his companions, there was Mark, and his three sons. Stephanus was the oldest, he was fourteen. Lucius was eleven, and Thomas was nine. Mark explained to his wife who Simon was, and she was very friendly. She had met Mark's Uncle Tobias on two different occasions, and she liked him immensely. Her affection for the uncle worked in Simon's favor.

As they ate, they talked. Simon told Mark and his sons about the land he came from. How close to the sea it was, and how flat the land was there (unlike the mountainous region where Jerusalem was). He talked about raising horses, and farming the land, and how many men and their families lived within the boundaries of his farm. He explained that it took five hours of riding on horseback to get from one side of the farm to the other. They listened in awe. The boys never had an opportunity before to talk with someone from a foreign land.

Simon explained that he had come to Jerusalem because he hoped to see this man they called Jesus. Mark's face became serious, which Simon noticed immediately. He questioned Mark, fearful of offending him in some way. "Mark, does it bring trouble to you that I seek out this man Jesus?"

Mark replied instantly, "It does not trouble me that you seek him, Simon. He is a good man, and I believe him to truly be the Son of God, but I am troubled by the sentiments of the Rabbis and the Sanhedrin. They give no consideration to the things this man does. They only concern themselves with their control over the people, and this man, Jesus, is taking control away from them."

Simon listened carefully. "Is he taking away their control, or, do they simply think he is doing this?"

"There is some truth to their losing control. Mobs of people follow this man wherever he goes. They bring their relatives who are lame, or blind, to him."

"And what does he do," Simon felt his heartbeat speeding up, "when these crippled and blind are brought to him?"

Mark's eyes widened in excitement. "He cures them!"

Simon was absorbed. "All of them?" The tone in his voice indicated that what he was hearing was difficult to believe.

Mark spoke faster now, "Yes, all of them. I myself have witnessed some of these things. I know a man my age who was born with a deformed leg. He was lame, and unable to walk. He was a childhood friend, and as he got older, he would beg near the temple. I knew him well, and I knew he was lame. But one day, this man Jesus came by and took note of him. He touched him, and told him to get up and walk. And the man did. He told me later that in an instant, it was as if someone had cut off his lame leg and put on a new one. He was beside himself with joy, and so were his parents; however, when they went to the synagogue to make a sacrifice for their son's miraculous recovery, the Rabbis were furious with them. He would not recant that he had been healed by Jesus. The Rabbis threw them out of the synagogue, and told them they were no longer welcome."

Simon hung on every word, as did his two companions.

Mark continued, "It is said that the Sanhedrin has plotted to kill this man."

Simon looked surprised. "How would they do such a thing? It is my understanding that Rome holds authority here, and that the Jews have no rights of execution."

"What you say is true, Simon, but these men are clever, and they are desperate. They will find a way to manipulate the Romans into doing their

bidding, I am sure."

There was a long silence as Simon took this all in. His companions saw a sadness in his eyes they had rarely seen. Simon looked at Mark and spoke imploringly, "Mark, I must see this man. It is very important. Do you know where I can find him?"

Mark saw the desperation in Simon's face. "I don't know where he is, Simon, but a man with whom I do much business might know. His name is Ben Joseph, and he does not live far from here. He has a very large home, and it has been said that Jesus and his followers are going to eat the Passover meal this year in his house."

"Could you take me to him tonight?"

Mark nodded. "We could leave right away. It is a short walk from here."

Mark's oldest son spoke for the first time since sitting down for the meal, "Father, may I go with you?"

Mark looked lovingly at the boy. "Stephanus, you must stay here and care for your mother, and brothers." The boy seemed willing to accept the answer.

Simon softened the blow. "Quartus and Jason will also stay here, Stephanus, so you will have company." The boy's eyes lit up and Simon's companions were relieved to not go back out. It had been a long journey, and they were looking forward to sleeping on soft beds tonight.

A few moments later, Simon and Mark stepped out of the house. It was twilight, and the streets seemed much less crowded. They walked down several streets, turning as they went, and Simon hoped he wouldn't have to find his way back to Mark's house by himself. They stopped in front of a very large house. It was obviously the house of someone of great wealth.

Simon looked at the house. "What does Ben Joseph do, Mark?"

"He is a lender of money, Simon, but he is very honest and fair. Most people in need of money come to Ben Joseph because of his fairness."

They walked a few steps to a large wooden door. Alongside the door was a small table, and on the table was what looked like a small club. Mark picked it up and banged on the door with it. It made a loud sound. He put the club back down on the table. A moment later, the door opened and a man stood in the doorway. He immediately bowed, which indicated that he was a servant in the house. When he stood back up he looked at Mark without saying a word.

Mark spoke to the man, "Could you tell Ben Joseph that Mark the tanner is here to see him on a matter of great importance?" The man immediately turned and walked away.

Simon and Mark waited at the door. The man had not closed it. Simon could see that the house was opulent. Everything looked to be trimmed in gold. The floor just inside the doorway was inlaid tile.

The man returned to the door, opened it wider, and asked the men to follow him. Mark and Simon entered the house, and the servant shut the door behind them. He walked down a hallway and through a large room. At the other end of the room, he walked through a doorway that led out into a garden. There were several benches near each other in the garden, and sitting on one of the benches was a little old man. It was Ben Joseph. He didn't get up from the bench, but as the two men approached, the old man greeted Mark. "Tanner, how good to see you, my friend. To what do I owe the honor of this visit?"

Mark replied as he continued to walk closer, "The honor is mine, Ben Joseph, that you allow one as unworthy as me into your home."

The old man chuckled. "You flatter me, Tanner. I if I did not know better I would think you here to borrow money, but I do know better. There are few in Jerusalem more worthy than you, my son. You are one of the few who take my money because I owe it to you." And he chuckled again. Now the old man directed his attention to Simon. "And who is this that you have brought?"

"This is Simon of Cyrene, Ben Joseph. He is a dear friend of my Uncle Tobias, who works with him. Tobias sent me a letter, Ben Joseph, and Simon brought it to me." He spoke of the letter with obvious pride.

The old man nodded his head several times. "Ah, a letter, such a delightful thing. All the way from Cyrene! This is truly a special day for you, Tanner. Tell me though, what is the purpose of your visit?"

Simon felt it right to speak. "Ben Joseph, I would like to express my gratitude for you taking the time to see us tonight with no formal notice of our visit. It is most kind of you."

The old man nodded his approval and agreement.

Simon continued, "I have traveled to Jerusalem for one purpose, to see this man Jesus."

Ben Joseph's face didn't change at all; he maintained the same smile. Simon had watched very carefully for a hint of a different facial expression. The old man seemed to make no attempt to speak, so Simon went on.

"It is very important to me that I have an opportunity to speak to this man. If you know where he is, or if you can help me, I will be very grateful to you. I assure you, I mean this man no harm."

The old man's smile disappeared. He seemed to be deep in thought. His eyes were closed, and for a moment Simon was afraid he had fallen asleep. But suddenly he opened his eyes and looked directly into Simon's eyes. He stared for a long moment, trying to read something of the man.

Finally he spoke, "Simon of Cyrene, and you too, Mark, the son of Nathan, what I tell you, you must swear to keep in the strictest confidence." Both men nodded. The old man went on. "You must tell no one. Do you understand?" The two men nodded again. The old man looked directly into Simon's eyes as he spoke, "This man you seek will be here tomorrow as the sun sets to celebrate the Passover with the twelve he travels with. He has requested the use of a large upper room in my home. They will arrive shortly before the sun sets. If you are here, I am sure that he will see you briefly as a favor to me."

Simon was beside himself. "Thank you, Ben Joseph. I only hope that some day I may be able to return such a kindness." The old man smiled and nodded.

Mark spoke up, "Thank you, Ben Joseph, for so much of your time. We will return tomorrow shortly before the sun sets." With that, the two men turned and walked back through the garden to the doorway where the servant was standing in wait for them. He showed them back through the house to the door that took them back to the street.

When they got out onto the street, Mark looked at Simon as if to say: "See, I told you I knew how to find him."

Simon put his hands on Mark's shoulders. "Mark, you have done me an indescribable service. How can I ever thank you?"

Mark seemed embarrassed. "There is no need to thank me. My uncle says in his letter that you are a very kind and righteous man, and I am honored to be of help to you."

They returned to the house quickly, as it was now dark, and it was dangerous on the streets at night. When they got back to the house they were careful not to reveal anything, as they had sworn to Ben Joseph. They said that they were going to return to Ben Joseph's house tomorrow, to see if he could arrange a meeting.

Simon finally lay down on a comfortable bed as a guest of Mark, the son of Nathan, the tanner, in Jerusalem. He had been journeying for seven days, sleeping on the ground. Simon never slept as well outside. He was exhausted, and though his mind was reeling, he quickly fell asleep.

The next day, Simon and his companions walked through the streets of Jerusalem looking in the shops. There were craftsmen of all kinds in Jerusalem. One could buy gold and silver jewelry. There were many shops that sold wooden household items, pots and bowls of all sizes and shapes. There were shops selling many types of woven cloth. Some of it was quite remarkable, with beautiful printed designs. Simon bought many things for his family, and for the other families. Stephanus had accompanied them to be sure they didn't get lost, and Simon bought things for him and his brothers, as well. By the time they returned to Mark's house, they were all loaded down with bundles. Before leaving for Ben Joseph's house, Simon washed and put on a special garment he had brought along for the occasion. It was a long white robe, in the customary dress of the Jews. A dark blue sash tied around the middle. Simon looked distinguished.

Mark and Simon arrived at the house of Ben Joseph half an hour before the sun was due to set. Simon was nervous, which was unusual for him. Mark knocked on the door, as he had done the night before. The same servant showed them in, and led them into a different room in the house. The servant asked Simon to wait in the room, and asked Mark to follow him. Mark and the servant left. Simon looked around. It was a large room. He estimated that he could lay across the floor at least three times, in each direction. The ceiling was so high he could not reach up and touch it. There were two couches in the room, both looked comfortable. There was a table at one end of the room, and two chairs at the table. There was a bowl on the table, and it was full of fresh fruit.

Simon suddenly turned back toward the door, and standing before him was a young man. He was dark-skinned, as if he spent much time in the sun. He had a full beard, as was the custom in these parts, but his beard was neat, his hair clean, and his eyes bright. Simon felt something he had never felt before, and he thought to himself that his lifetime had been over four thousand years long! He felt inadequate. He didn't know what to say, or how to say it. The man seemed willing to stand there and wait. He looked unhurried, and at peace. Simon realized he needed to speak. He remembered Ben Joseph stressing that he could arrange a brief meeting.

He looked into the man's eyes, and in those eyes he saw a wisdom beyond anything he had known. He knew that he himself possessed a greater wisdom than any other man he had met, strictly on the basis of his life's experience. But in this man, he sensed far more. It brought to his mind the times he had spoken with the man by the beautiful place, once by himself, and once with Noah.

He forced himself to open his mouth and speak. He thought he must sound like a little boy. "You are the man they call Jesus?"

The man smiled slightly, "I am he."

Simon came close to him, so he could speak softly. He wanted no one else to hear this conversation. He almost whispered, "I am Simon from the land of Cyrene."

Jesus looked into his eyes for a long moment, "Yes, you are Simon from Cyrene. But I knew you first as Hacaliah, the son of Adam." As he spoke, he held his arms out slightly, his palms uplifted. The two men were standing less than a foot apart, and Simon's reactions to those words were like the release of floodgates of emotion. Simon fell toward the man as a son might fall into the arms of his father, and Jesus put his arms around him as Simon cried. The two men stood together for several minutes as Simon sobbed. Those words told him that there was more to his life than just the coincidental timing of his birth. It told him that this truly was the Son of God, and that he knew of Simon (or Hacaliah or any one of the other dozens of names he had used over the years). Jesus continued to hold him and comfort him, until he regained control. Finally, they released the embrace, and faced each other again. Simon felt foolish, and started to apologize. Jesus put his hand up, to signal that Simon shouldn't apologize. He looked at Simon and smiled, gesturing toward the couches. "Come," he said, "let's sit and talk."

They moved to the couches, and sat so they were facing each other. There was not a lot of space between them. Jesus spoke first, "So tell me, Hacaliah, why do you seek me out?" It felt so strange to have someone calling him Hacaliah. When he left Noah and settled by the Great Sea over three thousand years ago, he stopped using the name Hacaliah. He had used the name Melchizedek all the time he lived near the Great Sea, and, when he moved over to the mountains, where he now sat talking to Jesus. But that had been thousands of years ago. The area was called Salem then. Abraham had referred to him as the King of Salem, which he thought amusing, considering there were less than thirty people living in Salem at the time. Regardless, he had been very hospitable to Abraham, and Abraham had rewarded him with some of his spoils of war. That was the beginning of his accumulating great wealth for himself.

Simon answered the question. "I have heard so much about you. Your ability to heal the sick and blind, and to raise the dead. I've heard that you speak of the kingdom of God. That you claim to be the Son of God, which I have no doubt you are. And I had to see you. I hoped you could help me understand what my purpose is. How can I continue to live, while everyone around me dies? How long will this go on?"

Jesus listened thoughtfully. "Hacaliah, long before I came to this earth as a child born to a woman, I existed in the heavens with my father. Do you understand this?" Simon nodded, but he wasn't sure he fully understood it.

Jesus continued, "I was fully aware of your birth, and that you were capable of living forever, because you are a perfect man. We watched you grow, and progress. We tried to protect you, and help you stay alive. The Father's holy spirit moved the ancients to write what we have today as the holy writings of God. Nowhere in those writings are you mentioned, because your survival depends on others not knowing who you are. I know I don't have to tell you this. But listen to me, Simon of Cyrene, or Hacaliah, or who ever you will be hundreds, or thousands of years from now. You must continue to do what you have done. Live quietly. Do not draw undue attention to yourself. You have the mental powers of a perfect human. Use it to help your fellow man in every way you can, without revealing yourself. Do good Hacaliah, and the day will come when you will no longer have to hide yourself from the world."

Simon didn't really understand. "What do you mean?"

Jesus sat back on the couch and smiled, "I mean, my brother, that all of mankind was supposed to be as you are. My father wished none to die. Now the time has come for me to die, so that all that my father has willed can be accomplished."

Simon was more confused. "I don't understand, how will your dying be of any benefit?"

"Simon, my death will cover over the sin of your father. You see, I too, am perfect. My conception was by Holy Spirit. I inherited no imperfection from a human father. Your father was perfect, and his disobedience caused the loss of perfection, thus all of your fellow men have died. My death, as a faithful son, will open the way for everlasting life to be offered again in the future. So, Hacaliah, be patient. Continue to live a good and upright life, and my father will watch over you." He rose off the couch as he spoke these last few words. "It is sundown, I must go and celebrate the evening meal with my disciples. I know you well, my brother. I am very happy that we had this opportunity to talk face to face." He opened his arms, and the two men embraced again. This time it was like two friends saying a final farewell.

Jesus left the room, and in a moment the servant was back with Mark. He asked them both to follow him. He led them through several other rooms, to a smaller room where Ben Joseph was sitting. Next to him, was a man dressed in formal religious garb. Ben Joseph introduced him as Nicodemus, a member of the Sanhedrin. Simon greeted Nicodemus, and then turned to Ben Joseph.

"Ben Joseph, this night you have done me a great service. Tell me how I can repay you."

Ben Joseph looked up at him. "There is no need, Simon. When I spoke to the Master about you he told me that he had hoped to meet with you before his time had ended, and he feared that time would run out before he had the opportunity. So you see, Simon, you are the one who has done a great service to me. You have given me an opportunity to please the Master."

Simon felt tears starting to well up in his eyes, and he thought he should make his exit before making a fool of himself. He and Mark left Ben Joseph's house. As they started down the street, he turned back and looked up toward a lighted room on the second floor. He could hear Jesus singing one of the Passover prayers. As they walked back home, Simon felt as though a weight had been lifted off his shoulders. He had so much to think about. He wondered if he would ever fully understand the importance of the conversation he just had.

Late the next morning, they left the house of Mark the tanner. Each horse carried a load of items for others back home. Before he left the tanner's home, Simon took Mark aside and gave him a small pouch. It was obviously a money pouch, and Mark held up his hand to refuse.

Simon reasoned with him. "Mark, you have been more than kind to me. Money is something I have in great abundance. I cannot give you life, or health, or protection. Please, allow me to repay your kindness in a way that is available to me."

Mark reluctantly accepted the pouch. It contained ten pure gold shekels, a common monetary denomination in Jerusalem. It was the equivalent of more than two years' work for Mark.

They walked their horses through the city streets, as they had when they arrived. It was late morning, and Simon was surprised to find the streets quite empty. They went down and across several streets toward the central square, where they would turn onto the main road that ran north and south through Jerusalem. Their destination was south back through the mountains to the Great Sea, and then south and west, back to Cyrene.

The small palace that was occupied by the Roman governor was on one side of the square. As they got closer to the square, they could hear what sounded like the yelling of a large crowd. As they got closer the noise grew louder. Eventually, they were within sight of the square, and could see a mob of people. The mob were all yelling and motioning with their arms, but Simon could not make out what the center of the commotion was. They stopped at the back of the crowd, and realized they were going to have to work their way through it to get to the road they needed. Simon warned his two companions to stay close at all costs; they did not want to get separated in this crowd.

They started to work their way through the crowd slowly. The horses remained surprisingly calm in spite of the situation. They were well trained. Simon moved very slowly, being careful not to seem to push anyone. He was also concerned about a horse stepping on someone.

They worked their way to the main road, and Simon turned south, carefully pushing through the crowd. At one point, he looked over in the direction where everyone was looking, and he could see he was close to the front of the crowd. There was a wide-open space beyond them, and it was obvious that was the center of all this attention. Simon looked back to see where Quartus was. He was directly behind him, and Simon signaled for him to come up beside him, which he did. Simon handed him the rein of his horse, and told him to wait with Jason. He then pushed his way through the remaining crowd to the front, where he could see clearly what was happening. To his horror, he saw Jesus struggling to drag a large pole. It was almost as large around as a man's waist, and it was longer than the height of three men. Simon had no idea how the weight of the thing wasn't crushing him. Jesus was bleeding from his head and his back. He looked as though he had been beaten and whipped.

There were Roman soldiers walking next to him, and they were yelling at him, but Simon could not hear them over the noise of the crowd. Jesus was struggling to move the great pole forward.

For the first time in his life Simon didn't care if his action cost him his life. He stepped out of the crowd and ran toward Jesus, with no concern for what the soldiers might do. He stepped under the pole in front of Jesus, took the weight onto his own shoulders, and started to pull forward.

One of the soldiers approached him as he struggled forward, yelling so that he could be heard above the noise of the crowd. "And who is this that has offered his assistance to this criminal?"

Simon struggled to keep some forward motion, though he had no idea where he was supposed to be going, and he looked to the soldier and yelled back to him, "My name is Simon from the country of Cyrene. I am only a visitor to this place and I know of no crimes this man has committed. I only know that he cannot move this pole alone, and that even with my help we will be unable to carry it far."

The soldier seemed to accept Simon's answer, and see him simply as a sympathetic observer, so he allowed him to stay under the pole and help. He even went to the edge of the crowd and pressed several other young men into service to assist.

As they struggled forward Jesus spoke to him, "We meet again, Hacaliah." Simon felt an ache in his heart he had never felt before.

Jesus continued, "Do not fear for me, my brother, for this is the will of my father, and soon I will be returned to him. Stay the course, Hacaliah, and the blessings of the kingdom will be yours."

Simon felt a strengthening effect from the words, and they dulled the aching in his heart. Under the direction of the soldiers they carried the great pole outside the walls of the city to a low hill that, from a distance, looked much like a human skull.

When they arrived at that place, there were two other poles. They were lying on the ground, and much to Simon's horror, he saw there was a man nailed to each pole. A large nail had been driven through their feet, one foot crossed over the other. Their arms had been stretched out high over their heads, and their hands were nailed in a similar fashion, one crossed over the other.

Simon had once heard that the Romans executed people by crucifying them, but it had been described to him as a pole with a cross beam of some sort. After arriving at the destination, the men who had been pressed into service, including Simon, were allowed to go. Simon was exhausted and filthy from the sweat and dust, but otherwise unharmed. He looked around to see if Quartus and Jason had followed him, and he saw them standing far off on a hill with the three horses. He started to walk toward them, and as soon as Quartus saw him coming he got onto his horse, took the reins of Simon's horse, and rode to him. Simon struggled onto the horse and they rode back up the hill to where Jason was still standing.

The three of them stood and watched as they nailed Jesus to the great pole, just as they had the two other men. They then took the pole with Jesus on it and lifted it into the upright position, the bottom of the pole dropping into a hole. They did the same with the other two. It was now about midday as they looked down at this terrible sight. Suddenly, the sky darkened as though it were night. The three men looked up, expecting to see a great cloud blocking the sun, but there was none. It was as though the sun had simply disappeared. Soldiers lit torches. Tears were streaming down Simon's face. Neither Quartus nor Jason could remember ever seeing Simon cry.

He looked at his two young companions. "It is both a sad day and a glorious day for the world."

Jason looked at Simon. "Who is he, Simon?"

Simon continued to look down at the man on the middle pole. "He is the Son of God."

Simon turned his horse south, and with his two companions, headed away from Jerusalem back toward the Great Sea. Simon promised himself he would never return to this place.

Chapter 27

Ken stared at the pages of the journal, wishing he could read the entries. He had taken one of the books without looking in it first, and now he found it written in a language he could not understand. The earliest entry in the journal was 03-12-1744, and the last entry in the journal was 09-28-1778. Most of the entries were short, as if just historical notes of events. But a few were longer, and he would like to be able to read them.

He had explained to the group he was sure that Adam would pay big money to get this book back. No one was thrilled at the prospect of blackmailing him, but Ken assured them that they could make serious money. He explained three times that these journals spanned a period of almost four hundred years, and they were all written by the same person.

Everyone told him he was crazy. He couldn't get them to accept that the same person was making all the entries. Even when he brought up the point about Lester not being able to find anything on him beyond the nineteen fifties, they didn't buy it. They all said the handwriting was probably just similar.

Ken looked at his watch. It was four-thirty. He pulled out the local phone book, and found the number for the city university. An operator answered, and Ken asked for the language department.

The receptionist asked, "Modern or ancient?" Ken wasn't sure, but he didn't think the seventeen hundreds would be considered ancient, so he said modern. The phone rang again, and a woman answered. Ken explained that he had come upon a journal of some sort, and it was in a foreign language, but he didn't really know what language it was. He wondered if someone at the university could take a look at it, and tell him what it said. The woman asked if the journal entries were dated, and Ken told her they were. She asked what the dates were, and he told her they ranged from 1744 to 1778. There was a pause at the other end of the phone.

Finally the woman spoke, "Could you bring the journal in for us to look at?"

"Sure," he said, "when would be a good time?"

"We'll be here for another couple of hours. Could you come over today?"

It was a fifteen-minute drive. "Sure, I'll be there in half an hour." The woman gave Ken directions to the language department. She told him her name was Sarah Smith, and he should ask for her. He told her he was on his way.

Ken walked in to the language department about twenty-five minutes later, with the journal under his arm. A young woman was sitting at a desk reading. She was very attractive, and Ken hoped this was Sarah Smith. He walked over to the desk and she looked up at him.

"Can I help you?"

"I'm looking for Sarah Smith." Ken smiled hopefully.

The young woman started to get out of her chair. "I'll get her for you." She turned and walked down a hallway. A few minutes later, she returned with another woman who was obviously older, but who was also quite attractive. With her was a much older man.

She introduced herself and the man. His name was Phil Levy. She asked Ken for his name, and he said simply, "Ken." He didn't want anyone to know his last name. They asked him to follow them and they walked back down the hallway into a room that was small, but comfortably furnished like a living room. There was a table with four chairs around it, and a couch on one end of the room. Sarah and Phil sat at the table, so Ken did as well.

He laid the journal on the table. Sarah and Phil looked at it. Sarah spoke first, "Is that the journal you told me about?"

"Yes."

Phil spoke, "Where did you get it?"

Ken didn't like the question, but he could tell that it was simply from curiosity, there was no accusation in his tone.

"I just came by it."

Phil extended a hand. "May I see it?"

"Sure," Ken said, as he slid it across the table.

Phil opened the book slowly, and looked at the first page. Sarah was sitting next to him, and she was also able to see the writing. Phil turned the pages, carefully looking over the writing.

"It's French," he said. "The grammar is a little odd, but it was probably correct for the time. I would say this is authentic, because people today wouldn't be familiar with some of the language usage I see here." Sarah nodded her agreement. They continued to flip through the pages.

Phil eventually came to a page, stopping to read. After a minute or so, he spoke, "Listen to this," he said with a tone of excitement. "Here is an entry dated May 30, 1778."

> Today my friend Francois Marie Arouet, who preferred to be called Voltaire, passed away. I found him to be a most interesting and enlightened fellow. He had a keen sense of reality in a world that seems to possess none. He had an appropriate disdain for religion, while maintaining a sincere love and appreciation for God. I found him to be refreshing in every sense, and I will miss his company.

Phil and Sarah looked at each other. Sarah spoke, "Wow, this guy new Voltaire!"

Phil continued to turn the pages. He turned them more quickly, and suddenly stopped again.

"Hey," he said, "here's an entry dated 1785 and the language has changed to German!" He kept leafing through the pages. Eventually he stopped. "Listen to this, the entry is dated April 10, 1786."

> Today I heard the new opera by Mozart. It is called the marriage of Figaro. It was quite good. The music was exquisite. This composer promises to be someone who will be taken notice of.

Phil and Sarah looked at each other again, and then they both looked at Ken. Sarah spoke this time, "Ken, really, where did you get this?"

Ken reached across the table and slid the book back to himself. "I told you, I just happen to come by it. It's none of your business exactly how."

Phil spoke in what Ken thought was an attempt at a fatherly tone, "Ken, look, this thing is possibly worth a lot of money. I believe it's authentic, and we would like a chance to review it."

Ken thanked them for their interest as he got up from his seat, but he explained he really wasn't interested in having the thing appraised. He just wanted a little information on what was in the journal, and they had already helped him with that. He thanked them and, in spite of their urging to the contrary, he left with the journal.

As he drove home, he thought to himself that he had a win-win situation on his hands. If he couldn't get Adam to pay what he wanted, he could always sell it to someone else. He decided that he would call Comtec in the morning to see what he could get.

Chapter 28

He was in a room that seemed unfamiliar to him, but the other people in the room with him were all people he knew. It was a boardroom of some sort. There was a long table. Yes, they were people with whom he served on the board of directors. They were in the middle of a discussion, but he was unable to understand what was being said. It wasn't that he couldn't hear it, it was just that he couldn't understand. He finally spoke up, and told everyone that he was having a problem. They stopped and looked at him as if they were the ones who didn't understand. He was trying to make them understand, and he was getting frustrated. "What's the matter with you people?" he heard himself yelling. They sat there staring at him.

He could see his hands on the table in front of him, and suddenly, with no explanation, his hands started to age. He was only in his forties, but his hands suddenly transformed into the hands of someone in their eighties. He screamed that something was happening to him, but no one even flinched. He was frightened and he didn't understand what was happening. The person sitting next to him handed something to him, and he took it in one of his shriveled up hands. It was a hand mirror, and when he looked in it he saw that his face, too, had become that of an old man. Everyone around him remained the same age they had been. He started to moan, "No, oh no. What's happening to me? Why am I getting old, and you're not? No, please no, no, no!"

And then he heard a voice from somewhere out of his view. It was a soft voice, as if from a far off place. It was saying, "Mr. Pearson."

Where was it coming from? He couldn't see who was calling his name. "Mr. Pearson?" There it was again. "Mr. Pearson."

Harris Pearson opened his eyes. It took a moment for his vision to focus clearly, and he saw a nurse standing over him. He realized he was in a hospital. There was an oxygen mask over his nose and mouth, and he could hear the faint beeping of a heart monitor in the background. He closed his eyes for a moment, and thanked God it was just a dream. He opened them again, and tried to speak, but it was difficult with the mask over his face. This made him angry, but he caught himself. He knew that he had to remain calm, or he might die. He tried lifting his left hand to his face, but it was taped up with an IV tube. He tried his right hand, and it seemed to be free. He lifted the mask off his face, pulling it down under his chin. He looked at the nurse.

"Where am I?" he asked.

The nurse answered him calmly and softly, "You're in County General Hospital. You had a heart attack yesterday afternoon. I'll go get the doctor." Harris nodded, and the nurse left the room. Harris looked at his right hand, as if to confirm that he really was an old man. That part wasn't a dream.

A few minutes went by, and the doctor came in. He was a very young man, although Harris thought that at his age, everyone looked young. The doctor introduced himself and explained what had happened. They were going to do some tests to determine if there was any permanent damage. He was in intensive care, where he would stay until at least Friday, and probably Saturday. Harris asked about his wife, and his daughter, and son-in-law. The doctor explained that they had waited to hear what the prognosis was, and they had left. It was now only seven-thirty in the morning, and he was sure they would be back shortly.

Harris watched the doctor as he spoke, and he seemed to be a nice young man. Harris decided to take a chance with him. "Doctor, I would like you to do me a favor."

The young doctor was a little surprised. "Sure, Mr. Pearson. What is it?"

"Do I have a phone here in the room?" the old man inquired.

The doctor nodded. "Yes you do, sir. Right here on your side table."

Harris didn't bother to look at it. "Doctor, I need you to contact the CIA for me." As he said this, the doctor started to smile. Harris figured he thought he was an old crackpot. "This is no joke, Doc, so listen closely."

The sharp tone of his voice caught the doctor by surprise, and he realized the old man wasn't kidding around.

Harris continued, "Got a piece of paper?" The doctor took out a prescription pad from his back pocket, ripped off the top sheet, and turned it over. He took the pen from his pocket. "OK. Call the CIA. Tell them it's urgent that they get a message to Frank Saunders. He's a retired assistant deputy. Tell Saunders that I'm in this hospital, and I need him to call me immediately. Tell him that it's important. Give him the phone number to this phone." As he spoke the doctor was writing. "Now, Doc, don't screw around with me, OK? If the phone doesn't ring in a half hour I'll know you didn't do what I'm asking you to do. I know you're a busy man, but this is really important. Hey, you don't want me to get all excited and have another heart attack do you?"

The doctor finished writing, and looked at the old man lying in the bed. "Mr. Harris, I'm going to go make the call right now."

The old man smiled, "Thanks, Doc, I appreciate it." The doctor turned and walked out of the room. Harris closed his eyes and tried to recall exactly what he saw yesterday. Was it really Adam Adamson? He was sure it was, he even had the same black man with him. What was his name? Harris thought for a minute, and remembered that his name was Gus. He looked older, but not as old as he should have been.

The doctor went into his office and sat down at his desk. He wanted to follow through on the old man's request because he saw the seriousness in his face, but he didn't want to get himself in any trouble, and he didn't know anything about the CIA. He didn't even know how to get in contact with the CIA. He pulled a phone book out of a desk drawer. He looked under "C" and there was nothing for CIA or Central Intelligence Agency. He looked in the blue pages under government, went to U.S. and found no listing for the CIA. He looked for the FBI, and found that number listed. He called the FBI and asked someone for the number for the CIA. They put him on hold for a couple of minutes, and then someone came on the line and gave him a number. He tried to thank them, but before the first word was out of his mouth they had hung up. He dialed the number to the CIA. The phone rang three times, and someone picked it up. It was a man's voice. "May I help you?"

"Is this the CIA?" the doctor asked.

"Yes it is. May I help you?"

"Yes, I need to get a message to a Mr. Frank Saunders. I understand he is a retired member of the CIA."

There was a momentary pause at the other end. "What is the message?"

The doctor felt his heart beat a little faster. They weren't denying there was a Frank Saunders. Maybe the old man was really on the level. He gave the man the message Harris had asked him to deliver. He then waited for a reply. The voice on the other end said nothing. The doctor wanted to be sure he had the message. "Did you hear me?"

"Yes I did. Is there anything else?"

"No."

The phone went dead. The other person had hung up. The doctor laughed. It seemed to almost be a spoof on the "spy" stereotype. He thought he had done all he could, so he got up and went back to his rounds.

Fifteen minutes later the phone next to Harris Pearson's bed rang.

Chapter 29

Adam was looking through a checklist of items he needed to take care of as Gus drove to Comtec. He had been able to make nearly all the necessary arrangements yesterday afternoon and evening. He kept most of the work from his home computer on floppy discs for security reasons. The few things he had on the hard drive, he transferred last night.

He also had packed all of his clothes, except for what he would wear for the next few days. He left a note for Elizabeth, asking her not to do any food shopping today. It was Tuesday, and she usually bought a little more on Tuesday as she planned meals for the week. Adam had no idea where he might be, or if he would have time to be home for dinner, so he asked her to stay this evening until he got home, because he wanted to talk with her. He was going to tell her tonight that he was leaving on Friday. He decided to leave five hundred thousand dollars in her checking account. It was one of the things on his checklist. He was meeting with the moving company tomorrow, and he made note of that on his list.

They pulled into the Comtec garage at eight-fifteen. Gus had his own list of things to do now that he had committed to the move. Adam already told him that the moving company would include all of his belongings, but still, the concept of leaving a place and starting as someone else in another country presented some challenges that Gus wasn't sure about. Gus and Adam had spent some time discussing things last night. Gus wasn't sure why he had to assume a different identity, but Adam explained that it would be possible for someone to find him by knowing where Gus was. He also explained that having bank accounts where your social security number is keyed to the account, or traveling on a passport ties you to your whereabouts. In today's computerized world, those things are accessible in just minutes.

Adam had all the information regarding Gus' finances, and he was going to give it to Roy Hazelton this morning, when he came in for the IMA charter. He was going to ask him to set up an account for Gus in one of the Swiss banks Adam used. Adam told Gus not to worry about the apartment. IMA was the landlord, and he would have them sell off the possessions and contribute the money to the charitable fund. Gus asked if he would be able to take a charitable deduction on his next years' taxes. They both had a good laugh over it. Even though Gus lived well for all these years, it was hard for him to think of himself as being wealthy to the point where an apartment full of belongings was of no consequence.

Adam went into his office to take care of some matters before his series of meetings. He had Tim Groff and Roy Hazelton at nine. He wanted Tim to hear the entire new charter arrangement from Roy. Roy could spend some time explaining, if need be. He had the board meeting at ten. He had scheduled the meeting with Tim and Roy in one of the smaller meeting rooms, so it wouldn't interfere with the board meeting.

On his desk was a note from Nancy confirming the two flights to London for Friday morning at nine o'clock. Adam made a series of phone calls, and he made a note to himself to make two more calls in the afternoon. By the time he was done with the calls, it was five minutes to nine.

He went to the smaller meeting room. Roy Hazelton and Tim Groff were already there. Each had a fresh cup of coffee. They both stood up as Adam walked in, and he quickly encouraged them to sit down, which he also did. It was obvious to both of them he was in a hurry. He was usually much more friendly, and relaxed. Adam looked at Roy.

"Are you all set, Roy?" Roy nodded. Adam looked over at Tim. "Tim, I want you to know that I think you've done a wonderful job at IMA. Since its inception, you have handled the fund just as I hoped you would. The organization has done some wonderful things for people, and I'm confident that it will continue to do so."

Tim got a little red in the face. "It sounds like I'm about to be replaced."

Adam chuckled. "No, quite the contrary. I'm being replaced." Adam gave that a minute to sink in.

Tim looked mildly shocked. "Adam, how is that possible?"

"I'm going to be leaving the area, Tim, and it will be impractical for me to continue my association with IMA. I've asked Mr. Hazelton here to draw up a new charter that will allow IMA to continue to function the way it has all these years. You will remain as the president. Your current salary will be increased at the same rate as the consumer price index each year. There will be a new arrangement for the chairmanship, which Roy is going to explain to you in detail." Adam looked at Roy. "All the changes have been made?"

"Just as you requested, Adam." Roy slid the new charter to Adam as he answered.

Adam opened the book and turned to the specific changes he had requested, after which he turned to the page at the back where his signature was required. He looked at Tim. "Tim, you'll witness my signature." He signed his name. "If you have any questions after Roy is done explaining things, you come see me." He stood up as he spoke.

Tim also stood. "OK, Adam, thank you." They shook hands.

Adam looked at Roy. "Everything else all set?" Roy told him that all the other arrangements had been taken care of. "Good, here's one more thing I need you to do, and it has to be done by tomorrow." He handed Roy a piece of paper with instructions regarding Gus' money. He and Roy shook hands, and Roy knew that he probably would never see Adam again.

Adam returned to his office and made several more phone calls. There were three phone messages for him, two he recognized. The third was from someone who wouldn't leave his name, or a return phone number. The message simply said that he would call back. That struck Adam as being a little strange.

Nancy came into his office and put two plane tickets down on his desk. He thanked her, and she went back out. He looked at the tickets. Everything seemed to be in order. His intercom buzzed. "Mr. Adamson." It was Nancy's voice.

He answered without picking up the phone. "Yes, Nancy."

"It's that man who wouldn't leave his name or number on line four."

"Thank you, Nancy." He picked up the phone, and pushed the button for line four. "Adam Adamson."

The voice on the other end sounded nervous. "Mr. Adamson, I'd like to talk to you about something I think you will be interested in."

Adam wasn't sure what to make of this call. "Who is this?"

"It's not important who I am, it's only important to know what I have."

"I'm not in the habit of doing business with people who don't want to tell me who they are." Adam really had no time for games, even under the best of circumstances.

The voice at the other end seemed a little irritated. "I don't care about your habits. Why don't you talk to me about what I got and then decide if you want to do business with me."

Now Adam was becoming a little irritated, but there was something in this voice that told him he should hear whatever it was he had to say. "OK, let's do this your way. What exactly is it that you have that you think I might want?"

"I've got a journal written in French and German with entries that date from 1744 to 1778. What's interesting about this journal is that I think it might be in your handwriting."

Adam froze for a moment, not believing what he was hearing. "And where did you happen to get such an unusual item?"

The voice at the other end was suddenly a little cocky. "Let's just say I happened to find it, and I thought I would be a nice guy and offer it back to the original owner first."

"First? What does that mean?" Adam couldn't believe the timing of this. He thought to himself that for the first time he might actually be tempted to kill a person, but he told himself it would be impossible.

"That means if you don't want to pay my price, I believe there are plenty of people or organizations that will."

"And what is your price exactly?"

There was a little hesitation at the other end. "One million dollars in small, unmarked bills."

Adam couldn't believe he was being shaken down by some punk hood somewhere, who had somehow gotten hold of one of his journals. He wondered how in the world he had gotten it. Then he wondered if he really had it at all. "Look, I have to think about this. Call me back in two hours, OK?"

The voice at the other end hesitated, perhaps expecting an immediate yes or no. "OK, two hours, but after that I go to my next bidder." And he hung up the phone.

Adam put his head in his hands for a minute. How could such a thing as this be happening now, when he barely had enough time to do all that he had to do? He picked up the phone and dialed Gus' extension. Gus picked up on the first ring.

"Gus, get the car ready. We're heading back to the Aegis. I'll be right down." He hung up the phone, and left the office. He poked his head into Nancy's office, she was working on the computer and she stopped, looking up at him. "Nancy, I have to go out. I'll be back in about an hour and a half."

"What about the board meeting? It's scheduled for fifteen minutes from now."

"Nancy, this is an emergency. Apologize to everyone for me, and change the meeting to tomorrow at the same time." He left before she could say anything more.

The limo pulled out of the garage, and they headed across town to the Aegis building. On the way Adam explained to Gus about the phone call. Gus couldn't believe it. He reminded Adam of the conversation they had a few days earlier, about Sally's brother and his gang. Gus said maybe they got into the penthouse somehow, and took the journal. They both agreed they would know in a few minutes.

It took about twenty minutes to get to the Aegis in the middle of the morning, when the traffic wasn't too bad. They parked the limo in front where there was short-term parking. They both went up.

Elizabeth was surprised to see Adam in the middle of the day, and the look on her face indicated that she thought something must be wrong. Adam didn't want to alarm her, so he assured her everything was fine, and that he just needed something. He and Gus went into his study and closed the door. Adam looked at the shelf, and he immediately saw that one journal was missing. It took only a minute to determine that it was the one the voice had described. He was furious that this person had gotten into his private living quarters. He wondered what else might be missing. He and Gus went back out into the living room, and he stood and looked around. Everything seemed normal. He went back into the study, and swung the picture that hid the wall safe away. He dialed the combination, and opened the safe. The contents seemed untouched. There were several bundles of cash, and a few other papers that he wanted to protect. He closed the safe, spun the dial, and put the picture back. He and Gus went back into the living room. Elizabeth was standing there, looking very confused. She could tell Adam was upset about something, and she couldn't remember ever seeing him that way before. Adam walked over to her and took her hand. He became his sweet, calm self.

"Elizabeth, everything is fine, really. Listen, don't forget about tonight. You and I are going to talk a little tonight, OK?" She nodded and smiled. He patted her hand, and then he and Gus left.

The limo pulled away, heading back to Comtec. Adam was trying to figure out how best to handle this situation. Could the journal harm him if it got into someone else's hands? Should he just tell this guy to get lost? Should he offer him ten thousand dollars? Gus spoke up from the front seat, "Adam, what do you want to do?"

"I don't know yet."

"Listen, let's talk with Sally and see if she can give us any idea who might be pulling this stunt."

Adam thought that might be a good idea. "OK. As soon as we get back, bring her to my office." Adam looked at his watch. They had been gone almost an hour. He had one more hour to figure this out. It was an hour that he really couldn't afford.

Chapter 30

Frank Saunders, Jr. sat at his desk deeply engrossed in a report on the latest intelligence regarding several Middle East terrorist groups that were continually threatening the United States. It was a large office on the third floor of the Central Intelligence Agency in Langley, VA.

Frank was the assistant deputy director of the CIA. His father had held the position twelve years ago when he retired. Three years ago Frank, Jr. had been promoted to the same position. He had been in the Special Forces, and had done two tours in Vietnam. He was promoted to Colonel shortly before joining the CIA. His father had been the deputy director when he made the move. Frank, Jr. was a very hard working and competent man. He earned every promotion he ever got, and refused to ever let his father grease the way for him. It just wasn't his style. No one in the CIA ever thought that Frank, Jr. got the promotion because of his father. They knew it wasn't true.

Frank was married with two children, both in their teens now. He and his wife attended the Presbyterian Church in Falls Church, Virginia, every Sunday with the kids. Frank wasn't really much into religion, but he had always known that religion played an important part in the stable image that had to be portrayed by military men who wanted to move up. It was a political thing. It wasn't that Frank didn't believe in God, but he didn't ever look to God for any help. He was a big believer in self-sufficiency.

His intercom buzzed. "Mr. Saunders." It was his secretary.

He stopped reading. "Yes?"

"It's your father, sir."

Frank put down the report, picked up the phone and sat back, half swiveling around so he could look out the window.

"Dad, how's it going?" He sounded cheery. He and his father were good friends.

"Great, Son. The weather out here is the best. When are you coming out to play some golf?"

Frank laughed, "Soon, Dad, real soon. What's up?"

His father's voice got serious. "Son, listen, I've got a real situation I need to discuss with you, but I think we should discuss it on a scrambled line."

This took Frank by surprise. "Dad, a scrambled line? Why? You think your phone is being tapped?"

"No, Son, but I never trust the phones at your end. I've always figured they were being listened in on by someone."

Frank really laughed now, "Dad, look, I don't want to make you feel old or anything, but with the new technology, we would know if anything was being tapped here. Don't worry about it, tell me what's on your mind."

His father wasn't going to waste time arguing with him. "Son, you remember Harris Pearson?"

Frank closed his eyes and scrunched his forehead trying to connect the name to the past, but he couldn't. "No, I'm sorry I don't. The name sounds vaguely familiar, but I can't place it."

His father jogged his memory. "How about the name Avionics?"

Now Frank remembered. "Yeah, yeah, now I know the name. He used to be involved with the interior design of our planes. I remember him. He must be ancient by now, if he's still alive."

"Hey, be careful what you say. You're talking to someone who's only a few years younger than him!"

"OK, Dad. What's the point about Harris Pearson?"

"Well, I talked to him today. He's in a hospital recovering from a heart attack."

"Sorry to hear about it. Were you guys close, or something?" Frank was wondering where this conversation was going.

"No, not really, but there was awhile where we did a lot of business together. Anyway, that's not the point. Listen, he's old, but he's still mentally as sharp as a tack."

"OK, I'm glad to hear that, but what is this all about?"

He could sense a little irritation in his father's voice now, and that made him really pay attention because it was very unlike his father. "Son, I'm getting to that. Harris was in a restaurant yesterday in California with his wife, daughter, and son-in-law. They were having lunch, and all of a sudden old Harris looks over at another table in the place and sitting there is a man who was the president of Avionics from nineteen fifty-six until about nineteen sixty-five."

There was a momentary pause and Frank felt like he should say something. "What about him?"

"Well, when this guy came to Avionics in fifty-six he was in his early forties, so by now he should be in his mid-eighties, right?"

Frank had no idea where this was going. "Well, I didn't do the math, but that sounds about right."

"Yeah, well, it's right all right. The thing is, he's sitting at the table and he looks exactly like he looked in nineteen fifty-six! It shook Harris up so bad it caused him to have the heart attack!"

Frank sat back in his chair and scratched his head with his other hand. "Dad, what you're saying is impossible. If he would be in his eighties, couldn't he have a son in his forties who looks a lot like him?" Frank felt quite confident that he had just thrown a big bucket of cold water on his father.

"That's exactly what I asked old Harris, but he said that he had a young black driver that he took with him when he left Avionics. That guy was sitting right at the table with him. Harris said he looked older than he had been in fifty-six, but not anywhere as old as he should have. I'm telling you, Son, this is no joke. I know Harris. He's an intelligent man, and he hasn't lost his marbles. I talked with him this morning and he was lucid and calm. He made perfect sense, except that what he was saying seemed impossible."

Frank could tell from his father's tone that he should be taking this seriously, but he was having a hard time doing that. "OK. What's this guy's name?"

His father shot right back, "Adam Adamson."

"It seems to me that Avionics changed its name a few years back." Frank was going to check the story out; it was the least he could do.

"I think they call themselves Aviation Interiors, but they're still in Massachusetts."

"OK. Give me a couple of hours and I'll call you back. Are you home?"

His father said he was home, and he would wait for the call back.

"Tell Mom I love her."

"OK, I will. Thanks for checking it out for me."

"No problem, Dad." They hung up.

Frank picked his phone back up and dialed a three-digit extension. Someone at the other end picked it up on the second ring. "Ben, it's Frank. I want you to do me a favor. Contact a company out in Massachusetts called Aviation Interiors. They had a president in the fifties and early sixties when they were called Avionics, and his name was Adam Adamson. Get his social, and then run a check on him. I want everything that a status one check brings up, and I'd like it in the next twenty minutes — Great, thanks." He hung up the phone and picked up the report that he had been reading. He thought about his father and how much he loved him. Was his dad getting so old that he was going to start to get these kinds of calls?

He laughed at the thought of someone looking the same fifty years later. What was his father trying to say, that the guy doesn't age? What does *that* mean? Is he hundreds of years old, or thousands? He shook his head and went back to his report.

Chapter 31

Sally Dreason was nervous as she followed Gus off the elevator and down the hallway to the executive suite. They walked in, and went directly into Adam's office. Adam stood up and came around to the front of his desk. He extended a hand to Sally, and gestured toward the couches. Gus and Sally sat on one, Adam sat on the other. Adam was sure Sally was not involved in any of this, and he didn't want her to feel like she was under suspicion. He decided to start carefully.

"Sally, I'm hoping you can help me out with a little problem."

Sally looked surprised there could be anything she could do for him. "Sure, Mr. Adamson. Anything."

"I got a phone call from a man this morning who claims to have something belonging to me. What he claims to have is, in fact, missing from my apartment, so I believe he really does have it."

She looked confused. "How can I help?"

Gus spoke up, "We believe he might be mixed up with your brother and his group. For all we know it is your brother."

Sally couldn't believe what she was hearing. "My brother and his friends are probably stupid enough to try anything Mr. Adamson, and I did tell Gus that I was dumb enough one day to tell my brother about your apartment. I'm really sorry if I contributed to this."

Adam could see that she was terribly upset at the prospect of contributing to the problem, and he wanted to put her at ease. "It's not your fault, Sally. We know that, but we need you to help us. Do you know where these people hang out?"

"Usually at Phil's apartment. He lives on Mechanic Street over on the west side of town. It's a green house. His apartment is the second floor."

Adam continued with questions, "Did your brother say anything to you about their breaking into my apartment?"

"Not at all. I would have told Gus immediately. He only asked me about your place one time a couple of weeks ago."

The phone on Adam's desk buzzed. "Mr. Adamson." It was Nancy again.

"Yes, Nancy," Adam answered from where he was.

"It's that man again, who won't give me a name."

"Thank you, Nancy." Adam looked at his watch. He was calling a half hour early. His being impatient was going to work out well.

Adam looked at Sally. "Sally, I want you to pick up this phone at the same time I pick up the phone on my desk." He pointed to a phone on the table next to the couch he was sitting on. "When I pick it up, I'm going to hit a privacy release button on my phone. You hit line four, and pick up at the same time. Now don't say anything just listen and tell me if you recognize the voice, OK?"

Sally nodded and moved over to the phone. Adam went around to his desk, sat down, looked at Sally to be sure she was ready, and pushed the button, picking up the phone at the same time. Sally picked up at exactly the same instant.

"Hello," was all Adam said.

"Well, what did you decide? I'm in sort of a hurry."

Adam wanted to extend the conversation. "Well, I've decided that we should negotiate the price, a million dollars seems a little high."

"I already got others telling me the book is worth a million, so don't jerk me around. Do you want it or not?"

Sally's face showed she definitely recognized the voice. She shook her head up and down to indicate that she knew who it was.

Adam continued, so as not to raise suspicion, "All right, I'll pay you the million for the journal, but listen, even *I* can't come up with a million dollars in small bills in a few minutes. Where can we meet tomorrow?"

There was silence at the other end as he thought. "I'll meet you at Wilshire Park, by the fountain, at noon. And don't try anything funny."

Adam wondered what he would do if he did try something funny, but he knew it wasn't going to matter. "No, I'm not going to try anything. I'll be at the park at noon." He hung up and he looked at Sally. "Well, who is it?"

Sally looked excited like she really was helping. "It's a guy named Ken, I don't even know his last name, but he is one of my brother's friends."

"Do you know where he lives?"

"I think he lives at home with his family; he's got a bunch of brothers and sisters. Whatever he has of yours, I'd bet he's keeping it at my brother's place."

Adam thanked her for her help, and asked her to write her brother's address down. He then asked her to be sure not to say anything to her brother about any of this, and she assured him that she wouldn't. She apologized again as she left the office, and went back to her desk.

Adam told Gus they would go take care of this problem themselves, tonight, on their way home. Adam placed a call to Tim Groff, who had just gotten back to his office. Adam asked him to have the elevator people come over and put a key switch on the elevator from their office to the penthouse. He made sure that Tim understood it was to be done today. Tim told him he would handle it immediately. He and Gus had figured it was the only way they could have gotten in. They must have watched for Elizabeth to go to the store. Gus left to take care of other things in anticipation of their departure. Adam went back to the telephone. He had a lot to do.

Chapter 32

Frank, Jr. had been reading his report for about fifteen minutes when there was a brief knock on his door as it opened. Ben came in with a thin oak tag file. Frank looked up at him.

"There isn't much on your guy, but what there is, is kinda weird."

"Really? Weird how?"

"Well, the record shows he came to the United States in 1955 from Switzerland. Used a Swiss passport to get a social security number because he was going to work in this country. We gave him a number, and pretty soon he's the president of Avionics. The application has no date of birth, no place of birth, no record of parents, nothing."

"How did he get a social security number?"

"Good question, but that's not the weird part. The weird part is that when I called Aviation Interiors, they said that their records showed him starting in mid '56, and their records showed him to be forty-two."

"So what's weird?"

"Well, when you track his places of employment, his last place was a major satellite manufacturer in California called Comtec. He became the president there eight years ago. That means they hired him as the president when he was seventy-nine. That really seems weird to me."

Frank, Jr. could see the point. "Ben, check with the Swiss embassy. See what they can find out about this guy, and ask them to rush it, will you?"

"Sure, but what's with him, anyway?"

"I'd feel better waiting to see what you come up with, then I'll let you know why I'm looking."

"No problem, Frank, I was just curious. I'll get right on it." He left the office and closed the door behind him.

Frank picked up his phone and dialed the field office out in Los Angeles. "Hey, Dino, it's Frank. Yeah, everything is good. How's everything with you? How's the wife? Great, yeah she's great too, thanks. Hey listen, Dino, I need you to do me a favor. Are you familiar with a 'Big Sky Bird' maker called Comtec? You are? Good. I need you to run a check for me on their president, a man named Adam Adamson. Don't ruffle any feathers, but I'd like to know a little about him. Is he old, young, tall, short, bald, full head of hair, whatever you can find out for me. Well, yes, I'm kind of in a hurry. No, not this minute, but if you could get back to me by tomorrow I'd really appreciate it. Great. Thanks." He hung up the phone.

He opened the file that Ben had left on his desk. He looked at Adam's social security number. He picked up the phone again, and dialed. It was the number for Todd Beacher's office. He was a top man at the IRS, and he was Frank's handball partner. The phone rang twice. "Beacher."

"Todd, my man."

Todd recognized Frank's voice instantly. "What's the matter, you still mad about getting beat this morning?"

"No way, I have to let you win once in a while or else you wouldn't play!" They both laughed.

"What's up, Frank?"

"I need a real quick favor."

"Let me have it."

"I need a read out of taxable income on a social from 1956 until now."

"Gee, and I thought it was going to be something tough. You want it faxed or e-mailed?"

"E-mail is probably quicker."

"Give me about three minutes. What's the number?"

Frank gave him the number, and hung up. In two minutes the e-mail symbol lit up on his computer. He punched a few keys and the information he wanted was on the screen.

He spoke, but there was no one else in the office, "Now you want to talk about weird? This is weird."

His taxable income each year from 1956 through 1999 showed as $0.00.

Frank left his office and walked down the corridor to Don Alexander's office. Don had been in the agency for a lot longer than Frank, and he had dealt with some interesting cases over the years. Frank respected his viewpoint. Don was sitting at his desk, looking over some papers. He looked up, and greeted Frank as he walked in. Frank flopped down in one of the big chairs Don had in front of his desk.

"Hey, I need to bounce something a little weird off you."

Don looked interested. "OK. Shoot."

"A man in his forties goes to work for a company in Massachusetts in nineteen fifty-six. A few days ago, this same man is seen in a restaurant in California, and he looks exactly the same as forty-four years ago."

Don thought for a second or two. "Maybe the guy is Dick Clark's brother." He smiled widely.

"No, seriously, he doesn't just look young for his age, I mean he looks exactly the same. Like instead of it being 2000, it's 1957."

Don stared at him. "Is this a joke?"

Frank looked dead serious. "Nope." He then filled Don in on everything he knew so far. Don sat back in his chair and looked up at the ceiling, put his hands up and behind his head, in a classic deep thought stance. He didn't say anything for about a minute.

"Well, my first take would be that the guy might be the son of the man, and 44 years later, look just like his old man."

"And what would be your second take?"

Don sat back upright and looked at Frank, rather than the ceiling, "My second take moves into the realm of somewhere between fantastic and impossible, so I'd rather not say."

Frank wasn't letting him off that easy. "Don, I respect your insight. That's why I'm coming to you with this. What's your second take?"

Don slapped both hands palms down on his desk in an emphatic gesture, "Well, I would have to say you have a man who didn't age in forty-four years, which might just as possibly be a man who hasn't aged in a hundred and forty-four years, or in a thousand years."

Frank didn't quite know how to react to that suggestion. "So, which do you think that theory is? Fantastic, or impossible?"

Don thought for longer than Frank expected. Finally, he said, "Fantastic."

Frank was a little shocked. "You're telling me that you don't think it's impossible?"

Don just stared at him. Frank shook his head side to side. "I must be crackin' up, or else I've been in this business too long. You're sitting here telling me that you think it's possible someone could be hundreds, or even thousands of years old?"

Don looked at him without speaking. It confirmed to Frank that was exactly what he was saying.

Finally, Don spoke very quietly, "Frank, did you ever read the Bible?"

The question caught Frank by surprise. "Sure."

"No, I mean *really* read it, with a view to understanding it?"

Frank thought about it for a few seconds. "No. I would have to say I haven't. Don't tell me you're some kind of born-again or something. How would I not know that?"

Don smiled and held both hands up. "No, Frank, I'm not anything of the sort. I'm a good Catholic who goes to church every once in a while and couldn't care less what the Bible says."

Frank couldn't resist the opportunity. "That's what I thought. You had me worried there for a minute."

Don went on, "But my brother-in-law, Dee's sister's husband, is one of those Jehovah's Witnesses. So is Dee's sister. At first, I thought they were crackpots, but I have to say that I've had some pretty interesting conversations with them. He knows the Bible like nobody I've ever talked to, and he's not some hyped-up person. He's very calm and normal."

Frank had no idea where this was going. "What's your point?"

"My point is, he's mentioned things in the Bible saying that humans were supposed to live forever, and that someday they *are* going to live forever. He really believes it. My point is, that I don't believe it, but I have to admit that my brother-in-law is a pretty normal intelligent person, and if he believes it there's probably some basis for it. That's why I don't put a guy living for hundreds of years into the 'impossible' category."

Frank thought about this for a minute while Don sat quietly. Frank shook his head. "This is getting weirder and weirder. You know, I pulled an income statement on his social for the last forty-four years. All these high paying jobs he's had, he's never taken a nickel in income. Zip. Zero. Zilch!"

Don's reaction to that was, "Oh baby, *that is* weird."

Frank headed out the door, and as he left he said without looking back, "I'll be back to you. Maybe we'll go see your brother-in-law."

Chapter 33

Philip, Ken, Lewis, Todd, and Lester were all sitting in Philip's kitchen. The journal was on the table. Ken had explained to everyone the phone conversations he had with Adam. He first explained about his trip to the university the night before. He was obviously excited about the prospect of getting a million dollars for the journal. No one else seemed all that excited, and he couldn't understand it. He looked around at everybody else. "What's your problem? You don't think a million bucks is pretty interesting?"

Lester spoke, "You know, Ken, you're the one who always thinks of everything. I don't think you're thinking of everything this time." The others shook their head in agreement.

"Why not? What am I not thinking about?" Ken said, irritated.

Lester continued, "For one thing, you want us to believe that this guy, in the year 2000, is the same one that was writing in your book three hundred years ago. Are you nuts or something?"

"Look, I told you I can't explain it, but I saw the different journals and all the writing looked the same, even the latest one a few days ago!"

Lewis spoke, "OK, Ken, let's go with your theory. This guy, who is worth millions of bucks, has been alive for hundreds of years. Forget whether we believe it, let's just go with it. OK, now, if this guy is some kind of super human, which he must be, and he has unlimited financial resources, should we be messing with this man? I mean, what's to stop him from having us all killed? I say we give him back the book, tell him it was all a big mistake, and hope we come out of it alive." No one disagreed.

Ken argued his side. "Come on, guys, you think he's going to blow us all away in a public park? That's why I set it up in a public place. There are laws, you know. He would never get away with it. He'd be screwing himself by killing any of us."

Todd chimed in, "But, Ken, you're asking us to believe that this is something other than a normal man, and then you're asking us to accept that he's going to play by normal rules. I agree with Lester, I say this is a bad idea, and I don't want to have any part of it."

"So, if I get a million bucks out of this guy you don't want any part of *that*, either?" Ken thought this was logical reasoning.

Todd gave him a look of disbelief. "Ken, we got a quarter of a million bucks in Phil's bedroom that we came away with free and clear. No risk. And, we can't even spend that money because we don't want to draw attention to ourselves. What good is another million going to do us? And what good is it going to do you if you get killed trying to collect it?"

Everyone voiced their agreement that this was a real bad idea, and Ken finally agreed to drop the plan. They decided that tomorrow morning he would call Adam again, and tell him that he was withdrawing his request for any money, and that he had put the journal in a plain envelope with Adam's name on it and had a friend drop it off at IMA. He would apologize, and tell Adam that the whole thing had been a big mistake.

Lewis spoke up, "It's six o'clock, and I'm hungry. Let's take a hundred bucks out of the box and go out and get something to eat."

They all agreed, and Todd went into Phil's bedroom. On the floor next to his dresser was the box full of money. He reached in and took out two hundred dollars and walked back into the kitchen. "Hey, I got two hundred just in case we want to eat somewhere really decent." They left the apartment, went down the stairs, and jumped into Phil's car. In a few seconds they were gone. None of them noticed the black Ford Explorer parked a few houses down the street.

Chapter 34

Gus and Adam had been watching the house for about forty-five minutes. Sally had been right on the money as to the house and the floor of the apartment. She told them the entire second floor was his apartment.

It was obvious to them they had all left. The apartment was dark. Gus and Adam got out of the car, and walked casually to the house. They tried the front door, and it opened into a common hallway. There were two doors off the common hallway. One had a number 1 on it, and the other had a number 2. They went up the stairs, and the second floor had only one door.

Gus and Adam were both wearing leather gloves. Gus tried the door, and it was locked as they expected it to be. Gus took a lock pick set out of his pocket and unzipped it. He chose what he thought would be the right pick for the type of lock, plus a tension tool. He handed the set to Adam, and proceeded to play with the lock. It took him two minutes to get the door opened. Locks had been one of the courses he took on his computer in his spare time, a few years earlier.

They entered the apartment and closed the door quietly behind them. Gus took the pick set from Adam, put the two tools back in, and zipped it closed. He put it in his pocket, and took from the same pocket a little flashlight. It produced a powerful, but narrow beam of light that let them see.

It only took them a few minutes to find the journal on top of a Budweiser beer carton. Gus opened the box, because it obviously had been opened before, and he wanted to see what was in it. After all, it was a strange place to find a case of beer. He was a little surprised to find it full of cash.

"Hey, boss," he whispered loudly, "look at this."

Adam came over and looked down into the box.

"Wow," he said, "I wonder who they stole that from?"

They looked at each other for a second and Adam said, "Let's take it with us."

Gus picked up the box, and they left. Gus didn't bother to try and lock the door again.

They drove off and headed back to Comtec to return the Explorer. It was a Comtec maintenance vehicle. As they drove, Adam opened the box and took out a bundle of cash. He estimated it was probably ten thousand dollars. He opened the window, and threw it onto the sidewalk. He was sure it wouldn't take long for someone to find it. He did that all along the way back to Comtec. Before they got back, the box was empty. They threw the box into the dumpster behind the building, returned the vehicle, and drove off in the limo. Adam had the journal safely in hand.

Chapter 35

When Adam got back to the penthouse, Elizabeth was waiting for him. She had his favorite dinner prepared. It was fresh broiled salmon, with a small potato, and a salad. It smelled delicious, and tasted the same. She ate with him, and he listened to her talk about her children who were all grown up, and her grandchildren. He was sure he had heard the same thing a dozen times, but he didn't mind.

They finished eating and she cleared the dishes, putting them in the dishwasher. A few minutes later she came into the living room where he was sitting and looking at the paper.

"Did you want to talk to me about something, dear?" He liked the way she called him "dear."

He put the paper down and looked at her. "Yes, Elizabeth, I did want to talk to you for a few minutes. Please, sit down." She sat on the couch so she was looking directly at him.

"Elizabeth, you've been taking care of me now for eight years."

She nodded. "That's right, eight years next month to be exact."

"Well, I must tell you, you have been very good to me."

"Oh, it's been my pleasure, Adam, you know that."

"Thank you. It's nice of you to say. But listen, here's the thing. I'm going to be leaving on Friday, and I'm not going to be coming back." He could see the look of surprise on her face. Her eyes started to well up, and her face became flushed.

"Now, Elizabeth, I don't want you to worry. I'm going to be leaving you a little something as a token of my appreciation for your years of loyal service."

"Oh, you don't have to do that." She was dabbing her eyes with a tissue she had taken from her apron pocket.

"I know I don't have to, but I want to. You have the household checkbook don't you?"

She looked at him not sure what he was asking. "Oh yes, of course, do you want me to get it right now?"

He smiled at her, "No, I want you to keep it. It's really a checking account in your name anyway; I was never on the account."

Elizabeth was a little confused. "But what would I want with your household checking account?"

"Elizabeth, the checking account only has your name on it, doesn't it?"

"Well, I guess so, yes."

"So, it's really your account. Now, I've deposited two hundred thousand dollars into that account. It's for you to use in any way you want."

Elizabeth was shocked. "Adam, I could never accept such a gift!"

"Oh yes, you can, Elizabeth, and you will. You don't want me going off and worrying about you, do you?"

The old woman didn't know what to say. She started to cry. She tried to talk in between sobs. "I'm … going … to miss you … so much!"

He moved over to the couch and put his arm around her shoulder. "I'll miss you too, Elizabeth."

She looked at him. "Where are you going?"

He knew he couldn't really explain it to her. "It's complicated. I'm going to be living in Europe for a while."

"Oh, I see," she said, drying her eyes. But he knew she didn't really understand.

They talked for a while and then they went down to the lobby, and he hailed a cab for her. She gave him a hug, and told him he was just like a son to her. Adam hugged her and told her how good that made him feel, and he really meant it.

Chapter 36

Frank Saunders, Jr. sat in his office with a cup of coffee, trying to get his brain sorted out. His father had called him yesterday with this crazy story. He had the zero income thing. Ben's research seemed to indicate this guy was hired by a high-tech progressive firm to be the president when he was seventy-nine years old. That seemed unlikely. He was still the president of Comtec, which would make him eighty-seven, and that seemed even *more* unlikely. He was up most of the night thinking about it. He tried to sleep, but his brain was unwilling to shut down.

Now it was a new day, and he hoped he was going to be able to sort this out and be done with it. As he sat drinking his coffee, Ben came in and sat down. He had another file in his hand, and he wasn't smiling. Frank looked at him. His look said: "I'm tired and grouchy, so don't jerk me around."

Ben sat there not saying anything. Finally, Frank couldn't take it any longer. "What?"

"Adamson used a Swiss passport when he applied for a social security number. According to the Swiss government, that passport had only been issued to him the year before. He applied for it as a French citizen. We checked with the French government, and they never heard of him."

"So whatever papers he used in Switzerland were forged."

"It would seem so. I can't think of any other explanation."

"So technically, his Swiss passport is invalid."

"Yup. But listen to this. I dug a little more. He's the founder and chairman of the board of the International Multicultural Assistance."

Frank looked lost.

"IMA," Ben said, and Frank's face came alive.

"Oh! IMA. I never knew what the letters stood for. They're the ones who donated all the new vests to the FBI a few years back."

"One and the same. Seems this guy is loaded, and always has been. Rumor has it he doesn't take any salary in these high paying jobs, and all his salary goes to the charity."

Frank's eyebrows raised as he contemplated this. It certainly explained the zero income statement he received. It was suddenly a little more difficult to think of this man as a criminal, or a threat.

"So, let's think about what we know. He comes to this country on a phony

Swiss passport in fifty-six. Switzerland has no real background information on him, and neither does France. His social security application contains no background information, so basically, before fifty-six he didn't exist."

Ben looked at him with a funny look. "That about sums it up."

Frank started thinking out loud. "OK. He's an outstanding person in the community. Success-oriented, big time philanthropist. On the issue of a phony passport, I might be tempted to just let the whole thing go. I mean who really cares? He certainly isn't hurting anyone. On the contrary, he's helping all kinds of people through his charity."

Ben just sat and listened. He could tell this was not a two-way conversation.

"But, this business about him not getting older over almost fifty years really worries me. I mean what's that all about? When something is completely outside my ability to understand it at all, it worries me." He looked over at Ben. "What do you think?"

Ben shrugged his shoulders. "I don't know, Frank. It seems impossible to me. I figure there has to be some logical explanation."

Frank looked back from looking out the window, and looked at Ben. "I'm not so sure this time Ben. I'm really not so sure."

Ben got up from the chair. "Well, I've got a lot to do. Let me know if I can do anything else for you on this case." And with that, he walked out the door.

Frank turned and stared out the window. He looked at the people walking along the sidewalks, two stories below. He wondered, could there be people down there who have been alive for hundreds of years? Maybe it was just an element of existence he was unaware of. Then he wondered how he could be standing there wondering such strange things. Just then his phone rang. It was his direct line in. He went over to his desk, sat down, and picked up the phone. "Saunders."

It was Dino Argento from the California office. "Good morning, Frank."

Frank looked at the clock on his office wall. It was nine-thirty. He calculated that it was only six-thirty in the morning there. "Dino. What did you do, stay up all night?"

"No way, man, we come in early here to beat the freeway traffic."

"So what's up? You got anything for me?"

"Yeah, this Adamson is a funny guy. Big time job, heads up a huge charity out here, but he keeps a very low profile. Very few people have ever seen him. He doesn't go out in public much. I couldn't find a picture of him anywhere."

"That doesn't surprise me."

"Well, we did talk to a few people who know him. We talked to his attorney and we talked to the guy who heads up the charity."

Frank was not pleased with this news. "Dino, I asked you not to ruffle any feathers. I was hoping you guys could do a little surveillance, and snap a picture for me, or at least get a look at the man. I didn't want you talking to people. You know that's going to get back to him, and I didn't want him to know we were even *looking* at him."

"Gee, Frank, I didn't understand that from our conversation yesterday. I'm really sorry."

"Yeah, me too. What did you tell these people about why you were asking?"

"I really don't want to answer that, now."

Frank had a sinking feeling in his stomach. "Oh boy, that doesn't sound too encouraging."

"We told them we were just looking for a little information at the request of the Washington office."

Frank gritted his teeth. "OK. OK. I'm not happy about how you did this, but at least tell me you have some answers for me."

Dino cheered up a little. "Oh yeah, we do. He's in his middle forties, he's about six-foot-two, or so. The guesses on his weight range from two hundred to two twenty, so he's not fat or anything, and he has a full head of hair."

Frank knew that he couldn't undo anything Dino had done, and there was no sense in making him feel any worse. "Thanks, Dino. I'll get back to you if I need anything more."

"Good enough, Frank. Take care." They hung up, and Frank leaned back in his chair. He knew that Adam Adamson would know by this morning that the CIA was snooping around asking questions. His attorney would certainly inform him immediately. So would the charity guy. But the age that Dino was giving him seemed to agree with the story Harris Pearson had told his father. Now, Frank felt a need to learn more about the possibility of someone living beyond a normal life expectancy. He dialed Don Alexander's extension. It rang once.

"Alexander."

Frank took note that everyone he knew answered the phone with their last names. "Don, it's Frank.

"Frank, how's the million-year-old man coming?"

"Very funny. Listen, I know this sound nuts, but I want to set up a meeting with you and your brother-in-law."

There was a pause at the other end. "Really. You can't make this go away with any logical explanation?"

"Don, how long have you known me? Would I be telling you I want to talk with your Bible-thumping brother-in-law if I could make this go away?"

"Good point. OK, when do you want to do this?"

"The sooner the better. I'd meet with him in ten minutes, if he had the time."

"I'll call and find out what his schedule is. He's usually working during the day. I'll call you back." And he hung up the phone.

Frank wondered if this was going to be a big waste of time. He really didn't believe the Bible anyway; but then, he didn't know much about it. Then another thought struck him. Suppose this person had been alive for hundreds of years, or more. Who really cared? Why was he pursuing this? Did it matter? Certainly it wasn't a case of national security. Or was it? Maybe the whole thing was a waste of time. Suppose he was able to determine that this man somehow had been alive for hundreds of years, or even longer. What would they do, arrest him? On what grounds? Wouldn't it be better to try to get this person to let them in on whatever he knows that allows him to live so long? He thought it was possible that he was overreacting to something just because it was so unfamiliar to him. Then he asked himself if he should simply depend on his own judgment. Should he call some military people he knew, and bounce it off of them? But it was so complicated, and so bizarre.

His phone rang and he grabbed it. "Saunders."

It was Don. "You're in luck. My brother-in-law is on vacation this week. He said if we want to come out to the house, he'll be happy to help in any way he can."

"How long a drive is it?" Frank didn't want to make this a long, drawn out thing.

"Half an hour or so. You want to go now?"

Frank sighed, "Yeah, let's get it over with. I think this may be a wild-goose chase, but I'll meet you in the garage in a couple of minutes." Frank hung up the phone, and shook his head. He had been telling Jehovah's Witnesses for years he wasn't interested when they came knocking on his door. Now he was going to them. He thought that his father had better appreciate all the things he did for him. He grabbed his jacket from behind his office door, and walked out.

The trip out to Don's brother-in-law's house took twenty-five minutes. It was the middle of the day, and traffic was light. He lived in a beautiful neighborhood in the Washington suburb of Gaithersburg, Maryland. His name was David Cipriani, and he was an attorney. That alone blew Frank Saunders' concept of Jehovah's Witnesses. Frank was impressed by the beauty of their home. David led them to what seemed to be a combination family room and study. One wall of shelves was loaded with books. A desk with a computer was at one end of the study. The computer used a screen saver that looked like a fish tank, with fish swimming around. Frank thought that was kind of cute.

David offered them something to drink, which they politely declined. He sat in a chair, and Frank and Don sat on a couch. David looked at the two men inquisitively. "So, gentlemen, what can I do for you?"

Frank spoke up, "Well, I'm looking for an opinion, or maybe I should say some information on a situation I'm looking into."

David looked at him as he spoke, and Frank couldn't help but wonder how often he would do this as an attorney. He found himself wondering what type of law he practiced. David kept looking at him. He hadn't heard a question yet.

Frank continued, "Here's what I would like your viewpoint on; could someone possibly live for hundreds of years, or even longer?"

David thought about the question for a moment. "Are you asking me if humans have ever lived for hundreds of years or longer?"

"No, not really. Although I guess I would be interested to know that too, but what I really mean is *now*. Could a person alive *today*, possibly have been alive for hundreds of years?"

David scratched his head. "Well, I have to tell you that the framing of your question certainly has my curiosity. Let me say this to get our conversation going; the answer to your question would *not* be an absolute no."

"So, it's possible then?"

"Well, it's not that simple. I'd like to show you some information in the Bible to help you understand my answer to your question. I'm not trying to preach to you, but I get the impression that you're looking for exactly this kind of information, am I correct?"

"You're right on the money." Frank could see what Don meant about his brother-in-law being a pretty interesting person.

David took a Bible off one of the shelves. "Now, Frank, I'm going to assume that you have some basic knowledge of Bible stories, right? I mean you know that the Bible says that God created Adam and Eve. Even if you don't believe in creation, you know that the Bible says that, right?" Frank nodded in the affirmative.

David continued, "OK, now let me show you a verse in the book of Genesis. It's here in chapter 5, verse 5. Notice what it says." He turned the Bible so Frank could follow along as he read. "So all the days of Adam that he lived amounted to nine hundred and thirty years and he died." David stopped and let that information sink in for a moment.

Frank didn't really know what to think. He had never read anything in the Bible that said men had lived that long. "Is it possible that they counted time differently back then?"

David smiled, "That's an excellent question, Frank. Let me show you the answer, also in Genesis. This time the first chapter, when God was creating the sun, the moon, and the stars, notice what it says here in verse 14 of the first chapter." He pointed as he read, and Frank's eyes followed along. "'And they must serve as signs and for seasons and for days and years.' So you see, Frank, the rotation of the sun and the moon has always been the same, so years have always been roughly the same as we know them today."

Frank was actually finding this interesting. "So, why was it that they lived so much longer back then?"

"Well, to understand that, you need to understand what God had in mind in the first place. You see, the Bible helps us to understand that when God created humans, he intended for them to live forever; they weren't supposed to die at all."

"How's that possible?"

"Well, think about it, Frank. Science today is just beginning to understand that when a person is in their thirties, a change occurs in their ability to regenerate cells. This is when the aging process begins. Science still doesn't understand why the change occurs, they just know that it does. If that change never happened; if the human cells in the body continually regenerated themselves with that process never breaking down; hypothetically, a person could live forever. When humans were created, they were perfect. And as such, that is what would have occurred. But the Bible says that they sinned, they were disobedient, and they lost their perfection because of it."

Frank thought he knew a little about this part. "Isn't that when they had sex, or something?"

David chuckled. "Well, that's what some people may lead you to believe, but no, Frank, sex had nothing to do with it. What exactly constituted disobedience or sin isn't particularly relevant to your questions. Just accept for the moment that the Bible teaches when Adam and Eve sinned, they lost their human perfection. The aging process kicked in, but they were so close to perfection that it took Adam almost a thousand years to age and break down, to the point of death. Some, in those times, lived even longer. When Noah built the ark he was six hundred years old, and then he lived another three hundred and fifty years after the flood. But the point is this; when Adam and Eve lost their perfection, they also lost the ability to pass human perfection to their offspring. Can you understand that?"

Frank nodded. He was surprised that he really did understand what David was saying.

"Now," David continued, "the Bible never mentions Adam and Eve having children until after they were disobedient, when they had lost perfection. But let's suppose, just for the sake of your question, that unknown to us, Adam and Eve had had a child *before* they were disobedient. That child, theoretically, would have been perfect. And had they had such a child, it would be possible that that person could still be alive today. I'm not saying I think such a thing is likely, because I don't. But your question was: could it be possible? And I'm trying to show you that yes, it could be."

Frank was overwhelmed. He knew the evidence indicated that Adam Adamson was unusual, at best. He seemed not to age for almost fifty years. Suddenly, even his name was like a cryptic message; Adam Adamson. Adam the son of Adam. Frank felt his head starting to spin. He looked at David. "I'd like to take you up on that glass of water now."

David left the room to get the water. Don looked at Frank. Frank spoke softly, "He knows his stuff. I never knew any of this, and I've been a Catholic all my life!"

David came back in with a glass of water and handed it to Frank. Frank drank it down like he hadn't had a drink in weeks. "Thanks, I needed that."

David said, "Sorry, Frank. I didn't mean to overwhelm you."

Frank held up a hand. "No, no, no don't apologize. You're giving me exactly what I need, and exactly what I came here for. I want to thank you for your time, David. You've been a real big help." Frank stood as he said this, and extended a hand. David shook it.

"I was happy to be of help, but I was hoping you might give me some idea of what brought this all up."

Frank shot a look at Don. Don just shrugged. It was a shrug that said: "Hey, it's up to you." Frank sighed, and sat back down.

"Well, David, without naming names, I got a call from my father who used to be with the agency. He told me about an old friend of his who called him. He claimed that a man who used to be the president of his company in nineteen fifty-six, when he was in his forties, still looks exactly the same today in 2000. He hasn't aged in almost fifty years. We've done a little background check on him, and the information we came up with leaves a lot of unanswered questions. It seems it is possible that this is the same guy, and he simply hasn't aged. I'm trying to figure out how that's possible."

David thought for a moment. "Well, with today's medical capability, a good plastic surgeon could keep someone looking pretty much the same for almost fifty years."

"We thought of that, and that would have been my first inclination. But it seems that we're not talking about a person not looking as old as he should. We're talking about looking *exactly* the same fifty years later."

David stood up this time, and extended his hand to Frank. "Well, I'm glad that it's your problem, and not mine. It sounds like a tough one. Just keep one thing in mind. If this person is alive on the basis of what we discussed today, it means that he's been alive for over six thousand years. It would also mean that you're dealing with a man who has one hundred percent use of his brain when science says that at best we use three-tenths of one percent. You wouldn't want to do anything that would risk harming such a man."

Frank shook his hand, thanked him again, and he and Don left. On the way back to the office they talked about the visit. Frank was surprised there was so much in the Bible he didn't know anything about. His head was swimming with possibilities. Was he onto a man who has been alive since the beginning of humans? What about evolution, he wondered? Don't scientists believe that humans have been around for millions of years? He thought about a movie he remembered from when he was a kid. Raquel Welch played a cave woman. It was entitled "One Million Years B.C." Were there humans alive a million or more years ago? Frank didn't know what to think. He decided he first had to make decisions on his earlier questions. Was this even worth pursuing? OK, maybe Adam Adamson used a phony passport fifty years ago, but so what? Look at all he's done for so many people. What was the benefit of going after him?

They got back to the office, and Frank had a message waiting for him. He had received a call from General Clay Edwards, one of the Joint Chiefs. Frank knew it had really hit the fan now. His father must have called him. He could feel his options being yanked away as he picked up the phone.

Chapter 37

Adam spent Wednesday morning with Bernie from the moving company, going through the apartment room-by-room, item-by-item. The man had been very impressed by the penthouse. He voiced concern over the desk in the study, how they would get it out the door. Adam explained that the legs came off, and when the top was stood on end, it was smaller than a refrigerator. It shouldn't be a problem, and the man agreed. They would be by the next morning to take everything. Adam explained he would have a trunk with clothes, also. They discussed where everything was going, and how long it would take to arrive. Adam had no problem with the time frame. Bernie told Adam what the cost would be, and Adam gave him a check. It was agreed that he would be there before eight in the morning to get started. He had already been in Gus' apartment, and the price included his things.

Adam had instructed Gus to pack only essentials for the trip. A few clothes and toiletries, and things like that. They could buy whatever else they needed once they got where they were going. Gus knew they were going to England, but he had no idea exactly where. He didn't really care.

By ten o'clock, Adam was at his desk. He had made several calls overseas the day before, and was expecting some confirmations today. He already checked with Roy Hazelton, and everything was taken care of. Adam had very little in the way of assets left in the U.S. He had over twenty thousand dollars left in the safe in the penthouse, and he expected that to be more than he would need between now and Friday morning. He still had a personal checking account that had just enough cash in it to cover certain checks he had either written out in the last few days, or would still be writing out. He figured to leave the account with nothing in it when he left. It was Wednesday, and most of the costs associated with his departure were already taken care of.

When he and Gus arrived this morning, and had gotten out of the car, he asked Gus for his driver's license. Gus looked a little confused as he opened his wallet, giving it to him. Adam assured him that he could get through a little more than one day without it. Now in his office, he took the license, along with his own picture Comtec ID card, and put them in an envelope. Adam didn't have a driver's license. It was one of those things he had just never gotten around to. He took the envelope and, along with two plane tickets, put them into a larger envelope. He wrote someone's name on the front of the envelope. He called Nancy into his office and asked her to take the envelope down to the main receptionist and to tell her the person whose name appeared on the front would come to pick up the envelope. Nancy took the envelope and left.

A little after noon, Adam received one of the phone calls from overseas he was expecting. The caller confirmed everything he had requested was arranged. At about one-thirty he received the other call. When he finished with that call, he sat back and relaxed. He knew everything was set.

Chapter 38

The phone on Mary Turner's desk rang just as she was taking a sip of hot coffee. She thought the timing could not have been more annoying. She let it ring twice while she tried to swallow the hot liquid without burning her mouth. She picked up the phone half way through the third ring. "General Edwards' office. May I help you?" She recognized the voice on the other end. It was Frank Saunders from the CIA.

"Good morning, Mary. Is the General in?"

"Good morning, Mr. Saunders. He's been waiting for your call, I'll put you right through."

She put him on hold and buzzed the General. "General Edwards, Mr. Saunders is on line two."

General Clayton Edwards was one of the last of the "old school" military leaders. No one was totally beyond suspicion as a potential enemy. Even though the U.S. stood alone as the world military power to be reckoned with, and there were no wars looming on the horizon, General Edwards believed that the military budget should be at least twice what it was. He wanted to see new submarines, tanks, and helicopters pouring out of factories. He suspected the entire break up of the Soviet Union was only a ruse to lull the U.S. into a false sense of security. He had a solution for the problem with homosexuals in the military. Just take them all out, and shoot them. Get the women out too, he thought, and we'd be back to the kind of Army a man could be proud of. He picked up the phone. "Saunders, what's going on?"

Frank Saunders really didn't like this man, but he had to be careful because he was in a very powerful position. "Good morning, General. That's a very broad question. You tell me, what's going on?"

"Come on, Saunders, you know exactly what I'm talking about. I talked with your father this morning. You know I've known your father for a long time. He's a good man, and when he tells me a story about somebody not aging in fifty years, I take it very seriously. Now, I understand you've known about this since yesterday morning, is that correct?"

"Yes, General. I spoke with my father yesterday morning."

"Well, what have you found out?"

"Not a lot. The man in question is the top executive of one of the largest developers of communications satellites in the country. They've developed the last two major military satellites we've deployed."

"Is that so?"

"Yes, sir, that is so. He's also the chairman of the board of a charitable organization called the International Multicultural Assistance, commonly referred to as IMA. They help out anyone from an individual who loses a home in a fire, to entire cities that are flooded or suffer from some other disaster. They also fund entire federal organizations that are underfunded. Some years ago, they provided the new technology bullet proof vests for the FBI after an agent was killed in the line of duty by a vest piercing bullet."

"All right, Saunders, so let's say this guy is a real do-gooder. Let's agree that he's not out to hurt anyone. Do you think we should just forget the possibility that he has somehow figured out how to stop himself from getting old?"

"I don't think that's what we're dealing with, sir."

"You don't, huh? So your father is just off the wall with this?"

"No, sir, I'm not questioning the validity of what my father told me or you. I haven't spoken with his friend Pearson myself, but I expect that my father was pretty convinced of the facts before he called me."

"So then what exactly is your point, Saunders?"

"Well, General, I'm not sure what my point is. I've been gathering information since yesterday morning trying to come up with a logical hypothesis."

"Screw the logical hypothesis, Saunders. Go pick him up and talk to him. How do we know that there aren't more like him out there?"

"With all due respect, General, the man is a highly respected person who has never so much as had a parking ticket. How can we just go 'pick him up' as you say? On what grounds?"

"Saunders, you're the assistant deputy director. Do I have to teach you how to do your job? I'm not suggesting you barge into the man's office with a swat team, throw the cuffs on him, and haul him away. Call him. Make an appointment for him to come in to see you. Talk to the man, Saunders. Find out what's going on with him. If he doesn't want to come in to your office, you go to his."

"But, General, just for a moment, let's suppose this guy is hundreds of years old. How is that really a concern to the United States government?"

"Saunders, is that a serious question?"

"Yes, sir, it is."

"You don't think it should be of any interest to us how he's lived so long? You don't think that maybe he's somehow figured out a way to slow down the aging process, and that this is something that should rightfully be shared *at least* with the government? Probably with the world?"

"But, General, suppose it has nothing to do with something he's discovered?"

"What is that supposed to mean? How else could he be alive for hundreds of years?"

"I'm not sure, sir. That's what I'm still trying to figure out."

"I don't follow you at all, Saunders. What other options are there?"

Frank really didn't want to get into this with him, but he didn't see any way to avoid it.

"Well, sir, it could have simply been a genetic fluke." There was a long pause at the other end. Frank had no idea what the General's reaction was going to be.

The General's response was quite subdued. The concept had obviously sent his mind in a very different direction. "What do you mean a 'genetic fluke'?"

"Well, sir, suppose he was born with the genetic makeup that simply never started the typical aging process of a man in his thirties?" Frank was already glad he talked to Don's brother-in-law this morning. "Suppose he just found that he wasn't aging like everyone else around him?"

There was another long pause, and then the General was mentally back to his previous position. "Listen, Saunders. I think you've been watching too many science fiction movies. I'm done with this conversation. I want you to talk with this person directly and see what you can find out. If in fact he's really been alive for anything more than the life span of a normal man I want to know how and why. I want to know if there are others like him, and if so, *where* they are and *who* they are. Do I make myself perfectly clear?"

"Yes, sir. You do."

"Good, I want to hear back from you by the end of the week." With that, the General hung up. Frank sat back and reflected on the conversation they'd just had.

Clayton Edwards also reflected on the conversation. He was a "black or white" type of man. In his world there was no gray. Something was good, or bad. There was little in his world he was indifferent about. He had an opinion on everything. He was an intellectual of sorts. He liked to read, and he enjoyed interesting conversation, although never for the purpose of changing his point of view. Simply for the exercise of defending it. He was not a religious man. He considered religion to be a crutch for the weak. The comment that Saunders had made about a "genetic fluke" stuck in his mind, because it was such a foreign concept. He wanted to simply dismiss it, but he couldn't. He picked up his phone and dialed a number. The phone rang twice, and a woman answered.

"This is General Edwards. Is Dr. Bennett in, please?"

Bill Bennett was the Chief of Staff at Bethesda Naval Hospital. He was the top medical man in the country, as far as the General was concerned. He gave the President of the United States a physical exam every year. That was good enough for him. A moment later the doctor came on the line. "Clay, how are you?"

"I'm fine, Bill, just fine. How's everything with you?"

"You know how it is. Just trying to keep up. So, what's up?"

"Bill, I need to bounce something off you, but I need you to understand that this question might somehow fall under the category of national security, so I need you to keep it strictly to yourself, OK?"

"Sure, Clay, no problem."

"That's great. OK, so here it is. I want your opinion on the possibility of someone having a genetic disorder that prevents them from getting old. They just get to a certain point in their lives and then they don't get any older."

"For how long, Clay?"

"Oh, I don't know. Let's say a couple hundred years."

There was a pause. "It's just about noon. You haven't been hitting the sauce have you?" The doctor was laughing a little as he said this.

"Come on, Bill, I'm serious"

"Well, if you're serious I'll give you a serious answer. First, if there was such a person, they wouldn't really have a 'genetic disorder.' Technically, the human aging process is a genetic disorder. We know it happens, but we don't really know why. If a person didn't age, they would actually be *free* from the genetic disorder we all have. Why do you ask, Clay?"

"Oh, I'm just on a fishing expedition, trying to sort something out." He didn't want to tip his hand to anyone. "Thanks, Bill, for taking the time to talk with me."

"Any time. How's the golf game?"

The General chuckled. "As bad as ever. I think I'm responsible for keeping the golf ball manufacturers rich."

"Hey, I hear you."

"Thanks again, Bill."

"No problem."

The General hung up. He decided he would just wait to hear what Frank Saunders had to say on Friday.

Chapter 39

Adam's intercom buzzed, which meant Nancy wanted him to pick up the phone, rather than have her message be heard through the speaker. She didn't always know if there was anyone in the office with him, and this told him the message was not routine. He picked up the phone. "Yes, Nancy."

"Adam, there's a Mr. Saunders on the phone for you. He says he's with the CIA."

"Thanks, Nancy." Adam looked at the blinking line for a moment and then punched the button. "This is Mr. Adamson. May I help you?"

"Mr. Adamson, my name is Frank Saunders, I'm the assistant deputy director of the CIA in Washington. How are you, sir?" Frank was making every effort to sound non-threatening. He was well aware of the public perception of the CIA.

"I'm very well, Mr. Saunders. What can I do for you?"

"Well, Mr. Adamson, I know this may seem a little unusual, but I wonder if I might get a few minutes of your time to meet with you in person?"

Adam thought for a moment before answering, "Did you say you're in Washington?"

"Yes, sir, I did, but it would be no problem for me to fly out tonight, and we could meet tomorrow morning, if that would be possible for you."

Adam didn't want to sound evasive. "Might I ask what this is in reference to?"

"Well, sir, it's something that I would like to discuss with you privately and in person, as soon as possible."

Adam sensed this would be a good thing to avoid if possible. "How about first thing Monday, Mr. Saunders?" He knew by Monday, Adam Adamson would be non-existent.

Frank had been in the business a long time, and he had developed a keen sense of perception, even in phone conversations. The slightest alteration in a man's voice could speak volumes. He sensed this man was looking to avoid this meeting. He didn't want to alarm him. "Sure, Monday morning would be fine. What time would be good for you?"

"How about ten o'clock?"

"Ten would be fine. Thank you."

"You're welcome, Mr. Saunders. Goodbye."

They hung up, and Adam breathed a sigh of relief. He thought about Harris Pearson. He must have recovered. He could just imagine what he was saying, and to whom he was probably saying it. They had done work almost exclusively for the military back in the fifties and sixties. When he left Avionics, they were doing about eighty percent military work, designing the interiors of the planes that flew the big brass all over the world. He had always followed the progress of every company he worked for. He knew that Avionics had merged with another company about fifteen years ago and changed their name to Aviation Interiors. They still did huge numbers with the military. There was a rumor that they were working on a new Air Force One, but it was unconfirmed.

Adam knew that Harris Pearson must still have some connections with the top military in the country. This call from a CIA assistant deputy was no coincidence. He ruled out any possibility that the call was IMA related. Since he'd founded IMA, he had never gotten a call about IMA directly. They all went to the IMA offices. No, he knew Pearson had started some ball rolling, and he was going to be gone, before it rolled into him. He looked at his watch. It was nine-thirty. He wished it was Thursday, instead of Wednesday. The rescheduled board meeting was in half an hour. He picked up his phone, and dialed the receptionist at the front desk. Her switchboard identified every in-house extension. She knew this was Adam's call. The phone barely rang. "Yes, Mr. Adamson?"

"Good morning, Jennifer. Did Mr. Jenson pick up the envelope I left for him yesterday?"

"Yes, sir, he did."

"Good, thank you."

"You're welcome." He hung up the phone. Adam met Mike Jenson three years earlier. One of his senior management people had remarked one day about a man on a TV commercial who looked exactly like Adam. He actually had thought that Adam was doing commercials on the side. Within a week, two other people made the same comment. One had taped a program, and the commercial was on the tape. He brought it in, and Adam watched it. They were right. The likeness was uncanny.

Adam had put a call in to the manufacturer of the product and gotten the name of the agency that produced the commercial. From them, he got the name of the actor, and the actor's agent. It took several phone calls, but he was finally able to convince Mike Jenson to come in and meet with him, without his agent. It had been an interesting meeting. It had taken Nancy by surprise when she saw him. And when Mike was shown into Adam's office, he was speechless. It was like meeting himself. They were even close to the same height. They talked for several hours.

Mike had been a struggling actor for many years. Then one day, he landed a small part on a weekly TV show, and he did pretty well. He did some high quality commercial work once in a while. Adam asked if he could call on him some time if he needed the services of someone who looked like him. He offered Mike a ten thousand dollar "retainer" for his personal phone number and for his willingness to be available if the need ever arose. Mike told him to keep his ten thousand dollars. He was doing quite well, and then he wrote his number on the back of his agent's card. He told Adam to call him anytime at all.

He was true to his word. When Adam had called him last week, he had been very willing to help.

Chapter 40

Sally Dreason couldn't believe the story Gus told her. Neither could she believe that the bundle of money she was holding in the palm of her hand was from her brother's apartment. She was in Gus' basement office. He had called her and asked her to come down. He told her the whole story, including how he and Adam had thrown all the money out of the car along the street on their way back to Comtec. Then, he pulled out the one bundle he had kept for her with Adam's approval, and gave it to her. He told her he had saved one for her. But he wanted her to be aware of everything that had happened, because her brother was probably going to be pretty angry. He might even suspect that she was somehow involved in Adam's knowing where to go. She couldn't stop looking at the money. She looked at Gus.

"How much do you think there is?"

He laughed, "I'm not sure, but I think they were bundles of ten thousand."

She looked at the money. "Wow, ten thousand dollars. What am I supposed to do with it?"

Gus laughed again, "Anything you want to do with it, Sally. It's yours now. But remember, you don't want to have to explain to anyone how you suddenly came to have ten thousand dollars in cash. That might be a little suspicious. And if your brother finds out, you know he's going to figure you were involved in his money disappearing."

She nodded her agreement. "What am I going to do with it, Gus?" I only have a little pocketbook. This big wad will never fit in it, and besides, it's still up at my desk."

Gus looked around the little office. On a shelf there was a small cooler pack. It was just large enough to put a sandwich and one can of soda in. He took it off the shelf, and opened it. He hoped there wasn't a sandwich in there he had forgotten about months ago. To his relief, it was empty and clean. "Here, you can use this. Everyone will just think it's your lunch." He handed it to her. The money just barely fit.

She said she was going to go out and put it in the trunk of her car, before she went back to work. Her car wasn't locked, so she could access her trunk. She could lock the car without the key, which was in her pocketbook. She got up from the chair and walked over to Gus who was still sitting. She put her hand on his head. It was shiny like a bowling ball. She caressed his head gently, and in her sexiest voice, she said, "How can I ever thank you, Gus?"

Gus knew where she was going with this, and he knew it was a real bad idea. He looked up at her. "We'll go out to dinner Saturday night, Sally. You can find a way to thank me then."

She smiled at him, bent over and kissed him on the top of his head. "You've got a date."

Chapter 41

Frank Saunders called the travel coordinator, and arranged for a flight out to the West Coast for late that afternoon. He had a ticket for a five-thirty flight. With the time zones being three hour's difference, he would arrive in LA less than two hours after he took off. He knew it was going to make him extremely tired the next morning, but he didn't think he had any other choice.

He called out to the LA office, and told Dino he was coming out. He gave him the flight number and arrival time, and asked Dino to pick him up. He also told him to clear his schedule for the next morning, Frank needed him with him. He told his secretary he was leaving to go home and pack. Besides, he wanted to spend a little time with his wife if he was going to be gone for a few days. In the old days when he was first in the agency, he would sometimes be gone for days or weeks on agency business. There had been many times when he had spent weeks in a foreign country, under an assumed name, doing the government's bidding. He thought about Adam Adamson possibly living for thousands of years under one alias after another. He couldn't help but have respect for the man. He intended to appear at the man's door in the morning, and hope for the best.

Chapter 42

Adam entered the board meeting at exactly ten o'clock. Everyone was present. Edward Keaton sat immediately to Adam's right. Adam wasted no time getting to the point.

"Ladies and gentlemen, thank you for rearranging your schedules. I first want to apologize for the sudden cancellation yesterday. It could not be avoided. As you have not received an agenda for this meeting, I'm sure you're all wondering what the purpose of this meeting is. I won't keep you in suspense. As of the end of business today, I am resigning as the President of Comtec."

There was an audible hush among the twenty-four people in the room. The only one who wasn't surprised was Keaton. Adam could tell from the response that he had told no one of their conversation.

"I am recommending that Edward be reinstated as the President and Chairman of the Board. Are there any questions?"

A young woman toward the other end of the table raised her hand. Her name was Ann Kelly, and she was the head of purchasing. "This is probably not relevant, Mr. Adamson, but are you leaving to take another job somewhere?"

All heads had turned to her when Adam called her name. Now, as if rehearsed, they all turned back to him for the answer.

"No, Ann, I'm not. I know it seems unfair to not offer you a logical explanation, but those of you who were here when I first came to Comtec know this is part of how I operate. I appear, I do my thing for a while, and then I disappear. It's the way I have always been. Please don't take it personally. I have enjoyed working with all of you very much."

A man down near Ann raised his hand. His name was Paul Atkins, and he was the head of Product Development, which was a division between Sales, and Research and Development. His people took sales concepts, and finalized them. Then the R&D people figured out how to make it work. Everyone looked at Paul when Adam called on him.

"The thing is, Adam, we really like our jobs here, but if we have a choice, we'd rather go with you wherever you go." Everyone recognized that he was joking, and they all had a little laugh. Even Adam laughed.

"I appreciate your loyalty, I really do. I'm confident that you'll continue to give the same support to Edward, just as you did before I came here." Everyone was silent. " I have one final request. I would appreciate it if you would not mention one word of this meeting to anyone. Please consider this confidential. Monday, I don't care who knows, but until then, I would like to keep my leaving under wraps."

Everyone nodded and looked at each other, signifying their agreement. With that, Adam stood up. As he did, so did everyone in the room. "Thank you all for everything." He stayed and shook hands with everyone in the room as they left. He knew every one of them by name. He knew their wives or husband's names, if they were married. He knew most of their children's names. He cared about these people like they were family. He cared about *all* people like they were family.

When he got back to his office, he had messages from Tim Groff and Roy Hazelton. Both were marked urgent.

Chapter 43

Frank Saunders' flight touched down at L.A. International at 7:30 in the evening. Every time he came out to the West Coast, he was surprised by how much better the weather was than on the East Coast. It made him realize that he always came out west during the winter.

Dino was waiting for him at the gate. He was younger than Frank. He was a handsome enough man, and he always had a great tan. Frank had heard that he was a serious golfer. They made small talk through the airport. Dino's car was parked in an area marked "Official Business Only." He had a small card that said, "Official Government Business" lying on the dashboard. They got in, and drove onto the freeway, which was the thing Frank disliked the most about the West Coast. The traffic was bumper to bumper, five or six lanes wide, and all moving at seventy-miles per hour. It made him nervous.

Now that they were alone in the privacy of the car, Dino wanted to know what was going on. Frank didn't want to seem secretive, but he knew how incredible the whole thing was going to sound. It made him reluctant to answer right away. He found himself avoiding getting into details. "I need to follow up on some information regarding Adamson."

Dino thought about that for a minute. "Look, I checked the guy out, he doesn't even have a parking ticket on his record. If he was a little more visible, he might have been the "Citizen of the Year" by now. Time magazine might have put him on the cover, if he was more of a public person."

Frank knew he was right. "Look, Dino, my coming out here is in no way a commentary on your work. You did exactly what I asked you to do, even if you did talk to some people I didn't want you to talk to. There are some aspects to this case that are so bizarre, I think it's best not to discuss it with too many people."

Dino had been in the agency for a long time, and he was not going to be easily brushed off. "Frank, not telling too many people is one thing. Not telling me is bogus. You ask me to clear my schedule, come out to the airport and pick you up, go with you tomorrow to see this person, and you don't want to tell me what it's all about? Come on. That's insulting."

They drove for a minute or two without another word. Frank could see that Dino was upset. "Look, Dino, you're a good guy. We've had some great times together, and we've taken care of a few interesting cases together. I'm telling you this thing is going to flip you out if I explain it to you."

Dino looked over at him for a long time, which made Frank nervous because they were still on the highway encased in traffic. Finally, Frank said, "Hey, watch the road, OK?"

Dino looked back out the windshield. "Look, Frank, if there's something about this that *is* crazy, it'll be *my* problem. But your keeping me in the dark is going to be *our* problem. Don't you think it's better for just *one* of us to have a problem?"

At this point, Frank realized that he wasn't going to let it go. "OK, Dino. You win, but here's the deal. No matter what you think about anything I tell you, it goes no further than this car. You understand that?"

Dino shook his head. "Sure, Frank, that's no big deal."

"You say that now, Dino, but you're not going to be saying that in a few minutes. But I'm warning you, if you leak a word of this to anyone else, in or out of the department, I'll personally see to it that you're discharged from the agency."

Dino looked at him in disbelief, but he could see Frank was not joking. "It's that serious?"

"Yes. It's that serious."

"OK, Frank. I agree to your terms. I swear I'll discuss this with no one but you. What's the deal?"

"I have reason to believe that Adam Adamson has possibly been alive for over six thousand years." Frank let the words roll off his tongue, like it was no big deal. He thought he sounded like Jack Webb, from the old "Dragnet" TV show. Dino kept driving as if he hadn't heard him. Frank sat quietly and waited.

Finally Dino spoke, "Frank. Seriously. What's the deal?"

"I just told you the deal."

"I'm supposed to believe that *you* believe that some guy has lived six thousand years?"

"I didn't say I believe. I said I have *reason* to believe."

"Frank, I don't think we're talking about the technicality of *exactly* what you said. I think we're talking about *what* you said in general. I'm supposed to buy that someone is six thousand years old. That's ridiculous!"

"You're probably right."

"I'm probably right! I'm *absolutely positively* right! If I'm not right, I'll resign from the agency, you won't have to worry about bootin' me out!"

"Be careful what you promise, Dino."

Dino looked back over at Frank. "Frank, you're not really serious."

Frank looked Dino straight in the eyes, and resisted telling him to look at the road. "I'm dead serious."

"Jeez, Frank. You said bizarre, you didn't say insane."

"Look, Dino, maybe I'll get this all cleared up tomorrow, or maybe I won't. We'll see."

Dino was watching the road again, much to Frank's relief. "When's he expecting you?"

"Ten o'clock on Monday."

"Oh boy." Dino shook his head as these words came out. They drove the rest of the way to the field office in silence.

When they got to the office, Frank made some calls. He called his wife, to let her know he made it safe and sound. He called his father, to bring him up to speed on what was going on. His father told him he had talked to Harris Pearson once more since they spoke, and Harris was absolutely positive it was the same man. Frank's father said he had purposely reminisced with the old man about some of their past dealings, just to confirm the man still had his mental faculties. He assured his son that Harris Pearson was a dependable witness. Frank wanted to make sure his father hadn't made any promise to Harris.

"You know, Dad; as far fetched as this whole thing seems, even if this is the same guy, he's not technically breaking any law."

There was a brief silence as his father pondered the point. "But, if he isn't getting any older, who knows how old he really is? He could be considered a national security risk. He might know things he shouldn't know. How do we know he didn't operate under different names in classified jobs?"

"Dad, there's no indication at all that he's been involved in anything, but high level corporate jobs. And, he's donated over a hundred million dollars to charity in forty-something years. Did you discuss any of this national security crap with Clay Edwards?" He knew the answer by the pause on the other end.

"Yeah, I think I said something to him about it, why?"

Frank knew he was going to have a lot more trouble on his hands. "I just wondered, Dad. That's all. Listen, I'll call you when I know more."

They hung up, and Frank tried to play out in his head all the possible scenarios. He knew that Clayton Edwards tended toward paranoia anyway. Now, if his father has been feeding that paranoia, he knew Edwards wouldn't be happy unless Adam Adamson was in a cell somewhere. Or, better yet, on a dissecting table in some lab.

Dino offered to have Frank to his house for dinner, but Frank politely declined. For one thing, he didn't want to talk about this for hours with Dino, and secondly, he was going to have a jet lag problem tomorrow if he didn't get to bed early. Dino dropped him off at the apartment the agency kept in downtown L.A. Frank took a quick shower, ordered a pizza from a local shop that delivered, and settled down to watch a little TV. By ten o'clock he was fast asleep. His body thought it was one in the morning.

Chapter 44

Adam was just about finished packing what he intended to take with him. It all fit into a medium-sized suitcase. Gus had asked him if he needed to limit his luggage to a carry-on, or if it could be a suitcase that would need to be checked. Adam had told him it could be any size he needed, but it would be good if he could limit it to one. Adam had also taken all his journals, and packed them into a large box. He taped the box carefully, so there was no chance of the box breaking open.

He opened the wall safe, and emptied the contents. There were several files of papers he wanted to take with him in his suitcase, and there was cash. He counted it quickly, just to be sure he knew how much he had with him. It was twenty-two thousand dollars. Twenty-two packets of fifty; new, twenty-dollar bills. He put them in his suitcase. All his other clothing and personal things he had packed already. The movers would take care of the rest.

He expected this would be his last night in this apartment. He looked around and thought about the eight years he had been here. He found himself reflecting on the forty-four years he had been in the United States, and how much he had enjoyed himself. He thought he would like to come back as soon as it was safe to do so. Under a different identity, he could probably do so in seventy or eighty years, with no cause for concern. In all his life, this situation with Harris Pearson had been a first. Both his attorney, and Tim Groff had called him to let him know they had gotten inquiries from the CIA. He had no idea why they would be involved, but he knew it was now dangerous for him. He was glad to be leaving on Friday. He just had to get through one more day.

He decided not to use the name Abel Cain. He thought that if the CIA was suspicious of him, they might eventually pick up on the cryptic quality of his name, so he felt it unwise to do the same thing. He contacted the agent making the transfer on the property they were moving to on Friday, and instructed them to change the purchaser name to Benjamin Nathan. He would transfer the other properties over the next several months. There was no hurry.

He also placed a call to someone he used to procure documents for him. The person was very expensive, but the documents were absolutely perfect. It would take deep research to reveal the fact they were not real. This issue of passports and citizenship had only been a problem in the last few hundred years. Before that, it was never an issue. All the necessary documents for him and Gus would be waiting for them.

Adam looked around to make sure he had taken care of everything. He even cleaned out the food from the refrigerator, although there wasn't much in there. He went to bed, and ran through a checklist of things he needed to do tomorrow.

Chapter 45

Gus had packed the things he wanted to take with him. He had a suitcase ready to carry with him, and he packed in boxes the things he wanted the movers to take. The rest he was going to leave, and eventually Tim Groff would get rid of it, as the apartment was part of their lease arrangement.

Gus didn't have any reservations about leaving the country, even though he had lived in the United States all his life. He had been with Adam for over forty years, and he felt a great attachment to him. He was no young man anymore, and knowing that Adam was always going to take care of him was an important part of his decision.

He knew it was getting late, but he had one last thing he wanted to do. He sat down at his desk and wrote a letter to his sister. He hadn't seen her in quite a few years, but he had her phone number, and every once in a while he would call her. He knew that his leaving and assuming a new identity would mean that he would never see her or talk to her again.

He had had a bank check made out in her name before his accounts were transferred. It was a check for a half million dollars. In his letter, he told her that circumstances had made it necessary for him to leave the country. He would not be back, and he was sorry he had not been able to visit her before he left. He also apologized for not having seen her more often. He knew that she wouldn't really understand why he had become so distant. He was a man in his late sixties, who looked like he was in his forties. He was afraid of the impact that would have had, or the possible attention it might have drawn. He wondered if he worried too much about that. He told her that he loved her and the kids, and he hoped this money would help in some way. He put it all in an envelope, and set it where he would remember to mail it in the morning.

He went to bed, and his mind was whirling at top speed. He wondered what it would be like to start a new life in a different country.

Chapter 46

Ken sat alone in his bedroom sipping a beer. He desperately wanted to think of a way to get back at Adam Adamson, but he had no idea what he could do without getting himself into big trouble, or killed. It had been quite a shock the night they got back after dinner to find Phil's apartment unlocked, and the money gone along with the journal.

Phil had been very thankful that Todd had gone into the bedroom for the dinner money. He was able to confirm the box was full of money, just as it had been for weeks. When the money was gone, Phil was not suspected. The fact that the book was gone left no question about who had been in Phil's apartment. The problem with being a thief is that when someone steals the stuff you stole in the first place, it's impossible to call the cops.

To add insult to injury, the next day the local paper ran a story about people finding bundles of money all over the streets. The papers said the money was unmarked, and in small denominations. Being untraceable, it would likely eventually go to the people who found it. They said almost a hundred thousand dollars had been reported found, so Ken knew that at least one hundred and fifty thousand didn't even get reported.

The rest of the gang was so mad at him, he thought they were going to beat him to a pulp. They didn't, but they told him to leave and not to come back until they called him. He wondered if they ever would. He had been hanging around with these guys for years. He had no idea what he would do without them. He had to come up with some way to redeem himself, and he knew that if he thought about it long enough, he would come up with a plan.

Chapter 47

The next morning, the movers were right on time. Adam briefly reviewed everything they were taking, and they went down to Gus' apartment and did the same. They filled out some official looking forms, and gave copies to Adam and Gus after which Adam and Gus took their suitcases, and headed for the garage.

When they got to the garage, Gus was surprised to see that the right rear tire on the limo was flat. He tried to remember if he ever had a flat before, and he didn't think he had. Adam looked at his watch.

"Well, this isn't a good start to the day."

Gus laughed at his words, "You don't think it's a good start! Who do you think is going to change this tire?" They both had a little laugh as Gus opened the trunk to get the spare and the jack.

At the same time he opened the trunk, a young man walked out from between two cars not far from the limo. He obviously had been standing in the shadows, and neither Adam nor Gus had seen him. He walked toward them, and stopped when he was about ten feet away from Adam. Both Adam and Gus looked at the young man, and they could see that he had something on his mind.

The man stood there for a moment before he spoke. "I have a bone to pick with you, mister."

Adam recognized the voice immediately. He was careful not to use his name, because he didn't want to implicate Sally. "Ah," he spoke slowly and calmly, "My friend, the bookseller."

Ken felt more scared than mad. He made every effort to sound threatening. "I'm not your friend. I want the money back that you took, or else."

Adam remained very calm, and he spoke quietly without his voice rising. "Or else what?"

He heard a sound, and he saw a knife blade appear in Ken's right hand. It was a switchblade, and the blade looked pretty long. Adam determined that this called for a forceful offense. He started to slowly walk toward the young man.

"Think about what you're saying, son. Are you going to be a murderer, as well as a thief?" He continued to walk slowly toward him. "Think about it.

You break into my apartment. You steal something from me, and then you demand a million dollars to give it back. Now you feel that you have a bone to pick with me, because I took something from you?"

He got to within three feet of the young man and stopped. "I'll make you a deal." Ken never took his eyes off of Adam's. "If you can tell me how you legitimately came by all that money, I'll write you out a check for it right now."

Ken didn't say a word. He tried to think of some plausible explanation for their having almost a quarter of a million dollars, but he couldn't. They were standing face to face looking at each other.

Adam spoke again, "That's what I thought. Now here's what you're going to do. Either take your best shot with that knife if you think it's going to help you, or turn around and get out of here while you still can. If you walk away right now, I'm going to forget this happened. I'm not even going to look closely to see why my tire is flat."

He stared directly into Ken's eyes, and Ken knew that he had made a big mistake coming here. He started to back up until he was ten feet away from Adam and then he turned and walked away.

Adam turned and looked at Gus, raising his eyebrows. Gus shook his head side to side. "I was a little worried when you walked over to him like that, boss. Why did you have to get so close? You knew the boy had a knife. Why did you have to get close enough to make it easy for him to stab you?"

Adam leaned up against the car next to the limo. "I just sensed that he wasn't really going to harm me. The kid is a thief, he wasn't going to stab anyone."

Gus just shook his head as he took the spare out and started to change the tire.

Chapter 48

Frank's alarm went off at six. He never did know how to get any music on the thing, so he always had it set to the "buzz" setting. It startled him, because at home he had a clock radio he knew how to operate, and he awakened to soft music. He slapped at the radio, and finally happened to hit the button that stopped the buzzing. He stared up at the ceiling thinking about meeting with this man today. He had no idea what he was going to say to him, or even if he was going to get an opportunity to see him at all. For all he knew, the man was going to be away on business. Or, being a Friday, he might be on a golf course somewhere. He was starting to second-guess himself. Maybe it wasn't a good idea to surprise the man on Friday when he had an appointment to see him on Monday.

He was talking to himself as he showered, telling himself that this was the right thing to do. Catch the man off guard. Get him to tell the truth. What did that mean? Did he think he could get this man to tell him the truth by surprising him a few days early? He remembered what Don's brother-in-law had said. If this man really was who they thought he was, he was using one hundred percent of his brain. To Frank that was a scary thought. He didn't want to bring his three-tenths of one percent brain up against a one hundred percent brain. It didn't seem fair.

He was just about ready to go, when Dino let himself into the apartment. He was dressed in a light gray suit, dark blue shirt, and a tie that seemed to blend the two colors perfectly. He was also very bright and cheery, for so early in the morning. He smiled when Frank came out of the bedroom.

"Good morning, Frank. How'd you sleep last night?"

"Like a baby, Dino. Just like a baby."

"I thought we'd stop and get a little breakfast on the way."

Frank wasn't a big morning-food person. "If we just pick up some coffee somewhere, I'm good."

Dino looked surprised. "Frank, this is L.A. People out here take time to eat."

Frank looked at him. "How long a drive to Comtec?"

"About an hour and ten minutes, plus a possible extra few minutes, depending on traffic."

Frank looked at his watch. It was ten minutes to seven. He didn't want to show up at Comtec too early. "OK, we'll stop and grab a bite."

Dino smiled broadly, "Great, I know a terrific place. The food is excellent and the waitress is the cutest little thing you ever saw."

They walked out of the apartment. Dino's car was parked right in front of the building, in a no parking zone. Frank wondered if Dino ever parked where he should.

They drove for a minute or two in silence. Frank was trying to figure out how to tell Dino that he was going to ask him to wait in the car when they got to Comtec. He knew that Dino wasn't going to like it.

Dino broke the silence. "Listen, Frank, I've been doing a lot of thinking about our conversation yesterday. You can't really think this guy has been alive for thousands of years. That's just an impossible theory."

Frank thought that maybe if he just didn't say anything, Dino wouldn't pursue it.

Dino realized that Frank wasn't going to answer. "Frank, come on, I need to understand this a little more. Are you serious about what you said yesterday?"

Frank looked over at him. "Look, I didn't want to discuss this with you at all, because I know how unbelievable it sounds. I think it's unbelievable, but there is some unexplainable evidence that I can't just ignore. I've tried to tell myself I should."

Dino shot him a quick look, and then turned back to the highway. Traffic was extremely heavy. Frank always hated driving on these roads. He wasn't used to this kind of traffic. They were moving at almost fifty-miles per hour, and they were literally bumper-to-bumper. There were two lanes on each side of Dino's car.

"What do you mean when you say you should ignore the evidence?"

"Dino, look. This whole thing started when some old coot my father did business with forty years ago calls him and starts jabbering about a man who ran his company back then. He saw this guy in a restaurant a few days ago, and he still looked exactly the same."

"So what? Dick Clark still looks exactly the same as he did forty years ago."

Frank smiled, "If I had a dollar for every time I've heard that in the last three days, I'd have an extra ten bucks in my pocket. I wish I could write this off to good plastic surgery, but I have a feeling that's not it."

"Really, and why not?"

"Well, my father grilled this old man pretty good. I wouldn't give you a nickel for the old man's reliability, if it wasn't for my father. He's still as sharp as he ever was, and he asked all the right questions. His evaluation of this old fella is that he still has all his marbles. And, he insists that it isn't that the man looks younger than he should. It's that he looks *exactly the same*." He stopped to let Dino ponder this information.

Dino seemed to be thinking about it, but he didn't say anything. They pulled off the highway onto a commercial strip lined with stores, restaurants, theaters, and motels. About a mile down from the highway, Dino pulled into a parking lot. It was a diner similar to what Frank was used to back home. It was called the "Sun Spot" diner. Dino parked the car, looked over at Frank and said, "You're in for a treat, buddy."

They had breakfast and made small talk. Dino was actually very professional, and he wouldn't talk about the case when there was anyone else within earshot. Frank had to admit the food was very good, and Dino was right about the waitress. She was very attractive, and she had a great personality. The tab came to about fourteen dollars, and Dino left her a ten-dollar tip. When they came out, Frank remarked about the tip. Dino told him he would have left three or four dollars no matter what, and for an extra six dollars, she would remember him when he came back in there.

He smiled a wide grin, "Now, Frank, wouldn't you think six bucks is a good investment to have a cute little thing like that remember you?" Frank shook his head. He knew Dino was a happily married man who loved his wife and kids. He wondered what made him think this way.

They headed back down the highway, and Frank noticed the traffic had lightened up. He looked at his watch, it was eight-forty. They should be at Comtec by nine-thirty.

They had been on the highway about two minutes when Dino broke the silence. "So, Frank, suppose this man is hundreds of years old, or let's say he's even thousands of years old. Now, I agree that that would be very weird, but I'm not sure exactly where the crime is, or where the threat to national security is."

Frank didn't look at him. "Now, you're coming around to where I was before breakfast. When I said I would like to just forget the evidence, that's exactly what I was driving at. This guy really hasn't done anything. Like you said on the phone the other day, he's practically a saint. The most we could dig up is that he probably entered the U.S. almost fifty years ago on a phony passport."

Dino seemed a little surprised. "Oh, is that so?"

"It seems that way."

"Well, I guess that's something, but you're right. It's thin. I mean really, Frank, if our concern is a phony passport, we should have turned this over to INS. Phony passports is their department."

"Yeah, yeah, you're right, but now there's an extra complication. Clayton Edwards."

Dino made a face as though he smelled something awful. "Oh no. Not the General. How did he get involved? You didn't call him did you?"

"No, my father got impatient. He called him."

"I thought you said your father was still sharp. He knows Edwards is a nut job."

"Well, I think he got upset when he talked to his old buddy. He had a heart attack you know, that's how upset he got when he saw this guy."

"Well, I guess we're supposed to take this guy out, right?"

Frank laughed, "No, not quite that bad, but he *is* looking for us to do something. I just don't know what."

"You were right about this being weird. I can't remember anything quite this strange. What are you going to say to the man?"

"I haven't figured that out yet. I'm just going to play it by ear, and see what happens."

Frank decided this was the right time to bring up the subject of Dino not going with him to see Adam. "Listen, Dino, I don't want you to get the wrong idea, OK? You're a good man, and you're a good agent, but I'm going to go see Adam Adamson by myself."

Dino didn't answer right away, which surprised Frank a little. He had expected an immediate reaction. Finally he spoke, "You really think that's a good idea?"

"Yes, I do."

"Why?"

"For one thing, I think one will be less intimidating than two."

"Less intimidating might not be better."

"No, I really think it will be better."

"OK. You said for one thing. What's another thing?"

"The other thing is I want the freedom to make whatever decision I feel comfortable with when I meet this man. I don't want to have to worry about putting you on some hot seat if I decide to walk on this."

"You think you might."

"Yes, I think I might."

Dino thought about this for a couple of minutes. "OK, I'll tell you what. I'm a little concerned about your safety. I know this person is a longtime 'do-gooder,' but we both agree this whole thing is beyond weird. We have no guarantee that he won't try to do something to hurt you."

He was going to keep talking, but Frank interrupted.

"I think the chances of that are almost zero, Dino."

Dino resumed, "I agree, so here's the deal. We both go into the main entrance. There's a big reception area. We go up to the receptionist, identify ourselves as government agents. We ask what floor your man is on. I'll stay at the reception desk, while you go up. If I don't hear from you in twenty minutes, I'm coming up. If you don't get in to see him in that time, you come back down, and we figure out what to do. If you do get in to see him, and you're going to be more than twenty minutes, you ask him to call down to the receptionist, she gives me the phone, you and I talk, you tell me everything is OK, and I wait for you. If you need to tell me you're in trouble without them knowing it, you call me Agent Argento when we talk. If you call me Dino, I know everything is OK. Deal?"

Frank smiled. This was why Dino was a good agent. "Deal."

They pulled into the Comtec driveway at nine-forty. It was a beautiful building, and Frank noticed the landscaping was impeccable. There were parking spaces marked for visitors. Through the parking lot, there was an entrance to what looked to be an underground parking garage. They parked in a visitor space.

Frank looked over at Dino. "What? Don't you want to park in a handicapped space, or something?"

Dino didn't understand what Frank was getting at. "What's that supposed to mean?"

Frank laughed, "Every time I've seen you park your car, it's in a no parking zone."

Dino laughed, "Come on, that's one of the perks, you know. I'm a government agent." He exaggerated the last few words. Frank was laughing, but he knew at this point it was more from nervousness, than a genuine reaction to something funny.

They walked into the main entrance of the building. The lobby was two stories high. The entire front wall of the building was glass. There were palm trees everywhere, and Frank could hear water running. There was a fountain in the lobby somewhere, but he couldn't see it. A large reception desk sat in the middle of the lobby. They could see a long hallway that went off from the back of the lobby, and it looked like the hallway was lined on both sides with elevators. Just before the hallway on the right side was another much smaller desk, and there was a security guard sitting at it. Both of the men sized up the security guard, and did not see him as a threat. He looked professional and very alert, but he appeared unarmed. He was probably well trained, and Frank knew that it was the improperly trained ones that could give them a hard time.

There was a very attractive young woman sitting at the reception desk.

She acknowledged them as soon as they approached. She smiled genuinely, and in a very friendly voice (which impressed Frank as "typical California"), she asked them if she could help them. They both reached into their jacket pockets, and brought out their federal badges. The badges were gold, set in rich black leather cases that made them look even more impressive.

Frank spoke very softly, "Good morning. We're federal agents. Could you tell us, please, what floor Mr. Adamson's office is on?"

She looked shocked and unsure what to do. Frank wanted to make this as smooth as possible.

"Look, miss, you don't want to make trouble for yourself by obstructing a federal agent, and we're not here to cause Mr. Adamson any trouble, so please just answer me."

She looked in his eyes, trying to see if she should believe him or not. She decided he was being honest with her. "His office is on the third floor." She didn't take her eyes off him.

He said as kindly as he could, "You're very smart young lady. What's your name?"

"Jennifer."

"Well, Jennifer, my friend here is going to stay with you, and I want you to pick your phone up only to answer incoming calls, OK? Don't make any calls until I come back down and tell you it's all right to do so. Do you understand?" She nodded.

Frank and Dino looked at each other, and Frank started to walk toward the elevator. Jennifer called out to him as he started to walk away, "Sir." He stopped, and turned back toward her. She slid him a visitor pass. "If you put this on you won't have to fight with the security guard over there."

He smiled at her, "Thank you, Jennifer."

He took the pass, and clipped it onto the outside pocket of his suit jacket. It was clearly visible as he walked past the guard and Jennifer was right, the guard didn't pay any attention to him. He punched the elevator button, and an elevator opened immediately. He stepped in and pushed the button for the third floor. He noticed there were seven floors. He took the visitor badge, and put it in his pocket. He thought it might take a little of the heat off the receptionist. In just a few seconds, the door opened on the third floor. There were signs on the opposite wall pointing toward the executive offices. He followed the signs, and in just a few seconds he was in the main sitting room of the executive offices. He couldn't help but take note of the quality of the offices. Everything was done in rich leather and mahogany. The receptionist's desk was a beautiful piece of furniture. She looked up from her work. "May I help you?"

"Yes, my name is Frank Saunders, I'm with the federal government. I'd like a few minutes of Mr. Adamson's time." As he was speaking, he brought out his badge and showed it to her briefly. He preferred to say he was with the federal government, rather than with the CIA, because people automatically thought of the CIA as a bunch of spies. No one ever looked at the badge closely. If they did, they would see it clearly said: "Central Intelligence Agency" around the edge.

Frank never carried a weapon either, although as an agent he was licensed to do so. With his identification, he could take a gun onto a commercial airplane, but weapons just weren't Frank's style. Neither was flashing his title. He never introduced himself as the assistant deputy director. He would simply say he was "with the federal government" or that he was a "federal agent."

The receptionist looked at him a little surprised, but Frank thought she did an excellent job of maintaining her professional composure. "Do you have an appointment, Mr. Saunders?"

"No, I'm sorry I don't, but it's very important that I speak with him."

She picked up her phone. "Let me see if he's available." She dialed two digits. Frank could hear a phone ringing in an office somewhere in the executive suite. He could hear a woman's voice pick up, but he couldn't hear what she was saying. He could only hear the receptionist's side of the conversation.

"There's a Mr. Saunders here to see Mr. Adamson." She paused. "No, he doesn't have an appointment, but he's a federal agent." She paused again. "Yes, he showed me a badge. No, I didn't ask him for identification."

As Frank heard this, he reached back into his pocket and pulled out his ID, which he proceeded to hold in front of her as she spoke to the person on the other end. She looked at the ID. "Well, I'm looking at it right now. No, it's the Central Intelligence Agency, and it says he's the assistant deputy director." There was another pause as she listened to instructions. "OK. Yes. OK, thanks." She hung up the phone and smiled, but Frank could tell it was an effort. "Mr. Adamson is extremely busy right now, his secretary suggested that perhaps Mr. Keaton, the senior vice president could help you."

The truth of the matter was that Adam hadn't even come in yet. It was very unusual for him to be late, but the flat tire, on top of meeting with the moving people, had made him so. Frank told himself it was important to stay very calm. It would make it more difficult if he appeared irritated, because that would cause them to be concerned for Adam's welfare.

"I'm sorry, but your vice president will not be able to help me. My reason for wanting to see Mr. Adamson has nothing to do with his being the president. I've come here to see Mr. Adamson, and he's the only one who can be of help to me."

As he was saying this, Adam walked into the sitting room. He had gotten close enough to hear the last couple of sentences, so he knew this person was looking for him. He was on guard, but his nature wouldn't let him walk away to try to avoid him. As he walked into the sitting room, the receptionist looked at him. Frank was still looking at her, but her eyes told him this was the man he was looking for. He turned and found himself standing face to face with the man he presumed was Adam Adamson.

Frank made every effort to seem casual. His brain was straining to take in every detail about the man, and analyze it all in a split second. They were about the same height, six-foot-two, or so. Adam was very trim, probably slightly under two hundred pounds. He was very handsome. He couldn't help but think of Dick Clark for a second. He had deep blue eyes, dark hair. He looked tan, and he had perfectly white teeth. Everything about him looked perfect. He remembered his conversation with Don's brother-in-law. He had said the only explanation for the long life was perfection.

Of course, all this analysis took a fraction of a second. "Mr. Adamson?" Adam looked him in the eyes. He knew Adam was sizing him up. Part of the agency training is to analyze body language, down to the tiniest eye movements, including pupil dilation.

He wondered, if this man was thousands of years old, and perfect, what must his analysis abilities be? Adam was dressed in an impeccable dark blue suit that fit like it was custom made. Frank quickly realized it *must* have been custom made.

Adam smiled, "I'm Adam Adamson, what can I do for you, Mr — ?" He paused, waiting for a name.

Frank wasted no time. He extended his hand and said, "Saunders. Frank Saunders."

Adam shook his hand. "What can I do for you, Mr. Saunders?"

Frank felt like he was in a dream. This all suddenly seemed unreal. This man looked to be in his middle forties. No wrinkles around his eyes. Barely any sign of crow's-feet. "Mr. Adamson, I really need a few minutes of your time in private, sir." He threw in "sir" in an effort to disarm him.

Adam snapped back, "I'm terribly busy, Mr. Saunders. Didn't we speak on the phone just yesterday?"

"Yes, sir, we did."

"And didn't we make an appointment for Monday morning?"

Frank was a little embarrassed. "Yes, sir, we did." He knew he had to come up with something good. He looked Adam right in the eyes. "But our meeting can't wait, Mr. Adamson. There are some very important things we need to discuss. And the people I have to report to are far less patient than me, and far less diplomatic than me. I honestly believe it is in your best interest to give me a few minutes of your time, right now."

Adam looked at him as he spoke. He looked at his watch. "Come in, Mr. Saunders. I'll give you ten minutes."

Frank felt an indescribable sense of relief. He realized as he was saying that last bit about Adamson's best interest, he really meant it. "Thank you, sir."

Adam turned and walked into his office, with Frank right behind him. Adam put his briefcase on his desk, and walked back over to the couch and chair at the other end of his office. "May I offer you a cup of coffee, Mr. Saunders, or water?"

"No, thank you."

Adam sat down in the chair, and Frank sat on the couch. They were facing each other.

"Well, Mr. Saunders, who are you with again? I believe you only told me yesterday that you were with the federal government. That could mean you're a mailman." He smiled when he said it, and Frank chuckled. It was a welcome relief.

Frank wanted to be honest with him. "Mr. Adamson, I'm with the CIA."

Of course Adam knew this all along, but he acted a little surprised. "The CIA. Isn't that spies, and national security? What in the world could you want with me?"

"Well, sir, I'm not really sure. Let me give you a little background about what brings me here." Before he could say anything more, Frank remembered Dino down at the receptionist's desk. He suddenly looked at his watch, it had been about fifteen minutes since he left Dino.

Adam misunderstood his reason for looking at the watch and said, "Don't worry, Mr. Saunders, it's only been a minute."

Frank looked at him. "That's not my concern, Mr. Adamson. I have another agent down at your main receptionist's desk, and I need to talk to him so that he doesn't call in the troops."

Adam looked at him with a genuine look of surprise. "My goodness, Mr. Saunders. You really have my curiosity now." He reached for the phone on the table next to the chair. He dialed two digits and waited. "Jennifer, this is Mr. Adamson, is there a federal agent standing there?" He paused for a few seconds. "Would you put him on, please?" He handed the phone to Frank.

Downstairs in the lobby the receptionist directed Dino to a house phone on the corner of her desk. He picked it up. "Frank, everything OK?"

"Fine, Dino, tell the young lady her phone restriction is over."

"You got it." Frank handed the phone back to Adam and he hung it up.

"Now, Mr. Saunders. What's this all about?"

"As I was starting to say, Mr. Adamson, I'd like to give you a little background. I'm the assistant deputy director, and years ago my father held the same position. He's a great guy, enjoying his retirement I'm happy to say. Over the years, he's known a lot of people from every walk of life imaginable. Now, why do I bring this all up? Because a few days ago, my father got a phone call from an acquaintance he knew from back when he was involved in the interior design of airplanes that were being built for the agency. He did a lot of work with a company called Avionics. I understand that you were the president of Avionics at one time?"

Adam seemed unflustered. "Yes I was. That was a long time ago."

Frank thought it surprising that he would say it that way. "Yes it was, sir, and I guess that's part of the problem. May I be perfectly frank with you, sir?"

Adam didn't flinch. "You certainly may."

"Good. You see, here's the problem as I see it: This fellow used to work with you back when you were the president of Avionics. The story I'm getting is that you two were about the same age. But now, this poor fellow is old, and on his last legs. I guess he's had several heart attacks, he's got emphysema, and he can hardly walk. But hey, he's in his mid-eighties, so what can you expect? The old man understands all that. He's generally at peace with it, you might say.

"But then, coincidentally, he meets his daughter for lunch in a restaurant, and who does he see at a nearby table, but his old boss. The only problem is that his old boss isn't old. He looks exactly the same as he did almost fifty years ago. It flips the old buzzard out so bad that he has a heart attack right in the restaurant! But it doesn't kill him. Personally, I hate to say it, but I wish it had.

"So now, he recovers enough to call my old man, and he jabbers about this whole thing, and my old man calls me and throws it at me. I do a little basic research, and I find out that you were the president of Avionics in 1956. Now, here we are in the year 2000, and I'm thinking you barely look old enough to be the president of *this* company. So tell me Mr. Adamson, how do I explain all this to anyone over my head who might be expecting an explanation?"

Adam stared at him for a long moment. "Is there such a person?"

"Yes."

"Who?"

"General Clayton Edwards of the Joint Chiefs of Staff." Frank realized that Adam was making no attempt to defend himself, or offer any explanation. His heart rate increased a little, as he contemplated the possibility that his suspicion might actually be correct.

Adam was now all business. "Tell me, Mr. Saunders, before you and I discuss anything that resembles an explanation; how does any of this become of interest to the CIA or the Joint Chiefs of Staff? Is there a national security issue that you've not yet explained to me?"

"No, sir, the truth of the matter is it's simply rotten luck that old Mr. Pearson knew my father, and was able to start this ball rolling. My father, bless his heart, was impatient when I didn't have answers for him in twelve hours, so he called Edwards, who is also an old friend of his. Edwards is the last of the 'Old Guard' paranoid military men who is convinced that everyone is out to destroy the United States. If he could figure out a way to eliminate shadows, he would do it."

Adam thought about his options. Saunders seemed genuine and he seemed inclined to find a way out of this situation that wasn't going to make trouble for him.

"Let me ask you, Mr. Saunders, what's your theory on all this?"

"Theory, sir? I don't really have a theory."

"Oh, come now, Mr. Saunders. You've had several days to mull this all over. You said you did some research. You made an appointment with me for Monday, and then flew out here at the drop of a hat to surprise me on Thursday. Surely, you must have some theory."

"Well, the only theory I have is too implausible. I would be embarrassed to tell you what it is."

Adam looked at him and Frank sensed a depth of wisdom he had not seen before. "Try me, Mr. Saunders."

Frank sighed deeply, "OK, but don't laugh at me. I think it's possible that you've been alive for a long time. Much longer than any other human. As a matter of fact, I believe it's possible that you've been alive for over six thousand years. I think you might be the only perfect human being on the planet. And I think that's why you don't age." Frank couldn't believe he was in this office talking with this man, saying what he was saying. He had rehearsed this in his mind, hoping this was how it would be, but now, when it was actually happening, he couldn't believe it.

Adam didn't laugh. "That is quite a theory, Mr. Saunders. Now, let me ask you something."

"Anything."

"If such a theory were true, what would you do?"

"I don't know. I guess I would try to get some assurance that if my theory were correct, in fact, there would be no threat to national security."

"What else?"

"I would try to figure out how to satisfy the inquiry of General Edwards."

Adam sat deep in thought for a minute. Frank broke the silence. "Do you have some logical explanation why you seemingly haven't aged in almost fifty years, sir?"

"I would say good genes, Mr. Saunders."

"Exceptional genes, Mr. Adamson."

"I get the distinct impression that you're not looking to make a big issue out of this."

"Your impression is correct, sir. I would actually like to make it go away. But, I would like to find a way to do that without jeopardizing my position."

"What if that way doesn't exist?"

"Then that would mean there is no logical explanation. Which would mean that my theory is correct." Frank had been staring off into the room while he was speaking, but now he turned back and stared into Adam's eyes. "It would also mean that you're a very unique individual, and something tells me that's a more important issue than my position."

Adam looked at him. "I don't know what to say, Mr. Saunders."

"Tell me my theory is insane."

"I wish I could, but that would mean I would have a better one."

Frank understood this was the closest thing to an outright confirmation he was going to get. He had a hard time concentrating on the moment, as his mind spun with the thought that this man, sitting across from him, was thousands of years old. He knew there was little left to say. The rest was up to him. He stood up from the couch.

"Well, Mr. Adamson, I appreciate your giving me so much of your time."

Adam stood up. "And what will you do now, Mr. Saunders?"

"Well, I'll go back to Washington this afternoon or tomorrow morning. I'll think about this conversation, and I'll start working on my report. I imagine I'll file it some time on Monday." He looked at Adam. He was sure that Adam understood what he was saying.

He extended his hand and Adam shook it. "It was a pleasure to meet you, Mr. Saunders."

Frank found it difficult to walk away. There was so much he wanted to ask. Frank was not a religious man, but he could think of an endless list of questions. He realized the power of being in the presence of a truly unique individual. He would swear later that what happened next was like an "out of body" experience. He felt as though someone took control of him. They finished shaking hands, and Frank looked into his eyes and spoke softly, imploringly, "Mr. Adamson, strictly between you and me, never to be repeated by me to anyone, is my theory correct?"

Adam looked at him for what seemed to Frank to be an eternity. "Yes, Mr. Saunders, your theory is correct."

Frank stared at him. He was speechless. He didn't know what to say. There was so much he wanted to say, so many things he wanted to ask. All he could say was, "Thank you," and that came out like a whisper. Frank finally forced himself to turn and walk out of the office.

He didn't look at the woman at the desk. He didn't look at anyone as he walked back to the elevator. He went back to the first floor, and walked to the receptionist's desk, where Dino was still standing. He handed the receptionist the visitor badge.

Dino looked at him. "You all right?"

Frank walked past him heading for the door. They stepped out into the sunlight. Dino was a few steps behind Frank. "Frank, you OK?"

Frank didn't look back. "Yup."

They got to Dino's car, he unlocked it, and they got in and drove away. Dino wanted to know everything. "So, what happened?"

Frank stared out the window. "We had a very pleasant talk."

Dino sounded a little surprised. "Really, well that's nice. What'd you two talk about?"

Frank wasn't sure how to handle this. "I have to sort it all out. I'll make sure you get a copy of my report."

Dino wasn't too happy about this answer. "Come on. You're killing me!"

"Dino, please, I'm not sure how to handle the information I got from him. I have to think about it. Give me a day or two, and I'll let you know. Besides, maybe it's best if you don't know everything. It reduces the possibility of you catching any flack."

"Jeez, Frank. You're sounding like he confirmed your suspicions."

Frank said nothing, and neither did Dino, all the way back to L.A.

Frank was on a two-thirty flight that landed back in Washington at ten-thirty. By the time Frank got to his car and got home, it was almost eleven-thirty. His wife and kids were all sound asleep. He put his bags down in the hallway. He went into his living room, and sat down without turning on a light. He tried to comprehend the enormity of what he now knew, and to justify it against the reality that he would never tell anyone.

He felt a tremendous sadness at not being able to have the opportunity to talk with Adam at great length. Not being able to get the answers to so many questions. He felt a sadness for Adam as well. What must it be like to always be on the move, in an attempt to keep your secret from the world. He thought about not being able to share this with his wife and children. And, he thought about how he was going to protect Adam from Clayton Edwards. He didn't have the answer to that, yet. The situation was overwhelming. He was going to have to write a report in the morning, and he had no idea what he was going to write. He finally climbed into bed and laid his head on the pillow. While his mind was running through all the questions he wished he could have asked Adam, he fell asleep.

Chapter 49

Mike Jenson finished packing at about four in the afternoon. Everything he would need fit easily into a bag he would be able to carry on. He expected to be back in just a few days. He put the bag on the floor in his entry closet.

Mike lived in an ultra-modern, three-bedroom house in Tarzana, a suburb of L.A. He bought the house about three years earlier, after landing a regular job on a weekly TV show. He wasn't the star, but it paid him ten thousand dollars a week to start, and the show had been going steady for three years. The studio had bumped the stars salaries from twenty-five thousand, to one hundred and twenty-five thousand, a week. Mike had been bumped from ten thousand, to twenty-five thousand. Based on a solid twenty-six week schedule, that was six hundred fifty thousand a year. Mike was still careful with his money. He saw his house as a serious investment. He heard about other houses nearby selling for enormous profits, after being owned for only five years. He did splurge on a car when he purchased a Porsche, but it was his only purchase he considered a real luxury.

Mike had been married when he was younger, but it didn't work out, and they divorced ten years ago. They still saw each other once in a while, and Mike dated different women, but there was no one serious in his life. His work was the thing he cared about most, so he knew it was best not to have any serious relationships.

At four-fifteen he got in his car and headed for Cleo's, a little restaurant frequented by television actors. He was meeting Darryl at four-thirty to discuss arrangements for the morning. Darryl Simmons was also an actor, but at the moment he had no steady part. He appeared in small parts in a wide variety of shows. One week, he would be a bailiff in a courtroom scene; the next week he might be just a man walking down the street, and the week after that, he might be a convict in a cafeteria scene.

He was a good actor in the sense that he took direction well, and was always on time. If he had a speaking part, he always knew his lines, and had the right inflection. He had a regular character part in a show a few years ago that lasted for three seasons, and he did pretty well. He invested some of his earnings, and that was a big help now. Mike met him when he had a small part that lasted for three weeks on Mike's show. They happened to sit together for lunch one day, and in conversation found they had a lot in common. They weren't what Mike would call close friends, in that they didn't see each other often, but whenever they got together for dinner or a night out, they always had a good time. Darryl had a wicked sense of humor, and Mike knew he didn't laugh enough in life, so he really enjoyed the time he and Darryl would spend together.

He had called Darryl to tell him about an opportunity to make some serious cash, for doing almost nothing. Darryl was very interested, but concerned that such opportunities usually required that the "almost nothing" be something illegal. Mike told him he would go over everything at dinner, but that Darryl should be ready to leave early Friday morning, and be gone for two or three days. He needed to have a passport, which Darryl said he had. Mike hadn't discussed any other details with him, and he was looking forward to seeing Darryl's face when he laid this on him.

Mike walked into the restaurant just after four-thirty and Darryl was already sitting at a table drinking a glass of white wine. In some ways, they were a real contrast. Mike was well tanned, with a full head of hair and piercing blue eyes. He looked like he might have been a golf pro. Darryl was a handsome black man, about the same height as Mike, but his head was shaved clean.

Mike sat down at the table, and looked at Darryl with a big smile. "Hey, been waiting long?

Darryl was willing to play along. "No, just got here a couple of minutes ago."

"So, what's new with you?"

Now, Darryl realized he was going to play this out indefinitely. "Come on, Mike, cut the crap. What's this all about?"

Now, Mike smiled even wider. He was like a little kid with a big secret. "OK. Did you clear your schedule at least through the weekend, like I asked you to?"

"It's been an open week, Mike. There was nothing to clear."

"That's good. OK, here's the deal. First, it's important that you understand you can't discuss this with anyone else, ever." Darryl looked at him strangely. Mike was emphatic, "I'm serious, Darryl. It's really important that you agree to that."

"OK. OK. I won't discuss it with anyone. Now, what is it I won't discuss?"

Mike looked around in a slightly exaggerated way, making sure no one was within hearing of their conversation. It made Darryl laugh out loud.

"I know a multi-zillionaire, and believe it or not, we look like identical twin brothers. He saw me in an old shampoo commercial, and actually tracked me down. He asked me to meet with him about three years ago. He's the president of a huge company, and he offered me ten grand just as a retainer to be available, if he ever needed a stand-in."

Darryl could hardly believe what he was hearing. "Jeez, ten thousand dollars for nothing?"

"Yeah, but I didn't take it. I just told him to call me if he ever needed me."

Now Darryl looked mildly annoyed. "You turned down ten thousand dollars for doing nothing? What's the matter with you?"

"It was shortly after I landed my job, I was making ten thousand a week, and I felt pretty flush."

"Well the next time that happens, remember your buddy Darryl, who's never that flush!"

"That's why you're here now, my friend." Mike grinned widely, and rubbed his hands together mockingly.

Darryl rolled his eyes back. "Oh boy, what are we getting into?"

"He called me a few days ago. It's simple. He gave me two first-class tickets to London for tomorrow morning. The trick is, I need someone who looks like the guy that the other ticket is for, because they ask for a photo ID, and the ID and the name have to match."

Darryl was listening intently. "So you're telling me that I look like this other person?"

Mike pulled two ID cards from his pocket. He took Gus' license, and handed it to Darryl. Darryl looked at the picture for a few seconds. "Hello, Gus Stoltz, whoever you are."

Mike smiled again, "Pretty amazing, isn't it? I figure that your shiny bald black head and the shiny bald black head in that picture is all anyone is going to look at. And even if they look closer than that, the picture is just bad enough to where it would be hard to tell it wasn't you."

Darryl was still staring at the picture on the license. He finally looked up at Mike. "Let's see your guy."

Mike handed him the Comtec ID. Darryl stared at it for a moment. "Man, this is really spooky. If someone showed me this ID, I would swear it was you."

Mike nodded. "Tell me about it."

Darryl handed him back both ID cards. "OK, so what's the deal?"

"You and I get on the plane tomorrow as these two men. Once we're on the plane, we're back to being who we really are. When we get off in London, we use our own names and passports. The most illegal thing we did is use phony ID to use two first-class tickets. I don't think it's even a misdemeanor, although it doesn't matter, because we're not going to get caught."

"And once we get to London, then what?"

"We do what we want. We can spend a few days there, or we can book the next flight back to LA and come home."

Darryl looked a little confused. "It sounds interesting, but a little expensive. I mean, a few days in London and a flight home. Who's paying for all this?"

Now, Mike put on mock surprise, "Oh, did I forget to mention the money?"

Darryl scrunched his eyes. "What money?"

"He paid me two hundred thousand dollars for this little gig."

Darryl looked shocked. "Is there something you're not telling me?"

"Like what?"

"Like he just murdered someone, and we're the decoys while he slips out of the country?" Mike laughed.

"Nothing like that, I promise. I figured we'll split the money, a hundred thousand for each of us. Of course, we have to buy our own tickets home with that."

Darryl looked at Mike with a smile, and a glint in his eyes. "I don't think so. You need me, buddy, you buy my ticket home. You're not going to find another fill-in for your second man too quickly."

They both had a good laugh. They ate dinner and finalized the morning plans. The plane left at eight in the morning. It was an international flight, so they needed to be there an hour early, Mike was going to pick Darryl up at five-thirty. He said he would bring Darryl's hundred thousand with him. He already cashed the check. That way, Darryl could stash most of it, and just bring what he thought he would need. They agreed they would probably do some sightseeing, and fly home on Sunday or Monday, but they would make the final decision after they were there.

At six-thirty, they left Cleo's and went their separate ways. They both knew they needed a good night's sleep. It was an early call, and they knew with all the time zones, it was going to be one of those weird things where they lost, or gained, a day — they couldn't figure out which.

Chapter 50

The morning arrived far too soon for Frank Saunders. The music came on softly at six-thirty. He instinctively hit the snooze button. The music came on again at six-forty, and again at six-fifty. At seven, his wife threatened him with bodily harm if he hit the snooze button one more time. He stumbled out into the kitchen, put on a pot of coffee, and then fell into the shower.

As he showered, he tried to figure out how he was going to put General Edwards off until at least Monday. His first thought was to wait for the General to call, and tell him he was working on the report, and he would have it on the General's desk Monday morning. The flaw in that plan was the General's total lack of patience. It had actually surprised him when General Edwards had agreed to wait, when they spoke a few days ago.

His plan "B" was to write that he had met with the person in question, and had found him to be considerably older in his appearance than he had been led to believe by his father, the former Assistant Deputy Director Frank Saunders, Sr. He expected such a report would have limited effect, because the individual in question should have been in his early-to-mid-eighties, and even if he looked considerably older than reported, it wouldn't explain why old man Pearson insisted he looked "exactly" the same as forty years ago.

It would come down to his word against Pearson's, and he thought that even his father would believe his assessment over Pearson's. If his hunch was correct, that Adamson was going to disappear, it would all become a moot point. But if he didn't take Adamson's inquiry correctly regarding his next move, and Adamson stayed in California where others would be able to check him out, he knew that his career with the agency would be over. He decided to put both plans into action by trying to stall the General, and filing what amounted to a false report.

After making that decision, his mind turned back to the enormity of the case. He was thinking about whether he could keep this information to himself, and wondered how he would be able to do it. He didn't want to treat his promises lightly, but he felt what he knew was going to affect him in some ways, for the rest of his life. He thought at the very least, he was going to have to confide in his wife. She would most readily see the effects, and if he said nothing to her, she would wonder why he was changing. He thought that would be unfair, and he knew it could have a long-term negative impact on their marriage. He also decided he would check on Adam later today, to see if he was *still* available. If he wasn't, it might be a sign he had disappeared back into the world. If he was readily available, he would try again Monday. If he was still available, he would assume that Adam planned to stick around, and ride this out. Then, it would be time for Frank to start thinking about a new career.

When he came into the kitchen, he was dressed for work. His wife, Sarah, was sitting at the kitchen table reading the morning paper. She had been an "agency wife" for a long time. She knew not to ask too many questions. She looked up as he came into the kitchen. "Good morning."

He came over to where she was sitting, leaned over, and gave her a kiss. "Good morning, to you."

"What time did you get in last night?"

"About eleven-thirty, or so. Then after a shower and wind down, I think I climbed into bed around quarter to one."

"So, how did everything go?"

"Everything went OK. One of these days we'll have to sit, and I'll tell you about it."

She looked up at him, as this unusual statement came out of his mouth. She was in disbelief. In all the years, she had never heard him say this before. "Really?"

"Yes, really. This is a most interesting case, and I should know in a day or two whether I can discuss it with you. Of course, even if I do, you can't discuss it with anyone else."

She frowned. "Oh, come on, I just signed on as a columnist at the Washington Post. This could be my first big story." He laughed as she mocked him.

"Yeah, well, you'll have to write about something else." He poured a cup of coffee.

"You ruin all the fun."

"Well, that's my job." He sat down across from her. She was reading, and he started thinking about his meeting with Adam.

When his wife looked back up, she could see he was a million miles away. He hadn't even taken a sip of coffee. "Frank," she said quietly, and he didn't respond. She tried a little louder, "Frank."

This time he looked at her. "Yeah."

"What are you thinking about?"

"Nothing."

"Nothing! You looked like you were in a different world for a minute." She was smiling about it.

"I probably was," Frank said, shaking his head. He took a drink of coffee, and sat back in the chair.

His wife sensed something was different. "Frank, are you OK?"

He looked at her. "I'm not sure."

She could see a slight quivering in his bottom lip, as if he was going to cry. "Frank, what's the matter? Talk to me."

He looked out the window, and took note of the trees and the birds flitting around. He saw a squirrel not far from one of the bigger trees in the back yard. He thought about how long he had lived in this house. His connection to the neighborhood, and the entire community. He tried to imagine what it was like to have to move every few years. To never be able to stay in the same place. He looked back at his wife. "I can't right now."

His eldest daughter, Kristen, came into the kitchen. She was a senior in high school, and on Fridays she didn't have to be in class until ten. School got out on Fridays at two, and Frank often remarked about how little sense that made. He used to say: "Why bother?" And his daughter would ask: "Is that your way of giving me permission to stay home on Fridays?" His pat answer was: "Can you stay home on Fridays, and still get straight A's?" This had long been a running joke. His daughter was a straight A student, and she was in the National Honor Society. She was very sensitive about her father working for the CIA, and she went out of her way to avoid telling people. When asked what her father did, she would say: "He worked for the federal government." If pressed, she would say she didn't really know: "It was top secret or something." Usually, if pressed beyond that, she would drop her friendship with the person asking. Only a few of her closest friends knew what her father really did, and they were sworn to secrecy.

She had explained to her father it wasn't that she was ashamed of what he did, in fact, she was actually very proud of him. But, her schoolmates had a weird view of the CIA, and she didn't want to be bothered with it. He told her he understood, and he did.

She came over and gave him a kiss on the cheek. "How's the world traveler?"

"Just fine. How's the number-one-daughter?"

"OK, I guess."

"Just OK?"

"Well, my father goes off to the West Coast, and doesn't even offer to take me with him." She put on a big frown to make the point. It was meant to evoke a laugh, and it worked.

"Sure, you would love to fly to California on Wednesday night and fly home on Friday afternoon."

She smiled at him, “Hey, if I had gone with you, we could have taken a couple of extra days and gone to the beach!”

Of course she was joking, but Frank couldn’t help thinking that might have been the perfect solution to his problem. He could have told everyone he was taking an extra day and making a long weekend of the trip, to spend some time with his daughter. “Believe it or not, honey, if I had really thought about it, I would have done that.”

She looked at him with a surprised, then dubious look. “Oh sure, you say that now.”

He knew he could not explain to her why he was serious. “I’m sorry, maybe next time.”

“Maybe next time, what?” said his younger daughter, as she came into the kitchen. She paid little attention to her parents. She went directly for the refrigerator, taking out the milk. Mackenzie was thirteen, and in her first year of high school. She was also a straight A student. She had to catch a bus in front of the house in fifteen minutes, and Frank was a little surprised she was first fixing a bowl of cereal.

Kristin answered her, “Next time, Dad is going to take me with him to the West Coast.”

Mackenzie looked over at her father. “Yeah, right!”

Frank looked at her. “What’s that supposed to mean?”

His younger daughter looked at him again. “When have you ever taken anyone on any business trip? We can hardly get you to take us anywhere when you’re on *vacation*.”

He tried to imitate the “know-it-all” way she made the statement. “Well, suppose I’ve decided that I should spend more time with my kids, huh?”

The young one was relentless. “I’ll believe it when I see it, Dad.”

Even his wife was starting to feel sorry for him, so she chimed in, “OK, girls, give your father a little break. OK?” And with that, they all went about their business.

Frank got into his office a little after nine. There were four messages on his desk. Two of them were from General Edwards, one was from his father, and one was from Colonel Thomas Bradford. Col. Bradford’s official responsibility was to be liaison between the military and several agencies of the federal government, particularly the FBI, the CIA, and the Secret Service.

Frank noticed one of General Edwards’ messages was from Wednesday afternoon, by which time Frank was on a plane to the West Coast. The second one was from Thursday, while he was in California. He didn’t want to talk to Edwards yet, so he decided to call his father first. That message was from yesterday. He dialed the number, and after two rings his father picked up. "Hi, Dad, it's me. I've got a message that you called yesterday."

"Well, I wondered how you made out on the coast. Did you get to see this guy?"

Frank figured he might as well begin to plant his story now. "Yes, Dad, actually I met with the man, and we had a very nice conversation."

There was a brief pause at the other end. "And?"

"And, what?"

"What do you mean, and what? You know perfectly well what. What's your take on him?"

"Well, for one thing he does look very good for his age, but he definitely doesn't look like he's in his forties. Not when you're sitting up close to him."

Again, there was a pause. "Really. So what are you saying? He looks fifty? Sixty? What?" His father was getting a little irritated.

"Dad, what are you getting mad about?"

"I'm getting mad because I think you're holding out on me, and I don't like it."

"Dad, I'm not holding out on you. I believe the man is very rich, and very vain. Sitting close to him I could see that his skin was stretched back, and his hairline has an artificial perfection to it. I'm telling you the man has probably had plastic surgery as many times as Joan Rivers."

"Who?"

"Joan Rivers. You know, the comedienne."

"Son, I don't have any idea who you're talking about."

Frank had to remind himself that his father wasn't a TV watcher, unless there was some big political story on the news.

"She's a television personality who's about sixty-five, and looks forty because she has had plastic surgery several times. I'm sorry, I forgot you don't watch TV. Anyway, the point is he could be quite old, even though he doesn't look it."

"So you think Pearson was just wrong?" Frank hoped his father wasn't going to push it.

"Well, I would rather think that Pearson's eyesight isn't what it used to be. That, combined with the work this man has had done on himself, probably made it seem like he hadn't aged. Believe me, when I met him, I knew I wasn't talking to some spring chicken." Frank closed his eyes and hoped his father would accept what he said.

Another pause at the other end. "OK, Son, I'm sure you know what you're talking about. I really appreciate you're checking it out for me."

"No problem. I was glad to do it."

They exchanged small talk, Frank asked to talk to his mother, and Frank,

Sr. explained that she was out with a couple of other ladies in the neighborhood doing their "power walk." Frank said he would call back. His father asked him to kiss Sarah and the girls for him, and they hung up. Frank wasn't sure if his father bought it or not. He told himself he didn't really care, as long as he was able to buy a few days. That was the least he could do for Adam, try to give him a few extra days to do whatever it was he did. He didn't know if he simply relocated with new identity, or if he was able to change his appearance.

Frank picked the phone up again, and dialed General Edwards. His secretary answered, "General Edwards' office."

"Hi, Mary. Is he in?"

"Hi, Mr. Saunders. No, I'm sorry, but he isn't in right now. Can I take a message?"

"Well, I'm returning his calls from Wednesday and Thursday."

"He mentioned yesterday that you weren't returning his calls. He was a little upset."

"What can I say? I was on the West Coast and had no idea he was looking for me."

"Well, he went out of here yesterday afternoon muttering something about taking care of things himself, and he's had a couple of different meetings today."

"What was he going to take care of himself, Mary, did he say?"

"Never did say. Want me to tell him you called?"

"Definitely. Tell him I'm in the office, and I just got back from California looking into the matter he and I discussed on Wednesday."

"I sure will, Mr. Saunders."

"Thanks, Mary." He hung up and put his head in his hands. What in the world was Clay Edwards pulling? The thought of him handling *anything* by himself was frightening.

He called Colonel Bradford. Tom was a decent guy. He and Frank hadn't had much reason to talk over the years, but on the occasions when they had, Tom had always been very professional and courteous. He answered the phone himself, "Bradford."

"Colonel, this is Frank Saunders returning your call."

"Hello, Frank. Thanks for getting back to me. Let me get right to the point. I got a call yesterday from General Edwards that worries me."

"Really? And why is that?" Frank was going to play dumb. He knew that any call from Edwards suggesting some type of action, would automatically be worrisome.

"Well, to be honest with you, he rambled about some ridiculous story regarding a man in California who might be thousands of years old. He wanted me to know he was going over your head at the CIA, side-stepping the secret service and the FBI, and sending military people into California to arrest this person so that he could be properly questioned by the government."

"What did you tell him, Colonel?"

"You know as well as I do that you can't tell General Edwards anything. I strongly urged him not to do anything until he heard back from you."

"I appreciate that. Do you think he listened?"

"I don't have to think, Frank. I know he didn't. He informed me late yesterday that he was empowering General Calvin Powers, who heads up the California National Guard to take eight of his top men, and go to where this man works to take him into custody this morning. He told me his men had strict orders not to allow any harm to come to the man, but not to let him get away. Edwards said he wanted him back in Washington, and that he wanted to talk to him, personally."

Frank's heart sank. Edwards was really going to throw a monkey wrench into the works. His father must have told the General more than he thought.

"Colonel, you wouldn't happen to have General Powers phone number, would you?"

"As a matter of fact I do, but remember it's three hours earlier there, so it's only a little after six in the morning."

"If Edwards talked to Powers yesterday, I can guarantee you Powers is up right now, wondering how in the world he suddenly has an order to go arrest a citizen for no real reason at all."

"You could be right. I suppose the worst that could happen is you wake him up."

"Tom, can I count on you to keep me informed of any information you get?"

"As long as I don't put myself on the hot seat, Frank, I'll do what I can."

"Thanks, I really appreciate it."

"No problem." They both hung up. Frank sat for a minute gathering his thoughts.

He dialed the number that Bradford gave him for General Powers. The phone rang twice, and Frank started to regret calling so early. Before it rang a third time, someone picked it up.

"Hello," was all they said. It was a man.

"Is this General Powers?"

"Yes. Who is this?"

"General, my name is Frank Saunders, I'm the assistant deputy director of the CIA. I'm very sorry to be calling you so early, sir, but it's urgent that we talk."

"What about, Mr. Saunders?"

"Well, did you receive a phone call from General Clayton Edwards yesterday?"

"I did."

Frank couldn't be sure, but he thought he sensed a defensive tone.

"In that conversation, General Powers, did General Edwards direct you to take any steps against a man named Adam Adamson, who is the president of a corporation called Comtec?"

"What business is that of yours, Mr. Saunders?"

"With all due respect, sir, it is very much my business. I am the person investigating a matter regarding Mr. Adamson. A matter I have found to be completely unfounded, and ridiculous. General Edwards, quite frankly, was acting out of impatience with the time it was taking me to complete my investigation. Mr. Adamson is guilty of nothing, and detaining him would be inappropriate."

"Mr. Saunders, are you trying to tell me that obeying the orders of my superior would be inappropriate?"

"Unfortunately, in this instance, sir, yes."

There was a long pause on the other end. "I don't see how I could not follow the General's order, Mr. Saunders."

"Sir, there are specific procedures that are to be followed in the event of national security issues that coordinate the activity of the military and the federal agencies. General Edwards has not followed those procedures. He is circumventing the proper channels for reasons known only to him. Detaining a man like Adam Adamson will be costly in the long run. His corporation is worth billions, and an unfounded arrest and detention will undoubtedly result in a substantial lawsuit, not to mention a probable media frenzy. When that happens, General Edwards is going to look to put the blame on someone else."

He was hoping Powers would buy this, and that the order to take eight men and go arrest this person had struck the General as quite unusual. There was a hopeful pause at the other end. "Mr. Saunders, you're asking me to disobey an order from the Joint Chiefs of Staff?"

"Meaning no disrespect, General, but actually I'm not. I'm asking you to consider the possibility that General Edwards' order is motivated by something other than an appropriate concern for the well-being of our national security. The other members of the Joint Chiefs probably have no idea that he's made this request. As a matter of fact, General, what I might suggest is that you ask General Edwards to issue a formal written request for this action. You might say something to the effect that the request seems a little unusual, and you would be more comfortable having it in writing so there is no misunderstanding."

Again, there was a long pause as the General contemplated this last suggestion. The General's tone seemed to soften just a little. "Tell me, Mr. Saunders, if this man is so clean, how does he come to be investigated by the CIA in the first place?"

"That's a fair question, General, and at some point I would be happy to go into great detail to give you an answer. For the moment, let me just say it involves my father, who happens to be retired CIA, getting a phone call from an eighty-six year old business associate from thirty or forty years ago. This man passed on some information that I felt compelled to look into, just to keep my father happy."

"Well, Mr. Saunders, I'm not sure what your stake in this is, but your point about having something in writing does have merit. I'll dash off a note requesting a written order, but I want you to understand one thing. If I get that request in writing, I won't hesitate for a second to do exactly what I'm ordered to do. I don't care how innocent the man might be, or whose head rolls later. Do I make myself clear?"

"Perfectly, General. Thank you for taking the time to talk with me. If I can be of any further help, you can reach me at the agency headquarters in Washington."

The phone at the other end went dead as the word "Washington" came out. He was surprised, because he thought the General had come around a little.

Frank looked at his watch. It was fifteen minutes to ten. He would like to have called Adam to warn him, but the time difference made it impossible. There wouldn't be anyone answering phones out there for another three hours, at least. He punched a few keys on his computer, and Dino Argento's home address and phone number came up on his screen. He dialed the number, and it started to ring. It rang three times, and Dino answered. It was obvious that he had woken him up.

"Hello?" Dino had an ability to throw a nasty inflection into one simple word.

"Dino, it's Frank Saunders. Sorry to be calling so early."

"Frank, what's the matter with you? It's not even seven o'clock yet." All of this was hissed out in an angry whisper. Dino was obviously trying to not wake his wife. "Wait a minute while I switch phones." He was not happy. A minute later, he picked up another line. Now he wasn't whispering, but the tone in his voice indicated he wasn't really a morning person. "Now wait, while I go hang up the other phone." And he was gone again. Frank heard the phone hang up, and a few seconds later Dino was back. "OK, Frank, this better be real good."

"I need you to do me a big favor."

"It's quarter to seven in the morning, and I'm sitting in my den talking to you on the phone. You mean you want me to do you a *second* big favor, in the same day?"

"Dino, I'm serious."

"So am I. I already have a sour taste in my mouth about this whole thing, and now you're calling me at this time of the morning. I know it's got something to do with this stupid case, and I don't like it." He wasn't joking, and Frank knew he was upset.

"I'm sorry this whole thing is so crazy, but you have to believe me, the less you knew, the better it was for you."

"What do you mean 'knew'?"

"Dino listen, I've got a real dilemma here, and I need your help. I just got word that Edwards has issued an order for his boys out there to pick Adamson up, and haul him back to Washington."

Dino's anger was replaced by disbelief. "Pick him up for what? Being old and not looking it?"

"You know General Edwards. Everyone but him is some kind of a threat to national security."

Dino sounded as though he was thinking out loud. "The old man's nuts. He's going to create a real problem if he arrests someone on the suspicion of being thousands of years old. That could be a real career-ender."

"Yeah, but in the process Adam Adamson becomes a freak show for the government. I'm telling you, Dino, if these people get wind of the truth, they'll invent some reason to kill him." There was a long pause on the other end of the phone. Frank wondered if Dino had fallen back to sleep.

"What exactly do you want me to do?"

"You ran him through a preliminary, you must know where he lives."

"Of course we know where he lives."

"Good. Go there. Warn him that the military is going to be coming looking for him."

"Frank, you're asking me to jump into the middle of this. You know my butt could be on the line here."

"I don't think so, Dino. Edwards has gone to the guard for this little dirty deed. He's not using his own. I'd be surprised if anyone in the National Guard would know you, so even if they see you coming or going, it wouldn't mean anything to them."

"OK, Frank. I'm going to give it a shot, if for no other reason than to meet this man myself."

"Thanks, Dino. How soon do you think you can get on this?"

"Man, you can be pushy sometimes."

Frank laughed, "Hey, what can I say? I'm anxious."

"This means that much to you, Frank?"

"Yes."

"Is it OK if I take a leak, and throw on some clothes?"

"I suppose so."

"Good, I'll be on the road in a half hour. I'll be at his building by," there was a pause as Dino looked at his watch and calculated his travel time, "a little after eight."

"Thanks, Dino, I really owe you one."

"You're going to owe me more than one, man."

"OK, you're right, but listen, one more thing. Call me the second there's anything I should know."

"I will, Frank. Don't worry." He hung up.

Frank sat back in his chair and looked out the office window. He contemplated going out to California again, just to choke Harris Pearson with his bare hands.

Chapter 51

From his second floor apartment, Darryl watched Mike's silver Porsche pull into his parking lot. It was five-thirty on the button. Darryl chuckled to himself as he thought about the first job he ever had with Mike. Everyone on the set made jokes about Mike's punctuality. Everyone respected his sense of professionalism, but he was fanatical about being on time.

He watched as Mike climbed out of the car. He had what looked like a duffel bag with him. Darryl was practically giddy at the thought of the bag being full of money. A minute later there was a knock on his door. He opened it, and Mike came in smiling. "How ya doing, big guy?"

Darryl thought he was awfully perky for five-thirty in the morning. The bag was bigger than it had appeared to be.

"Is that the money?" Darryl was anxious to put his hands on his share.

"Well, it's not *just* the money. My stuff is in here for the trip," Mike said this as he unzipped the bag. He pulled from the top of the bag packets of money, each about a half-inch thick. They were packets of one hundred dollar bills. There were twenty of them. As he pulled them out, he was throwing them onto Darryl's couch. They made a nice little pile.

Darryl looked at the pile. "That's it?"

"What did you expect, the bag to be full of money?"

"I don't know. I guess I did." Mike laughed.

"Darryl, you've been watching too much TV. That's what a hundred grand really looks like, right there." They both looked at it for a minute.

Darryl spoke softly, "It looks pretty good. It's a nice little pile." He scooped it up and made two neat stacks. He looked at Mike. "Fifty in a pack?" Mike nodded.

"That's five thousand each. I think one should get me through this weekend." He put one into his inside jacket pocket. "I'll be right back." He disappeared down the hallway to stash the rest. Mike looked around. He hadn't been to this apartment. It was a very nice place. Spacious, well decorated, and furnished. He liked Darryl's taste in furniture. High quality, but subtle. Darryl came back into the living room with one small suitcase. "Let's hit the road."

They pulled out of the parking lot at five-forty heading for L.A. International.

Chapter 52

Adam was up, and ready to go by six o'clock. He sat in his kitchen drinking a cup of coffee, reading yesterday's Wall Street Journal. Most of the furnishings were staying with the penthouse. The cost to move them overseas exceeded the cost to replace them. Only those few pieces that meant a lot to Adam were gone with the movers from the day before.

In the living room near the elevator, was one medium-sized suitcase and two large cardboard boxes. They were well taped with reinforced packing tape. These boxes contained his journals. He and Gus were leaving at eight. He had called for a rental limo.

When he and Gus left Comtec last night, they rode home in a cab. Adam had found the cab dirty, and the driver erratic. He didn't want to subject himself to that again, so he rented a limo for this morning's ride.

At about quarter to eight, the elevator opened and Gus walked into the living room, carrying a huge suitcase. He put it down next to Adam's things, and came into the kitchen. He walked over to a kitchen cabinet, and took out a cup. Then, he went to the coffee maker and poured. He sat down at the table across from Adam. They hadn't exchanged a word yet. When Adam looked up, Gus was staring at him.

"Something wrong, Gus?"

Gus looked directly into his eyes. "No, not at all."

"You look like something's on your mind."

"No, not really. I've just been thinking about all the mental and emotional aspects of doing what we're doing, and then I think about how many times you must have done this before."

Adam smiled, "Oh, Gus, you don't really want to think about that."

Gus took a sip of the coffee. "No, you're right. But it's hard not to."

The phone rang. Adam got up, went into the living room, and picked up the phone from the table. "Hello?"

"Adam, it's Tim." It was Tim Groff from downstairs.

"Yes, Tim."

"Adam, I wasn't sure what to do, so I called you. There was a man banging on our office door, so I opened it to see what was going on, and it turned out to be someone who's identifying himself as a CIA agent. He said it's urgent he speak to you, but he has no way to get up to your apartment, and there's no intercom up to you. What do you want me to do?"

Adam thought for just a moment. "Is it a man named Frank Saunders?"

"No, sir. It's a man named Dino Argento, but he said Mr. Saunders asked him to come and speak with you."

"OK, Tim, send him up."

"OK, he'll be there in just a minute."

Adam went back into the kitchen. "Gus, there's a man coming up to talk with me. Stay in the kitchen, I don't want him to see you. The less he knows, the better."

Gus didn't fully understand, but he nodded. He trusted Adam completely.

Adam went back into the living room as the elevator door was opening. A well dressed, well tanned person came out of the elevator, and walked over to him. He extended a hand, "Good morning, Mr. Adamson. My name is Dino Argento, and I appreciate you seeing me."

"Mr. Argento, I only have a few minutes before I have to leave. What can I do for you?"

Dino looked at the suitcases and the boxes. Even without knowing Gus was in the kitchen, it didn't look like a lot of luggage, even for one man. He looked back at Adam. "Going somewhere?"

"Just a short trip. What can I do for you, Mr. Argento?"

"Frank Saunders called me this morning, and asked me to come see you. He wants you to know that a General Clayton Edwards, who is a member of the Joint Chiefs of Staff in Washington, has issued an order for your immediate detention." Adam was surprised and still unsure of this man's intentions.

"And Mr. Saunders expects me to do what, exactly?"

"I don't think Mr. Saunders expects you to do anything. He just wanted you to have a heads-up, that's all. I think he figured that you would want to know."

"When do you anticipate these orders being carried out?"

"I don't know exactly, but I would expect it to be today. Probably this morning sometime."

Adam watched Dino carefully. He sensed he was telling him the truth. He extended his hand to Dino again. "Thank you, Mr. Argento. I appreciate you going out of your way to tell me this."

Dino shook his hand. "You're welcome."

They walked back toward the elevators. Adam pushed the button for the express elevator to the lobby. Adam looked at him. "Please tell Mr. Saunders that I thank him as well."

Dino simply nodded as the elevator door opened. He stepped, in and

Adam explained the elevator would take him directly to the lobby. The elevator door shut. Adam walked back into the kitchen.

He could tell from the look on Gus' face that he had heard everything. Gus spoke first, "Well, no one can say we're leaving too soon." They both smiled, but Gus could tell that Adam was concerned. "What's the matter, boss?"

Adam looked at him. "Nothing really, Gus. I just didn't expect this. I talked with this Saunders from the CIA yesterday. He was waiting for me when I got in. I never expected anything like this to happen so quickly. I expected to have at least until Monday. I suppose as long as the Army doesn't show up here in the next ten minutes, it probably doesn't matter.

They both sat for a few minutes in silence. The phone rang again. This time it was the limo driver. Adam had given them his number. He was calling from the car, and he was parked out in front of the building. Adam asked him to come into the lobby. He was going to send someone down for him. He hung up the phone.

Gus looked at him. "Who you going to send?" Adam smiled.

"Very funny."

Gus got up from the table, walked over to the elevator, and pushed the button. The door opened a few moments later. Gus stepped in, and pushed the down button. The elevator door closed. Adam went into the bathroom. When he came back into the living room, Gus was back with the limo driver.

He was a man who appeared to be in his fifties. He was well dressed and had a neatly trimmed full beard. It was quite gray, as was his full head of hair. Adam asked him if he could take the two suitcases, which he did. Gus and Adam each took a box. Adam took one last look around, both to remember the place, and to make sure he wasn't forgetting anything. Gus pushed the button and the elevator door opened immediately. They all stepped in, and in less than a minute they were in the lobby.

The limo was relatively new and it was black. That had been Adam's only request. The car had to be black. He had nothing against cars that were other colors, but he didn't care for white limos. He thought they were good for weddings only. The driver opened the trunk, and put the two suitcases in. Both boxes also fit in the trunk. He opened the door, and Adam and Gus got into the back seat. He closed the door, and as he was walking around the car, Gus said to Adam, "This is different." They both laughed.

The driver got in and fastened his seat belt. Without looking back he said, "L.A. International?"

Adam said, "Just head that way." The limo pulled away from the Aegis building. It was eight-twenty.

Chapter 53

At ten-thirty the IBF Teletype machine in the corner of Mary Turner's office came to life. This equipment was only used for high-level communications that were considered classified. It was rare that the thing ever got used these days, and when it started to print, it startled Mary for a moment. She walked over to it, just as it stopped. She pulled the paper up and to the right, and it cut clean from the machine. She looked at the message. It was addressed to General Edwards, from General Calvin Powers of the California National Guard.

Gen. Clayton Edwards: Joint Chiefs: Washington.

Please forward written request regarding matter discussed yesterday. Personnel standing by to execute upon receipt of written request.

Powers

Mary read it twice, to be sure she read it correctly. Who was General Powers, and what order was he talking about? There was very little General Edwards did these days that he didn't actually have Mary do for him. She usually made his phone calls, and typed any requests he made to anyone. She had no idea what this was about. She knocked on the General's office door, and he barked, "Come in."

He was sitting at his desk, reading some papers that had been delivered to him earlier in the day. He stopped, and looked up at her. She walked over to his desk, and handed the paper to him. As she did, she said, "It's off the IBF." His eyes widened a little, and he took the paper and read it. She stayed for two reasons. One was that she wanted to see his reaction because she didn't know what it was about, and secondly, she expected it was going to result in his asking her to do something. She watched him as he read it, and his face became noticeably red. She could see that the message was making him angry. He looked up at her, and she knew he was mad.

"I can't believe this little pip-squeak is asking this. What is this Army coming to? Mary, send him back a message."

She looked at him and shrugged. “Hold on, General, let me get a pad and pencil.” She walked back to her office and grabbed a pad and pencil. She returned to his office. She sat down in a chair in front of his desk. He started to speak immediately.

“General Powers: As per our conversation yesterday, I officially request that you seek out and detain one Adam Adamson, who is reported to be the president of Comtec Corp. He is to be transported FWP to Washington for interview.” He looked at Mary. “Put my name on the thing, and send it off right now.”

Mary went back to her office. She rolled the chair from behind her desk over to the IBF terminal, and sat down. Each terminal had its own code number. When a message was sent through the terminal, it went into a computerized system that scrambled the message, sent it to its destination, and unscrambled it at the receiving terminal. She punched in the terminal number from which this message had originated, and then typed in the General’s message.

She tried to remember the last time she had entered anything into this system, and she couldn’t. When she was finished, the terminal printed out a confirmed copy of the message, and about ninety seconds later, it printed a confirmation that the message was received at the other end. She walked both these documents into the General’s office and put them on his desk. This time he didn’t look up from what he was doing.

Chapter 54

Mike and Darryl arrived at the airport at six-thirty. They parked the car in long-term parking, and walked over to where the shuttle picked them up to deliver them to the TWA terminal. They both had only a carry-on so they went to a departure monitor to see which gate they needed for flight 1166, departing for London via New York City at eight-ten. The monitor told them it was Gate 20, and that the flight was on schedule. They walked to Gate 20. It was a longer walk than from the long-term parking lot to the terminal.

When they got to the gate, there was no one in line at the counter. There was a middle-aged woman on duty, who looked like she had worked a double shift. She looked very tired. Mike walked up to the counter, and she greeted him with the standard line. "Has anyone given you anything to carry on board with you, and have you had your luggage in your possession at all times?" Mike said no to anyone asking him to carry something on board, and yes to watching his bag at all times.

He handed her his ticket, and she seemed to change her attitude when she saw that it was a full fare first-class ticket. She was definitely friendlier. "Thank you, Mr. Adamson. Could I see some photo identification, please?"

He reached into his jacket pocket, and pulled out a wallet. "I don't drive, so I can't show you a license, but here is my company ID." He handed it to her. He smiled as he thought to himself there was no chance that she was going to hassle a first-class fare.

She looked at the ID briefly, looked up at him, and handed it back to him. "Thank you, Mr. Adamson. We'll be calling for first-class boarding in about twenty minutes."

He thanked her, and stepped aside, but waited to be sure that she understood he and Darryl were together. Darryl handed her his ticket, and she went through the same routine about the luggage. He answered the same way Mike had. She saw that his ticket was also a full fare first-class ticket, and that they were seated together. "Mr. Stoltz, could I see some ID please?" Darryl took out his wallet, and handed her Gus' license. She looked at it briefly, looked up at him, looked back down at the picture again, and then looked back up at him a second time. She handed the license back to him. "If you don't mind my saying so, Mr. Stoltz, that picture doesn't do you justice. You're a much nicer looking man than that picture shows."

Darryl smiled, “Why thank you for saying so.”

She smiled back, “You’re welcome, sir. We’ll be calling for first-class boarding in about twenty minutes.” Darryl and Mike walked over to the chairs and sat down.

Mike looked at Darryl. “Well, that was pretty easy.”

Darryl nodded. “I’ll still be much more comfortable when we’re in the air.”

Mike looked at his watch. It was seven-ten.

Chapter 55

At seven thirty-five General Powers was reading the IBF dispatch from General Edwards. He had been giving a lot of thought to his conversation with Frank Saunders, and he hoped this written order might not come at all. He had nine of his best officers with him, and he had already briefed them on the mission.

There had been several questions indicating that his men were also confused by the order. They were not given any reason for detaining this individual. They didn't know if he was dangerous. They didn't know how they were to treat him. It was a very vague order, and it made the men uneasy. Powers wouldn't admit it to them, but he felt the same way.

They headed out in three Suburbans all painted dull Army green. He, and three of his men were in the front car. There were three men in the middle car, and three men in the rear car. The plan was to put Adamson in the middle car once they picked him up. He estimated it would take them an hour and twenty minutes to get to Comtec.

At nine they pulled into the Comtec driveway. They turned into the circle that came around to the front entrance, and parked there. The drivers each stayed with the vehicles. The other men got out and went into the building. They walked up to the receptionist, and General Powers introduced himself. He explained that he was there to see Mr. Adamson.

The receptionist picked up the phone, and dialed Nancy's number. Nancy picked it up on the first ring. "Nancy, it's Jennifer. There are men from the Army here, and they're asking for Mr. Adamson." She paused while she listened. "No, I didn't. I wasn't sure what to do. OK, yes, I will."

She hung up the phone and looked up at General Powers. "Take the elevator to the third floor gentlemen. Nancy will be waiting for you there." General Powers turned and walked toward the elevators with six men following. They stepped into an elevator, and went to the third floor. When the door opened on the third floor, there was a woman waiting for them. She smiled at General Powers, recognizing him to be in charge.

"Hello. My name in Nancy Drummond. May I help you?" This wasn't exactly what Powers had expected, and he had no intention of going through layers of people explaining he was here for Adamson.

He looked at her in what he hoped was a glare. "Didn't your receptionist explain why we're here?"

"Well, she said you were looking for Mr. Adamson."

"That's correct. Where is he?"

She looked a little uncomfortable. "I'm sorry, but Mr. Adamson is not here. Could Mr. Keaton help you?"

General Powers was getting irritated now. "Who is Mr. Keaton?"

"He's the president of Comtec."

"I thought Adamson was the president of Comtec."

"Well, sir, yesterday was Mr. Adamson's last day at Comtec. Mr. Keaton is now the president. Is there something wrong?"

Powers was visibly upset. "Where would I find Mr. Adamson?"

Nancy shrugged her shoulders. "I wouldn't have any idea. Who did you say you were?"

"Powers. General Calvin Powers, U.S. Army. What is Adamson's home address?"

Nancy looked at him with defiance. "I'm sorry, General, but without a warrant we wouldn't give that information out to anyone."

Now Powers was furious, and he started to raise his voice, "Lady, it's probably information I could get off the Internet in two minutes."

Nancy wasn't backing down. As a matter of fact, she was starting to get a little irritated herself. "What you get off the Internet is your business, General. What information comes out of these offices is mine, and if you don't have a warrant for the information you're seeking, you're not going to get it here. So, I suggest you leave before I call the police, and you can all shoot it out in the parking lot."

General Powers wasn't sure what to do. He had never come up against a civilian with this type of attitude before, and he already felt this entire mission was on shaky ground. He decided to retreat, and think it through. He and his men turned and went back into the elevator. As the door closed, and they went back down to the first floor, all the people at desks close enough to have heard the entire scene broke into applause. Nancy grinned widely and walked back to her office.

Powers and his men exited the Comtec building, and got back into their cars. Powers dialed General Edwards' number on his cell phone. It rang twice and Mary picked up. "General Edwards' office."

"This is General Powers in California calling for General Edwards."

"One moment, sir." Mary put him on hold, and buzzed to the General. "General Powers on one, sir."

General Edwards picked up the phone. "Edwards."

Powers was clearly upset. "General Edwards, it seems that our man is no longer employed at Comtec."

This took Edwards by surprise. He leaned back in his chair. "Really!"

"No one will give me his home address without a warrant."

Now General Edwards started to feel a little irritation. "Is that so?"

"They're a tough bunch in there, General. What do you want me to do?"

"Hold on a minute." He pushed the hold button on his phone, glanced at his Rolodex and dialed a number. The phone on Frank Saunders' desk rang.

"Saunders"

"Saunders, this is General Edwards."

"Yes, General, what can I do for you?"

"Your people did a preliminary investigation on this guy Adamson, right?"

"Yes, sir."

"Then you went out there, I understand."

"Yes, sir, I did."

"OK then, what's his home address?"

Frank thought for a moment. He tried to come up with an excuse to not give it to him, but he would have to make himself look like a complete incompetent. That would work against him later, when he tried to defend himself. He knew he had no choice but to give him the address. He gave the address to Edwards. The General didn't even say thank you. He simply hung up.

Edwards pushed the blinking button, and gave General Powers the address.

Powers and his caravan pulled out of the Comtec parking lot and headed for the Aegis building.

Chapter 56

The limo was nearing the airport. Adam directed the driver to pass the main entrance to the airport, and continue down the road. There were several air express companies, and trucking companies. Adam told the driver to take the next right into a driveway. The sign out in front said: "World Link." The limo pulled in, and drove to the end of a low steel building, then turned left, pulling up to a chain link fence. Through the windshield, Gus could see a runway, and several small jets. He looked at Adam. "Where in the world are we?"

Adam smiled, "Where does it look like we are, Gus? It's the airport."

Gus chuckled, "It's not quite what I was expecting."

"Well, I have to keep you guessing once in a while." They got out of the car and the driver opened the trunk. Adam took out one of the boxes and handed it to Gus. He took the other himself. The driver reached in and took out the two suitcases.

A young man dressed in casual pilots' attire came out of a side door of the building. He looked to be in his thirties. He was wearing dark pants, and a short sleeve white shirt with epaulets, that pilots wore. He looked at Gus and Adam. "Good morning, gentlemen, who's Mr. Nathan?"

Adam extended his hand. "That would be me."

The pilot shook his hand. "Nice to meet you, sir. The plane is ready to go." He took the suitcases from the driver.

Adam tipped the driver, and thanked him. He and Gus walked through a gate in the fence, and followed the pilot toward what looked like a brand-new jet. The pilot opened a side compartment, and put both suitcases in. He took the boxes from the two men and put them in, as well. He closed the compartment and asked them to follow him. He then walked up a set of steps that led into the plane. He ducked and stepped in, turning as he did to warn them to do the same. When they had all climbed in, he directed Adam and Gus to the right, which was the passenger compartment. As they stepped in to the compartment a young woman emerged from the cockpit and greeted them. The pilot introduced her as the co-pilot and part-time stewardess. They both laughed when he said it. Adam and Gus could tell that they must have used that routine a hundred times before.

In the passenger compartment there were eight seats that seemed to be very luxurious and comfortable. They were set in four rows of two, and there was plenty of space between the seats in each row. The pilot explained that each seat could be swiveled around, and reclined. The only request was that they face forward and upright during take-off and landing. He took them through a door at the back of the passenger compartment, to a small kitchenette. Off to one side was a bathroom. The kitchenette had a sink and a refrigerator, which was stocked with food and drinks of all sorts.

They walked back into the passenger compartment. The pilot showed them a control panel that lowered a television screen from the ceiling. He showed them how to use the VCR, if they wished to. He explained how the stereo system worked, and pointed out that there was a set of headphones in a side pouch on each seat. There were ten different channels, offering every kind of music. He asked if there were any questions. Adam and Gus both said no.

"Good. We'll be departing in about ten minutes gentlemen. Make yourselves comfortable."

Adam and Gus sat in the two seats that made up the first row. They buckled themselves in. Gus looked around, and looked at Adam. "All these years, we never traveled like this."

Adam laughed, "We never had to, Gus. At least we traveled first-class, didn't we?"

Gus laughed, "I used to think so, but now I'm not so sure."

The engines started, first one and then the other. They had a high-pitched whine that was common with high-rev engines. The cockpit door was open, and Adam could hear the pilot talking to the tower. He couldn't quite hear what he was saying, but he could hear when he spoke. In a few minutes the plane started to move, and they taxied out to a runway that seemed to be used mostly by several small air carriers. Adam could see the airstrip they were on was attached to the International Airport.

They were still for a few minutes while the pilots went through their pre-flight check. Adam felt the engines rev up, then idle down. The plane then moved again, and pulled out onto the strip, turning sharply right. In only a few seconds, they could feel the torque of the plane as the engines were pushed full throttle. Quickly, the planes wheels were off the ground, and the pitch of ascent was much sharper than anything they were used to. It seemed as if they were going straight up. It was amazing how quickly the ground fell away as they looked out the window, and in about two minutes the plane leveled off, although they could tell it was still climbing. When they had been in the air for about five minutes, the co-pilot came out of the cockpit. She looked at the two men and smiled. Adam figured for how much he was paying for this flight, it was no wonder they were smiling. "Gentlemen, can I get you anything?"

Gus asked for a cup of coffee, and Adam said he would like a bottle of water. She disappeared into the kitchen. Moments later she was back with the water and the coffee.

She explained they could walk around if they desired, but that while they were sitting it was a good idea to have their seat belts on loosely. She told Gus that there was a fresh pot of coffee in the kitchenette, and he should feel free to help himself. He thanked her, and she went back into the cockpit. At the door she stopped and turned back toward the two men. "Next stop, New York City." She disappeared into the cockpit.

Chapter 57

Mike and Darryl were settled into their seats in the first-class section. Both men had flown many times, but neither had flown first-class before. They were finding it to be quite an experience. They were allowed on the plane fifteen minutes before anyone else. They were offered whatever drinks they desired. Both men opted for coffee. The coffee was served in a china cup, with a saucer. They both thought that was funny. Darryl made a crack about a fifteen hundred dollar cup of coffee, after he figured out that was about the difference between first-class and coach. They were also given menus to look at, so they could place their breakfast order. It was explained breakfast would be served after take-off, but in the meanwhile, they could have as much coffee, juice, or any type of alcoholic drink they wanted.

The first-class seats were far wider, and more comfortable. Mike took note that there were six rows in the first-class section. Twenty-four seats in all, and all were taken. He felt a little self-conscious as the rest of the passengers got on the plane and came through the first-class section. He couldn't help but think about what always went through his mind when he was walking through the first-class section. Now, he was one of the people sitting in the first-class section, and it made him wonder how many others in first-class were flying on someone else's money.

Eventually everyone was on the plane, and the plane backed away from the boarding gate. In a few minutes they were taxiing out to a runway. Mike and Darryl had already discussed the fact they both loved to fly.

As they were taxiing out, Darryl turned to Mike and said, "This is a tough way to make a living, man." They both laughed.

The pilot's voice came over the speaker to tell the passengers they were second in line to depart, and that they would be doing so in about two minutes.

Shortly after the announcement, the plane moved forward and turned sharply left onto the runway. The engines revved, and there was suddenly the feeling of being pushed back in the seat, as the plane accelerated down the runway. After a little more than thirty seconds, the noise of the wheels on the runway stopped as the plane lifted off the ground. Mike was sitting next to the window, and he looked out to see the airport fall away beneath them. Within a few minutes, they had started to level off, although the plane still had an upward tilt to it that indicated they were still climbing.

As soon as the plane leveled off, a stewardess appeared to refill their coffee cups and to ask if they wanted anything else to drink. They both said no. A minute later another stewardess appeared. She was carrying a tray of hot, damp, rolled-up washcloths. She also had a set of tongs, and she was coming down the aisle offering a hot washcloth to each passenger. They saw that others were using them to wipe their faces and their hands.

Mike and Darryl each accepted a towel, and used them to wipe their faces. They both went through the motions as if they had done it hundreds of times before. Before long, the stewardess was back to collect the used towels. After she had done so and moved up the aisle, Mike and Darryl looked at each other and started to laugh. Mike finally asked Darryl what he was laughing about.

Darryl said, "Two things. One, I don't know if I'm going to be able to stand this treatment all the way to London. Two, I think I'm going to have to buy myself a first-class ticket back, because I don't know if I'll ever be able to fly coach again." They both laughed even more.

Chapter 58

The caravan of green Suburbans pulled up in front of the Aegis building. The men got out, creating the appearance of a mini-invasion. Frank Saunders had given General Edwards the address, but he had neglected to mention that he lived in a penthouse apartment on the twelfth floor.

The men walked into the lobby and stopped at the directory. Powers scanned the directory, and found nothing that would indicate Adam Adamson lived there. He went down a hallway until he came to the first office entrance. It was a law firm with six names on the door. He walked in while the rest of the men waited in the hallway. There was a receptionist at a sliding window. General.Powers approached, and the woman asked if she could help him. He explained that he was looking for someone who supposedly lived in the building, but he didn't see their name on the directory. The receptionist explained that she only knew of two people who actually lived in the building. One lived on the eleventh floor, and the other lived in a penthouse above the eleventh floor. General Powers thanked her and walked out.

As he came out into the hallway, he explained to his men that they were going to the eleventh floor. They walked back into the lobby and pushed the elevator button. One of the elevators opened immediately. They all got in one elevator, although it was a little tight. When they got off on the eleventh floor, there was a man standing at the elevator waiting to get on. He looked like he might be a lawyer, so General Powers approached him.

"Excuse me," he said, "do you work on this floor?"

The man wasn't quite sure what to make of this sudden crowd of military personnel. He looked a little nervous. "Yes I do. Why?"

"I understand that there's a penthouse above this floor. Could you tell me how to get to it?"

The man seemed to relax a little. "Sure, you have to go into the IMA office, which is right down the hallway over there." He pointed them down the hallway. "They actually own the penthouse."

Powers thanked him, and they all went down the hallway until they found the office door marked: "International Multicultural Assistance." They all walked in. There was a young woman sitting at a counter who Powers guessed was also a receptionist. She looked up when the door opened, and was a little surprised to see ten men, all dressed in military garb, come walking in. She put on a smile in spite of the surprise, "Good morning. May I help you?"

Powers made every effort to not be aggressive. "Yes, good morning. How are you this morning?" This seemed to put the woman at ease.

"I'm fine thank you, how about yourself?"

Powers was using everything he had to be nice. "Oh, I'm pretty good, but I need a little help. You see, I'm looking for a man named Adam Adamson, and I believe he lives in this building, but I have no idea exactly where. Can you help me at all?"

The woman continued to smile and Powers took it as a good sign. "Let me see what I can do for you, sir." She picked up her phone and dialed three numbers. When someone picked up, she said, "Mr. Groff, it's Betsy. There are some gentlemen here asking about Mr. Adamson." She waited a few seconds. "They're military, sir. I believe they're Army." As she said this she looked up at the General with an inquiring look, and he nodded. She waited again, and then she looked around. "Ten of them, sir." She paused again. "No really, there are ten of them." Another pause. "Yes, sir." She hung up and looked back at the General. "Mr. Groff will be right out, sir."

Powers wanted to ask who Mr. Groff was, but he thought better of it. He decided to just wait and find out from Mr. Groff himself. He didn't have to wait long. In less than a minute, Tim Groff came through a door and into the lobby. General Powers approached him. "Mr. Groff?"

Tim looked at him. "That's me. How can I help you?"

"My name is Calvin Powers with the U.S. Army, and we're looking for Adam Adamson."

Tim looked around the room for a moment assessing the situation. He realized Betsy was right, there were ten of them. He had no idea what this was about, but he had a gut feeling it would be good to stall this for a few minutes, if he could. He saw the stars on Powers' shoulders, and assumed he was a General. "General, why don't you and I go talk in my office?"

He turned and started to walk back to the door. Powers wanted to grab his shoulder, spin him around, and say: "Listen you little twerp, just tell me where Adam Adamson is and I'll get out of here," but his experience at Comtec had taught him that such a tactic probably wasn't going to work. He told his men to sit tight, and he followed Tim to his office. General Powers could not help but be impressed with it. It was large, beautifully finished and furnished. But more impressive than that were pictures on the wall of very important people, all with notes of thanks to Tim Groff.

There was one he recognized as being from the head of the FBI. There were two from Presidents. One of Reagan, and one of Clinton. There were two he could see were from Governors of various states. He saw one from George Bush, the Governor of Texas. There was one from Mario Cuomo, the Governor of New York. There were probably thirty or more, and many of them were from police and fire chiefs all over the country. He sat down in a chair in front of Tim's desk. Tim Groff sat down behind his desk. He leaned back in his chair, and put his hands together so his fingertips touched. "Now, General, help me understand what this is all about."

Of course General Powers didn't want to discuss the matter with him, but neither did he want to find himself at another dead-end.

"Well, Mr. Groff, it's a matter involving Mr. Adamson that I'm just not at liberty to discuss with anyone else. I understand that you folks own the penthouse above you, and that Mr. Adamson lives there. What I need to know is how I get to the penthouse." He was being very calm.

Tim looked at him for a long moment. "Well, General, you are correct that we control the penthouse. This organization was founded by Mr. Adamson. To date we've donated over one hundred million dollars to various individuals and organizations who have certain financial needs not being met through conventional means. Several days ago, Mr. Adamson resigned as the chairman of the board of IMA, and to the best of my knowledge he has moved out of the penthouse."

Powers was getting angry. "So you're telling me he's not in the penthouse right now?"

Tim looked completely confident. "I'm quite sure that he's not in the penthouse right now."

"Would you mind if we went in and checked?"

Tim thought for a moment. "Tell me, General, do you have any kind of a warrant?"

Powers couldn't believe he was hearing this for the second time this morning. "No, I don't."

"Well, I'll tell you what I'm willing to do." Tim was speaking slowly and calmly. "I'll take you alone up to the penthouse, under one condition."

Powers went along, "What condition is that?"

"That you give me your word you won't touch anything. I have no idea what's up there, and I don't want you to start touching things. I'll let you look around so you can be satisfied that Mr. Adamson isn't there, but you have to give me your word you won't touch anything."

"I give you my word, Mr. Groff. I'm only looking for Mr. Adamson."

"All right then, let's go." Tim got up from his chair and walked out of his office, Powers following right behind him. They came back out into the lobby, and he explained to his men he was going to the penthouse alone with Mr. Groff, and to wait for him. Tim pulled a small key chain from his pocket and stepped over to the elevator, which Powers hadn't noticed. He put a key into a key switch next to the elevator, gave it a half turn, and the door opened. He stepped in, and General Powers stepped in behind him. Tim pushed the up button, and in a few seconds the door opened into the penthouse. Again, General Powers was impressed with what he saw.

Tim stepped out of the elevator and moved toward the kitchen. "OK, General, let's see if there's anyone here."

The General followed him into the kitchen. They turned and walked back into the living room, then down a hall to a bedroom. Tim walked into the bedroom, and put his arms up as if to say: "look around." There was obviously no one there. They did the same with all the rooms, including both bathrooms. General Powers realized Tim had been telling the truth.

He turned and looked at the man. "Tell me, when do you think Mr. Adamson will be back?"

Tim beckoned for the General to follow him, and he walked back down the hallway to the master bedroom. He went to the closet and opened it. It was empty. "Honestly, General, I don't think Mr. Adamson is coming back."

Powers was a little confused and very irritated. "What exactly do you mean you don't think he's coming back? Don't you know?"

Tim sighed a heavy sigh, "General, Adam Adamson is man of immense wealth. His personal fortune is probably in excess of a billion dollars. He founded IMA, and funded it initially. For decades what would have been his corporate earnings have gone into the charity to enable us to do what we do. He gave me this job, which has been and will forever be, the best job I could ever hope for. Several days ago, he resigned from Comtec and IMA. I didn't ask him what he was going to do. It's not my place to do so. I can only expect that eventually I will get either a phone call or a letter from him, telling me what to do with the penthouse. Until then, it's going to remain as it is, on the outside chance that he might come back."

Powers knew nothing he could say was going to change anything he just heard. "OK, Mr. Groff. I understand what you're saying. You've been straight with me, and I appreciate it."

They walked back to the elevator, pushed the button and the door opened. As they stepped in, the General asked what the other elevator was for. Tim explained it went directly to the lobby. In a moment, they were back in the IMA lobby where the nine men were waiting. General Powers and Tim Groff shook hands, and the General thanked him again. He left the office and his men followed, like a mother duck and her ducklings.

When they got back to their cars, General Powers made a call to a friend who was an FBI agent in the L.A. bureau.

"Bob, it's Cal. Listen, I need a big favor, and I need it yesterday. I'm looking for a man named Adam Adamson, and I think he might be on a flight out of here today. Can you check with all the airlines and see if his name jumps out anywhere? Yeah, Adamson. How long do you think? OK, that's not bad. Call me back as quickly as possible. Yeah, thanks." He gave him his cell phone number. General Powers looked over at his driver. "He said it would take about twenty minutes. We're going to head toward the airport just in case." The lead car pulled out, and the other two followed.

They were almost to the airport when Powers' cell phone rang. He talked briefly and hung up the phone. He looked over at his driver. "He was on a TWA flight to London that left a little after eight this morning. The plane stops over in New York. It should arrive at JFK a little after four this afternoon, Eastern Time."

Powers looked at his watch. It was eleven-fifteen, so that would be two-fifteen on the East Coast. He instructed his driver to get off the highway, turn around, and head back to the National Guard HQ. He knew there was nothing more he could do. He was glad to be able to throw this back to General Edwards. He dialed his number and Mary answered the phone, "General Edwards' office."

"Yes, this is General Powers calling for General Edwards."

"One moment please, General." She put him on hold and buzzed into General Edwards' office. "General Powers on one."

General Edwards picked up the phone and punched line one. "Edwards."

"General, this is Powers."

"Have you got him?"

"No, sir, we don't. He left on an early flight this morning for London, but the plane stops at JFK in New York a little after four this afternoon, sir."

As he spoke General Edwards reached for a note pad and started to write. "What's the airline and flight number?"

"TWA flight 1166."

"OK, Powers, good work. I'll take it from here."

"Yes, sir, thank you, sir." And Powers hung up.

General Edwards buzzed Mary. "Yes, sir?"

"Mary, call TWA, find out exactly what time flight 1166 from L.A. to New York's JFK is due to arrive."

"Yes, sir."

General Edwards flipped through his Rolodex until he found the number he was looking for. It was the number for Skip Sunderland. He was the helicopter pilot assigned specially to the Joint Chiefs. He answered the phone on the second ring. "Skip Sunderland here."

General Edwards took mental note that he finally found someone who didn't answer with just his last name. "Skip, it's General Edwards."

"Good afternoon, General. How are you?" General Edwards didn't want to be rude, but he hated small talk. "Fine, Skip, thanks. Listen, Skip, I have a very unusual situation, and I need to use the baby."

There was a pause at the other end. "The baby," was a Bell 222UT helicopter the military kept expressly for the Joint Chiefs whenever they needed to be somewhere in a hurry. It had twin turbine engines, and it would cruise at one hundred sixty-miles per hour, plus. It didn't get used very often.

Skip finally spoke up, "Well, General, the baby's all dressed up with nowhere to go, so what have you got in mind?"

General Edwards was relieved he didn't bring up the issue of authority. They usually used the helicopter only under emergency circumstances.

"Here's what I need you to do, Skip, I'm going to have two of the top MP's from Andrews hotfoot it right over to you. When they get there, I want you to fly over here and pick me up."

"Right at the Pentagon, sir?"

"Right in the courtyard. Then we're going flat out, to JFK."

"In New York?"

"You know of any other JFK?"

"No, sir, but we'll require special clearance to fly into the airport's space."

"We're not only flying into the airport's space, Skip. We're dropping her on the tarmac at the TWA terminal."

Skip's voice sounded a little excited, "Are you serious, General? I didn't think we could get clearance for that."

"Skip, you'd be surprised at what we can get when we really need it. I'll get those MP's on the move. You be ready to go. We need to be at JFK by a little after four o'clock."

"Wow, that's cutting it close, General. Those MP's better be here in five minutes."

"Let me get going on that, and I'll see you in a few minutes." General Edwards hung up the phone. He immediately dialed the number for Colonel Barry Anderson, who oversaw the military police at Fort Belvoir just south of the city. This was also where the helicopter was housed and maintained.

A woman answered the phone, "Colonel Anderson's office."

General Edwards knew he had no time to waste. "This is General Clayton Edwards calling for Colonel Anderson."

"He's in a meeting at the moment, General."

"Is the President of the United States in that meeting with him?"

"No, sir."

"Then go interrupt the meeting and tell him I have to speak with him immediately."

"Yes, sir. One moment please," and the phone went dead.

He hoped that she hadn't hung up on him. He made a mental note to suggest that the military invest in music on hold. A moment later Colonel Anderson came on the line. "General Edwards, this is Colonel Anderson. How can I help you, sir?"

"Colonel, I'm sorry to pull you away from your meeting, but this is of the utmost importance. I need two of your best MP's to hotfoot it over to the hangar where the Joint Chiefs' helicopter is housed. I have an extremely important mission involving a fast-track into New York City to pick someone up and bring them back to Washington."

Colonel Anderson was a longtime military man, with a policeman's mentality. The two ideologies combined caused him to be terribly regulation oriented. "Sir, I'm not sure what you mean by 'pick someone up.' You're requesting military police, so I assume you mean 'pick them up' as in arrest them or detain them, is that correct, sir?"

General Edwards knew this wasn't going to be easy. "Yes, Colonel. That is correct. When we return to Washington, we'll need to keep him overnight in your detention center. This isn't a criminal, Colonel, so we'll want to treat him with respect and dignity. We're not going to throw him into a cell."

"We have several very nice rooms in the detention center, General."

"I know that, Colonel. That's why I'm mentioning it."

"Is this someone within the military community, sir?"

"No, it is not, but I am unilaterally taking military action for the purpose of detaining this individual for questioning. I have determined this matter is in the interest of national security, and I don't have time to get into a discussion with you right now. We have to be in New York City by about four-fifteen."

The Colonel looked at his watch. "I'm not sure that can be done, sir."

Now the General was getting angry. "It won't be possible if you and I keep talking about it, Colonel. Now listen, just get two of your top men over to the hangar now. We'll discuss the details of this later. I'll take full responsibility for the mission, and for your men. They'll be in no danger, I can assure you."

"Sir, am I to understand you're going to take the Bell all the way to New York City?"

"Yes"

"And where exactly are you going to land, sir?"

"At JFK."

"Well then, my men are already going to be endangered, sir. Meaning no disrespect."

General Edwards didn't want to argue the point. "I suppose you're right, Colonel. Just get them over there, the rotor's turning." He hung up, hoping the Colonel would obey his order. If he didn't hear from Skip in the next ten minutes, he was okay. He looked at his watch. It was almost twenty after two. He knew that if they were in the air by two-thirty and they pushed it, they could be at the airport by four. They would have to stop on the way back and fuel up. The helicopter only had a range of a little over three hundred miles.

In the next ten minutes he made phone calls to arrange for special clearance to land at JFK, and to stop at Fort Dix, New Jersey, to fuel up for the flight back. When he was done, he grabbed his coat and hat, and headed out of his office. Mary was sitting at her desk.

She looked up as he came out of his office. "Four thirty-five," she said.

He looked at her a little puzzled. "What's four thirty-five?"

"The time flight 1166 lands." He had forgotten he asked. "Oh good. That makes it a little easier. I'm going up to New York; I probably won't be back until late."

Mary wasn't sure she really heard him correctly. "Did you say New York?"

He kept walking as she spoke, and he was out in the hallway by the time he answered her. "Yes, I said New York." He rushed down the hallway to the elevator, and then down to the ground floor.

As he approached the door that led out into the central courtyard, he could hear the approaching helicopter. He walked into the courtyard, and there were several armed guards on alert, carefully watching the approaching helicopter. He yelled as loudly as he could to be heard over the sound of the incoming machine. They turned and saw him approaching, and for a moment they weren't sure what to do. Should they keep their attention on the helicopter, or should they salute their superior officer? Finally, their training won over; they stopped, and saluted. By this time he reached them, and explained the helicopter was approved, and it was for him. This caused them to back off.

Skip brought the helicopter down, dead center of the courtyard. As he approached, he saw the General talking to the guards. By the time he had the machine set firmly on the ground, the General was climbing in. He got in, closed his door, and fastened his seat belt. He turned and introduced himself to the two men sitting in the back. They each introduced themselves. Before they were done, Skip was back off the ground and heading north toward New York.

General Edwards looked at his watch. It was two thirty-three. He looked over at Skip, and realized he wasn't going to hear him unless he put his headset on. He reached up behind him, unhooked the headset, and put it on. He adjusted the mouthpiece and spoke, knowing Skip would hear him.

"We need to push a little, Skip, but not as bad as I thought. The plane comes in at four thirty-five. We need to be on the ground by four-fifteen or so. That will give us time to explain to the Port Authority exactly what we're doing." Skip nodded.

The General turned back toward the two men, and explained to them as little as they needed to know. The man they were going to pick up was a private citizen, he wasn't military. He hadn't broken any particular law, but there was enough information to believe he posed a possible threat to national security, and for that reason General Edwards wanted him questioned. When they had him in custody they were going to transport him back to Forth Belvoir, where he would be detained overnight.

General Edwards explained he would arrange to have him questioned at the base, as it was easier for those questioning him to come out to Belvoir than it was to get him transported safely to Washington somewhere.

He stressed that the man would not be armed in any way, would not likely resist arrest, and that under no circumstances was he to be harmed. He was satisfied the men understood the parameters of the mission. General Edwards then turned back around to enjoy the view. He always loved flying in this helicopter. It had been specially outfitted for the men who made up the Joint Chiefs of Staff. It was heavily soundproofed, so it was somewhat quieter than a typical helicopter. The seats were very comfortable and there was special communications equipment on board for emergency situations.

Edwards looked at the controls and saw they were moving at about one hundred fifty-five knots. He looked over at the pilot. "Skip, as soon as you're in range, let the New York traffic control know you're coming and give them an ETA on our arrival into their space. Let them know who we are, and that we received clearance through the defense department to land at JFK. You'll have to get landing directions from them to find the TWA terminal." Skip nodded.

General Edwards looked down and took note of the traffic along the I-95 corridor. He was happy he wasn't down there trying to get to New York.

Chapter 59

Mike got up out of his seat, and opened the overhead compartment. He retrieved his carry-on bag and sat back down. He unzipped the bag, and fished around for a small leather carrying case that he took out of the bag. He unzipped it, and Darryl saw it contained little toiletry tools, including a small pair of scissors. Mike took the little scissors out, and put the case back in the bag. He looked at Darryl, and said he would be right back. He walked a few steps to the back of the first-class section, and went into the bathroom.

He noticed the bathroom wasn't any bigger in first-class. He sat down on the closed toilet and took out his wallet. From the wallet he took out Adam's company ID badge he had used to board. The boarding pass they had been given was going to cover them at New York also. They wouldn't even have to get off the plane, so he thought this would be a good time to get rid of the ID.

He was ready to cut it into little pieces when he started to think about it. What if there was a problem with the plane? What if they had to switch planes? Would he need to show the ID again? What if they had to stay overnight? He decided not to cut the card up, yet. He would wait until they were done in New York and back in the air on the way to London. Then, he could be sure he wouldn't need the ID anymore. He put the card back in his wallet, and put the little scissors in his pocket. When he got back to his seat he spoke softly to Darryl so others wouldn't hear him. "I was going to cut up the ID, but I decided we should wait until we're in the air after New York."

Darryl nodded. "Makes sense to me."

There was the sound of a chime and the pilot's voice came over the speaker telling them that they were right on time, they would be landing at JFK at four-thirty, and they would be at the gate by four thirty-five. He also told them that the weather in New York was clear, and the temperature was sixty-five degrees. Mike looked at his watch, and saw it was three-thirty.

Chapter 60

Gus was reclined in his seat with a headset on, and his eyes closed. It looked to Adam like he was sleeping, and he assumed he was listening to the channel playing jazz. Adam was reading the Wall Street Journal. The pilot came out of the cockpit, and walked through the cabin into the kitchenette area. Adam heard the door to the restroom open and close. A few minutes later, he came back through and stopped to talk for a moment.

"We'll be stopping in New York for refueling. We should be there in about forty minutes." He turned and went back into the cockpit. Adam looked at his watch, it was twenty-five after three.

He thought about the castle on the east coast of England. He hadn't been to the castle in over a hundred years. He hadn't lived in the castle in over three hundred years. A little over a hundred years ago, he visited the castle, posing as an agent for the owner. He said that he was there to be sure the castle was being kept up, as it was supposed to be. He had found the family living there doing an excellent job with the upkeep. The ownership of the castle had changed hands many times over the years, as Adam's identity had changed. Adam owned the castle since the middle of the seventeenth century. He first moved into the castle in sixteen-sixty.

Chapter 61

The castle stood at the top of a hill on the east coast of England overlooking the North Sea in the town of Winterton by the Sea. It was a beautiful castle, built in the late fourteen hundreds. It sat in the middle of a thirty-acre estate full of gardens. There was also an apple orchard, and a small vineyard that produced enough wine to supply the household for a year.

He called himself Andrew Smith when he moved from France to the castle in sixteen-sixty. Moving was easier then. There was little in the way of documentation in those days. People tended to take your word for who you claimed to be. When you came to an area bringing with you great wealth, it was even easier because no one dared to question you. Even then there was great wealth, and Andrew Smith lived quietly in Winterton by the Sea for thirty-three years.

In sixteen sixty-three, Andrew traveled to Cambridge on business. While there, he stayed at an inn owned by a man named Henry Graham. Graham was a man in his forties who not only owned the inn, but also was a professor of philosophy at Trinity College. He and Andrew spent several evenings in deep discussions. Henry Graham thought Andrew was the most intriguing man he had ever met. He found the conversations to be enormously stimulating, and found Andrew's knowledge of the world, and his insight into humankind to be without equal. On the night before Andrew's departure, Henry brought a student from Trinity home to the inn for dinner, expressly for the purpose of meeting and talking with Andrew.

His name was Isaac Newton, and he was in his third year of study at Trinity. Henry had found Newton to be an exceptionally bright student with great interests in mathematics and science, particularly astronomy.

Andrew Smith, like Henry, thought Newton an interesting young man. They talked for hours on theories Newton had in the area of mathematics. Andrew found he could steer Newton's thinking in a slightly different direction, and that Newton would then expand his thinking on his own, to gain a much greater understanding of the issue. Andrew recognized the superior intelligence of the young man, and they both found they genuinely enjoyed each other's company.

Before Andrew left to return to Winterton by the Sea, he exchanged addresses with Newton, and with Graham. They all promised to keep in touch, which they did over the next several months. Isaac would often write to Andrew with his theory on something or other. Andrew would write back with his viewpoint on the theory, commending him when he knew Newton was on the right track, and offering suggestions when he thought he needed a little redirection.

In the early winter of sixteen sixty-five, Newton mentioned in a letter a disease that was becoming a concern in his area. They were calling it the plague, because it was killing a great number of people who caught it. Andrew wrote back, inviting Newton to come out to his home in Winterton by the Sea, and to stay for as long as it took the plague to pass. He urged Newton to accept, and assured him he would have no concern about finances. Newton accepted the invitation and left Cambridge in late May, having received his Bachelor's Degree.

The plague ravaged the more populated areas of England and other parts of Europe for almost two years. During that time, Isaac Newton and Andrew Smith exchanged ideas in endless hours of conversations. Andrew felt he had found a mind able to absorb much of what he knew, and he was sure this young man could be a channel, through which he could pass on valuable understanding to mankind without drawing attention to himself.

He helped Newton understand mathematics that had not been imagined by mankind up to that time. He explained such things as tangents in curves, and how to calculate the area of a curve. He found Newton to be an able student of geometry, which had been developed by the Greeks, and which was considered to be the highest form of mathematics at the time. He was able to expand his understanding of mathematics far beyond that, to what the modern world eventually began to call calculus.

They discussed areas of science that also fascinated Newton. He had long wondered about the earth and its motion. Andrew helped him understand the earth, like all other planets and stars in the universe, are affected by gravitational pull from other heavenly bodies. Andrew called it "universal gravitation," and it was the first time Isaac ever heard the word "gravity."

Andrew taught him about light, and color. He helped Newton understand that light contains all colors, in what he called a "spectrum." He demonstrated this to Newton by taking a large prism, and allowing sunlight to pass through it, causing a reflection on the wall consisting of all the basic colors in a neat row. He explained how light reflects and refracts on different surfaces, and how different components on the same surface can change the reflected and refracted colors, causing the human eye to "see" a particular color. This was the principle behind paints and dyes. Andrew helped Newton understand that a wall painted red, is simply covered with a substance that absorbs all the colors in the spectrum except red, which it reflects. The reflection is what humans see as a "red" wall.

By the time the plague had faded out and Newton could return to Cambridge, he felt he had gotten a vastly superior education at the castle on the hill. The relationship that had developed between them over the two years was as close to a father and son relationship as Isaac ever had. They continued to write for years, and Isaac càme out to the castle to visit many times.

In sixteen eighty-seven, Newton published a book entitled "Philosopiae Naturalis Principia Mathematica," in which he explained his theory that all bodies in space and on earth are affected by the force called "gravity." His theory was the result of years of conversation with Andrew. The book marked a turning point in the world of science, and launched Newton into a world of celebrity, with which he was never comfortable.

In the spring of sixteen ninety-three, Andrew determined it was time for him to move on. He had been at the castle for thirty-three years, and he knew it was the longest he could stay in one place, before people he dealt with noticed that he didn't age. His heart was heavy with the thought of simply disappearing from Isaac Newton, whom he had come to love like a son. But, he saw no other way.

He made arrangements to financially provide for the upkeep of the castle, including a staff of servants who would continue to live there. His instructions included Isaac Newton's use of the castle as often as he might want, for the rest of his life. This information was only to be given to Newton, should he arrive at the castle looking for Andrew. Details of Andrew's departure were not to be given to Newton, or anyone else. A simple statement: "No explanation regarding Mr. Smith's departure was given," would be the answer to any inquiry.

The financial arrangement with the Bank of Norwich, which was the closest major city to Winterton by the Sea, was that it would cover the maintenance and upkeep on the castle in perpetuity, and Andrew Smith's instruction to the bank was that this was to be the case even as ownership of the castle changed hands. Smith's instructions were that such upkeep was to continue until the bank was instructed to do otherwise, which may never happen. The bank was given a code they were to keep confidential. Smith explained that anyone in the future authorized to control the account, would know that code.

In July of sixteen ninety-three, Isaac Newton came to Winterton by the Sea to find out why his last two letters to Andrew Smith had gone unanswered. The unexplained departure of Andrew, and the arrangement regarding the castle, threw Isaac into a state of shock and depression. He had come to love Andrew Smith like the father he never had, considering his own father had died when he was only a year old. His mother had farmed him off to be raised by his grandmother when he was three. His depression caused him to develop poor eating and drinking habits, which in turn, caused him to become ill. It took over a year to regain his health and some control over his mental outlook.

In 1704, he published a book on the mathematical formulas and understanding of light that he had discussed years ago with Andrew. He hoped that somewhere out in the world, Andrew would eventually get a copy of the book and enjoy reading it.

Late in the same year, Andrew did get a copy of the book, and for several days he sat and read it with tears streaming down his face.

Chapter 62

The pilot came out of the cockpit and told Adam and Gus that they would be landing at JFK in about five minutes. They were going to refuel, and head right back out. There was no way to know how quickly they would get a fuel truck to fill their tanks. He explained that at times, they were in and out in fifteen minutes, and other times, it took more than an hour. Adam assured him it didn't matter to them how long it took. The pilot asked them if they wanted any special food brought on board while they were in New York. Both men felt the food in the refrigerator of the plane was plenty. The pilot asked them to fasten their seat belts for landing, and went back into the cockpit.

Gus and Adam were both looking out their respective windows at the sprawling city below. The plane banked sharply left, and then leveled off. The plane's altitude was now only about three thousand feet, by Adam's estimate. The plane banked left a second time, and leveled off again. The altitude of the plane was dropping sharply as they approached the airport.

Suddenly, the cars were quite distinguishable moving along the various highways below, and then the highways disappeared, and there was a brief moment of grass and lights. The plane's wheels touched down with a little chirp, followed by the familiar sound and feel of the reverse thrusters that brought the plane to a stop.

They taxied for several minutes, and they could see various parts of the airport go past the windows. The plane finally came to a stop in an area designated for private jets waiting for fuel. This was where planes waited if they were not dropping off or picking up passengers. Adam looked out the window, and in the distance he could see planes pulled up to the various gates. They were TWA planes.

Chapter 63

General Edwards looked at his watch as New York City came into view. It was ten minutes after four. Skip had already spoken several times with the tower and at first, there was some question by the traffic controllers as to whether they did have clearance to fly into the airport's airspace. That was cleared up with a quick phone call, and arrangements had been made for the Port Authority to meet them on the tarmac at the TWA terminal.

Katherine Trantalis was the assistant manager of the airport, and this was her watch. When information about the Army landing a helicopter and using the Port Authority to capture someone on an incoming flight came to her attention, she wanted to be involved personally. She had been told that the individual they were looking for was on flight 1166, due in from L.A. at four-thirty. She was very concerned about potential danger to the other passengers on that flight, but the General had assured her there was no danger. She was also concerned about what might happen in the gate when the passengers came off the plane. The Port Authority explained there was not likely any need of force.

As she stood at Gate 36, where flight 1166 was due to arrive in about ten minutes, she looked out the window and saw six Port Authority cars pull onto the tarmac in an already designated area. All had their lights flashing, and they formed a large circle. The sun was starting to set. She carried a walkie-talkie, and it came to life. "TCT to number 2. Come in."

She pushed a button on her device. "This is number 2. Go ahead."

"We have a visual on the chopper, we've put air traffic for runway approach 22 on a holding pattern for the next five minutes or so. The chopper should be down in three. Over."

She pushed the button again. "That's affirmative TCT. Over." She stayed at the window until she saw the chopper drop down into the circle of police cars.

Chapter 64

The pilot's voice came over the sound system to inform the passengers and the crew that the plane would be landing momentarily. Everyone was asked to move their seats into the upright position.

Mike and Darryl were listening to music on headsets, but they could hear the pilot's instructions over the music system. They took the headsets off, and looked out the window at New York. They felt the plane slow down as the flaps were lowered, and a few moments later they could hear the whining sound as the landing gear was dropped. Darryl felt his ears popping as the pressure in the cabin changed. The pilot's voice came over the speaker again, advising the attendants to prepare for landing.

Darryl patted his packet of money in his jacket pocket. He smiled as he thought about this weekend adventure to London, and that he had an additional ninety-five thousand dollars stashed away at home. He looked over at Mike. "Hey, Mike, this is a great gig, you know?" Mike nodded.

Darryl continued, "I'd be happy to have a gig like this every week."

Mike laughed, "Who wouldn't?"

Darryl said, "A trip to Europe every week for a hundred thousand. Boy, that's a tough way to make a living." They both laughed.

Mike was sitting next to the window, and he could see the highways and buildings below moving past the window quickly. Then there was grass, and in a moment they were touching down.

Chapter 65

As the chopper touched down, Katherine walked over to a door, swiped her security card in the reader, and pushed against the door with her shoulder. The door opened, and she was in a stairway that brought her down to runway level. As she approached the door that led out to the tarmac, she saw the group approaching. There were three men in military uniform, and twelve Port Authority policemen. She couldn't help but wonder what kind of fiasco this was going to be. She opened the door, and they came into the receiving area.

She targeted the military man with the most fancy stuff on the front of his jacket. He was also the only one who had stars on, and although Katherine knew very little about the military, she had seen enough movies to know that stars meant a General of some sort. She was tall for a woman at five-eleven, and she looked Edwards square in the eyes. "General, I'm Katherine Trantalis, the airport manager," and she extended her hand.

General Edwards took her hand and shook it firmly, but not too firmly. "My name is Clayton Edwards, U.S. Army, Joint Chiefs. Ms. Trantalis, we're here on official government business."

Katherine smiled, "I already knew that, General, just by where your chopper landed."

Edwards smiled a little himself. "I guess that was sort of a give away, wasn't it?"

"Yes, sir, it was. Now, I would appreciate having some idea of what it is you intend to do."

General Edwards' gut instinct was to tell her it was none of her business, and that she should just stay out of his way, but he knew that would only make this process take longer. He could tell that she wasn't a woman who was easily intimidated.

"It's simple, Ms. Trantalis. There's a passenger on TWA flight 1166 due in any minute who we are going to take into custody. He's not dangerous, he's not armed in any way, and we don't anticipate any trouble. At which gate is 1166 due?"

"Gate 33, which is right up these stairs. It'll only take a few seconds for us to get there and the flight hasn't landed yet." As she said these words, her communicator came alive. "TCT to number 2. Come in."

She put the thing to her mouth, and pushed the button. "Number 2. Go ahead."

"1166 is on the ground, Gate ETA: two minutes."

"Roger, TCT. See if you can stretch that a minute or two. Stall them for crossing traffic."

"Roger number 2. Revised Gate ETA: four minutes."

General Edwards liked this woman immediately. He smiled at her with obvious approval of her quick thinking that gave them an extra few minutes to get ready.

She looked at General Edwards. "Are any of your men armed?"

He nodded. "My men are trained military police. They carry standard Army issue hand weapons."

"There has to be an understanding, General, that there will be no firing of weapons in this airport."

"I don't anticipate any need for firing weapons, Ms. Trantalis."

"With all due respect, General, I don't care what you anticipate or don't anticipate. What I'm saying is if something you don't anticipate occurs, there will still be no firing of weapons. Is that understood?" She wouldn't take her eyes off his.

The General was thinking to himself that this was one heck of a woman, and he noticed her eyes were bright green. He wasn't going to mess with her. "Yes, it's understood." His men were able to hear the entire conversation clearly, so there was no need for him to repeat anything to them.

"OK, then. Follow me," she said, and turned to the stairs.

As they emerged from the door into the gate area, everyone waiting for other flights or waiting to greet passengers coming off flight 1166 stared at them. It was startling to see so many police officers together, and the three men in Army uniforms added intrigue to the scene.

General Edwards immediately saw the effect this crowd of uniforms was having on people around the gate. He suggested to the senior Port Authority officer that they spread out a little, to be less conspicuous. He ordered his men to stand at each of the columns around the gate area, which they did. General Edwards and his two men, along with two of the Port Authority officers, stood at the gate area as flight 1166 rolled up.

They watched as the motorized walkway worked its way out to the door of the plane. A few minutes later, passengers started to emerge, and it suddenly occurred to General Edwards that he didn't know what Adam Adamson looked like. He realized the man could walk right past him, and he wouldn't know it. He should have made them keep everyone on the plane while he went on board. They would have known what seat he was in. He knew there was nothing he could do about it now. The plane was going on to London, so even if Adamson got off, he would have to get back on.

He stood, waiting for all the passengers to disembark. When they stopped coming out of the plane, he looked over at Katherine. "I have a suggestion," he said in her direction. She looked at him, waiting to hear the suggestion. "Why don't you go to the plane and ask the man we're looking for to come with you. I don't think he would give you a hard time."

"What's his name?"

"Adam Adamson."

She looked at him for a moment and he could tell she was thinking about the name.

"All right, I'll go get him, but I have another idea. Two gates down, across from Gate 31 is an executive lounge that's empty most of the time. Why don't you take your men and a couple officers down there, and I'll bring Mr. Adamson there. That way, we can avoid some scene right here in the gate area."

Edwards thought it was a good idea, and headed down the corridor with his two men and two of the officers.

Katherine spoke into her communicator, "Number 2 to terminal B-3 security. Come in."

In a few seconds there was a response, "Security. Go ahead."

"Who have I got?"

"It's Fred, Katherine. What's up?"

"Fred, how close are you to the executive lounge by Gate 31?"

"Not far at all, why?"

"Get over there as quick as you can and let some people in. You'll find three Army men and two Port Authority officers."

"Roger. I'm on my way."

Katherine headed down the gate walkway to the plane, wondering what she was about to get herself into. She made sure her Airport ID badge was facing the right way on her jacket lapel. She got to the plane and there was a stewardess and co-pilot standing at the door. They both greeted her, and she motioned for them to step out of the plane. They understood she wanted to talk with them without passengers hearing. They approached her and leaned in. She spoke in a hushed tone.

"I'm Katherine Trantalis, the assistant airport manager. I believe you have a passenger named Adam Adamson on the plane. Can you confirm that for me?"

The stewardess spoke up, "Yes, we do. He's in first-class, seat 7-A. He's traveling with someone, Gus Stoltz, a black man, in seat 7-B."

"Are they both in their seats at the moment?" The stewardess put up her index finger as if to say: "wait a moment," and she stepped back into the plane. Katherine watched her as she walked directly left into the cockpit. Katherine thought that was clever. A few seconds later, the stewardess came out of the cockpit, and glanced into the first-class area before coming back out of the plane. "Yes," she was excited, "they're both in their seats."

"How have they been on the flight here?" The stewardess looked a little confused, as though she didn't fully understand the question, so Katherine elaborated, "Have they been drinking at all?"

Now the stewardess understood. "Oh no, they've been very polite. Coffee or juice is the strongest thing either of them have had. They've been as nice as first-class passengers can be."

Katherine breathed a sigh of relief. At least she didn't have to deal with someone intoxicated. "OK, here's the deal. I need to take Mr. Adamson with me for a few minutes. The scheduled stop for this plane is an hour and ten minutes. It's possible that Mr. Adamson will not be back, but I'm not sure. I'll communicate through the control tower one way or the other. What's your flight designation out?"

The co-pilot answered, "1220."

The stewardess spoke again, "What do you want us to do?"

"Nothing, I hope. I don't expect any problem here, but if for any reason there is a commotion, just run out to the gate. You'll see about ten Port Authority officers. Bring some of them down here in a hurry."

The stewardess's eyes were open wide with excitement. "OK," was all she said.

Katherine took a deep breath, and walked into the plane. Her eyes scanned first-class very quickly, and she saw her passenger sitting in seat 7-A. She was taken aback by how good-looking he was. She had the strangest feeling that she had seen him somewhere before. He was reading a magazine, but for a moment he looked up and their eyes met. He smiled, and looked back down at his magazine. She approached their seats. "Mr. Adamson?"

For a split second, Mike didn't react, but then he remembered that for this flight he was Adam Adamson. He put the magazine down, and looked up at the woman. He thought she was quite attractive and he couldn't help but notice her green eyes. He smiled again, "Yes, I'm Adam Adamson. Can I help you?"

Katherine put on her most professional air of apology. "I'm very sorry, Mr. Adamson, but I have to ask you to come with me."

Mike was a little surprised. "I'm sorry, I don't understand."

"I'll explain it to you, sir. But I would like to do it in private, so if you could just come with me I would really appreciate it." She hoped she seemed non-threatening.

Mike wondered if they had found out he wasn't really Adam, but he dismissed that as being impossible. "Do I need to take my bag with me?"

Katherine thought that if she said yes, it would be cause for alarm. "No, sir, that won't be necessary. We'll only be a few minutes." She didn't like to lie, but she felt that whatever she had to do to keep the situation completely under control was justifiable. She noticed the man sitting with him hadn't said anything, and she was grateful because she could tell that he was a very big man, and she would not want to have a problem with him.

Mike looked over at Darryl. "Well, Gus, I guess I'll see you in a few minutes."

He put the slightest emphasis on "Gus." Darryl picked up on it immediately.

"OK, Adam. I'll just wait right here."

Mike stepped out into the aisle past Darryl, and followed Katherine out of the plane.

Chapter 66

Adam sat in the comfort of the small jet and looked out the window at all the police cars with their lights flashing. He wondered what was going on. He was surprised when he saw the helicopter land in the circle created by the cars. It was unmistakably a military helicopter. He watched as three men climbed out of the helicopter and spoke with the policemen. Then, all of them walked into the terminal.

The pilot came out of the cockpit, and told Adam and Gus they were scheduled for refueling in ten minutes, and that they should be back in the air by five o'clock. Adam put his headset on and went back to his music.

Chapter 67

Stanley Wentworth eased the automobile into the driveway of his apartment house and parked in the space designated for him with a little sign on a stick that simply read SW. There were four parking spaces for the other tenants, and each space had a modest car parked in it. It was not a particularly good neighborhood, in the North of London. Stanley could remember when it was a very nice neighborhood. He remembered when the apartment house he now lived in was a single-family house. The Woolsey's had lived there for as far back as he could remember. Mr. Woolsey was a banker. Stanley delivered coal to the house when he was young. Mr. Woolsey had three daughters, and they were all teenagers when Stanley was a coal deliveryman. He could close his eyes and see them as if it were yesterday. They were all beautiful, and his heart used to ache that his station in life was so far beneath them. It would have been foolish to think he could develop a relationship with any of them.

Stanley had the largest parking space because he had been a chauffeur for many years, and usually had a large luxury car parked in the space. Tonight was no exception. As a matter of fact, Stanley considered it to be the pinnacle of his experience, as a professional driver. He got out of the car, and closed his eyes as he gently let the car door shut. He closed his eyes, because he wanted to concentrate on hearing the sound of the closing door. The tight "thunk" the door made was a thing of beauty to Stanley. He opened his eyes, and looked at the car. The sight of it made him giddy, though he had been driving luxury cars for almost forty years.

It was a brand-new Rolls Royce Park Ward touring saloon. It was dark blue, although now that the sun had gone down, it looked black. The engine was a 5.4 litre V-12 producing well over three hundred horsepower. Stanley had never driven anything like it before. When he got a call last week from the agency he worked through, he could not have imagined the opportunity about to be presented to him.

Stanley had been married for thirty-eight years. His wife Margaret was a wonderful woman, and they were very happy together. They had two children who were now grown. Their son was a violinist with the London Symphony, and their daughter lived in Liverpool with her husband and two children. Stanley and Margaret had enjoyed a good life together, but Margaret got sick three years ago, and had passed away last year.

Stanley had been the driver for the Peterson family for the past eight years. They were very kind and generous to him. When his wife died, they insisted on paying all the costs of the funeral. Three months ago, Mr. Peterson passed away, three days before his eighty-seventh birthday. Mrs. Peterson went to live with her daughter in Paris, and that left Stanley unemployed. Mrs. Peterson gave him a severance package equal to a years' salary. Stanley had always been very frugal, and had managed to save quite a bit over the years, so he didn't need to work. But, he loved to be part of a family, and couldn't see himself sitting around watching television all day. He had called the driving agency to let them know he was available.

Three days ago, the agency called him and he went down to see them. A new client was moving into the country, and was looking for a driver. The position was for a live-in driver. He would have no responsibilities but to drive and maintain the car. The wages offered were far more than such a position normally paid, but emphasis had been put on the need for the driver to be mature and responsible. The agency knew Stanley's reputation was impeccable, and they called him. Stanley accepted the position immediately. He was told to report to Rolls Royce of London at five o'clock on Friday afternoon to pick up the car. He was then to go home and pack what he could take in one suitcase. Just the essentials to begin with. His new employer would arrange to have all of his belongings moved to his new home after he arrived. He was surprised to learn his new home was going to be the old Balmoor Castle at Winterton by the Sea. He was told to be at the Stansted Airport in Sawbridgeworth at five o'clock tomorrow morning, where he was to wait for his new employer. His name was Nathan. Benjamin Nathan. That's all the agency knew.

When he arrived at the Rolls Royce dealership on Friday, he was treated like the king of England. He knew the people knew he was only the driver, but it didn't matter. He was taking the very first Park Ward to leave their dealership. Three hundred and seventy thousand pounds had been wire-transferred two days earlier. The Park Ward was a brand-new model, and this was the only one they had. It was purchased sight unseen, and there had been no haggling over the price. Stanley couldn't believe it when he saw it.

Now, he stood in his driveway looking at the car. It was truly magnificent. He forced himself to walk away from the car. He knew he had to finish packing. He had informed his landlord he would be leaving at the end of the month. He checked his maps to be sure he knew exactly where he was going tomorrow. Stansted Airport was a small airport about twenty miles north of London on Route M-11. He was surprised this was where he was picking up his new employer. Heathrow was the major airport in London, and he couldn't remember ever picking anyone up, or dropping anyone off at Stansted. As he went into the apartment house, he glanced back at the automobile parked in his space. He shook his head as he walked in. He couldn't believe he held the keys to that car in his hand.

Chapter 68

Mike followed Katherine Trantalis up the walkway, into the gate area, and down the hallway to a secure door with a sign on it that said: "Executive Lounge." As he followed her, he was trying to think of what she could possibly want with him. As he had stepped into the gate area he took note of what seemed to be an awful lot of police, but he didn't imagine it had anything to do with him. Katherine took her lapel badge off and swiped it through a reader next to the door, and the door opened. She walked in with Mike behind her. In the room Mike saw three men in military uniforms and two more policemen. He was a little surprised to see all of these people. One of the men in military uniform approached him. Mike sensed immediately he was mildly hostile.

"Are you Adam Adamson?"

Mike knew that he only had a split second to make a decision. Should he say yes and carry on a charade, or should he say no, and identify himself as Mike Jenson? He decided that he could get into a lot more trouble trying to convince these people he was Adam Adamson. All these cops and military people milling around told Mike this was something big. He knew he couldn't really get in trouble for using someone else's plane ticket, but he could get into big trouble for trying to jerk these people around, and he wasn't about to take that chance.

He looked at the man who had posed the question. "No, my name is Mike Jenson." He saw the stars on the man's shirt collar and knew he was a General.

Now he saw a look of utter shock and disbelief on the man's face. "What do you mean, no? Are you, or are you not, flying under the name of Adam Adamson?"

Once Mike made the mental decision to be on the level with these people, he felt he had a little latitude to have some fun with this situation. "Oh, well, yes I am using Adam's ticket, but that's not what you asked me. You asked me if I was Adam Adamson, and the answer is no." He could see the General's face getting red.

"Do you know the penalty for falsely using someone else's ticket?"

Mike could see he was serious, and Mike couldn't help but laugh, because he was sure the penalty couldn't be very serious.

"No," he said with a little chuckle, "I have no idea."

Now the General was *really* mad. "You think this is funny? Let's see some identification, Mr. Jenson."

Mike took his wallet out, and pulled out his California driver's license, handing it to the General. "What's this all about, anyway?" He figured he might as well take an active part in whatever this was.

The General didn't look at him as he spoke. He was concentrating on the license. "Don't you worry about what this is all about."

Mike didn't like his attitude, and decided to let him know it. "Look, unless I'm mistaken this is New York. I believe that New York is still part of the United States, isn't it? Last I knew citizens in this country have rights. I have a feeling my rights are being violated right now, so someone better tell me what this is all about." He looked around at the faces of the cops and the other soldiers and he got the impression they were as much in the dark as he was.

He looked over at Katherine. "We better clear this up in the next few minutes, or by the time my attorney is finished with this, you'll be looking for a new job." He could tell she was nervous.

The General finally finished with the license. "You got any other ID, Mr. Jenson?"

Mike looked at him. "Sure, what do you want?" He started pulling things out of his wallet. "Here's my social security card, here's my SAG ID."

The General took these. "What's SAG?"

"Screen Actor's Guild. I'm an actor."

Katherine's eyes widened as she suddenly realized why he looked so familiar. "Jeez, now I know where I recognized you from. You're on that HBO show 'The Sopranos.'"

Mike smiled, "Yes, I am."

Katherine confirming his appearance on a television show made the General's heart sink with the prospect this wasn't Adam Adamson. "OK, Mr. Jenson, suppose you explain to us why it is you're traveling under Mr. Adamson's name."

"That's quite simple, General, Mr. Adamson is a friend of mine. He had two tickets to London that he wasn't going to be able to use, and he asked me if I might want to use them. You see it came to our attention some years ago that Mr. Adamson and I look a lot alike. Adam knew that with one of his photo ID's, I would have no trouble using the tickets. They were first-class and he hated to see them go to waste. I naturally jumped at the opportunity to fly to London for free so … here I am."

"So you're telling me that you are in possession of one of his ID's?"

"I'm not sure if I should answer without a lawyer present."

"Look, Mr. Jenson, if you're really who you say you are, I couldn't care less that you're getting a free flight to London. I hope you have a great time. I just want to see this ID to confirm your story."

"So, I show you this ID. You see that I'm telling you the truth. You give me back the ID, I get back on the plane, and that's the end of it? Is that what you're telling me?"

"That's exactly what I'm telling you."

Mike looked at Katherine. "Are you vouching for what he's saying?"

She looked at the General, then back at Mike. "I guarantee you the plane will not take off without you on it."

Mike took the Comtec badge out of his wallet and handed it to the General. He looked at it, looked up at Mike, then back down at the ID, and then back at Mike again.

"That's unbelievable. They say everyone has a twin somewhere." He handed the ID to Katherine and she looked at it. She handed it back to the General. He spoke to Katherine, "Does he need this ID to get back on the plane?" She shook her head to indicate that he did not. The General looked at Mike. "Mr. Jenson, I need to make a small adjustment on our deal. I need to keep this ID, but other than that you're free to go."

Mike knew it wasn't worth making an issue, so he turned to leave with Katherine.

One of the two policemen spoke as he walked toward Mike, "Excuse me, Mr. Jenson?"

Mike turned back. The cop reached into his jacket pocket and pulled out a little spiral notebook. Flipping open to an empty page, he smiled and handed it to Mike. "Could I have your autograph before you go? I never miss your show."

Mike smiled and took the notebook. "What's your name?"

"Steve."

Mike wrote on the page: "It was nice to meet you, Steve." And he signed his name and handed it back to the man.

He followed Katherine back to the plane where she got him on board without his boarding pass. At the door to the plane, she apologized for the hassle. She told him she hoped he understood she had no control over the situation. He said he did, and they shook hands. With that, she turned and walked away. He went back to his seat. Darryl looked at him as he stepped past him to sit down.

"What was that all about?"

"I'm not sure."

"What do you mean, you're not sure?"

"It was weird. They took me to a room full of soldiers and cops. They were looking for Adam, and they figured I was him because I was flying under his name."

"Man, I thought you said this guy was OK."

"He is. That's what's so weird about it. I'll be interested to call Adam when I get back and ask him what the heck this was all about."

"You OK, man?"

"Yeah, I'm fine. Really."

They sat quietly as the plane was prepared for the overseas flight. They couldn't see any of the runways out the window, because they were facing the terminal. They took no note of the small Lear jet that took off on the runway behind them.

Chapter 69

General Edwards was silent all the way back to Fort Belvoir. He was beaten, and he didn't like it. He had obviously underestimated this man, and now he would probably never find him. By the time they touched down at Belvoir, he resigned himself to the fact that he wasn't even going to try. It was bad enough he was going to have to explain a wild-goose chase to New York. All the strings he had pulled for clearances, and extra police. He was going to have to find a way to explain it without sounding like a nut.

He could picture himself explaining he had done it to capture a six thousand year old man before he left the country. What had he done? Oh, nothing really, just lived for six thousand years. Isn't that enough reason to pull out all the stops to take this man into custody? He knew that such an explanation would result not only in his losing his position, but might even result in him being thrown into a mental institution. No, he had to come up with something better, and he had no idea what it was going to be.

General Edwards had stopped drinking about five years ago. He didn't consider himself to be a "problem" drinker, but he had noticed that he was drinking more than he thought he should, so he just stopped. Tonight, he couldn't wait to get home and pour himself a scotch.

Chapter 70

Stanley's alarm went off at three-thirty in the morning. He shut it off, and sat up, swinging his legs around so he was sitting on the edge of his bed. He reached over and turned on the lamp on the nightstand next to his bed. He looked around, and thought about this being his last morning in this bedroom. He brewed himself a cup of coffee, took a shower, got dressed, and left his apartment, with one small suitcase. He locked the door securely.

The sight of the car still took his breath away. It was still dark, but the magnificence of the automobile was clearly discernible. He pushed a button on the control that came with the keys, and the boot opened. It didn't spring open; it opened in a slower, controlled way. He put his suitcase in, and it looked tiny in the cavernous space for luggage. He pushed the button again, and the boot closed just as it had opened.

At the dealership, they had showed him how all the controls worked. He unlocked the car and got in. Again, he closed his eyes as he turned the ignition key. He wanted to focus his hearing on the glorious sound of the V-12 engine coming to life. It was a joy to behold. He sat for a long time with his eyes closed. The sound of the engine was barely perceptible, but to him it was like the sound of the symphony when he went to hear his son play. He backed the car out of his space and eased down the narrow driveway. He headed out of London on Route 4.

It would take him about fifteen or twenty minutes to get to the airport at this time in the morning. There was no traffic to contend with. The feel and smell of the automobile was almost more than Stanley could bear. It was a wonderful feeling to drive this automobile, the quality of which he knew would be driven only by a tiny portion of humanity.

He looked at the clock on the dash. Even it was elegant. It read four-twenty.

Chapter 71

The Lear entered Great Britain controlled airspace at three-fifty in the morning London time. The pilot conversed with the traffic control tower at Heathrow, identifying himself and the plane, and explaining that he was on course to Stansted Airport. The tower gave him flight parameters, and he made the necessary adjustments. He knew his two passengers were sleeping and he didn't feel any need to wake them up. Their ETA was four forty-five. He had researched the airport when his client first made the arrangements. Stansted was a very small airport. It was not capable of handling large commercial flights, but quite a few private jets flew in and out of Stansted regularly. It was a way for the super-wealthy to avoid all the hassle and publicity. Because there was a fair amount of international travel coming through, the airport did have customs agents there at all times, and they had their own control tower. He would make contact in a few minutes.

Ten minutes later, the lights of London came into view. He checked in with the Stansted tower, and they instructed him to drop to fifteen thousand feet and stay on his present course. They cautioned him that the approach traffic to Heathrow overlapped the approach area to Stansted, and he should watch his altitude carefully. His course took him just right of London. He could see the flashing lights of Heathrow off to the left. He banked slightly left after passing the immediate city, then straightened out. He could see the flashing lights of Stansted up ahead. He was approaching from the correct direction for landing, and he was given landing clearance straight in. He was on a visual landing, although the tower commented regularly on his altitude, to be sure he didn't come in too high, or low.

At four thirty-five, they touched down so gently he didn't think his passengers were awakened. He wished he didn't have to throw the reverse thrusters on, because that was probably going to wake them up. But, he didn't want to find himself running out of runway. He taxied around as directed by the tower, to an area close to the only terminal. It was small, and reminded the pilot of the terminal on St. Croix.

He shut the engines down, and the plane interior became quiet. He walked out of the cockpit, and found both passengers asleep. He gently nudged Adam on the shoulder, and he awakened immediately looking at the pilot.

"We're at Stansted airport, sir," the pilot whispered.

Adam looked over at Gus, who was still sleeping, then back at the pilot. "OK."

He looked at his watch and saw it was four-forty. He reached over and nudged Gus. Gus opened his eyes and looked at Adam. "What's going on?"

"We're here," was all Adam said.

Gus stretched and got up from his seat. "Man, that's a comfortable seat. I don't think I sleep that good in my own bed."

They gathered their things and stepped out of the plane. The pilot was coming back from the terminal with a small handcart. He opened the luggage compartment, and took out the two suitcases and the two boxes of books. He had a large manila envelope in his hand, which he handed to Adam. "Someone in the terminal asked me to give this to you." Adam took it and looked at it. The envelope had the name Benjamin Nathan written on the outside. He told Gus to come with him, and they went back into the plane.

In the passenger compartment, he opened the envelope. Inside was a British passport in the name of Benjamin Nathan. It was perfect. Completely indistinguishable from the genuine article. Even the picture was excellent. There was also a British driver's license, a Master Card, Visa, and an American Express, all with the name Benjamin Nathan. There was also a passport for Gus. The passport was in the name of Gustave Stoltzen. Again, a perfect forgery, with a very complimentary picture. There was a license and credit card in his name, as well. They took a few minutes to put all the new cards into their wallets. They each put their passports in their jacket pockets. Their old identification had been destroyed the night before.

They came back out of the plane, and walked with the pilot and co-pilot toward the terminal. The terminal was as small as it looked. There were only three people in the terminal: the Customs Inspector, a ticket agent, and one baggage handler. The Customs Inspector asked if they had anything to declare. They both said no. Adam showed him his passport, which was already stamped to show they left the country and went to California three months ago. He looked briefly in Adam's suitcase and waved him by. It was the same routine for Gus. In three minutes, they were through customs. The two boxes of books didn't interest him. Adam assumed the man was trained to look for signs that someone was hiding something.

Adam made small talk with the pilot on the way out of the terminal. He told Adam that he and his co-pilot were going to get a cab into London, and grab some sleep before heading back. Adam thanked him outside the terminal, shaking hands with both of them.

He looked in the parking lot and saw the car in a corner of the parking area, all by itself. At the same time he saw the car, the door opened, and someone got out. It was a man, and he was walking toward them. When he got close enough, Adam could see that he was in his late fifties. He came up to him and Gus, looked at both of them, and said, "Mr. Nathan?"

Adam thought it was very clever that he went out of his way not to assume the white man was the one with all the money. This man was obviously well trained. He extended his hand. "I'm Mr. Nathan."

They shook hands. The man introduced himself as Stanley Wentworth. Adam introduced Gus.

"This is Gus Stoltzen." Stanley shook his hand. "Pleased to make your acquaintance, sir."

Adam looked over at the car. "So how's the car, Stanley?"

Stanley smiled, "That's no 'car,' Mr. Nathan, that there is an automobile. The finest I've ever driven, I might add."

Adam laughed, "That good, is it?"

"Better, sir," Stanley said, without skipping a beat. Stanley picked up one box of books, and put it under his arm. He then reached down with the same arm and picked up one of the suitcases. He tried to pick up the other box with his free hand, but he couldn't get his hand under it.

Gus said, "Hey, Stanley, I'll get that one."

Stanley looked at him. "Much obliged, Mr. Stoltzen," and he instead, picked up the other suitcase.

Gus picked up the box of books. "It's Gus, Stanley. OK?"

Stanley started walking toward the car. "Whatever you say, Gus."

When they got to the car Stanley put the suitcase down, and with that free hand, reached into his pocket and pulled out the control for the car. He pushed a button, and the boot opened. It was impressive the way it opened. He put the suitcases in, with the two boxes of books. Even with those items and his suitcase, the boot was half empty. He pushed the button again, and the boot lid closed slowly and tightly. Adam and Gus looked at each other, and then over at Stanley.

Adam spoke up, "Pretty impressive."

Stanley smiled, "Yes, sir, it truly is." He walked around and opened the back door, Adam motioned Gus to get in the back with him, which he did. Stanley shut the door, walked around, and got in behind the wheel. He turned back and looked at Adam. "Balmoor Castle?"

Adam looked at him. "That is correct, Mr. Wentworth."

Stanley said, "Please, call me Stanley."

"OK, Stanley, let's go home."

"Yes, sir, Mr. Nathan."

"Stanley, it's Ben."

"Yes, sir, Ben."

The car eased out onto Route M-11 and continued north up to Route A-11. There, Stanley turned right, onto Route A-11, which took them northeast to Norwich. In Norwich, he turned east onto Route A-47, taking them to Great Yarmouth. At Great Yarmouth, Stanley turned north onto Route A-149, into Winterton by the Sea. In the center of town Stanley turned right, onto the Old Sea road. About a mile up the road was the driveway that led into Balmoor Castle. Stanley turned into the driveway, which was a well kept gravel drive.

The castle was quite large. It was built of magnificent stone blocks. As they approached, Stanley counted seven chimneys coming from the roof of the building. The gardens along the way were spectacular, and there were large rolling lawns. They pulled into a circular drive that allowed them to turn the car around and stop relatively close to the front entrance. Before the car came to a stop, four servants had emerged from the house. Stanley smiled. He knew he was really going to enjoy this.

Chapter 72

On Monday morning, Frank Saunders filed his report with the director of the agency. In the report, he explained the initial phone conversation with his father and his resulting investigation. The summary of his report was there was no foundation for any further investigation into the matter. He had personally met with Adam Adamson, and concluded that any accusations against the man were completely unfounded.

Frank knew this report was eventually going to be considered, along with an investigation into General Clayton Edwards' trip to New York. People were laughing about it all morning. Frank was relieved that General Edwards had not gotten his hands on Adam. Some had expressed the opinion that the General's judgment on this matter was going to result in the end of his career. Frank felt his outlook on so many things would be different for the rest of his life. He realized he wasn't going to be able to forget what he now knew.

Frank had called his father, and discussed his findings with him. At first, his father had been argumentative, but eventually Frank helped him see that his old friend had probably exaggerated the situation. He might have seen his old boss, and he might have looked younger than he should have, but he certainly didn't still look like he was forty. Frank assured his father he had met with Adam personally. He told his father he looked like he was a young sixty-five, with skin stretched back probably from surgery. His father accepted his explanation. Frank hoped that was the end of it. Frank also had a long talk with Dino Argento, and he was relatively certain Dino was going to keep quiet.

Chapter 73

They had been in the castle for three days. Adam was pleased to find the building had been beautifully maintained. Victor Munson was the head butler, and man about the house. He had been living at Balmoor for ten years and his wife, Mattie, was the cook. He had hired all the other present staff members. He explained to Mr. Nathan that he preferred to avoid the term "servant." Besides himself and his wife, there were four staff members. A grounds keeper; a young woman who was his wife's assistant; and two other women, a mother and daughter, who cared for the rest of the house.

Balmoor Castle was a lot to care for. It consisted of twenty-nine rooms on two floors, and a partial third floor at one end of the building. On the second floor on the northeast side of the building, you could see the North Sea from every window.

In recent years, the building had been modernized with electricity and modern plumbing. Adam couldn't help but notice that it had been done in a way as to maintain the original look of the building. Stone walls had been opened to install electrical wires and plumbing, and then closed up.

Adam found Victor to be a very competent, and fair man. He spoke with him at length, and asked many questions he thought the new owner of a castle would ask. He knew the answers to many of the questions, but not all of them.

One of the questions was what it cost to modernize. The kitchen looked like it could be in an exclusive L.A. restaurant, and all eleven bathrooms looked relatively new. Victor explained that a previous owner, back in the late sixteen hundreds, set up a maintenance account with what had been the Bank of Norwich. The account was to generate income to pay a permanent staff to care for the castle. The bank had set up a trust in the name of the castle, when the owner abandoned the building. The trustee oversaw the finances for the staff at that time, and that trusteeship has continued to the present.

Victor told Adam that the old Norwich Bank had been bought out thirty years earlier by the Bank of Scotland, but that the trust account for the castle had not only remained in tact, but had grown over the years. Four years earlier, a newly appointed trustee visited Balmoor to see the place for herself. She thought the building was well maintained, but she was disappointed it had not been modernized in many years. There was already electricity and plumbing, but it was very old.

She explained to Victor that the trust account over the centuries had grown to more than three million pounds. She strongly recommended a thorough modernizing, and assured Victor that all expenses would be approved. In all, the renovations including the kitchen and all the bathrooms had cost about a million pounds. There were new light fixtures installed to replace most of the old ones. Many of them were reproductions custom-made to maintain the original appearance.

A new well had been drilled, and a sprinkler system was installed in all the gardens and lawns. Telephone wires were run in the walls as well, so there could be phones more conveniently located throughout the building.

All the fireplaces had been checked and repaired. All the chimneys had been pointed, so every fireplace was useable. New heating equipment had been installed, including a large commercial boiler, located in what had once been the "shield" room. Hot water pipes had been installed on the first floor and holes had been cut in the ceiling at strategic locations, to allow heat to get to the second floor. All the holes were finished with antique iron gratings, making them look like they were original.

Adam was also pleasantly surprised to find that several new outbuildings had been added. One was a small winery. The vineyards had been well maintained, and expanded. They were now producing enough grapes to yield over three thousand bottles of wine each year. The trustee had entered into a business arrangement with a local man to lease the vineyards and the winery. They produced a red table wine called "Balmoor." Victor showed a bottle to Adam. The label had a picture of the castle on it. Adam made a mental note to talk with the trustee about the lease on the vineyard. He thought he and Gus might want to become vintners themselves.

He knew that the account set up all those years ago did not include any authority on the part of the trustee that superseded the authority of any owner. When he established the account, he included a code number that would be passed down from generation to generation, through his family. Should a future owner know that code, it would tell the bank they were dealing with someone who had the authority to change, or even discontinue the trust. He wondered if the code had been passed down all these centuries.

Today, Adam was going to spend some time in the library. The library at Balmoor was large. The room was twenty-six feet wide, and forty-two feet long. There were shelves from floor to ceiling on all four walls. In the middle of the room was a large table. It was kin to the desk Adam had taken with him when he left the castle. That desk was due to arrive back in its original home in a few weeks. Around the table were four large overstuffed chairs. The library was on the southeast corner of the building, and sunlight came in the east-facing windows all morning, and the south-facing windows for a good part of the afternoon.

Adam had not spent time in this room in over three hundred years. Many of the books on the shelves were brought here by him, when he first purchased the castle in sixteen sixty. Some of his earlier journals were on the shelf where he left them. He looked down at the two boxes on the floor. Soon, those would be on the shelves with the others. The books on the shelves only covered brief periods of time.

Some of the books were there from previous owners of the castle. There were books that went back to the middle fourteen hundreds. There were several early Bibles that were massive. Adam thought he should donate them to some museums. He browsed the shelves, reacquainting himself with the books. When he had lived here previously, he knew every book. His eyes traveled from one end of each shelf to the other, as he familiarized himself with the books again.

He came to some of the books he and Isaac Newton had discussed so many times, years ago. Some were the earliest written theories on the universe, and some were the earliest texts on mathematics.

As his eyes passed over these books, something caught his attention. There was something in between two of the books that he did not recognize. He pulled it out, it was an envelope. It was sealed, and on the outside was written "Andrew Smith — personal." Even though it had been three hundred years ago, Adam recognized the handwriting as that of Isaac Newton. He took the envelope over to a chair and sat down. He stared at it for several minutes before opening it.

Chapter 74

Celia Harris opened her front door, and reached around to the mailbox that hung alongside the door. She pulled out the small bundle of envelopes with a rubber band around them. She noticed the arms under the mailbox held a catalog, and she grabbed that, too. Celia lived in Connecticut with her husband Rodney, and two of their four children. Two were grown and married, with children of their own, and they lived in Massachusetts. She and Rodney had moved to Connecticut eight years ago, when Rodney's company moved. Keeping his job required that he relocate, and although they had been hesitant, they were now very happy in Connecticut. They had many new friends, and they still lived close enough to all their old friends that they could see them several times a year.

Of their children who still lived at home, one of their daughters had married someone she didn't know as well as she should have. The marriage lasted only a year, and she moved back home. She was divorced, and soured on relationships. Celia figured she and Rodney would have her living with them until they were in an old-folks home.

Their youngest son, Matt, was twenty, and in his second year of college. They expected one day he was going to be either a lawyer, or a ball player. They weren't sure which. He was a talented ball player, and he was a starter on the varsity team. Celia and Rodney were of the old school that sports was great as a learning experience, but it was no career.

Lately, Matt had been telling them about all the multi-million-dollar-per-year deals baseball players were making, and they had to admit times had changed. A good baseball player in the Major Leagues was now able to make more money in one year than most lawyers would make in a lifetime. Of course, they all agreed that being a good ball player and being in the majors were two different things.

Celia flipped through the envelopes as she walked into the kitchen, where her cup of coffee was on the table. She sat down as she looked through the envelopes, and was surprised by one of them. It was addressed to her. The envelope was addressed by hand, to their old address, in Massachusetts. Their old address had been crossed out, and a label with their new address had been put on, along with a stamp that said: "Forward." The return address simply said: Gus. No address, just the name. It was from her brother. She stopped and tried to remember the last time she had seen him. She thought it was right after Matt had been born, so that would be about twenty years ago. She remembered he had called a couple of times after that.

She opened the envelope and took out a single page. As she unfolded it, something dropped onto the table. She picked it up and looked at it. It was a bank treasurer check made out to her in the amount of five hundred thousand dollars. She gasped, and felt a pounding sensation in her head as she looked at the check in disbelief. She put the check down and read the letter. It was dated last Thursday.

My dear sister,

I am writing to you because I am going to be leaving the country tomorrow, and I expect that I will never have the opportunity to return. Please don't worry about me. Life has been very good to me, and I'm not in any trouble. It's just that circumstances have arisen that I have no control over, and so I will be leaving. I'm sorry I haven't seen you in so long, or that I haven't even called you in the last six years. Sometimes I wonder where the time goes. I haven't been anywhere near as good a brother as you have been a sister. I hope that Rodney and the kids are all well. I am enclosing a check that I want you to use any way you see fit. I have done quite well for myself, and I feel better sharing it with you before I go.

I love you, Sis, and I will always miss you. Please give Rodney a big hug for me, and kiss all the kids.

Your brother,
Gus

Celia read the letter three times with tears streaming down her face. He was right. She *had* been a better sister than he had been a brother, but she loved him all the same, and it was clear from this letter she would never see him again.

She picked the check up, and looked at it for a long time. There was certainly plenty she could do with the money. She had a fleeting thought the check wasn't real, that it was some sort of a bad joke, but Gus had never been a practical joker. She was sure that the check was real.

Rodney had a good job, and they were not careless with their money. They had plenty of bills to pay and they were paying for Matt's college, which was a big chunk of money every month. She looked at the check. A half million dollars. She wondered how much of that would have to be paid in taxes. She thought that even if it was half, it still meant that there was two hundred and fifty thousand dollars.

She thought about all the things they could do with the money. She thought they would want to pay off the mortgage, although they only owed about thirty thousand dollars. They had sold a house when they moved, so their mortgage was fairly small.

The idea struck her like a bolt of lightning. Her husband had taken his car in for servicing recently. It was a six-year-old Honda. She had followed him to the dealer, because they were going to leave the car for the day. He insisted that she come into the showroom and look at the new two-seater convertible on the floor. She had to admit it was a beauty, but it also had a price tag of thirty-four thousand dollars, and they had a son in college.

Rodney assured her he had no thoughts of buying it, but he did say that it would be the first thing he would buy, if he ever had the money. She took the phone book out of a drawer and looked up the number for the dealer. She looked at the clock. It was ten-thirty in the morning. She was sure they could have that car in the driveway before her husband came home at five. She dialed the number and as the phone rang she picked up the check and looked at it again.

Chapter 75

Adam sat in a chair in the library, and carefully opened the envelope in his hand. It was a letter written to him. Looking at it brought back memories of the profound sadness he felt when he left over three hundred years ago.

September 20, 1693

Dearest Andrew,

I have been here at Balmoor since late April. When you did not answer my letters from February, I had to come and find out why. How surprised and shocked I was to find that you had gone and left no forwarding address, much like a scoundrel might do. I cannot imagine what has precipitated such an unexpected turn of events.

I have remained here now for almost five months, hoping that your return might be as sudden as your departure, but it seems that such is not to be. I regret that I have never expressed to you over the years the fondness I have felt for you. At times, I have considered you as a brother, while at other times, I have thought of you much as a father to me. I never knew my father, or any father for that matter. My childhood recollection is that of being raised by my grandmother on my mother's side. She was a kindly old woman who took good care of me, and I shall always be grateful. However, you have been the closest thing to a father I have ever known, and my heart is heavily burdened with the sadness of your departure, and my inability to find you.

To whom shall I look for inspiration? Who will enlighten me so that I may pass the enlightenment on to others, and claim it as my own? Never before have I known anyone to possess your intellectual generosity, nor have I been acquainted with anyone who has your understanding of grand things.

You are, in a word, irreplaceable, my dear friend, and I fear that I shall never see you or speak to you again.

I can only hope that you are well and that you will think of me fondly, as I shall think of you. I leave this letter here in hopes that one day you will return and find it in between these, our favorite subjects of discussion, mathematics and the universe.

Goodbye my dear friend, wherever you may be.

Your Friend,
Isaac N.

Adam folded the letter carefully and put it back in the envelope. He slid the envelope back in between the two books. He could not help but feel sadness as he recalled those times, but it was three hundred years ago, and the passing of so much time was a welcomed buffer from the profound sadness he had experienced.

He unpacked the two boxes of books and found space for them on the shelves. He folded the boxes flat, and took them out to the kitchen where Mattie was working on the evening meal. He asked her where he should discard the cardboard, and she pointed him toward a large trash bin out behind the garage.

Today, the local movers were due to arrive with Stanley's things from his apartment. Stanley was given two rooms of his own on the first floor, plus a small bathroom. Adam was very pleased with Stanley, although he and Gus had gotten into an unexpected discussion about why they suddenly needed a new driver. Gus told Adam he thought half the reason he wanted him along was to be the driver. Now they get to England, and Adam hires a new driver.

Adam explained to Gus he was concerned about his learning to drive on the other side of the road. He didn't want to be causing accidents. Gus assured him that he would have had no trouble learning to drive on the left. Adam explained the real reason he asked Gus to come with him was because of his need of a friend. He told Gus he could always hire a driver, but he could never hire a friend, and that was what Gus was, a friend. Besides, Gus was getting older, and it was one thing when the car he was driving was a company car, but now, Adam said, the car was his. When they both stopped laughing, Gus finally acknowledged he had gotten sick of driving anyway.

Adam called the bank and spoke with someone in the trust department. He explained he was the new owner of Balmoor, and that the castle had been owned by a distant relative back when the trust account was originally set up. He was told the woman who oversaw the account would call him back shortly.

They were true to their word, because the woman phoned only twenty minutes later. Her name was Barbara Grady, and she sounded young. She told Adam how excited she was to have an owner living in the castle. To the best of her knowledge, there hadn't been an owner living there in over three hundred years. He told her that she was correct, and he commended her on her knowledge of the place. April, sixteen ninety-three was the last time his distant relative Andrew Smith lived in the castle. "In fact," he explained, "he was the one who set up the account to maintain the castle in the first place." She commended *him* for *his* knowledge of the castle, and then asked him if he had ever heard any stories about a secret code that would enable a person to control the trust account. Adam told her that he not only had heard the stories, but he was quite familiar with the code himself.

There was a long, awkward pause at the other end. "So then, that is to be the end of the account, I imagine," she said. Adam could picture the frown on her face. He assured her such was not the case at all, but he would like to meet her. She was going to be out to see him at two this afternoon. He asked her to bring all the records she had. She told him that would be several boxes, and he said it didn't matter. She agreed to bring it all with her, and she would see him at two. Adam looked at the grandfather clock in the corner of the room. It was one-thirty.

Chapter 76

Barbara Grady was on Route A-47 heading to Great Yarmouth from Norwich. She had two large boxes of papers in the back seat of her car. She was anxious to meet Mr. Nathan, who seemed to know quite a bit about Balmoor. She had taken over as the trust conservator five years ago. She researched the castle at Balmoor once she became responsible for its upkeep. She was the kind of person who wanted to know everything she could about such a place, once it was in her charge.

Barbara was thirty-three years old. She had never been married, but she did have several boyfriends at various times, including one she had presently. Shortly after she had taken over the trust for Balmoor, her supervisor had advised her to go out and check on the place. He suggested she think about modernizing the castle to help maintain its property value. He also reminded her that the estate had grown quite large, and it could appear to be negligent if the building was not properly maintained.

She had overseen the entire renovation project, even staying out there for days at a time, while the work was being done. The renovation had taken eight months. She felt like the castle was her second home.

She knew construction on the castle had begun in fifteen fifty-five by King Edward the Sixth, as a summer home. Edward was the son of the infamous King Henry the Eighth. In fifteen fifty-six, King Edward died and his half-sister Mary Tudor became Queen Mary the First. She had the castle at Balmoor finished, although she never set foot in it. She appointed her cousin the first Duke of Balmoor, and he lived in the castle from fifteen fifty-eight until his untimely death, in fifteen sixty-three. The castle then remained abandoned for many years until it was offered for sale by the royal family in sixteen sixty-two. That's when it was purchased by a relatively unknown person named Andrew Smith.

Rumor had it that Sir Isaac Newton had spent a great deal of time at Balmoor when he was young, but Barbara never found any proof of that. She loved the castle, and felt that she had really contributed toward its being a useable residence with the renovations she had undertaken.

She pulled into the drive leading to the castle a few minutes before two. It was a beautiful fall day. The sun was shining brightly, and she noticed how beautiful the gardens were. As she pulled into the circular drive in front of the castle, she noticed the Rolls. There weren't too many cars like that in this territory. She parked near the front entrance and got out of her car. As she walked to the front entrance, she felt a little nervous. She took hold of the massive knocker on the door, and gave it three sharp wraps.

Victor's face lit up when he saw her there. She had been delightful to work with on the renovation project, often asking for his opinion and taking his advice. She had made him feel like he was part of the process. It had been a boost to his sense of dignity, and he would be forever grateful.

Barbara liked him, equally. He was a wonderful husband to Mattie, and Barbara knew that good loyal men were far and few between. She had tremendous respect for him. She also knew, from others, how fair he was to everyone on the staff. She hugged him and kissed him on the cheek. She hadn't been out to the castle in almost a year. "Victor, it's so good to see you. How's Mattie?"

"She's still the best, Miss Grady. How are you?"

"I'm great, Victor, thanks. I guess you have a new tenant?" She was smiling widely.

"That we do, a Mr. Benjamin Nathan, from the States."

She looked at him with a quizzical look. "The United States?"

He nodded. "Those are the ones."

"My, what makes him come all the way out here?"

"I believe he's related to one of the original owners, actually."

Barbara looked at him. "So he says. I can't wait to meet him, Victor. Where is he?"

"In the library, miss. Why don't you follow me?"

"No need. I know where the library is," and as she said this, she headed down the main corridor to the library.

When she got there she peeked in and saw a man sitting in one of the chairs, reading a book. She knocked on the trim around the door and he looked up. He got up, and walked over to her. He was younger than she expected. Her guess was mid-forties. He was good-looking, and he seemed friendly. As he approached her he extended his hand. "You must be Miss Grady. My name is Ben Nathan."

She took his hand and shook it with a firm grip, "Hello, Mr. Nathan. Please call me Barbara."

"All right, Barbara. Thanks for coming out to see me."

"Are you kidding? I'm thrilled to have someone living in this place besides hired help. And from our conversation I take it you go back to the original owner other than the Royals, Andrew Smith. I'm hoping you can tell me a little about him."

Adam looked at her with an apologetic look. "I'm afraid I don't really know any more about Mr. Smith than you do. He goes so far back that no one in my family really could tell me anything about him."

She looked genuinely disappointed. "I'm sorry to hear that, Mr. Nathan. I was hoping to fill in some blank spaces."

"Please, call me Ben. I wish I could help you, but I don't know much about him. I do know that he was friendly with Isaac Newton for a time."

Her eyes widened. "Really? I've heard that he spent time here, but I couldn't find any proof. I've wondered if it was true."

Adam was glad he could give her some information she didn't already have. "Oh, it's true all right. As a matter of fact, I happened to stumble on this letter a little while ago," as he spoke, he pulled the envelope back out from between the two books. "It's a letter from Isaac Newton to Andrew Smith from over three hundred years ago. Apparently they were close friends, and then Smith just disappeared." He handed the envelope to her.

She looked at it as if she were holding something extremely fragile. She looked at him. "May I read it?"

"Sure, help yourself."

She opened it carefully and stood reading. Adam watched her. She was an extremely attractive young woman. She was dressed in a beige business suit. Her skirt was hemmed stylishly right at her knees. The jacket fit perfectly over a white silk blouse. A simple strand of pearls were the right complement.

He watched as tears suddenly started to run down her cheeks. She made no effort to wipe them. She was unashamed. When she had finished reading the letter, she folded it back up and put it in the envelope. She looked at Adam as she handed it back to him. He found that her unashamed display of emotion made her even more attractive. He walked over to the table, where there was a box of tissues, and picked the box up. He extended it to her without a word, and she pulled several out, dabbing her eyes. "Wow," she said as she wiped away the tears, "I didn't expect anything like that."

Adam chuckled lightly. "I had the same reaction when I read it, so don't feel bad."

He asked her if she had all the papers with her, and she told him they were in the car. He excused himself and found Victor. He asked him to have someone get the two boxes and bring them into the library. He then went back in. They spent several hours going over the trust account. Most of the old records were very simple, and some were not well explained, but she told Adam it was all that could be expected from so long ago. She thought it was quite amazing the trust had remained in tact at all, and that someone hadn't pilfered it a century or more ago. He agreed.

She finally pulled an old file out of the bottom of one of the boxes. It was leather bound, and tied with a strand of leather. Adam thought it was probably several hundred years old. She untied the file and opened it in front of her. Adam was sitting at the other end of the table. He could not see anything in the file.

She looked at him and smiled, "OK, Ben. This is the real moment I've been waiting for. You said you know the code that controls the trust fund. I'd like to hear it."

He laughed, "Oh, you would, would you? And what are you going to do when I tell you what it is?"

She was obviously enjoying this. "I don't know, but it's sort of like that 'Back to the Future' movie where the Western Union man comes up to Marty in the rain, and gives him an envelope from back in the eighteen hundreds.

Adam told her he didn't have the slightest idea what she was talking about.

She looked at him like he was joking. "You never saw any of the 'Back to the Future' movies?"

He shrugged his shoulders. "Sorry, I've hardly ever been to the movies, at all."

She thought about that for a moment while she stared at him. "Really?"

"Really," was all he said in return.

"Well then, let's just say it's intriguing that you might know a code passed down for over three hundred years, just among a man's family members."

Now he was toying a little. "Why is that so intriguing?"

"Oh, come on, Ben. Quit torturing me. If you know the code, I want to hear it."

He got a more serious look on his face. "All right, Barbara, the code is zero, one, one, four, three, three." He watched her as she looked down at the file and then up at him.

"You're right, that *is* the code. My god, I can't believe it. You really do know it. I just can't believe it."

He laughed, as he found her amazement amusing.

She looked for a long time across the table at him, and they didn't speak. Finally, she broke the silence, "What are you going to do?"

He didn't understand her question. "What do you mean?"

"With the trust. What are you going to do with it?"

"Nothing."

"Nothing?"

"Well, almost nothing. I would like to suspend any payments toward the maintenance of the place while I'm living here. I can take care of things on my own."

"Anything else?"

"Well, if I ever leave, I want the maintenance arrangement put back in place."

"Why?"

He was surprised by the question. "What do you mean, why?"

"I mean why would you want to do that? If you leave this place, why wouldn't you just let it be maintained by whoever buys it? Why wouldn't you take the money out of the trust for yourself? It's a little over two million pounds."

"I don't need the money, Barbara. And I might leave here, and leave the place to some relative who will show up a hundred years from now. I would want them to find things as I did, well taken care of."

She accepted that answer, and they discussed other aspects to the property. He expressed his interest in the vineyards, and she explained the lease arrangement was only year-to-year. He could start next spring if he chose to, but this year's harvest and wine would rightfully belong to the people leasing the vineyards presently. Their lease gave them storage rights in the barrels for their vintage for two years. She explained that each year, as they bottled a vintage, those barrels became ready for the next year's batch. The wine was fermented for two years, so there were enough barrels for three years' vintages.

Adam was impressed by how much this young woman knew. By the time they were done, it was almost four-thirty. He invited her to stay for dinner, but she declined, saying that she really needed to get back. Adam had the boxes put back in her car. He told her she was welcome at Balmoor anytime, and he hoped she would be back soon. She shook his hand, and told him she would be back real soon. She asked him what he was going to do with the letter from Isaac Newton, and he told her he hadn't thought about it.

She asked if he would consider offering it to some museum, as it was an important piece of history, especially considering it confirmed that Newton had spent time at Balmoor. Adam told her he would think about it. She thanked him for his time and got into her car. As she drove up the drive heading back to the road, she thought about what an excellent day it had been, and what an interesting man Ben Nathan was.

Chapter 77

Paul Fenton didn't recognize the return address on the envelope. It was probably just another real estate group looking to offer their services, should there be a future vacancy. He was the Chairman of the Co-op Committee for one of the most exclusive buildings in New York City. The Central Park West address made real estate people a little crazy. A few years ago, an agent had contacted him representing Barbra Streisand. He remembered how sure that person was that he was going to get excited about the prospect of having her living in his building. The poor woman was quickly deflated when he told her that Ms. Streisand would have to appear before the committee, just like everyone else who might potentially live in the building, and he emphasized "potentially" when he said it.

They were particular about who they let live there. Of course, financial standing was an issue, but it was a given that when the apartments were selling for two million and up, interested parties likely had the financial qualifications. The committee was more concerned about individuals' reputations. Were they quiet people, or were there going to be problems with parties? Parties meant a lot of guests, and guests meant a lot of unauthorized people in the building. The committee tended to reject individuals who drew a lot of attention. They didn't want the media hanging around if they could help it.

Years ago, before the building went condo (which meant before the committee), John Lennon had purchased an apartment. He paid one million eight hundred thousand for it. It faced directly out to Central Park. Today, that apartment was worth over four million. Now, they had to deal with his widow. Paul had to admit she was actually pretty quiet, and never entertained, but there was a residue of photographers that often hung around hoping for a picture.

He slid his sterling silver letter opener under the flap of the envelope, and quickly sliced it open. It was not a solicitation at all. It was a letter notifying him that apartment 4-C, previously owned by Adam Adamson, had recently been sold to a Mr. Benjamin Nathan, and that a new Deed of Ownership had been filed with the clerk of Records, City of New York, Manhattan office.

To Paul, Adam Adamson was merely a ghost. He was another one who bought long before the building went condo. 4-C was a beautiful apartment that also faced the park. The building had been controlled by the condo association for eighteen years, and Paul had been the chairman of the committee for sixteen years, yet he had never met Adam Adamson. To the best of his knowledge, he had never set foot in the building other than the day he came and looked at the apartment. Paul wasn't sure that he came personally even then.

The records showed he purchased the apartment in nineteen seventy-three for two million dollars. As long as he could remember, the apartment had been maintained by a management company. People were in there cleaning every week.

As the chairman of the committee, he had the right to inspect any apartment once a year. It was a right he never exercised with the regular tenants, but two years ago he had notified the management company who took care of 4-C that he wanted to do an inspection. One of the senior people from the management company met him at the apartment. He was pleasantly surprised by what he saw. The furnishings were exquisite. The colors of the walls and drapes were wonderfully coordinated. The apartment was truly a showpiece, right out of a fashion magazine. Everything looked like it was brand-new, except some of it was obviously antique. He left hoping that every apartment looked like that inside.

He read the letter a second time. Well, Mr. Nathan might be the legal owner, but unless he gets approval from the committee he'll never actually be able to live here. This had happened one time since the building went condo. Mr. Barnesworth, who lived in 2-D, passed away leaving the apartment to his daughter who was his only surviving relative. Barnesworth had lived in the building since the late fifties. He originally rented, that's how far back he went. When the building went "condo" in the sense that the apartments could be bought, he purchased his apartment for six hundred thousand dollars. The condo association with a committee didn't form until nineteen eighty-two. When the old man died, his apartment was worth at least two and a half million, in spite of the fact it was in desperate need of a complete interior redo.

His daughter showed up six weeks after he passed away to look at her "new apartment." She was in her early forties, divorced, with three kids ranging in age from twenty down to eleven. Until her father died, her entire financial portfolio consisted of a checking account with an average balance of a few hundred dollars, a savings account with a thousand dollars in it, and a Dodge mini-van, which she owned outright. She also owned two French poodles she took everywhere she went.

When Paul first met her, he wasn't sure whether to laugh or be sick. He had shown her the apartment, and at least she had been on the same page with him regarding what the apartment needed. Of course Paul knew what it cost to get anything done in the city, but Barnesworth's daughter didn't have a clue. She rattled on about doing it herself, slapping on a coat of paint, some slip covers, etc., etc. He really thought he was going to be sick. After she had thoroughly inspected the apartment, he invited her to come to his office where they could discuss other issues related to the apartment.

"What other issues?" She wanted to know. There was a slight hint of antagonism in her voice.

He wanted to be as diplomatic as possible. "Well, the building residency is now governed by the condo association committee. They meet with each potential resident." He emphasized potential. "They determine who will live in the building."

Barnesworth's daughter wasn't stupid and she understood the implication. "You're telling me that even though my father left me this apartment, you get to decide if I can live here or not?"

"It's part of the agreement every owner signed when the association took over."

She was getting a little upset. "Well, let me tell you something, buster. My father also left me three million bucks, and if I have to spend it all on lawyers, that's what I'll do. I plan to live in this apartment."

Paul did not want this to become a yelling contest. He sat quietly while she ranted for a minute or so, and then she, too, sat quietly. He spoke in a calm and collected tone. Her name was Brenda Kent.

"Ms. Kent, there are many factors considered in our determination. Before you get too upset, let me tell you that even if the committee rejected your residency application, you would be in very good company. Six years ago, we told Michael Jackson no, and last year we turned down Madonna, so you shouldn't take it personally if we don't feel that you fit the criteria."

She seemed to calm down. "What criteria?"

"Well, for one thing, children are an issue. This is a very quiet building, and we all like it that way. We want it to stay that way, and this is a major consideration. You have three children, who are all going to have friends they want to bring home. We also have a strict rule regarding pets. Only one pet is allowed in each apartment, not counting birds in cages and fish. You would have to decide on one dog, and get rid of the other." He could see from the look on her face that this was something she considered out of the question.

It had eventually turned into a legal matter, and in the end the court found in favor of the condo association. The ownership agreements signed by every tenant clearly stated that residency of future owners was contingent upon committee approval, and the committee did not need to specify why or what played into their decision. It probably helped that several people who testified in court for the committee were extremely high-powered individuals. Barnesworth's daughter had an offer on the apartment for three million within a week of the court decision. The new owners were a Wall Street banker and his wife, who were in their late fifties. It took the committee ten minutes to approve their residency.

So now, Paul would write a letter to this real estate group informing them that Mr. Nathan would have to make an appointment to come in and talk with the committee before his residency would be accepted. Before coming in, he would also need to fill out an application that would accompany the letter, and certain financial information would also have to be submitted. Paul had never seen Mr. Adamson, but at least he would get to meet Mr. Nathan.

Chapter 78

Barbara Grady had been out to Balmoor Castle three times since she first met Mr. Nathan three months ago. Each time she went, she had a reason for going. Or perhaps, more accurately, she invented reasons for going.

Her second trip out had been with new trustee papers. Since Mr. Nathan had proven his right to control the trust by knowing the code, it seemed appropriate that new papers be drawn up naming him as trustee. Barbara had run this concept by her boss at the bank, and he agreed. She purposely left a little later in the afternoon to deliver these papers, hoping her late afternoon arrival might prompt another dinner invitation.

Ben had been genuinely happy to see her. She watched him read through the trustee papers in about three minutes, which she thought to be impossible. Her assumption was he merely scanned them. But when he finished, he said they were fine except for two minor typographical errors, which he then showed her. They were in different paragraphs on different pages, and they were simple words representing a wrong key hit. His seeing those errors told her he had read the document word for word, but she didn't think it was humanly possible to read eight pages of legal information in three minutes. He signed the papers and handed them back to her. They were sitting in the library, he looked at the clock in the corner, and saw it was late in the afternoon. He extended a dinner invitation, and she hesitantly accepted.

They enjoyed a wonderful dinner and spent several hours after dinner talking. It turned out that he knew far more about Andrew Smith than he had let on. She found his knowledge of the past fascinating. The truth of the matter was she found him to be fascinating. He was like a young/old man. He was so wise and interesting, but he seemed so youthful. She didn't think he was that much older than she.

Her next trip out to the castle was to discuss various investment vehicles the trust might use. In the past, the bank always chose the most conservative course, being responsible for the continued growth. Now that there was a controlling individual, not related to the bank, a more aggressive course could be considered. She arrived later in the afternoon, and again stayed for dinner and conversation. She thought he was showing signs of affection toward her, but she wasn't sure if it was just her wishful thinking.

Her most recent trip out was to bring him several boxes of the old records.

She explained they had just been audited, and that with new trust papers in effect, they were advised to get rid of the old papers.

The auditor explained that seven years was the usual length of time for retention of old records, and these were over three hundred years old! He was sure it was safe to get rid of them. She didn't want to simply discard them, so she brought them out to him.

Shortly after she arrived, it started to rain. By the time they finished dinner it was a terrible storm, and Ben asked her if she wanted to stay the night. It was a Friday, and she didn't have to be at work the next day, so she accepted the invitation. Barbara always carried a toothbrush with her in her purse. She liked to brush her teeth after a meal, no matter where she was. She was glad she did, because she would have been embarrassed to bring up the question of whether or not there was an extra toothbrush in the place.

They talked late into the night, drinking a bottle and a half of Balmoor wine. Finally, Ben said it was time for him to retire for the evening. She hoped he was going to invite her to his bed, but that didn't happen. They walked up the stairs together, and he stopped at a door to one of the guest bedrooms. He thanked her for coming out to Balmoor and bringing the papers. He told her she should find everything she needed in the guest room, and that he would look forward to having breakfast with her in the morning. She stared into his eyes as he spoke. His eyes were piercing blue. She wanted to kiss him, but she dared not. They locked eyes for just a moment, and then it happened. He leaned forward, putting his left hand gently on her right cheek, cupping her cheek and chin in his hand. She could feel his fingers on her right ear. Her heart all but leapt out of her chest. She thought he was going to kiss her. She closed her eyes anticipating what she had been dreaming of for months. And he did kiss her, but it was a tender kiss on her forehead. He took his hand away and stood up straight and their eyes met, again.

She concentrated on not letting her feelings show on her face. She felt both disappointment, and embarrassment for what she had hoped would happen. She was afraid she might have a look on her face he would interpret as her being upset that he had kissed her. She smiled, and he smiled back. She reached for the doorknob and opened the door, as he turned and walked down the hallway. She turned back, and watched to see which door was his bedroom. She watched him open the door and walk in. He never looked back up the hall. She went into the guest room.

The fireplace was lit. She thought that was very special. She had to remember to thank Victor in the morning. On the bed was a set of new silk pajamas. They were her size. She was amazed they would have such an item.

She went into the bathroom off the guest room, and on the vanity was a brand-new toothbrush, still in the box, a small tube of toothpaste, and a stack of towels. Two large bath, a hand towel, and two face cloths. There were three different packages of soaps to choose from. She laughed to herself. Well, if not Ben, maybe she could steal Victor away from Mattie. She washed up and changed into the pajamas. They fit her perfectly. She climbed into the large antique bed, and was amazed at how comfortable it was. She pulled the sheets and thick quilt over her, and lay there thinking about the kiss. She analyzed it, playing it in slow motion in her head. Yes, it had only been a kiss on the forehead. Very fatherly. But the way he had held her face in his hand. It was so tender. So … sensual. And the actual kiss itself. It wasn't a typical fatherly peck. His lips had made full contact, and lingered a split-second longer than "fatherly" would have merited. Yes, she was sure there was more to that kiss than a fatherly good night. She was sure there were feelings there. This was an ultra-conservative man, sending out the first little feeler. She would gladly move at whatever pace worked for him. She was in no hurry.

She had broken it off with her last boyfriend after her second trip out to Balmoor, months ago. It wasn't that she thought then anything would ever develop between her and Ben, but having spent time with him twice made her see the need to raise the bar of her expectations, and her boyfriend at the time wasn't even close.

Now, she was lying in this beautiful old bed hoping he would come sneaking into her room in the night. She would give herself to him without a moment's hesitation, and she told herself it had nothing to do with the money. To her, that was incidental. OK, so he was worth millions of dollars. Her last boyfriend was earning less than she did. Money didn't really matter.

He was charming, and seemed unpretentious. She hadn't found a single fault yet. Maybe *she* should sneak into *his* room. She thought about it as she started to drift off to sleep. The possibility of what might happen was intriguing. Even if he rejected her advance, certainly he wouldn't be upset with her. She was an attractive woman. What man would be offended by a sexual advance, even if unwanted?

She decided to give it a try. She didn't know how long she had been lying in bed, but she was quite sure it was long enough for him to be asleep. She got out of bed, and walked over to her door. She opened it slowly. It didn't make a sound. She peeked out, and looked both ways down the hall, listening for any sound. There was none. Her heart was pounding as she stepped into the hallway and closed her bedroom door behind her. She walked quietly down the hall to the door she saw Ben go into. Her heart felt like it was going to explode. She questioned her sanity, but she reached for the doorknob and slowly turned it. As she did, she wondered if it might be locked from the inside, but it wasn't. She pushed against the door and felt it start to swing open. She opened it just enough to allow herself to slip in, and she closed the door behind her. She was now standing in his bedroom and she was afraid the pounding of her heart might wake him up. She stood there for a few moments while her eyes adjusted to the darkness of the room.

The door to his bathroom was open, and there was a small night light in the bathroom. Finally she could make out the outline of furniture, and the bed. It was a large bed, and she could see him sleeping under the covers. She crept closer to the bed. He slept quietly. His breathing was even and he didn't snore. She took off her pajamas and stood naked by his bedside wondering if she had lost her mind. She very slowly lifted the edge of his bed covers and slipped into the bed next to him. He was facing the other way and as she brought her body up next to his she realized that, he, too, was naked. He started to stir and she reached her arm around him, and put it on his chest as she pressed her body up against his. He was obviously awake now and his arm reached back over himself, and came to rest on the back of her lower thigh. His hand rested there for just a second or two and he started to caress her skin, slowly moving his hand up her thigh. She slowly ran her hand from his chest to his belly, then even lower, where she received confirmation that he was as desirous as she was. He rolled over, and in one move was on top of her. She whispered into his ear, "Please make love to me." And they did. It was glorious and she knew she had never experienced anything like it in her life. Perhaps she had never had a physical relationship with someone she felt so strongly about. She wasn't sure why it was so wonderful, she just knew it was. And it seemed to go on for hours. When they were done and exhausted, she lay in his bed next to him. She thought she had to be the happiest woman in the world. If he never touched her again, she thought she could be happy with just the memory of this night.

There was a tapping sound. To her horror, she realized someone was knocking on the bedroom door. She knew he would not want anyone to know what had happened. Her pajamas were on the floor next to the bed. Why wasn't he moving? Didn't he hear the knocking? She reached over to touch him, and he was gone. She opened her eyes and the room was lighter. Daylight was coming through the drapes. She was surprised to find her pajamas back on her. The knocking on the door came again. She realized she was in her own bed, not Ben's. Had he put her pajamas back on and brought her back to this bedroom? Had she just dreamt the entire thing? There was a third knock on the door and she called out, "Come in."

Her door opened and one of the women staff members, Julie, stuck her head in. "Good morning, mum. Breakfast is served."

Barbara looked at her. "What time is it, Julie?"

"Almost ten, mum."

"Thank you, I'll be down in a few minutes." Julie closed the door, and Barbara closed her eyes for a minute. Her mind was reeling. Was it just a dream? If it was, it was so real it was hard to tell. She went into the bathroom and as she prepared to shower, she checked herself for any telltale signs that their lovemaking was not just a dream. There was no telltale sign.

Breakfast went wonderfully. Ben was his charming self. She was sure her night's activities were only a dream. There wasn't a hint of greater familiarity on his part. For a moment, she found herself wondering if the kiss in the hallway had been part of the dream, but she was sure it wasn't. That *had* actually happened.

Sometime after breakfast, she went into the kitchen for another cup of coffee and Victor was in the kitchen with Mattie. Barbara thanked him for the fire in the fireplace, and asked him how he happened to have new pajamas in her size. Victor told her that after her very first visit to Balmoor, Mr. Nathan had asked him to pick some up the next time he went into Norwich for anything. The little town of Winterton by the Sea had small shops and a little grocery store, but any major items required a trip to Norwich.

She stayed at Balmoor until mid-afternoon on Saturday, after which time she knew it would be awkward to stay. She thanked Ben for everything, gave him a hug, and then as she let go of the hug, kissed him on the cheek. He kissed her back on the cheek. She gave Gus a hug, too. She had gotten to know him pretty well, and she liked him very much.

Now she had run out of excuses to go out to Balmoor, and she wasn't sure what to do. She was desperate to be back in the warmth of Ben's company. She knew she was in love with him, and that he probably did not feel the same way about her. She also knew she could wind up making a real fool out of herself, and there was the likelihood of getting hurt. She knew she had never really been in love before. Her past boyfriends had really meant nothing. She hadn't loved any of them, she simply liked them.

She decided it didn't make sense to try to make up some excuse to go to the castle. Why not simply say that she came out there because it was where she wanted to be. It might be a little forward, but wasn't it time to take a chance? Let him know she had feelings for him? She packed a small overnight bag with some items that would allow her to stay a few days. It was Friday, and she was hoping to stay through Sunday. She would tell her supervisor she had to go out to Balmoor on bank business Friday afternoon. The money in the Balmoor trust was earning quite a bit, and with none of it going out in expenses, it was growing and compounding. The commissions being paid to the trust division were substantial. Her supervisor was so happy with the account and the way she was handling it, she knew she could do just about anything she wanted.

As she headed out for work, she told herself this weekend was it. She was going to tell Ben Nathan she loved him, even if it meant never seeing him again.

Chapter 79

Adam and Gus decided they didn't really want to be in the wine business. Adam was going to renew the lease with the people who were presently handling it. He would offer to provide financial assistance, if they wanted to expand the operation. He thought the wine they produced was very good, and he also thought it might be nice to produce a white wine, perhaps a chardonnay.

Adam had been a workaholic for over forty years, and he was enjoying a long-needed rest, but lately he and Gus had been talking about what he was going to do. They had been at Balmoor for more than four months, and Gus knew that Adam couldn't sit around and do nothing forever. He didn't mean literally forever, he meant figuratively forever.

There were two companies in Great Britain involved in communications and satellite related fields. This is what Adam had been doing for so long he was most comfortable staying with it, but he wasn't sure he would be able to avoid having to meet with any U.S. counterparts. He knew that could present a risk.

One company was British Technologies, just south of London. The other was Space Sciences, Inc., and they were located a hundred and twenty miles east of London in Bristol.

Adam had come to really enjoy the castle. Its original charm, combined with all the added modern conveniences, made the place irresistible. He wanted to make an offer to one of those companies, but he didn't like the idea of having to live close to them. He decided he was going to try British Technologies. If they accepted his offer, he would purchase a helicopter and hire a pilot. He figured he could fly from Balmoor to the office in about twenty minutes. There was ample space to land a helicopter at the castle, and they would have to make space at British Technologies.

Victor brought in the day's mail. Adam looked through it, and picked out an envelope from the property management agent in L.A. that handled all the property transfers. He was curious as to what this was about.

They received a regular retainer from him for several properties they maintained, but all their invoices went to his accountant and the accountant paid the bills. He opened the envelope, and read the letter. It explained their receipt of a reply from the New York property. They had forwarded the financial sheet to his accountant. The condo committee was requesting a return of the application, along with the financial sheet, and then he would need to make an appointment to go to New York City to meet with these people. He needed to talk with his accountant about what he wanted him to do, and he needed to talk with the property management people about what he wanted them to do. Adam felt it would be in his long-term interest to hold onto the Manhattan property. If it meant a trip to New York City, so what? No one there knew him, so it shouldn't be a problem.

He picked up the phone and called his accountant. They talked for five minutes. Then he called the property management people in L.A. He told them to wait for the credit information, go ahead and fill out the rest, and if they had any questions, call the accountant. He would get them the answers, and send it all back to New York with a note asking for notification as to when they wanted to meet. He required a two-week advance notice. When they got a call from New York, they were to call the accountant with the date and time, and he would pass the information on. He hung up the phone.

It was Friday afternoon, and Ben phoned the Bank of Scotland in Norwich. He wanted to ask Barbara to check into British Technologies for him to find out what their market position was, and what they were working on. Who was the head of the company? He could do it himself, but it was a reason to call her. He really liked her.

He was amazed to find that after centuries of living without the companionship of a woman, he was suddenly attracted to her. She was beautiful, so there was no surprise from *that* aspect. But he had known many beautiful women over the years. Some of them were exceptional, yet he never felt genuinely attracted to them.

The receptionist told him that Barbara had left for the day. He looked at his watch and found it was only one-thirty. He thanked her and hung up, a little disappointed. He decided to talk with Stanley about making a trip to British Technologies one day next week. He would give himself through Wednesday to find out what he wanted to know. Thursday would be a good day to make the trip.

He got up to go to Stanley's room. As he walked down the hall, there was a knock on the front door. The huge iron knocker could be heard through the entire castle. Adam was almost directly at the door when the knock came, and he walked to the door himself and opened it. He was surprised to see Barbara standing at the door, and she was equally surprised to see him answering the door.

He spoke first, "Barbara, what a pleasant surprise. I just called your office looking for you, and they said you were gone for the day. Come on in." He stepped out of the way and she came in. He closed the door.

She looked at him with a smile. "What did you do, give the help the day off?"

He realized she was referring to his opening the door. He laughed, "No, I just happened to be right here when you knocked. I couldn't see just walking by and waiting for Victor to run from wherever he was," as he said this, Victor did come around a corner, seemingly in a hurry.

He had heard the door, but he was upstairs and had hurried down to answer it. He was also surprised to see Ben had beaten him to it. He smiled at the both of them, "Good afternoon, Ms. Grady. How nice to see you."

She smiled back, "Hi, Victor, it's nice to be here. As a matter of fact, it's always nice to be here." Victor wasn't sure what to do with that comment so he simply smiled, turned, and walked away. This left Ben and Barbara standing in the hall.

He looked at her. "So, what brings you out here on a Friday afternoon?"

She had planned this moment over and over in her head on her way out here. She looked him in the eyes, and concentrated on not looking away as she spoke, "There simply wasn't anywhere else that I wanted to be, so here I am." She swallowed and tried not to look as frightened as she was. They stood looking at each other for a long moment. He had a serious look on his face. She wanted so much to know what he was thinking.

Finally his face softened, and he put his arms around her and hugged her. It was a long, wonderful hug. She could have melted into his arms, if it lasted a little longer. When they finally separated, he looked at her again. "You're interestingly bold. Do you know that?"

She smiled, "Why, because I know what I want and I'm willing to take the chance to express it?"

"That's reason enough, don't you think?"

"Look, Ben, I know you're older than me, but some things are different for women than for men. Men can get better looking with age. If they take care of themselves, they can be much sexier as they get older. That doesn't happen with women. I'm thirty-three, and I'm not going to get sexier or more attractive as I reach forty or fifty. Time isn't on my side like it is on yours."

Ben tried to think of how many times he had been in a situation similar to this. Women trying to take a relationship further than friendship. It was why he eventually tried to avoid relationships with women altogether. But for some reason he couldn't understand, he felt "different" about this woman. He wanted to take this relationship beyond friendship, but he knew the complications made it so difficult, if not impossible.

He knew he was falling in love with this woman. He could marry her, but he would have to tell her the truth first. She would grow older, and he would not. She was thirty-three. That would give them twenty years where things would be all right. He could alter her diet somewhat, and give her some supplements that would do for her what they did for Gus and she could probably look close to his age until she was at least sixty, or maybe even seventy. But at some point, she would simply get old, and eventually she would die. He had always felt that such heartache was not worth it. But with Barbara he felt differently. He wondered if some biological clock was finally kicking in, after more than six thousand years. Then, there was the issue of children. His father had warned him shortly before his death at the age of nine hundred and thirty, not to have children. That warning had stuck with him all these centuries. He knew any children he had would be perfect like him, and would only age to a certain point, then maintain that age. Jesus had confirmed that for him when they talked. He had explained his being born of a human woman didn't alter his perfection, because he was not conceived by an imperfect man. His conception had been through Holy Spirit, so an imperfect woman could give birth to a perfect human.

It was the same with Adam. He was perfect, so an imperfect woman, impregnated by him, would still be able to give birth to a perfect human. How could he explain all of this to Barbara? How could he tell her in a way that would make sense? He wasn't going to get older, while she would age and die.

How could he say their children would be like him, and never get old? If they had children, and they were like him, would it present the same danger today that it might have presented years ago?

He had financial resources today that were, for all practical purposes, inexhaustible. Even major economic depressions could only have a slight effect on him. He had thirty million dollars in gold bullion in a Swiss bank vault. He had twenty million dollars worth of diamonds in another bank vault, and that twenty million was based on values from twenty years ago. Today, they might be worth more than thirty million. He owned several valuable properties. He had over a hundred million dollars on deposit in each of three other banks, and he had over three hundred million on deposit with Credite Suisse.

In all, he estimated his net worth at the moment to be close to a billion dollars. There were far richer people in the world, but most of them were wealthy based on stock values and other intangible things. His wealth was solid and liquid. What would be the challenge to raise children under his circumstances? Eventually he would have to explain a lot of things to them, but that wouldn't be impossible. And his wealth would provide a permanent ability for his offspring to stay out of the limelight and maintain a very enjoyable and useful life, so why not have children? He didn't know the answers to any of those questions, but he knew now he would have to figure out the answers, because something was different about this woman.

They spent the afternoon talking, and Victor served them a delightful dinner. Gus ate with them, and Ben and Gus reminisced about some of their experiences in the recent past. Gus knew he had to avoid any discussion that went back far enough to make her wonder about Ben's age.

After dinner, Ben and Barbara took a walk outside. It was a beautiful night and she wanted to walk in the garden. Gus excused himself, saying he was retiring to his computer. He was teaching himself Russian. He had actually started a while ago, but he was finding it more difficult than expected.

Ben and Barbara strolled through the south garden. It was beautifully laid out, with low lighting along the paths. There were the typical comments about how nice the night was, and how lovely the stars were, and then, there were a few minutes of silence as they walked. Barbara felt this was the right time to continue her earlier conversation.

"Ben, I hope you're not upset with me for coming out here this weekend."

He hesitated for a few seconds. "I'm not upset at all, Barbara. I'm actually quite pleased."

"Really? You're not just saying that?"

He chuckled. "No, I'm not just saying that."

She took a deep breath. "You know I'm in love with you, don't you?"

He was silent for a little while as they walked. "I knew you had feelings for me, but I'm not sure I would say I knew you loved me."

"Well I do. So how does that make you feel?"

"I'm not sure."

"You're not sure? Is it that you're not sure if it makes you happy, or sad?"

"Barbara, please. You're a beautiful, intelligent, funny woman, and any man would be crazy not to want you. It's not a question of happy or sad, it's a question of desire balanced against fear."

She stopped walking and looked at him. "Fear of what?"

He looked at her. She was so beautiful. He was feeling desires that he had never allowed himself to feel before. "Barbara, it's so complicated, I don't know how to even begin."

She looked confused. "What could be so complicated? Is it the money? I'll sign a prenuptial agreement, I couldn't care less about your money."

He wanted to laugh, but he knew it wouldn't be right. She was so serious. "No, it has nothing to do with money. I could give you a hundred million dollars tomorrow and it wouldn't mean a thing to me."

He saw tears start to run down her cheeks as she looked up at him. "Then tell me. What is it that's so complicated it could stop us from sharing our love with one another?" she said, as she reached out with one hand, and touched his face. It was a tender caress, and it made him desire her even more.

He looked at her. "Let me think about all of this, Barbara. There's a lot that I have to sort out. I promise you; tomorrow we'll discuss all of this in great detail. Tonight, let's just enjoy the garden and each other's company." She agreed, and they walked to a bench in the garden. They sat. He pointed out many stars, and a few planets that were visible to the naked eye. She was amazed at how much he knew about everything.

As they talked, they held hands. The touch of his hand in hers was more satisfying to her than she could have imagined. Her hand in his brought him face to face with desires that he had managed to put in the back of his mind. He knew he was going to have to take a chance, and reveal everything to this woman. His heart told him that doing so would not endanger him. Even if it made her change her mind, he was confident that she would not reveal him to anyone else. He had to think about how to tell her.

Later, as they sat in the library, she asked him why he had called her office earlier. He explained his thinking about going to work and he needed information about this company just south of London, in a town called Chatham. She was delighted he had thought of her to do the research. She said she had the ability on her computer at work to dig up everything he wanted to know in a matter of minutes. He was impressed, and told her he would expect a phone call with the information by noon on Monday. She laughed, and told him there would be a slight "expediting fee" for getting the information that quickly. He asked her how much, and she told him ten million dollars. He laughed, told her that was a little steep, and he wouldn't pay a penny over five million and that was his final offer. They both laughed for a long time.

Eventually, they walked upstairs. He again stopped at her bedroom door. She looked at him, and he could tell her brain was speeding at a hundred-miles an hour. He looked at her. "What are you thinking?"

She waited a few seconds longer. "I'm thinking I don't want to sleep alone in this bed tonight. I'm thinking I want to sleep with you. That I want to make love with you, and I don't really want to sleep at all."

He looked at her for a long moment silently. "That sounds wonderful, but I can't do that."

"Why not? We're both adults, this is your home, why can't you do that?"

"I guess it's part of that complicated story I promised to tell you tomorrow."

She got a worried look on her face. "You're not going to tell me about some war injury, are you? If you can't have sex, I want you to tell me right now. I don't want to wait until tomorrow. I'm serious!"

Ben smiled, "Barbara, it's nothing like that. There are no war injuries, don't worry."

She lightened the moment by wiping the back of her hand across her forehead. As she did so, she said, "Whew!" They both laughed. Then, they stopped laughing and looked at each other with mutual desire. He leaned forward and kissed her. This time it was on the lips, and there was nothing fatherly about it. They put their arms around each other and kissed for a long time. Finally, they separated. She looked at him with longing, "You sure I can't convince you to spend the night in here, with me?"

"I'm sure, darling, although there's nothing I'd rather do. We'll discuss it tomorrow."

She knew he wasn't going to change his mind, and she didn't want to put him on the spot. "OK. Good night." She smiled, as she went into her room.

He walked to his room and went in. As he did, he looked back down the hall at the door to her room. He shook his head, went into his room, and closed the door.

She took a long hot bath and thought about all they discussed. She wondered what complication he could be talking about. She climbed into bed and found that she could not stop thinking about that last conversation. It seemed like hours before she fell asleep.

He took a shower and set the water a little colder than usual. He had conditioned himself long ago not to think about sex. He knew the problems that could result from dwelling on the subject. He had seen the sad results for thousands of years. He climbed into bed, and thought about tomorrow.

He had only revealed the truth of his existence to a dozen or so people in all of six thousand years. All of them had been fiercely loyal to him. None had ever revealed anything to anyone. He had been able to help these people, through diet and additional compounds that he knew of, to live far longer than average. One had lived to almost a hundred and thirty. He expected that Gus would live to well over a hundred. He was in his late sixties now, and he looked a little over fifty.

He had already decided he could trust Barbara with the truth. He had no idea what effect it would have on her desire for him. He would soon find out. He drifted off to sleep, thinking about a life with her. Having a family was such a strange concept to him. He had told himself for so long it would never be, until that time that Jesus had told him would come eventually. “Then,” Jesus had said, “you’ll be no different from anyone else.” Then, he wouldn’t have to worry about hiding himself.

Chapter 80

Frank Saunders sat in the waiting room. He was a few minutes early for his appointment with Doctor Ambura.

Peter Ambura was an Indian man in his late thirties. He had been a psychiatrist for five years, before branching off into family counseling. He found psychiatry too depressing. It always made him laugh when he thought about that. It was like an ice cream man with lactose intolerance. But the fact was, the people he dealt with started to have a negative impact on him, and he was intelligent enough to see the need for change.

He started working with people having marriage problems seven years ago. It was more uplifting, because he found he was able to help a good number of his patients. He was happily married, and felt he had a real handle on what made marriages work. His psychiatric training had already taught him to be a very good listener, and it seemed to be a natural move.

Frank had been having a problem with his wife ever since his encounter with Adam Adamson. He had changed. He couldn't put his finger on everything that had changed, but he knew he had started to take some things in life more seriously. He wanted to spend more time with his wife and children. It wasn't that they were opposed to it, but it seemed so contrary to the way he had been for so long, they found the change a little worrisome.

He was less interested in his work, and that had always been his life. He also had bought a Bible. It was a Bible written in modern English, and he was now reading it for an hour or so, every night. That really worried them, because Frank had never given two hoots about religion. He was bringing things up that he read, as if everyone else should be as interested as he was. And he talked about Adam Adamson all the time. He would say he wondered where he went. Or, he hoped he was all right. He would make comments like: "If I ever told you what I know, you'd think I was crazy." Of course, he made those comments enough, so they started to think he was crazy, anyway. The end result would be an argument with his wife, and this was getting to be a common occurrence.

He and his wife hadn't had a fight for fifteen or twenty years, and now they were arguing all the time. She had finally insisted he get some professional help. He didn't know what good it would do, but he agreed.

Peter Ambura came highly recommended. When he came out of his office, Frank was a little surprised to see how young, and small he was. To Frank he looked like he wasn't old enough to buy liquor. And, he didn't think he was taller than five-foot-five. Frank figured that soaking wet, this man weighed one thirty. Peter introduced himself as Doctor Ambura, and they shook hands. He followed the doctor into his office.

It was well furnished, with two large chairs facing each other. There was a low table in between the chairs, with a flower arrangement on the table. Interesting artwork hung on every wall. Frank figured it was designed to give the patient something to look at when they didn't want to look at the doctor. Peter shut the door to the office, and they sat down. He opened a thin file, took out his pen, and started writing, even though they hadn't spoken yet. Frank wondered what he could be writing.

As if reading his mind, Peter stopped writing and looked at him. "I'm making a note of the date and time of our first visit." He smiled, and it seemed to be a genuine smile. It made Frank smile. "So, tell me, Mr. Saunders, may I call you Frank?"

"Sure."

"Tell me, Frank. How can I help you?"

Frank thought about that for a minute. "I'm not really sure, Doctor. Say, is it all right if I call you, Doc?"

Peter smiled, "You can call me anything you want, except late for dinner." He smiled wider, thinking he was pretty funny. It made Frank laugh, because it was such a goofy thing to be coming out of an Indian psychiatrist. Besides, it was a typical comment from somebody who looked like they ate a lot, but this guy looked like he ate a steady diet of rice cakes.

"Thanks, Doc. Well, I don't really know how you can help me, because I don't really know exactly what the problem is."

"It is my understanding from our conversation when you made this appointment that you have been having frequent arguments with your wife." He was looking at his notes in the file.

"That's true, I am. But I think our arguments are merely a symptom, not the problem."

Peter nodded his head. "That sounds quite insightful, Frank. Often, I spend many weeks with someone trying to help them differentiate between problems and symptoms. You seem to be there already. That's excellent. Let's assume for a moment that you're correct. These arguments are symptoms. How do you think you might determine the cause, which will help lead us to the problem?"

Frank thought for a moment. "I'm not really sure."

"Not sure, or you don't know? There's a difference. If you don't know,

I take it to mean you have no answer. If you're not sure, I interpret that as you have one or more possible answers, but you're afraid to express them."

"I guess I'm not sure. I do have some ideas, and you're right, I am afraid to express them. Possibly because I don't want to deal with them, and possibly because they might make me sound like a crazy person."

"Ah, well, I take a dim view of anyone being crazy, so you don't have to worry about that. As far as being afraid to deal with these things, do they have the potential of being worse than losing your family?"

Frank thought about that for a few minutes, or at least it seemed that long. "No, I don't think they could be worse than that."

"So, give me one of your thoughts as to what causes these arguments that you are having with your wife."

"She says that I'm obsessed with someone I investigated about four months ago."

"Investigated in what capacity?"

"I'm a senior officer in the CIA."

Peter's eyes widened a little. "I see. Does your employment require that you carry a weapon?"

"Sometimes, but not usually."

"Are you carrying one presently?"

Frank looked at the little man, realizing where he was going with this questioning. "No, Doc, I'm not carrying a weapon. I will never come in here carrying a weapon, and I'm not on the verge of shooting someone. You have nothing to worry about."

"I wasn't worrying, Frank. I just like to know what the potential is in any given situation. So tell me about this person you investigated."

"I really can't tell you much."

"Really, why not?"

"I was sort of sworn to secrecy."

"By your employer, the CIA?"

"No."

"Then by whom?"

"By the man I found in the process of my investigation."

"I see. Tell me, Frank, you say that your wife thinks you're obsessed. How do you feel, do you think you're obsessed?"

"To some degree I guess I am, yes."

"It has been my experience that being obsessed is like being pregnant. One either is, or is not. There is no such thing as being pregnant 'to a degree,' and so it is with obsession. You are, or you are not."

"Well, then, maybe I don't really know what obsessed is. I do think about this person all the time. I know I mention him a lot, and that makes my wife angry. But it's partially because I haven't explained things to her, so she doesn't understand."

"And these things you haven't explained, these are the things that you are sworn to secrecy about?"

"Yes, I guess so."

"Tell me, Frank, do your feelings for this individual have anything to do with physical attraction?"

Frank looked at him with an incredulous look. "Doc, what the heck are you trying to say here?"

"I'm merely trying to categorize the obsession. Sometimes, after many years of marriage, a man may find that he has surprising feelings for another man."

"You're way off base, Doc, so pick a different direction. This man just happened to be the most unusual man I've ever met. What makes him so unusual is what I can't discuss, but it's also what makes it impossible for me to stop thinking about him."

"So then, Frank, this man that you met, why don't you talk with him and explain that you need to share what you know with your wife. Perhaps you could convince him of her ability to keep this information quiet, and then you could explain things to your wife so that she'll have a better understanding of the situation."

"That's impossible."

"Impossible is such an absolute, Frank. Why is it impossible?"

"Because he's gone."

"What do you mean gone? He's dead? He left the area?"

"He disappeared right after my investigation. He moved, probably to a different country and changed his identity. No one will ever find him."

Peter thought about this. "This sounds quite mysterious to me, Frank. A man who disappears and changes his identity. But tell me, if he's disappeared and changed his identity and you're sure no one could find him, what harm could there be in telling your wife about him?"

"I'm just afraid that if she ever slipped and told someone else, it could get to the wrong people."

"The wrong people. Who are the wrong people?"

"The people I work for."

"The CIA, Frank? The U.S. government? They would be interested in this man?"

"Very much so."

"And why would that be?"

"That's part of what I can't tell you, Doc. I'm really sorry, I wish I could."

"Well, you know, there is what they call doctor-patient privilege. By law I'm not supposed to discuss things you tell me directly with anyone, nor can I be compelled to tell someone anything you discuss with me."

Frank laughed, "Doc, what if the something was so big or so unbelievable that you couldn't help yourself? Tell me, Doc, do you ever buy a lottery ticket?"

"What's that got to do with anything, Frank?"

"Humor me. You ever buy one?"

"No."

"OK, suppose one day the Powerball lotto is a hundred million dollars, and for the heck of it you buy one ticket. A few days later you find out you have the only winning ticket. Now, part of you wants to scream from the rooftop that you just won a hundred million dollars. But another part of you says you want to make it to the lottery people without getting killed, and there are a lot of people who would kill you for a hundred million dollars. So, you say to yourself, I have to keep my mouth shut. Can you understand all this?"

Peter nodded. "Completely."

"So self-preservation wins out, and you keep quiet. That's the situation I'm in. If people find out what I know, I endanger myself, my wife, and the guy I'm talking about. Because if the government ever got wind of this information, they'd pull out all the stops to find him and they would probably eventually succeed."

Peter gave all of this some thought. "We talked earlier of more than one possible reason for all of this. Do you have another theory as well?"

"Sometimes I think that I keep talking about him because I want to find him."

"Do you think you could?"

"Possibly."

"Why could you find him so easily, and others could not?"

"Because I have certain information that would make it a little easier."

"And your purpose in finding him would be what?"

"That's the tough part, Doc. I don't know what the purpose would be."

"Would it be to harm him?"

"Absolutely not."

"So to what, be with him? Maybe like a disciple, or something. Is this man a deeply religious man?"

"No, he's not deeply religious. I don't know." Frank was suddenly in deep thought. He had never verbalized, or even come face to face with the idea of finding him himself, but he realized as he said it that it was exactly what he desired to do. He really didn't know why. What would be the purpose? What would he expect? It was all so crazy.

He was suddenly aware of the doctor speaking to him. "Frank, are you all right?"

Frank looked at him. "Yeah, I'm fine."

"Where did you go, Frank?"

"What do you mean?"

"Just then, you went off into your own little world. I could see in your eyes that you left the room mentally for a minute. What were you thinking, Frank, can you tell me?"

"I was thinking about what I said about finding him myself. When those words came out, I was a little taken by the reality or truthfulness of what I said. I think that's the whole crux of the matter, Doc. I have a drive to find him."

They talked for almost an hour. Peter thought he should wrap it up for this session. "Frank, we've discussed a lot for you to think about. You need to decide how much you can tell your wife without endangering anyone, and without feeling that you've compromised your principles. Remember, there are principles involved in your relationship with her, too. When you married her, you promised to love her, perhaps even to cherish her, is that correct?"

"Yes it is."

"Well, allowing this immense event in your life to dominate your thinking and not sharing any of it with her is destroying the trust that you two have built over the years. You shouldn't put your loyalty to someone you may never see again, over your loyalty to your wife who loves you."

Frank had not thought of it from that perspective. He was right. He owed his wife more.

"You're right, Doc. I need to find some middle ground where I can help my wife to understand this thing."

"Why don't we get together again next week, and we can try to sort this out a little more. How would that be?"

"I don't think so right now, Doc. You've really been much more help than I would ever have expected from *ten* visits. Let me try to take care of a few things, and I'll get back to you on another appointment, OK?"

Peter smiled, "Sure, Frank. That will be fine." He stood up and shook Frank's hand. "Good luck, Frank."

"Thanks, Doc."

"Say, one favor, OK?"

"Sure, what is it?"

"If you ever get to where this secret can be told, will you come back and share it with me?"

"You gonna charge me for your time, Doc?"

"No way, Frank. It'll be a freebie."

"You got yourself a deal, Doc." They both smiled and Frank left.

As he drove home, he thought about how he was going to approach the subject with his wife without upsetting her. He had a pretty good way figured out by the time he got home.

Doctor Peter Ambura sat writing in Frank Saunders' file for almost an hour. His notes included his grave concern for Frank's ability to deal rationally with the issues surrounding this mysterious individual.

Chapter 81

The U.S. Military Review Board was made up of four top military officers, one from each branch of the military, and three non-military people. At present its members were Admiral Nelson Coombs from the Navy, General Arthur Boyce, U.S. Marine Corp., General David W. Banyon, U.S. Army, and Colonel Angela DeBartolo, the highest ranking female at present in the U.S. Air Force. The non-military members were John Frye, the senior Senator from West Virginia, Ellen Clark, a Congresswoman from Illinois, and the Reverend William Myles, a well-known Baptist minister, who was currently the spiritual counselor to the President of the United States.

The review board had been established to consider any complaints against senior officers of any branch of the military that could result in a loss of rank or dishonorable discharge from the military.

Today, they were meeting to consider the case against General Clayton Edwards who, until recently, had been a member of the Joint Chiefs. Each member of the Review Board had received a document detailing the case, over two months ago. They had ample time to consider the case, and discuss it among themselves. Today, they would have the opportunity to meet with General Edwards and his legal counsel. It would be a formal setting, much like a courtroom.

The initial complaint had been filed by General Lawrence Fielding, who was the commander of Fort Belvoir. When the entire incident came to his attention, he was shocked at the number of breaks in protocol. Only one General, unilaterally deciding to use the Bell helicopter was one. Any use of that helicopter was supposed to be agreed to by the entire Joint Chiefs. Ordering the pilot to land within the Pentagon compound under anything other than red alert conditions was the second. Landing the helicopter at JFK, right in the middle of commercial air traffic was unprecedented. There was a National Guard terminal less than a half-mile away, where they could have safely landed the chopper, without requiring any special clearance. From there, they could have driven over in a National Guard vehicle, arriving at the TWA terminal only five minutes later than they did. The plane was scheduled to sit on the tarmac for another forty minutes before departing anyway, so it wouldn't have made a difference. The stop at Fort Dix on the way back to refuel was yet another break in protocol. There were certain channels Edwards should have gone through to requisition the fuel. Instead, he simply pulled rank on the personnel there. Several high ranking officers at Fort Dix were upset.

When all of this first came to General Fielding's attention, he did what a professional officer in the military should do. He called General Edwards to discuss it with him. He thought it was only fair to hear his side of the story. After all, no one wants to make more waves than they have to and General Fielding was certainly willing to try to clear this whole mess up without a formal complaint. The truth of the matter was that a few well placed apologies could have been the end of it.

When he called General Edwards, he wasn't in. He left a message, and asked the General to get back to him as soon as possible. When he hadn't called by the end of the day, General Fielding called again. General Edwards' secretary told him he still wasn't available, and General Fielding got the distinct impression he was purposely not taking his call. He left a message again, to please return his call. He *still* did not get a return call. When General Fielding called the third day, he was less polite. The message he left was that if he didn't hear from the General in one hour, he would be filing a complaint with the Military Review Board. General Edwards called him back in fifteen minutes.

To say that the conversation didn't go well would be an understatement. General Fielding tried not to let his irritation, over the difficulty of getting General Edwards on the phone, enter into the conversation. He wasn't used to being treated with such disrespect. General Edwards and he were the same rank, and owed each other the same respect.

He started to question General Edwards about the entire fiasco, although he didn't use that word in the conversation. That was simply his take on the matter. General Edwards basically told him the matter was one of national security, and he made the decisions he felt were prudent at the time.

General Fielding asked him to explain how national security was involved, and he was told he couldn't discuss it. General Fielding asked him if he had discussed this matter of national security with any of the other members of the Joint Chiefs, and General Edwards told him he had not. General Fielding asked if he had discussed it with the Secretary of Defense, and he told him he had not. Had he called the President, and discussed it with him? No, he had not. General Fielding asked him if he realized just how many areas of protocol he had violated, and General Edwards told him that he could take his protocol and do something that was anatomically impossible with it, and hung up.

General Fielding began working on the formal complaint immediately.

Such a complaint was no simple task. It required conversations with dozens of individuals. It required him to get all the facts of the case, and get them as accurately as possible. His complaint had to clearly spell out the action, or actions, and the violations of military code that were involved.

By the time General Fielding had completed the document, it was twenty-nine pages long. It was well done. He was careful to avoid any insertion of his opinion. From all appearances, it was a completely impartial explanation of the events and how they violated military code and procedure. General Fielding had been careful to explain everything in such a way that the three non-military members of the review board would understand the complaint. General Fielding was confident the end result would be General Edwards' relief of duty, and honorable discharge. He would have had to massacre a hundred civilians to receive a dishonorable discharge.

The U.S. Military Review Board met in a small conference room on the second floor of the Pentagon. The board sat at a long table, much like a Senate Committee hearing. The room was set up like a courtroom. There were two tables, one for the person who was the subject of the complaint and their legal counsel, and one for the military prosecutors. There were twelve rows of chairs behind the tables for spectators.

Often there were few, or no spectators in these hearings, because the matters they were dealing with were of little interest to anyone other than the people directly involved. This was a different case. The room was packed. This was a high-profile review.

The papers had picked up the story. The New York Post started the ball rolling when one of their photographers snapped a picture of the helicopter just as it landed, surrounded by all the police cars. He was in the TWA terminal expecting to see a certain infamous celebrity get off the plane from L.A. When all the commotion started outside with the police cars, he could clearly see everything from the window along the gate area. He put his camera lens right up against the glass to avoid the reflection from the flash, and the result was a perfect picture of the military chopper in the middle of a circle of police cars. A few minutes later, he had a picture of General Edwards and two military police with a crowd of Port Authority policemen in the gate area of the terminal. The Post ran the story the next morning, and all the major newspapers picked up on it and dragged it out over the following week.

It came out that the military was attempting to "capture" a businessman from California whose name was Adam Adamson. They wound up questioning a man who was flying under his name and ticket, but who turned out to be a television actor named Mike Jenson. It was surprising how little money it took to get information out of an airline stewardess. For several weeks the story was the topic of conversation on every talk show on television. By the time the review board was meeting with General Edwards, the story had been a national topic of discussion.

When the Review Board came into the room everyone was present. General Edwards sat at one table with several military people, and two men in civilian clothes. The General looked his dress-parade best. His jacket was covered with ribbons and medals of all colors, shapes, and sizes. At the other table were four military lawyers. Two were Army, one was Navy, and one was Marine Corps.

Admiral Coombs was the chairman of the Review Board. He opened the meeting with a brief statement reminding everyone of the serious responsibility of the military in defending the freedom of this great nation, and that, from time to time, in the heat of the moment, there can be a failure to follow procedure. It was the duty of this Review Board to consider the case before it in a fair and impartial manner, to determine the accuracy, and the seriousness of the charges before them, along with the appropriate corresponding action. It was also understood that as a military hearing, all testimony given in this room would be considered to be given "under oath."

The procedure then moved to the reading of the complaint. Legal counsel for General Edwards offered to waive the reading and agree that everything stated in the complaint was accurate, but the prosecution objected to the waiving, citing the packed room and the fact that the spectators had not had an opportunity to read the complaint. As spectators to the procedure, they had a right to know what the complaint was. The chairman agreed, and asked Congresswoman Clark to read the complaint.

Although the document was twenty-nine pages the actual "complaint" was only three pages. The rest was testimony and military procedure. Ellen Clark read the complaint. She had a pleasant voice, and she was a good reader. It took her twelve minutes to read the three pages. Everyone listened attentively. Several reporters in the gallery were writing furiously; no recording devices were allowed in the room.

Preliminary questions from various members of the Review Board dealt with General Edwards' history in the military. Where he went to school, where he served at various times, and when he had been appointed a member of the Joint Chiefs. Eventually the questions became more directly related to the complaint.

General Banyon threw out the first fireball. "General Edwards, a few minutes ago we heard your legal counsel stipulate agreement to the complaints listed in this document. Are you personally in agreement with the explanation of events as they appear in this document?"

The General was concise, "I am."

General Banyon continued, "So then, General, with your agreement to the events as they are listed you know our responsibility here today is to try and understand the reasons behind your actions, and to determine whether or not you were justified in those actions."

The General looked directly at General Banyon this time. "I do, General."

Senator Frye picked up the ball, and ran with it. "So tell us, General, how was it that this individual, a Mr — " at this point Senator Frye looked down at his copy of the document, "Adamson came to your attention in the first place?"

General Edwards related the initial phone call he received from a retired assistant deputy director of the CIA. He explained he had had many dealings with the man in the past, and he knew him to be intelligent, of sharp mind, and patriotic to the core. When he spoke those last few words he emphasized them. It sent a message to the Review Board and the prosecution that he was going to play the patriotic trump card. Edwards went on to explain the nature of the call. The retired CIA person had himself gotten a call from an old friend relating a wild story about this individual with whom he had worked almost fifty years earlier.

He related the entire story about Adam. How he reportedly hadn't aged in fifty years. Edwards explained how he first waited for the CIA to investigate, because as it happens, the retired man's son coincidentally currently fills the same position at the CIA. He told the Review Board that he had personally spoken with Frank Saunders, the current assistant deputy director, and that Saunders told him that he was investigating the matter.

General Boyce threw the next ball into the court. "Tell us, General Edwards, on what day of the week did you talk with Mr. Saunders?"

"As best I am able to recall, it was Tuesday."

"And when Mr. Saunders told you he was investigating the matter, did he agree to inform you of his findings?"

"He did. Yes."

"And how many days did he say his investigation would take?"

"He didn't say."

"Well, how many days did you feel it should have taken?"

One of the military men sitting next to General Edwards reached out and covered the microphone in front of the General with his hand. At the same time, he leaned toward the General and the two of them spoke briefly. The Review Board waited patiently. Finally the General answered the question, "I had no predetermined time frame in mind."

General Boyce continued, "It is the written testimony of Mr. Saunders that you requested he have some answers back to you by the end of the week, General. By the end of the week, did you mean Friday?"

"I suppose I did, General. Yes."

"And yet this incident took place on Friday, General?"

The expression on General Edwards' face changed just slightly. There was a hint of remorse. "Yes, General. It did."

"What made you decide not to wait for Mr. Saunders' report, sir?"

"I tried to reach Mr. Saunders on Thursday, and he was unavailable."

"Wasn't that because he was on the West Coast doing exactly what he promised you he was going to do?"

"Yes, as it turns out he was."

Reverend Myles spoke for the first time, "Tell us, General, what was it that caused you to be so concerned about this man Adamson?"

The General hesitated, weighing his words carefully. "I had received enough information to be quite sure we were dealing with an individual who had somehow been able to halt his own aging process. I believed it to be in the national interest to question this man, and find out how he had accomplished this."

Colonel DeBartolo chimed in, "So then, General, is it to be our understanding that you consider the 'national interest' and 'national security' to be one and the same?"

The General realized what he had said, and it flustered him. "No, Colonel, that is not what I believe. It was later, in contemplating the information that I had available, I realized if this man had, in fact, been able to stop the aging process, we had no way of knowing how long ago he had done that. He could have, at various times, worked in highly sensitive positions within our government, or other governments for that matter. It was then I came to the realization this individual was more than a national interest, and, in fact, he was a potential threat to our national security." He thought he had recovered from that quite nicely.

The Review Board questioned him on dozens of issues. The various breaches of protocol came up one by one, and the General explained his position on those issues usually citing his concern for national security as the reason for side-stepping normal procedure. He explained that, without exception, procedure or "protocol" always represented a time requirement. He explained if he had done everything "by the book," it would have been Sunday before he and those men would have been at JFK.

The Review Board listened carefully to everything the General said. They felt he answered their questions as fully and honestly as he could. They didn't agree with a lot of his viewpoints, but they respected him for being honest with them.

General Edwards was a highly decorated officer. He was fresh out of the military academy when the Bay of Pigs incident took place. He served three tours in Vietnam, and he was directly involved in the Gulf War under General Schwarzkopf. He was sixty-one and eligible for full retirement in a year. The Board agreed his judgment in the entire matter was grossly deficient. It would appear to be an exoneration if they took no action. By the same token, they did believe he was acting out of a misguided loyalty to the national security, so they wanted to temper their punishment. The decision was to relieve General Edwards of his duty, and recommend honorable discharge with full Army pension and benefits.

In the end, that's exactly what happened. Several major newspapers made note of the decision, but it was tucked away in a back section somewhere. General Edwards cleaned out his office and went home.

The General owned a modest home in a very nice neighborhood in Laurel, Maryland. His wife had passed away ten years before. He sat in his study and stared at the wall across the room. It was full of war mementos. There were several swords and knives. There were small flags from various battalions in which he had served. There were guns of all sorts. Five different rifles, one machine gun. Eight different types of handguns, including a German Luger semi-automatic.

General Edwards sat for a long time and replayed everything in his head. Eventually he decided that it all came down to one man. Adam Adamson. He was out there somewhere, and he had gotten the best of him. But Clayton Edwards was a big believer in the "he who laughs last" philosophy. In his heart of hearts, he knew there was something to this whole thing. Yes, the review had made him look a little crazy when he started talking about a man living for hundreds or thousands of years. But, he wasn't going to just sit in this house and die. No sir, not Clayton Edwards, warrior. He was going to find Adam Adamson if it took him the rest of his life. He would get to the bottom of this, one way or another.

Chapter 82

Ben watched the sun come up over the ocean from his bedroom window. He needed to think about the conversation he was going to have with Barbara, and how much of his life he was going to explain to her. He already determined he really did want their relationship to continue and grow. He would marry her, and even have children, but he felt a need to take everything slowly. He had known her about four months, and he had felt himself developing strong feelings for her very early in their relationship. However, in that time they really only spent a total of about four days together. Any real expressions of affection were only verbalized in the last day. He realized it was premature to start talking about wedding plans. He wanted to explain things to her, and then give it time to sink in. He would wait to see how she felt about him after that.

He knew when two people fell in love, they considered spending the rest of their lives together, even growing old together. How would she deal with the reality that they would not grow old together? Only she would grow old. He wondered if he should discuss it with her at all, but then he already promised her he would explain complications. What was his explanation going to be? He certainly wasn't going to lie to her. Then, there is the need to move every so many years. What was her relationship to her family? He had no idea. Would she be willing to move away and never see them again? How much more challenging would that be if they had children?

Ben thought about all the complications and possible problems, but they didn't make him feel differently about her.

They had breakfast together and he suggested they take a walk. They walked across the front circular drive, onto the lawn toward the ocean. There was a set of wooden stairs at the edge of the property that went down to the water. At low tide, there was twenty feet of rocky beach. At high tide, the bottom two stairs were under water. They had to be replaced every few years because the water would cause them to rot.

When they got to the edge and looked down, the tide was high. They sat on the grass by the edge of the drop. They could look down and see the water crashing against the rocks. They sat for several minutes in silence. Barbara was waiting for Ben to speak, and he was choosing his words carefully.

Finally he spoke to her calmly, "There's so much I want to tell you, that

I don't really know where to start."

She looked over at him. "I've always found that starting at the beginning is a good place."

He smiled, "What if the beginning is way too long ago?"

She didn't get his point. "Well, then, start wherever you feel comfortable."

There was another minute of silence before he spoke again, "Would you agree that we get to a point in our lives where we think we've pretty much heard it all? I mean, everything tends to be a variation of a theme we've heard before. You know what I mean? Nothing really new? I mean, totally, radically new?"

Barbara thought about the question, or what she thought the question was. "Yes, I agree we do get to that point."

"We also develop definite ideas as to what is possible, and what is impossible, wouldn't you say?"

Barbara was a little confused by all of this. She wondered where this conversation was going. "Yes, I suppose we do. But what's possible can be very subjective, don't you think? One person may feel that running ten miles is impossible, but if they trained they would probably be able to do it eventually."

Ben thought about that for a moment. "That's true, but some things we all agree *are impossible*. For example, man flying without the aid of an airplane, or hang glider, or something to assist him. That's simply impossible, wouldn't you agree?"

Barbara nodded in agreement.

"Think about those few primitive cultures that still exist in the world where they don't even have electricity. They don't even know about electricity. If we explained to them that in our culture we can flip a little switch, and a dark room lights up, they might think that such a thing was impossible. But, we know it's *not* impossible. We might say their insistence that such a thing was impossible was a result of their lack of knowledge and experience."

Barbara looked at him as he spoke. She thought he was so smart, and she loved to hear him talk about things, but she was a little confused about where he was going with all this. "Is there a point in all of this I should be getting?"

He laughed, "Yes, if I can ever get to it. I'm beating a pretty flat path around a big bush, aren't I?"

She laughed too, but she was relieved she wasn't just missing the point.

He looked at her, and the smile faded from his face. "Sometimes, as smart as we think we are, and as much as we think we know, there can be possibilities we will swear are impossible. I need you to be willing to take my word for it on this point, for now."

She realized he had suddenly gotten very serious and it made her a little nervous. "All right, Ben, I'll take your word for it."

"Barbara, I know how you feel about me based on our conversation last night, and I want you to know that I feel much the same about you. But if I really love you, I'm obligated to be fair to you in our relationship, and part of being fair is being completely honest. Wouldn't you agree?"

Now she was getting really nervous. She started to shiver, although it was mild outside. "Yes, Ben. I certainly would agree that honesty is very important between two people who love each other."

He nodded, "Yes, it is, even if some aspect of the truth might be overwhelming."

Now she was becoming frightened. She loved this man, and if there was some huge thing in his past he thought she had to know, she was starting to think maybe she didn't want to know. "Ben, you're starting to frighten me. What could there possibly be that is so important for me to know?"

He looked at her in a way she had not seen before. His eyes were more piercing, as if he were trying to read her mind. At the same time, she thought she saw an element of some profound sadness.

"There's something about me you must know if we're going to even consider having a life together."

"All right then, just tell me. Just spit it out, and we'll deal with it." There was an edge of feistiness in her voice. He wished it could be that easy.

"Do you remember asking me how much I knew about Andrew Smith, the man who bought this castle almost three hundred and fifty years ago? I told you I didn't really know very much about him?"

She nodded. "Yes, I remember."

"I wasn't truthful with you. I know everything there is to know about him. What would you like to know?"

She looked at him with bewilderment. "This is your big thing? You weren't honest with me about an old relative?

He looked at her with no smile on his face, and she knew he was speaking very seriously. "It's not that he was an old relative. It's that I was Andrew Smith almost three hundred and fifty years ago."

At first she didn't think she understood what he said. She looked at him expecting some explanation, or a smile that said he was joking, but nothing came. She realized that he was not joking. Finally, she spoke very softly, "I don't understand."

"It's not an easy thing to understand."

"People don't live for hundreds of years."

"That's true, although at one time they lived much longer than that."

"But somehow, you're the exception?" She watched for some sign that he was joking.

"Yes."

"How old are you, exactly?"

"Six thousand fifteen years old, give or take."

"Ben, you're asking me to believe the impossible."

For the next two hours he explained his birth to her, using several Bibles from the library shelves. He explained that he had been born while his parents, the first two created humans on earth, were perfect. He, therefore, as a perfect human did not age. He gave her a general overview of his life, the many places he had been and the need to keep on the move, to avoid having people notice he never got any older. He told her he left the castle back in sixteen ninety-three for the same reason. He opened several of the journals and showed her various entries. He took paper, and wrote the same entries on the paper so she could see the handwriting matched. He told her about his relationship with Isaac Newton, that Isaac had been like a son to him.

He explained the theories Newton had published that made him famous were all theories he had given him, and he was glad to have done it. Somehow, Barbara seemed willing to accept this unbelievable thing as the truth. She asked hundreds of questions, and he answered her questions patiently and clearly. "The code," she said, "to the trust. Did those numbers mean anything? We spent months at the bank trying to figure out what the code could have meant."

He smiled at her, "Do you remember the code?"

She nodded. "Zero, one, one, four, three, three."

"The code was the date I stood on a hill side with two of my traveling companions, and watched the impalement of Jesus. It was the first month on the fourteenth day, according to the Hebrew calendar and in the year thirty-three, by our current calendar."

She closed her eyes and started to cry. Through her sobbing she said, "You were right. It is overwhelming."

By this time they were both sitting on the couch in the library, and he put his arms around her and held her as she cried. She realized there were extraordinary circumstances they would have to deal with. She thought about all he must have seen and done in the lifetime of humanity. She wondered if she would ever stop asking questions, and she found herself wondering if she would be able to keep this information to herself.

Chapter 83

Clayton Edwards had two days to remove all personal effects from his office. He arrived at the office very early the morning after the Review Board's decision was handed down.

He sat and punched some information into his computer. He entered several codes and commands, in an attempt to access several high-level database files that were limited to use by only the highest security-code levels within the Defense Department. He was pleased to see the wheels of the federal government didn't work too quickly, because his access code was still valid. He typed for a few minutes, and eventually found what he wanted.

He punched in a request for all real estate transactions using the name Adamson between the middle of August and the present. The database he was using was international, and was compiled through the efforts of the CIA, Interpol, Scotland Yard, and several other organizations in the world dedicated to preventing terrorism and fighting crime. It was primarily used to track the purchase of "safe" houses by known terrorist organizations.

After about four minutes, the computer screen told him there were almost two hundred transactions using that name. He narrowed the parameters of his search by requesting a list of transactions between anyone with the name Adamson, and any other name common to more than one transaction. The computer worked for another minute or so, and finally brought up a screen with four transactions listed. One was in Great Britain, one in Spain, one in Switzerland, and one in New York City, in Manhattan. All transactions were from Adamson to a Benjamin Nathan. Edwards noticed the transaction in Great Britain occurred a little before the other three. He decided Great Britain was probably where Adamson was. But, he thought that it would be prudent to check Manhattan first, considering how close it was. He would have hated to travel to Europe, only to find the person he was looking for was in New York. He printed a copy of the list, logged off the computer, and left.

He knew if anyone ever checked the system, they would be able to determine he had logged on and taken this particular information. He knew it could one day be evidence against him, but he didn't care. Besides, there was nothing he could do about it. There was no way to get on the system without using a log-on code, and there was no way to purge the system of an entry. He told himself the only thing he was interested in was finding this guy, and talking to him. He would wait and decide if he needed to kill him after that. If he determined the man really was hundreds, or thousands of years old, the guy was dead, no matter what the consequences. The man would be a menace to the future of our society. He would be capable of being a super spy. Over many years, he would be able to infiltrate many different government agencies. Who knows what the man may already know?

When Clayton Edwards got home he started packing right away. He took out an old suitcase he hadn't used in years, and put in enough clothes to go at least a week before he had to worry about washing anything. He hated doing laundry. Ever since his wife died he sent his laundry out, but he knew on this trip he would have to wash his own clothes.

He also packed two handguns, both 45 automatics he had acquired over the years. He took a box of ammunition, although he wondered why he would need more than the two clips full. He laughed to himself, because he then had a counter-thought. Why would he need more than one bullet? What was he thinking, that he was going to wind up in some shoot-out? He took the box of bullets out of the suitcase and put it away. He was sure the two clips, which was eighteen shots total would be more than he would need.

When he was packed, he called an old friend from the military academy named Gary Flemming, who presently oversaw the military flights between the East Coast and Europe. Colonel Flemming was stationed at Fort Dix, and had tipped him off early that the top brass were upset with his requisition for fuel on his New York trip.

He told Gary he wanted to get away for a while, and he was looking for a ride to Europe. The U.S. Military flew planes back and forth almost daily to various parts of Europe, and a high ranking officer could usually "dead head" for free. Colonel Flemming was happy to extend the travel privilege to General Edwards, even if he was soon to be retired. He told him there would be a plane leaving Fort Dix and flying to Grafenwoehr Training area in Germany in two days, and there were several available seats if he was interested. The plane would be departing at five in the afternoon, and Edwards asked him to reserve a seat for him. If he wasn't there when the plane was ready to go, let it leave without him.

He hung up knowing he had a ride to Europe, if he needed it. He could well afford to travel on a commercial airplane, but he knew it would be impossible to take his guns with him. The military flights afforded him the luxury of simply throwing his suitcase in the luggage compartment. There was no security inspection to deal with. He would be getting off on a military base, so there would be no customs inspection at the other end. He would get someone to drive him to the nearest town, where he would rent a car, or maybe travel by train. He didn't know exactly what he would do, but he wasn't going to worry about it. All he really cared about was being able to get to Europe with his guns.

He closed up his house as if he were going out for a few hours. He threw his suitcase into the back seat of the car, and headed for I-95. He figured he could be in New York City in six hours, taking it nice and easy. He would stop in New Jersey somewhere for dinner to avoid driving in New York rush-hour traffic. As he drove toward the highway, he had a strange feeling, and it took him a few minutes to figure it out. It was a combination of feeling like he was on vacation, yet at the same time like he was on a mission. He was going to find Adam Adamson and vindicate himself if it was the last thing he did.

Chapter 84

There was something vaguely familiar about the return address on the envelope, but what got Paul Fenton's attention was that it was a nine by twelve business envelope, and it was addressed to him directly. Most realtor junk mail was addressed to the "Manager" or "Director," but whatever this envelope was all about, at least they knew his name. Inside the envelope he had found a letter that quickly refreshed his memory. It was regarding the transfer of apartment 4-C from Mr. Adamson to Benjamin Nathan. He had sent an application out several months ago. Now, he had the application back and it seemed to be filled out completely. There was a page behind the application. It was thick linen paper. There was a gold emblem embossed at the top. It was stationary from the Credite Suisse Bank's home office in Zurich, Switzerland, and was a letter of credit for Mr. Nathan in the amount of three hundred million dollars. Paul Fenton had never seen a document for so much money.

There was an additional letter from the California real estate firm informing him that Mr. Nathan would be willing to come to New York for a meeting with the committee, as long as he had a seven-day advance notice. He had written back with a date three weeks into the future on a Wednesday. Five days later, he received an e-mail confirming the appointment and acknowledging Mr. Nathan would be there, and would likely spend the night in his apartment.

The committee had been intrigued by this mystery man none of them knew. Usually, the people that applied for residency were well-known, either from the entertainment or business world, but no one had ever heard of Mr. Nathan. They all agreed the confirmation implied an overnight stay, and they were not going to make an issue over it. If they felt he did not qualify for residency, they would notify him through the mail and he could fight with them all he wanted. He was due in three days.

Chapter 85

Sarah Saunders sat in the waiting room, wondering how late her husband would be. It seemed he was never on time anymore, for anything. Just another one of many changes she had been dealing with for the last several months. She tried talking to Frank, at first. They had been together for many years and basically he had been a good husband and provider. He had always been more tied up in his work than she preferred, but that came with the territory. Working for the CIA was bad enough, but once you became management, or in Frank's case an A.D.D., the demands on your time were unreasonable.

Sarah had raised the two girls practically by herself. When they were young, Frank would often come home after they were in bed, and he would leave so early that sometimes they wouldn't see him for a week. That was part of what made his recent transition so hard. Suddenly, he wanted to spend time with the girls. He wanted to take them places and be with them, and it was very difficult for them. It wasn't that they didn't love their father, but in many ways they didn't know him.

There was also his obsession with Adam Adamson. At first, he talked about him all the time. When she got mad at him and made him see a psychiatrist, he seemed to be a little better about it. He talked with Sarah, and tried to explain there were things about the man that were very unique. When she asked him what kind of things, he said he couldn't discuss them with her. He was afraid she would be in danger if she knew what he knew, and there was also the possibility she would inadvertently pass information on to others. That might endanger Mr. Adamson. Of course, this only confused her, and it led to arguments.

Their relationship got much worse over the last few months, and Sarah told Frank if they didn't see a counselor together she was going to file for a divorce. Frank had agreed to the counselor, and she made an appointment with a woman named Maggie Benton, who had come highly recommended. Their appointment was for four o'clock, and Frank promised her he would be at the office by ten to four. It was now three minutes to four, and she was starting to worry.

The door to Maggie's inner office opened, and Maggie came out with a young couple. Sarah guessed they were in their twenties. She wondered if most of the people who came to Maggie were younger. Maggie only looked to be in her late thirties herself. She was attractive, but not overly so. As Maggie stood at the door talking with the couple for another minute, Frank came into the waiting room. Sarah was irritated he was so last minute, but she was relieved he made it before their appointment was to start.

The young couple left, and Maggie looked at Sarah and smiled. As she approached, Sarah stood up. Maggie extended her hand. "Hello, you must be Sarah. I'm Maggie Benton." They shook hands, and Sarah noticed Maggie had a very firm hand shake.

Sarah introduced Frank. "This is my husband, Frank," as she looked at Frank who was taking off his coat. Frank threw his coat over his left arm, and shook Maggie's hand.

"Well, come on in," Maggie said, gesturing toward her office. Frank and Sarah went in and Maggie followed, closing the door behind her.

The office was large. There was a couch and a chair. It was obvious the furniture was intended to require couples to sit together. Sarah and Frank sat on the couch. It was large enough for two people to sit on without having to be too close to one another. Sarah chose to sit a little closer to Frank. She didn't want to create the impression she was mad at him, because she wasn't. Maggie sat down, and took a note pad off the table that was next to the chair. She slipped a pen out of the note pad, and looked at Sarah and Frank. She smiled at them.

"How long have you two been married?"

Sarah answered, "Twenty-three years." Maggie looked at her for a moment.

"Any children?"

Again Sarah answered, "Two girls, one eighteen, and one about to turn fourteen."

Maggie looked at Sarah, and then at Frank.

"Sarah, do you work outside the home?"

"No."

"And Frank, what do you do?"

Frank looked up at her. "I work for the federal government."

She looked at him. "Really? Doing what?

He realized she wasn't going to accept his simple answer. "I'm with the CIA."

She raised her eyebrows. "Wow, does that mean you're a spy or something?"

He laughed, "No, I just supervise all the spies."

"Oh," she said, and made a few notes.

"OK. At what point in your marriage did you feel there was a need to get some type of help?" She looked at both of them, moving her eyes from one to the other. "Sarah, what do you think?"

Sarah didn't look up, she was fidgeting with her hands. "I would say the last four months, or so."

Maggie looked at Frank. "Frank, what do you think?"

He looked at his wife and then looked at Maggie. "I don't know, I guess I would have to agree with my wife."

Maggie made a few notes, and then she looked back to them. "So then, we have a couple married twenty-three years and they agree the problems only started about four months ago. That's pretty good. Most couples say their whole marriage has been a problem. So tell me, what's happened in the last four months?"

There was a long silence, and it was obvious to Maggie neither was going to be forthcoming. "Sarah, why don't you tell me what you believe to be the case."

Sarah looked over at Frank, and tears started to stream down her cheeks. She looked up at Maggie. "Four months ago, my husband was involved in a case. In all his years at the agency, he's been involved in hundreds of cases. He deals with them, he comes home and leaves them at the agency. Frank has never been one to let his work affect his relationship with me or the kids, as far as the particulars he had to deal with. Frank always worked too much. He put in long hours, and he really didn't spend any quality time with the kids. Not very much with me either, but he never seemed to let things he was dealing with at work affect him outside of work. Everything to do with his work was usually hush-hush and that's what I became used to. But ever since this case where he met this person, he's been different."

"How so?"

"At first, he talked about the guy all the time. He was like a teenager talking about their favorite rock star. I think if he had a poster of him, he would tack it up on our bedroom wall."

Frank had been sitting with a look of acceptance, but he was clearly irritated by this remark. "Come on, Sarah, that's ridiculous."

"Is it, Frank? I don't think you realize how obsessed you've become. For the first six or eight weeks, he was all you thought about. You went and saw somebody one time after I threatened you, and you came home like everything was going to be fine. You gave me some mumbo-jumbo about not being able to tell me things you knew, because it would be dangerous. Do you know how that sounds, Frank? Do you know how it makes me feel to know that you have some overwhelming thing that's eating you up and possessing your every thought, and you can't discuss it with me because you don't trust me?" She was now yelling at him. Maggie was seeing bitterness and anger that had developed over the months.

Frank looked at his wife. "It is not that I don't trust you, Sarah, it's that I — " And she cut him off in the middle of his sentence.

"Yes it is, Frank. It *is* that you don't trust me. You've told me a dozen times you can't tell me, because I might tell someone else and *that's* what could endanger me, Frank. I have it memorized by now, I've heard it so much. The bottom line is, after twenty-three years you don't trust me. And you know what, Frank? I wouldn't really care if you could just let it go. It's not like I have to know this thing. But it's with *us*, Frank. You've undergone this change in your personality. You want to spend more time with the girls, and that's a good thing. But the girls can't just magically switch on some new relationship, Frank. It takes time. And you seem so insistent, so desperate that it makes them nervous. It makes *me* nervous. And you give us no explanation. It's a little freaky."

Maggie felt the need to step in before things got out of hand. "Tell me, Sarah, what sort of things do you mean when you say Frank has undergone a personality change?"

Sarah sat for a minute or so, gathering her thoughts and calming down. She realized she was getting upset, and she didn't want to. When she spoke again, it was in a much quieter, softer tone.

"It's not even that the changes we've seen are bad changes in themselves. For the most part, they're probably changes that wives and children would appreciate … if they understood the motivation behind the changes. He suddenly has taken to staying around in the morning, and having breakfast with us. He used to be on the road by six-thirty or seven in the morning. He wants to know everything the girls are doing. Do they have boyfriends? How are their grades? Their teachers? How's the basketball team doing? … It's just a little overwhelming. And suddenly, he's become very … I don't know … spiritual or something. You know, years ago we used to go to church every Sunday. When the kids started to get older, every Sunday became every third or fourth Sunday, and it's been that way ever since. We go to church just enough for the people there to remember who we are. Now, all of a sudden, he's got a new Bible and it's in modern English, and he's reading it all the time. He talks about creation, and how it's really true, and that evolution is nothing more than an unfounded theory.

Frank had been sitting quietly and now he spoke up, "Well, that happens to be right."

Sarah looked at Frank with what Maggie saw as desperation. "Frank, it might be right, but that's not the point. The point is: I don't really care. The girls don't really care. To us, it seems like you're having some kind of a mental breakdown, and we're scared."

"Because I'm reading the Bible, I'm having a nervous breakdown?"

"It's not just the Bible, Frank." Sarah was remaining calm. "You also have all these new history books, ancient history books. You spend hours pouring over them like they're a treasure map you found. What are we supposed to think, Frank?" She looked at him waiting for an answer. He looked back at her, but he said nothing.

Maggie broke the silence, "Frank, do you love your wife and children?"

Frank looked over at her. "Of course I do."

"Can you appreciate that your behavioral changes without the benefit of some explanation seems to be what is really causing all this trouble?"

Frank was looking down at the floor. He didn't answer.

Maggie pressed a little more, "Frank, what can you tell me about this person you met?"

Frank looked at her and she didn't understand the look on his face. It was a sadness, but it seemed to go beyond sadness of his present situation, and it concerned her.

He finally spoke quietly, "He was a very unique individual. He was a very good man who seemed to just want to do good things for other people. He minded his own business, until someone made an accusation against him. That's where I got involved. It was up to me to investigate the accusation. I went and met with this man and talked with him, and he trusted me with information that I swore I wouldn't tell anyone. The problem is, I haven't been able to get him, or what he told me out of my head. It's like some kind of a curse. Knowing things you want to tell everyone, but being sworn to secrecy."

"And where is this man now, Frank?"

"I think he's gone."

Maggie didn't understand. "Gone. What do you mean?"

"I mean I think he's left the country, and probably changed his identity."

"So, he's a criminal of some sort? I mean, who else has to change their identity?"

Frank looked at Maggie and it seemed to her his sadness became even deeper. He spoke very softly, "No, he's not a criminal. But yes, he has likely changed his identity to protect himself. I wish I could tell you more, but I can't."

Maggie thought about this for a moment. "Frank, suppose Sarah left the office and you shared this information with me alone for now? I would be ethically bound not to discuss anything you tell me with anyone else. Even a court of law couldn't make me divulge anything we discuss in a doctor-patient capacity."

Frank was still looking at her. He thought about how naïve she was. He wondered how well she would keep a secret, after she had been injected with sodium pentothal? His experience told him it wouldn't take much to make her spill everything she ever knew, about everybody she ever knew. "I wish I could do that, but I can't."

"And you don't think you can discuss any of this with Sarah to help her understand?"

Frank shook his head slowly from side to side. "No, I'm sorry, but I can't."

Maggie looked at them sitting on the couch. She wondered what could have been so profound to destroy twenty-three years of marriage.

"Frank, you realize this could destroy your marriage. That it's close to doing that, now?"

"I don't see why it should. It's not like I've become some bad person, it's just that I've changed. I can't help it."

Sarah looked over at him. "Frank, I can't go on this way. It's like you have a part of your life that you can't share with us, but you force us to look at it every day. It's just not going to work."

Frank sat there and shrugged. "Well, if it's not going to work, I don't think there's anything I can do."

Sarah reached over and put her hand on his knee in a gesture of affection. "You can talk to me, Frank. You can trust me with this information, and we can work through this."

Frank sat still, without speaking.

Sarah looked at Maggie pleadingly. Maggie didn't know what to say. She spoke, "Sarah, you spoke about Frank's not discussing this with you, but you having to look at it each day. What exactly did you mean?"

"Well, Frank is different. He seems to be constantly preoccupied. Granted, he's taken to spending more time at home with me and the girls, but it never seems to be what I would call 'quality time.' It's like some inner voice is telling him he should be home with us, but he has no idea what he should be doing."

Frank spoke up softly, "I don't think that's true."

Sarah looked at him. It was obvious her anger was getting the better of her. "You don't think it's true? Then you tell me, what have we done that you feel represents 'quality time'?"

Frank just sat quietly.

"Come on, Frank, what have we done together as a family? What have you and I done as a couple? Have we gone to the movies? Have we gone out to eat? Have we had friends over to the house? Tell me, Frank, who are our friends? The guys from the agency? You don't even like them! Frank, don't you realize *our* life has revolved around *your* life? I've been willing to accept it all these years, and I think I would continue to accept it, but this is different. It's like making an appointment with a doctor, and then when you get to his office, you refuse to tell him what the problem is. I'm sick of it, Frank. You've been weird for months. You won't tell me what it's all about, and you won't stop acting weird." The anger in her voice was unmistakable.

Two weeks later, Frank was served papers at his office. His wife had filed for a legal separation. The papers cited irreconcilable differences, and said Frank had three days to remove his belongings from the house and find other living quarters.

Chapter 86

Clayton Edwards parked his car in a garage between West 63rd and West 62nd Avenue. He walked east, a half block to Central Park West, and turned left. He walked past the Society for Ethical Culture, and wondered how many wackos frequented that place. He crossed West 64th Street, and stood in front of the address his computer had given him as one of the addresses changing ownership from Adamson to Nathan. The place looked pretty exclusive. There was a doorman, and he not only wore a uniform that reminded Edwards of the guards at Buckingham Palace, but he wore a really strange looking hat. Edwards figured they had to pay the man a lot of money to wear that hat, and if they paid a doorman a lot of money, it had to be an exclusive place.

He approached the doorman and asked if a Mr. Nathan lived in the building. The doorman told him he was not allowed to discuss who lived in the building with anyone. Edwards asked him who he would have to talk to. The doorman suggested he try a Mr. Fenton, who was the Building Manager. The General asked him how to get in touch with him. The doorman stepped aside, and Edwards saw a phone box recessed into the wall. The doorman opened the box, and took out a receiver. He dialed two digits, and waited. He waited a few seconds, and someone picked up at the other end.

The doorman spoke, "It's Steve. There's someone here to see Mr. Fenton." He listened for a moment. "He's asking about somebody. Wants to know if he's a resident of the building." He listened again. "Yeah, I told him we don't give out that information." He paused again. "Yes." Paused again. "Yep." Paused again. "Well, then he asked me who to talk to, and I told him to talk to Mr. Fenton, so that's why I'm calling you. He asked how to get in touch with Mr. Fenton." Another pause. "OK. Yes, I will. Thank you."

He hung up the phone, and closed the box. He reached into his uniform coat pocket and pulled out a pen and a pad of paper. He wrote down a phone number and a name, ripped the sheet of paper off the pad, and handed it to the General. "Here's the person you need to talk to and his number. He's tied up right now. You'll have to call him and make an appointment. I'm sorry."

The General looked at him, and decided he was being sincere. He thanked him and walked away. Edwards walked back to the garage, and retrieved his suitcase from the trunk of his car. He told the garage attendant he would probably be staying the night.

He walked back to Central Park West, and turned right this time. Two blocks down, was the Hotel Mayflower. It was early in the week, and he had no problem getting a room. It was expensive, but he didn't care. He liked the convenience of being close.

He unpacked his suitcase so he could hang up the clothes that needed to be hung. He cursed his lifelong military training. Some habits were hard to break. He picked up the phone, and dialed the number on the piece of paper the doorman gave him. A woman answered the phone, "Mr. Fenton's office. May I help you?"

Edwards decided to try impressing her. "This is General Clayton Edwards, U.S. Army, calling for Mr. Fenton."

There was a short pause on the other end. "One moment, please." Edwards was put on hold. A few moments later, she came back on the line. "I'm sorry, Mr. Fenton is unavailable at the moment. Could I have him return your call?"

"Certainly, I'm at the Hotel Mayflower."

"Here in New York?"

"Yes."

"Your room number, sir?"

"Two-ten."

"Very good, General, Mr. Fenton will return your call shortly." She hung up without waiting for a reply. He understood it was her way of letting him know his reply didn't matter. These were people who were used to dealing with very wealthy, very powerful people. They had a sense of insulation. They didn't worry about upsetting anyone outside of their own residents.

He sat on the bed, and turned on the television. He flipped through the channels until he got to CNN. He looked at his watch. It was almost six o'clock. He could catch the news.

Chapter 87

Ben invited Barbara to travel with him to New York City. He explained he had to go for an interview regarding an apartment he owned and wanted to keep. When he bought it, there were no questions asked, but that was many years ago. Now there was a Condominium Committee, and no one could live in the apartments unless they were approved by the committee.

He didn't know when he might want to live there, so he was willing to take the chance of going there in person. No one had ever seen him, because he had only appeared once personally when he purchased the apartment. He had run a check on the committee. No one he had ever known was among them.

On top of the cost for the apartment and the annual taxes, it cost over four thousand dollars a month to maintain the apartment. That didn't include the condominium's maintenance fee of five thousand a month. He thought it would be nice to spend at least one night there.

Barbara said she didn't think she could get the time off from her job, and that made Ben laugh. She looked at him, and realized how funny it was in light of all they had been discussing. He told her to call her supervisor, and tell him she was going to New York with Mr. Nathan on business. The bank could bill her time to him. When Barbara talked to her supervisor, he told her that Mr. Nathan didn't have to worry about her time being billed. He was the most valuable customer they had, and if he needed her in New York, it was fine with the bank.

Barbara expressed concern she didn't really have the right clothes for New York. Ben told her not to worry. What she had would be fine, and she could go shopping when they got there. Ben had always been a very generous man, giving away millions of his own money each year to others. But he had never had the opportunity to spend lavishly on one person before. True, he often bought things for Gus, but this was different. This was a woman he was in love with, and it was fun to tell her not to worry about clothes. He enjoyed telling her she could go on a shopping spree in New York City.

Ben called the Credite Suisse Bank in Geneva. He identified himself with a series of codes, and had one hundred thousand dollars transferred to the New York City office. He instructed them to convert the money into five hundred dollar traveler's checks, and that he would pick them up in the New

York City office on Wednesday. Ben thought it would be good to take Gus along. Gus was familiar with New York City, and besides, maybe he would want to go see his sister in Massachusetts. When he asked, Gus said he would be happy to go along.

Ben made a phone call and booked three first-class tickets on a 10 a.m. flight from Heathrow to JFK on Wednesday. One interesting thing about flying from London to New York was that the flight lasted five hours and the time difference was five hours. When you left London at ten in the morning, you arrived five hours later in New York at ten in the morning. Ben's appointment with the committee was at three in the afternoon.

Chapter 88

The ringing phone woke Clayton Edwards from a light sleep. He looked at his watch. It was six thirty-five. He answered the phone, "Hello."

"General Edwards?"

"Yes."

"This is Paul Fenton returning your call. How can I help you?" He sounded a bit snooty to Edwards.

"Well, Mr. Fenton, I was wondering if you could tell me if you have a resident living in your building named Nathan?"

"I'm terribly sorry, General, but we don't give that sort of information out."

Clayton thought to himself that he wasn't terribly sorry at all. He hated it when people said that. They never meant it. "Look, he's an old friend of mine and I'm in New York for the first time in years, and I thought if he was there we could get together for a drink and dinner. You know how it is." The General thought he had done a pretty good job of making up that story. He thought he sounded very sincere.

"I wish I could help you, General, but we have very strict rules, and it's my responsibility to make sure the rules are followed. How could I break them myself? I'm sure you can understand." And with that, he hung up.

The General sat, stunned by the rudeness. He wasn't used to being treated this way. A week ago, he would have identified himself not only as a General, but also as a member of the Joint Chiefs, and *then* he would have gotten what he wanted. To say you're a member of the Joint Chiefs is to say your one of the President's closest confidants. It gets things done. Now, this snotty apartment building supervisor basically told him to take a hike, and then hung up on him. He was batting zero in New York that was for sure.

Chapter 89

Ben had run through the trip in his mind and was sure he thought of everything. The return flight was Thursday afternoon. Of course, on the return flight, they left New York at five in the afternoon and arrived in London at three in the morning. Stanley would be waiting for them. Stanley had turned out to be a gold mine. He knew every road in Great Britain. He knew all the shortest routes to anywhere, and he was a wonderful driver. Not overly slow, but very safe. He took wonderful care of the car, and he loved to garden, so in his spare time he did the gardening.

Ben decided to call Mr. Fenton personally. He didn't want to have any problem because he had a black man in his party, and he didn't know what the policies were in this building. It had been no issue at all when he bought the place, but things changed, and he didn't want to take a chance. He thought of calling the agency he was dealing through, but decided against it due to the sensitive nature of his concern. It was four in the afternoon on Tuesday, and eleven in the morning in New York City. He dialed the number he had been given. A woman answered, "Mr. Fenton's office. May I help you?"

"Good morning," Ben said cheerily, "Mr. Fenton please?"

"May I ask who's calling?"

"Mr. Nathan. I have an appointment to meet with him tomorrow."

"One moment please, Mr. Nathan." She put him on hold. Within ten seconds a man picked up. "Mr. Nathan, this is Mr. Fenton. What can I do for you, sir?"

"Well, Mr. Fenton, I have a question for you, and it's of a sensitive nature. I feel I have to ask to avoid any unpleasant confrontations."

Paul was immediately concerned he was going to ask about the questions the committee might want to ask him. "Anything I can do to help, Mr. Nathan, I'm only too happy to do so. Feel free to ask me anything. I assure you your inquiry will be held in the strictest confidence."

"I appreciate that, Mr. Fenton. I'll get right to the point. One of my closest traveling associates is black, and I want to be sure there isn't going to be any problem with him staying in the apartment with me tomorrow night."

Fenton was relieved. Of all potential questions, this was a real easy one. "Mr. Nathan, we have no concern whatsoever regarding anyone's race. In considering residency qualifications it is not a criteria, at all. I will tell you that we presently have two African-American families living here, along with one Chinese family, and two Japanese families."

"Well, that's very encouraging to hear. Thank you for your time, Mr. Fenton."

"It was my pleasure, Mr. Nathan. I'm looking forward to meeting you tomorrow. By the way, sir, coincidentally an old friend of yours called me yesterday looking for you. He said he was in town and wanted to have dinner with you. He wanted to know if you lived in the building."

There was a momentary pause at the other end. "Did he leave a name?"

"General Edwards. I believe he said his first name was Clayton."

"What did you tell him?"

"I told him we don't give out such information, sir. That's our strict policy."

"Did General Edwards happen to say where he was staying?"

"As a matter of fact, Mr. Nathan, I had to return his call because I was tied up when he called. He was staying at the Hotel Mayflower, just two blocks down on Central Park West. He was in room number two-ten."

"Thank you, Mr. Fenton, I appreciate your letting me know. If you run your building with this same courteous service, I may move in permanently."

"Thank you, sir," Fenton replied, although what he was thinking was: "We'll be the ones to make that decision." However, he had to admit he liked Mr. Nathan based on the phone call. That was a plus for Mr. Nathan.

Ben hung up the phone and thought about this information. General Clayton Edwards, in New York City, snooping around this particular building and asking about his "old friend" Benjamin Nathan. Somehow, the General had figured out his new identity. Because he was in New York, he knew he had somehow searched back into the real estate transfers and came up with the transfer from Adamson to Nathan. He must have been able to isolate same-name transfers. He made a mental note to do it differently next time. He would transfer each property into different names. Then he would wait a few months, and transfer them into whatever name he chose for the time. He would eliminate anyone being able to run a same-name isolation on the transfers in the future.

But, that didn't do him any good now. If Edwards was looking for him in New York City, then he knew about the other properties as well. He was probably starting with New York because it was easier. He knew that eventually he would find his way to Balmoor. He couldn't have a man like this stalking him. It could be disastrous. He took a small book out of his desk drawer. It was names and phone numbers he had accumulated over the years.

He flipped through a few pages until he came to the name he was looking for. He dialed a different number first. The phone rang twice, and the call was answered by an automated system. A recorded voice asked for his personal identification number. He punched in eight numbers. He waited till the recorded voice said, “thank you.” He had another dial tone. Now, he dialed the number he wanted. He was on a scrambled signal line that was untraceable to where he was. The phone rang three times and a woman answered, “Mr. Saunders’ line.”

Ben spoke softly, “Frank Saunders, please.”

Chapter 90

The intercom on Frank's phone came alive. "Mr. Saunders, a call for you on line four."

"Who is it?"

"I'm sorry, sir. He wouldn't give me his name."

Frank thought that was a little odd as he picked up. "Frank Saunders."

"Is this line secure, Mr. Saunders?"

Frank thought he recognized the voice, but he wasn't sure. "Yes it is a secure line, who is this?"

"It's Adam."

Frank felt a chill run up his spine, and at the same time his heart rate increased by about thirty percent. He hadn't felt this way since he was in his first year of high school, and he was calling a girl he liked for a date. He had no idea why he reacted this way. "Mr. Adamson, is that really you?"

"Yes, Frank, it's really me. How are you?"

"Well, to tell you the truth, I'm not really very good."

"I'm sorry to hear that, Frank, is something wrong? Are you sick?"

"No, not exactly. Ever since we spoke I've been very confused and I guess, according to my wife, I've been acting really weird. The problem is I just can't stop thinking about you."

"Me, Frank, why?"

"Why? You have to ask me why? Think about what you told me. How can I forget that?"

"Well, I don't know about forgetting, but I don't understand why anything we discussed would make you 'act weird' as you put it."

"Come on, I find out there's a person been alive for thousands of years and it's not supposed to make me a little crazy?"

"Well, let me say this; if I thought it would make you a little crazy, I never would have told you anything. I judged you as a man who could handle it, and I don't believe I ever make judgment errors, Frank. Maybe the problem is you think there should be some profound revelation connected to what you know, but the bottom line is there is no profound revelation to it. It's just a fact you know that no one else knows, that's all. You should go on with your life."

"Yeah, well, I'm sure you're right, but I'm having a little trouble with it.

I'm sure I'll sort it all out. So tell me, why are you calling me? You're taking a chance that this call could be traced."

"I thought you said it was a secure line."

"It is, but a line being 'secure' is relative when you're in the CIA."

"Not to worry, Frank, this call is untraceable, even by the CIA. The reason I'm calling is because I have a problem I'm hoping you might be able to help me with."

Frank couldn't believe his ears. He would do anything for this person. "You name it, Adam."

"I apparently have Clayton Edwards snooping around looking for me in New York City."

"Are you *in* New York City?"

"No I'm not, but I do own property there and I'm traveling there tomorrow on some overnight business. I called on a non-related matter, and I was told the General was there yesterday, looking for me."

Frank Saunders shook his head. General Edwards had really flipped. What did he think he was going to accomplish?

"You happen to find out where he's staying?"

"He was at the Hotel Mayflower, in room two-ten."

"I'll take care of it."

"Are you sure, Frank?"

"Absolutely. It will be my pleasure."

"Frank, tomorrow night, I'll be one block further up at sixty-eight Central Park West. Why don't you come by. Tell the doorman you're there to see Mr. Nathan in apartment 4-C. We'll talk then. OK, Frank?"

"Sure, that would be great. Thank you."

"No, thank *you*. I was worried about the General."

"Forget about the General, sir."

"Thanks, Frank, I'll see you tomorrow." He hung up.

Frank hung up the phone and contemplated the situation. He wasn't much for believing in fate or signs, but he had to wonder what the odds were that his wife would serve him with papers one day, and he would get a call from Adam the next.

He looked at his watch. It was ten. If Edwards was checking out of the Mayflower, he would already be gone. He got the number for the Hotel Mayflower, and dialed it. When the desk answered he asked for Clayton Edwards room. The phone rang and he hung up immediately. He figured they would have told him if the General had checked out. That meant he was staying at least another day. He could go home, pack some things and be on the road in an hour. He would be in New York by four o'clock.

There was no one home when he got there. He packed a bag with clothes for a couple of days. He unlocked a gun locker in his closet, and took out a leather case. In it was a special assignment weapon he hadn't used in the fifteen years he owned it. It was a nine-millimeter automatic with a silencer. He put it in his bag and left. He didn't leave a note. He wouldn't have known what to say. He had no idea if he would ever be back in this house, or if he would ever see his wife and children again.

He thought, as he drove up I-95 toward New York, about what he was going to do with the General. He really just wanted to kill him. If it hadn't been for his insistence, he would never have followed up on his father's story. He would never have met Adam and he wouldn't be in the situation he was in with his wife and kids. The problem was, he never killed anyone, and he didn't think he could do it. Besides, if the General turned up murdered in New York City that would just draw more attention to the whole thing. And how did the General even get wind of where Adam might be? He said he was going to be staying under the name of Mr. Nathan. How did the General find that out? If he was searching in top security databases, his code would be in the memory system. If he turned up murdered, someone could go snooping to see what he had been doing the few days before his death. It was possible they might find any inquiries he made in the system.

Frank tried to remember exactly how the system worked. When he used it he was never concerned with who knew, so he never gave it much thought. He thought if they removed the General's access code in the next day or two, any memory of his use of the system would be eliminated. The truth was, he didn't care. The General was a threat to Adam, and if he had to kill him that's what he was going to do. It didn't matter what the consequences were.

Frank arrived in New York City a little after four o'clock in the afternoon. He found his way to the Mayflower Hotel, after parking his car in a garage a few blocks away. He went to the desk clerk and pulled his ID from his jacket pocket. The CIA ID was very impressive with a small gold plated badge. He gave the clerk enough time to read the ID, so he knew he was talking to a CIA agent.

"Do you still have a man named Edwards in room two-ten?"

The clerk hesitated for just a second and Frank thought he was trying to decide if he should say they don't give out that information. But he thought twice about the CIA and that he already knew the room number, and decided against it. He punched a few buttons on the computer and looked at the screen.

"Yes, sir, he's still here. According to the system he's in his room."

"How do you know that?

"The computer logs every time the door opens. It shows a door unlocked from the outside differently than a door opened from the inside. Based on the readings, it looks like he went 'in' last. Of course, if he opened the door just to look and never actually went in, then he wouldn't be there. But, chances are he's in his room."

"Thanks. And, we never had this conversation."

The clerk understood exactly what he meant. "What conversation?" he asked, and smiled at Frank.

The Mayflower had a large sitting area with overstuffed chairs, couches, and tables everywhere. Frank sat in a chair in the corner of the lobby, where he would be able to see everyone coming and going. He took a newspaper off one of the tables and started to read it, as a cover for his face. He tried to remember the last time he had done this. He kept the paper spread open and just low enough for him to see over the top. Several people came out of the elevator at different times and a few went in, but none of them were Edwards.

An hour and a half later the elevator door opened and Clayton Edwards stepped out into the lobby. Frank saw him immediately. He raised the paper slightly to be sure Edwards didn't see him. Edwards stepped out the front door and turned left onto Central Park West. He walked up a few blocks, and Frank followed him. Edwards stopped in front of the building where Mr. Nathan supposedly lived and he looked at the entry. Frank watched him and wondered if the General was doing the same thing to Adam, that he was doing to the General. Frank stayed back and watched.

The General stood there for about ten minutes, then turned and started to walk back toward Frank. Frank turned and walked briskly to the next street, where he turned the corner and put his back to the wall of the building. His heart started to race, because he had no idea where the General was going. He knew he could possibly walk right around the same corner, and they would be face to face. What would he do? He reached into his jacket and took out his weapon. He was wearing his shoulder holster. He had put the silencer on. He thought about the irony; he had never been in this type of a situation in all his years in the agency, and here he was ready to kill a man and it had nothing to do with the agency whatsoever.

He held his breath knowing that the General had to be close to the corner and, sure enough, the General walked past him, continuing down Central Park West. Frank breathed a sigh of relief, stepped back out onto the sidewalk, and continued following him. The General walked past the Mayflower, and at the next corner turned right. When Frank came to the corner he continued walking as if he was going to go past the street. That was how he had been trained. When he got to the other side of the street he glanced over, and saw the General continuing up the street. Frank crossed back over and followed. When they almost reached the end of the block, the General turned in to a parking garage.

Frank followed him in, but he didn't like parking garages because of the echo footsteps made. He realized he should have been wearing soft-soled shoes. He concentrated on stepping very lightly. He watched as the General walked over to the elevators. He stayed back until an elevator opened and the General got in. When the doors closed, Frank went over and saw the elevators had level indicators. He watched until the elevator stopped on level three. He pushed the elevator button and the other door opened. He got in and pushed level two. When he got to the second level, he got out and climbed the stairs quietly to the third level. He looked around, but didn't see anyone immediately.

From the location of the elevators he could walk several yards to the left and see all the way down the parking row or, he could do the same to the right and see all the way up the other row. He slowly moved to the left and saw nothing. He moved to the right and about halfway up the row he saw a car's interior lights on. Frank broke into a sweat. What was he going to do? He hadn't really thought this out. If this was the General, was he going to confront him? What would he say? He knew there was nothing he could say that would stop the General from pursuing whatever he was after.

As he slowly moved toward the car, he decided the only solution was to kill him. He didn't know how that would play out in the end, but he really didn't care. He wasn't going to let this person open a can of worms that might result in Adam being exposed to the world. He approached the car and saw the passenger door was open. Someone was sitting in the passenger's seat and as he got close enough he realized it was the General. He was counting money. The glove box was open. It must be where he kept his money. Frank's heart was pounding, and he was sure the General would be able to hear it, but he was almost to the car and Edwards hadn't looked up. He took his weapon out of the holster and stepped around from behind the car next to the General's. Hearing someone so close startled the General, and he looked up to see Frank standing right next to him pointing a gun at him. Frank saw a frightened look on his face for a second, then he obviously recognized him and the look on his face changed to one of confusion.

Edwards must have wondered why Frank was following him and why in the world he was pointing a gun at him. He started to speak. The name Saunders was half out of his mouth when Frank pulled the trigger. The bullet hit him in the neck almost at the collarbone. The look on his face changed to one of shock. He tried to speak, but couldn't. Frank pulled the trigger a second time and the windows on the driver's side of the car were instantly splattered with red. The second bullet had caught the General just over his right ear. He slumped over toward the driver's side. Frank saw the windows of the car were darkly tinted. He reached in, and checked the General's jacket pockets. In one of them he found the room entry card to the hotel. He took it, then took a handkerchief out of his pocket and pushed the button on the door that locked all the doors. He pushed the door closed with his elbow, careful not to touch the car. The interior lights remained on, and for a moment Frank was afraid he wouldn't be able to shut them. But, as he pondered this dilemma, they faded off.

The lighting in the garage was not particularly good, and it was impossible to see into the car. Frank was sure he had a few days before anyone would discover the General's body. He would go back to the Mayflower and check the General's room just to be sure he hadn't left anything behind that might point to Adam.

Chapter 91

The Rolls pulled up to the departure terminal for TWA at Heathrow. Stanley jumped out and came around to open the door. Ben, Gus, and Barbara stepped out while Stanley took their luggage out of the trunk. Stanley shook hands with Ben and said he would be back to pick them up tomorrow night. A skycap took their bags and they walked to the departure gate.

The plane took off from Heathrow at nine-fifty in the morning. Ben and Barbara sat together in first-class and Gus sat across the aisle. The flight took almost five hours, and with the time zone change, the plane would arrive in New York at nine thirty-five. They would get to New York fifteen minutes earlier than they left London. Ben thought about how tired they would be by ten at night, when their bodies knew it was really three in the morning. His meeting with the Condominium Committee was at three o'clock. He and Barbara were going to do some shopping before that. He had to stop at the Credite Suisse office on Fifth Avenue, to pick up the money he had transferred there. He arranged to have a limo waiting for them at JFK.

Ben thought about some of the conversation with Barbara the day before. He had explained to her why it was important to him to wait until they were married, before they had any sexual relationship. At first she had looked at him like he was crazy, but she accepted the fact that he was a unique person, and if she was going to be with him she was going to have to accept that many things might be different.

He told her he felt a personal relationship with God, even though he didn't practice any religion. He was completely familiar with the Bible, as he was with the Koran, the writings of Muhammad, and the Vedas.

He believed the Bible to be inspired and to represent God's view of matters pertaining to humans. He felt many other religious writings had some positive elements to them, but that only the Bible was truly inspired by God. He knew all of the arguments and criticisms directed toward the Bible, and he knew the explanations to all of them. He also knew how accurate the Bible was about so many ancient events.

He had never had an opportunity to meet Moses, and he knew that much of his writings dealt with events that occurred thousands of years before he lived. Somehow God had passed that information down to him, because it was amazingly accurate. There were times in the Bible when men had more than one wife and God seemed to allow it. But the Bible always condemned sexual relations without the benefit of marriage, and Ben felt a need to avoid anything that he knew to be condemned in the Bible. Barbara had reluctantly agreed, and he promised her they could get married soon. When she pushed him about what "soon" meant, he just smiled and said that "soon" meant "soon."

Chapter 92

It had been a long time since Paul Fenton felt nervous about an interview with a prospective resident, but Ben Nathan made him a little nervous. He was very wealthy and absolutely unknown. Fenton could find no meaningful background information on him and he wondered if he might be someone else, using an alias. He checked into his financial position as much as he was able and simply received verification he had enormous wealth.

Fenton had always been impressed by the staff that maintained 4-C when it was owned by Mr. Adamson, even though no one ever saw him. It seemed the same staff was still maintaining the apartment, and that pleased him. He played his brief conversation with Mr. Nathan over in his head a dozen times. Mr. Nathan had sounded pleasant enough.

While he mildly resented the question about racial discrimination, he couldn't help but appreciate the man's attempt to eliminate any type of unpleasant situation. His experience with the wealthy was that most didn't care about anything but themselves, and would have simply assumed they could do whatever they wanted. So, all in all, the phone call was a plus in his favor.

Fenton looked at the clock and saw it was a little past nine-thirty. The other members of the committee would start filing in shortly. Their first interview of the day was at one, and Mr. Nathan was due in at three. It was unusual to have two interviews in the same day. When they did, the association bought the committee lunch, which was brought in by a small caterer at eleven-thirty. They would eat and discuss any preliminary issues having to do with the candidates.

The committee only scheduled one meeting a month and most often there was no need to meet, because there were no new applicants. Today's meeting was unusual on two fronts. One was that there were two interviews, and the second was how intrigued everyone was about Mr. Nathan. There were many rumors flying around. One was he was actually a movie star using an alias, or perhaps using his real name which no one knew. Another was he was either a big-time movie director or producer. Of course, these were simply rumors, but they did make for interesting possibilities and they insured all committee members would be present today.

Chapter 93

Frank Saunders sat in his car and watched. He was parked in the same aisle as the General's car, but he was closer to the other end of the row. He had driven up and down the parking garage for well over an hour to find the space he was in. Now he could see the General's car, and he knew on one side of it there was a white BMW 528i and on the other side a blue Buick Century. He was waiting for either of those cars to pull out so he could take the space.

He had gone back to the General's hotel room yesterday. He found a computer readout that confirmed his suspicion. The General had accessed the pooled data files used by various branches of the federal government. He found the other real estate transactions in the name of Benjamin Nathan. He ripped the paper into little pieces and flushed it down the toilet.

He decided to use the room, rather than go out and rent one on his own. He was surprised that it didn't bother him more that he had killed someone. He washed up, and went out to find a place to eat. He walked south on Central Park West and found himself down around Times Square. There was a restaurant called the Times Square Brew Pub, and it looked appealing to him. Along with dinner he sampled several different types of beer and when he came out, he was feeling pretty good.

He walked around for a while and then headed back toward the Mayflower. Walking up Central Park West he looked across the street, and realized that he had never been in Central Park. It was one of those places that everyone knew of, but many never visited. He crossed the street and entered the park. It was well lit, and he wondered about all the muggings and rapes he heard about. He didn't walk too far into the park before he sat down on a bench. He thought about the rough element that might cruise through a little later looking for victims. He put his hand up, felt his weapon under his left arm, and silently dared anyone to give him a hard time. He knew he had seven shots left in his clip, and with the silencer, he could drop an entire gang and no one would hear a thing.

He looked up at the stars and started to contemplate the universe. He wondered what it was all about. He had never been a real believer in God, until he met Adam. Once he understood Adam's origin his entire thinking changed. But he had come to realize that it was like the brain injury some people suffer when they're in an accident where their forward motion is stopped too suddenly, and their brain, because of the momentum, slams up against the front of their skull. He had gone from being a person who really knew nothing about God, the universe, or some divine purpose, to being someone who knew too much in a blink of time. He hadn't been able to make the adjustment. He instantly became a "lost soul," knowing there was something he should do with what he knew, but not having a clue what it was.

Now he had killed a man to protect another man. He was trying to understand how he had gotten to this place in his life when it all became crystal clear to him. His relationship with his wife was over, and as much as it hurt him to admit it, he never really had a relationship with his daughters. He didn't want the General's murder to lead to some big investigation that could possibly lead to Adam.

While the press had no clue, many people within the loop understood the animosity between him and the General when the investigation was ongoing. It had been Frank's report, which so sharply contradicted every action the General took, that got the ball rolling in the first place. The General had come to hate Frank, and he had been verbal about his feelings. Frank had always considered Edwards to be incompetent and, he, too, had expressed his view to others.

Frank came to the conclusion that the only way to tie this entire situation up neatly was to kill himself. When he and the General were found, it would be obvious from ballistics that Frank had murdered the General, then taken his own life. There would be talk about Frank's depression and odd behavior over the past six months. It would come out he had seen a psychiatrist, and he and his wife had been to a counselor. His wife's filing for a legal separation would also become public, and the puzzle pieces would all be there. A crazy man goes to New York, kills the man he hates, and then kills himself. Would anyone wonder why the General was in New York, or how Frank found out he was there? He didn't think so. That would take real investigative initiative, and he didn't think anyone on the New York Police Department would care enough. He knew the military and the CIA would both be too embarrassed by it to dig deeper.

There was a woman walking up the aisle from the elevator. Frank watched as she passed his car. It was difficult to be sure, but it looked as though she had gotten into a car up by the General. Sure enough, he saw the white BMW back out of the space and drive away. He started his car, pulled out into the drive lane, and moved up slowly, easing his car into the space next to the General's car. He backed up a little, and straightened his car out so it didn't look out of place. His car also had dark tinted windows, and he hoped that it would be days before either of them were discovered. He wanted Adam to be out of the country first, even though he thought there was little chance of anything pointing to him.

He shut the car off and sat for a few minutes. He was nervous, but it wasn't what he would have expected to feel in the last few minutes of his life. He was sorry he wasn't going to see Adam again, but he knew doing so would increase the risk. Should his picture appear in the paper, he didn't want someone to say they had seen him the night before going into an apartment building just off of Central Park. He was surprised by how calm he felt. It was as if this had been the destiny he was searching for.

He had considered writing a note to his wife and daughters, but what would he say? He thought whatever he said wouldn't be right and would probably be misunderstood. His wife would think he was trying to make her feel guilty. Better to leave no note at all, and let everyone think whatever they wanted.

He took out his gun and slumped slightly in his seat. He put his duffel behind him on the rear seat. One advantage to being a trained CIA agent was that he knew exactly how to shoot himself to ensure a painless, instant, and relatively neat death. He knew putting the muzzle of the gun into his mouth, and pointing it only slightly up toward the back of his neck would cause instant severing of his brain stem. He slumped down in the seat so the bullet wouldn't pass through him, and out the rear window. The way he was sitting ensured the bullet would wind up in the duffel, or the back seat of the car. He put the muzzle of the gun far enough into his mouth till he could feel the end of the silencer against the back of his throat. He knew he had to do this quickly, or he would talk himself out of it. He adjusted the level of the gun so he felt it was pointed exactly where he wanted it, and as he squeezed the trigger, he told himself that it really wouldn't hurt at all.

Chapter 94

The limo driver was waiting at the gate holding a small sign that said "Nathan." Ben approached him and introduced himself. The driver accompanied them to the baggage claim area, and then walked them over to the customs counters. He spoke briefly to the inspector who asked Ben the basic questions. He looked at the three passports and waived them through without opening a suitcase.

Within minutes they were in the limo heading into the city. Their first stop was the bank and Ben went in, while everyone else waited in the car. Five minutes later, he was back in the car and he had one hundred thousand dollars worth of traveler's checks. It was ten-forty when they entered Bloomingdale's. Ben spent over five thousand dollars on clothes and accessories for Barbara. A few minutes before noon, they entered Brooks Brothers. Ben bought clothes for himself, and Gus. Gus kept arguing, saying he had his own money, but Ben kept joking, saying his money was "no good in New York." At one-thirty they were in Tiffany's. Barbara picked out some diamond and sapphire earrings. They looked at diamond rings just for the fun of it, and Barbara tried on a dozen different ones. They were all beautiful. At two-thirty they were back in the limo heading for Central Park West.

Chapter 95

There were six members of the Residency Committee. Paul Fenton was one of the members, and he was the Chairman of the Committee. He had lived in the building for seventeen years, and they made him the Chairman of the Association about a year after he moved in. He was very interested in the building and its residents, and he had inherited his apartment along with eleven million dollars from his grandmother. He had a degree in accounting, and had been working for an accountant in Darien, Connecticut, when his grandmother passed away.

He spent the first three years of his newfound wealth as somewhat of a playboy, making all the upscale party scenes, but he discovered he had a strong sense of civic duty and it resulted in his serving on several boards of directors. One was for a small art museum that met twice a month. They decided what exhibits to bring in and how long they could be on display, and they handled the day-to-day business of the museum, as well.

While serving on that committee, he met a woman named Andria Sebastian who became a board member a year after him. She was attractive and intelligent, and she was a real asset to the board. He also learned she was independently wealthy and working part-time as an investment counselor. They started to see each other, and she helped him diversify his investments with amazing results. Within a year of their dating, she had helped him earn an additional million and a half dollars. He joked about what they could do if they combined their fortunes, and she asked him if that was a proposal. He told her it was, and she accepted. She told him her one condition was that they were married in a private civil ceremony. She had no desire to get all dressed up in a fancy wedding gown, and she didn't want to agonize for months making plans to spend tens of thousands of dollars to feed people they hardly knew, and would probably never see again. It made him love her all the more.

They were married two weeks later, and she moved into his apartment on Central Park West. After the wedding, he found out her wealth was almost double his. Her grandfather had invented Velcro. She dabbled in the stock market on the computer when she felt like it. Between the return on their investments, and the money she made with her dabbling, they were earning a little over three million a year.

The rest of the committee was made up of three women and two men. It was simply coincidence it worked out that way. One of the women was Frances Cantor. Her husband was the president of a large insurance company. They lived in 3-A. She was a fifty-eight year old woman with the emotional makeup of a sixteen year old. She was always complaining about some physical problem, or how her kids never called her except to ask for money. In spite of her personality faults, Paul found her to be very fair when it came to the Residency Committee.

Another of the women was Ann Vellone, who lived in 2-C. She was one of the younger members of the committee. She was in her early forties and she had lived in the building for six years. She had previously lived in West Palm Beach, Florida, with her husband, who had been a landscaper with all of his customers in the community of Palm Beach. He had been a hard working man who provided only the best service to his clients. Life had been good for them, and their children. One day, her husband received a letter in the mail from a law firm in Palm Beach. It informed him one of his clients had passed away, and *h*e had been named in the will. His presence was requested at the reading of the will.

That day came, and her husband found himself sitting in a room with the man's three sons, each of whom was the size of a pro football player. None of them were happy to see him there. They all saw him as representing some money they were not going to be splitting. The will was read and the bulk of the man's estate went to his sons, which was a relief to Ann's husband. However, the old man had really loved his estate and the beauty of the grounds. He used to talk to Ann's husband every week, and her husband would humor the old man and spend time talking with him about the grass, or the palm trees, or the old fichus tree at the back of the yard. He had altered his will several years earlier and left the property and three million dollars to the landscaper. He was a shrewd old man who knew his sons, because the will stipulated if they contested the will in any way, their portion of the estate would divert to charity.

Ann and her husband decided to sell the property because they were perfectly happy with their home and they had no desire to live in such a huge place. The estate was appraised at four and a half million dollars, but they sold it to one of the sons for three and three-quarter million just to show that there were no hard feelings. Of course, selling to the son eliminated the need for an agent, which saved them almost a quarter of a million.

A year later, her husband was killed in a high-speed boating accident. It turned out the accident was caused by a defect in the fiberglass molding of the boat, and the manufacturer settled with Ann for three million dollars. Ann had a sister living in Rochester, New York, who was happily married to a dentist, and Ann decided to move up North. Her daughter was working in Key West and had no desire to move, but her younger son came to New York with her, and was attending a private school.

The third woman on the committee was Claire Auwood. She was the oldest member, and she was Paul's idea of a beautiful older woman. She was seventy-one, but looked like she was in her late fifties. Rumor had it that she had been in several movies when she was young, but she was never a star. She had been married for forty-six years to a criminal lawyer who practiced in New York City. When he had a fatal heart attack five years ago, it was the first time Claire had any idea about their financial standing. His will left everything to her, and his net worth was just under five million dollars, including the apartment, which was valued at one point eight million. She was a very kind woman, always sending money to various causes she would hear about. The checks were never large, perhaps a hundred dollars being the largest, but she would send out a dozen or more of them each month. She was a very refined woman who wanted the apartment building to be refined. Her analysis of each candidate was particularly directed toward his or her impact on the quality of the building.

The two men on the committee were Alan Shapiro and Ron McGory. Alan Shapiro was a retired violinist from the New York Philharmonic Orchestra. His parents had been living in the building for about twelve years when his father died. Two years later his mother also died, and left the apartment to him along with an estate of several million dollars. Alan gave violin lessons in his apartment with the committee's permission, but they limited his hours of lessons to between ten in the morning and three in the afternoon. He only accepted the most gifted students, and he was an excellent teacher. Alan had never married and was too old and set in his ways to think about it now. He did see various women socially and, for a man in his late sixties had a fairly active sex life, or at least he thought so.

Ron McGory was the newest member of the committee, and the only member still working full-time. He was in his middle fifties, and he was an equipment broker. He dealt mostly with equipment used in large manufacturing such as robots, cranes, hoists, and metal molding systems. There was a huge demand in developing countries for the type of machinery that was being replaced every three or four years by manufacturers in the United States, Canada, and several European markets. He moved over a hundred million dollars of equipment a year in a bad year, and his commission was ten percent. His wife had lived in the building for nine years before they met. When they married, he moved in with her. The committee had no control over new residents under those circumstances. They were married for two years when she became ill. She died eight months later. Her will left her entire estate to her two children. Neither of them was interested in the apartment, and they agreed to sell it to him for a million dollars. It was worth two. When the ownership of the apartment changed, he technically fell under the control of the committee and it was the only time that Paul could remember when the committee waived their consideration. Ron sent them a thank you note with an offer to serve on the committee, if there was ever a need. Eight months ago, one of the members had become ill and had to resign from the committee. Ron was invited to take her place. She had died recently, and the couple desiring to buy her apartment represented their first meeting today at one o'clock.

The committee had concluded its meeting with them in only twenty minutes. They were a couple from Philadelphia and their financial credentials were impeccable. Lots of money inherited from parents on both sides. He was about to be the new president of CBS. Their children were all grown and on their own. One was a doctor in Los Angeles, and one was an airline pilot flying for American Airlines. They were approved unanimously.

The way it worked with the committee was interesting. The decision to accept a resident did not have to be unanimous. There could be one dissenter, and the applicant could still be accepted. Two dissenters or more, and they were rejected. When there were one or more dissenting votes, they always discussed it at length. Among themselves, they were very candid about how they felt, and why. When an applicant was rejected, they were never told why. They were simply told that their application "had not been accepted." They believed wording it that way made it easier to accept.

It was fifteen minutes to three, and they were all looking forward to meeting Mr. Nathan. They weren't sure, but they thought he was the second wealthiest applicant they had ever interviewed. Three years earlier Michael Bloomberg, the sole owner of Bloomberg News Network and Bloomberg Publications, had applied for residency. His net worth at the time was about five billion dollars. He reluctantly agreed to meet with the committee. The building is posted clearly with "No Smoking" signs at the front entrance and the lobby. Of course, residents are free to do whatever they please in the privacy of their own apartments, but the lobby, hallways, and elevators are strictly "No Smoking."

Fenton's office on the first floor, which includes the committee meeting room, is also clearly marked with "No Smoking" signs. When Mr. Bloomberg came into the building, he was smoking a cigar. He continued to smoke the cigar throughout his interview with the committee. It took them five minutes to agree to reject him. They had no doubt that, as a resident, he would smoke in the lobby and the elevator and the halls. Paul had anticipated hearing from his attorney when he received the letter, but he never did.

They expected Mr. Nathan at any moment.

Chapter 96

The limo pulled up to the front of the building at fifteen minutes to three. The doorman came over to the limo, and opened the door. He had no idea who they were, but he figured he couldn't go too far wrong. The limo was a stretch Mercedes, and even in New York, there weren't many of them around. Ben stepped out first, and helped Barbara out. Gus climbed out the other door and walked around. Ben introduced himself to the doorman, and the doorman acknowledged he was expecting him.

"Apartment 4-C I believe," he said with a smile.

Ben looked at him. "That's the one."

The doorman seemed genuinely friendly. "Why don't you go on up, Mr. Nathan. I'll get the luggage and be up in a minute." He took a key out of his pocket. "A man from the agency that cares for the apartment dropped this off to me this morning, and told me to give it to you."

"Thanks," Ben replied. "What did you say your name was?"

"Steve." And he extended his hand, which Ben shook.

"Thanks, Steve, I'll see you in a minute. I have to meet with a committee at three."

"No problem, Mr. Nathan. I'll let them know you're here and that you'll be along."

"Thanks, Steve," Ben said, and he handed him a folded bill, which he put in his pocket immediately.

"You're very welcome, Mr. Nathan. Welcome to the building."

Ben smiled at him, "Don't be hasty, I haven't talked to the committee yet."

"Don't you worry, Mr. Nathan, they do whatever I tell them." His laugh assured Ben he was joking, and Ben found it amusing.

Ben, Barbara, and Gus went into the building. Steve went into the lobby and took a small cart kept just for luggage, and walked back out to the limo. The driver had already put the luggage on the sidewalk and was standing, waiting. Steve looked at him. "Hey, how you doing?"

"Good, how about you?"

"Great. My name's Steve." And he extended his hand.

The limo driver said, "Ken." And they shook hands.

Ken said, "Take care of that guy, he's a good one."

Steve wasn't sure what he meant. "Really. Why?"

"I picked him up at JFK this morning and I've been taking them all over town shopping. He told me to stay on call tonight until ten. He took my cell number and he told me to be back at ten tomorrow morning, if I don't hear from him tonight. And to plan to drive them around all day until they have to be back at JFK at five in the afternoon. He just tipped me three hundred dollars for today."

Steve reached into his pocket and pulled out the folded bill. He opened it and found that it was a hundred. "Man, I better get this stuff up to him. Nice meeting you, Ken. I'll see you in the morning, I guess." He tossed the three suitcases onto the cart and headed into the building. He stopped at the phone just inside the entrance and called into Paul Fenton's office. Paul answered the phone himself.

"Mr. Fenton, this is Steve"

"Yes, Steve."

"Mr. Nathan just arrived. He'll be at your office in a couple of minutes."

"Thank you, Steve."

"One more thing."

"Yes, what is it?"

"If you reject this guy, I quit."

Paul laughed out loud. He had never heard such a thing from Steve in all the years he was the doorman. "He's that good, huh?"

"Yes, sir, that good."

"Big tipper, I imagine."

"You got it."

"Thanks for the input, Steve, I'm sure it will make all the difference." He hung up the phone and related the message to the committee. They all had a good laugh. It was obvious they were inclined to accept this mystery man unless he did or said something to make them feel otherwise.

Chapter 97

Ben unlocked the apartment and was extremely pleased with what he found inside. He had not seen it since the first day he looked at it. It was run down then, but he recognized the potential. He put several of his people to work hiring designers and contractors and he had given them no limit on the spending, but he required they come to him with a fairly accurate estimate before they did a thing. The estimate was for three hundred thousand dollars, which was a lot of money back in the late sixties when he bought the apartment, but he had given them his approval. They had also discussed an annual cost of maintaining the apartment with no one ever living there. That represented an additional one hundred and seventy thousand dollars a year. Five years ago, he had the entire apartment repainted.

They walked into a beautiful bright living room filled with a wonderful mix of new and antique furniture. The color coordination between the walls, drapes, and furniture was exquisite. The hardwood floors were polished to perfection and there were subtle Aubusson rugs placed everywhere. Each room was delightful, and there were fresh flowers in every room. The refrigerator was full of food and bottled water. There was a liquor cabinet in one corner of the living room, stocked with a bottle of twelve-year-old single malt scotch, Courvoissier, top shelf vodka and gin, and several bottles of expensive white and red wines. There were also two bottles of Balmoor wine. When Barbara pointed it out to Ben, they both laughed. Ben made a mental note to thank the agency. He encouraged Barbara and Gus to each settle into a bedroom and relax. He had to run off for the committee meeting.

He left the apartment and went down to the first floor on the elevator. Steve was waiting at the elevator when the door opened. He had their luggage on the cart. He looked at Ben as he came out of the elevator. "Hello, Mr. Nathan, I was just on my way up. Mr. Fenton's office is right over there, sir." And he pointed toward a door at the end of the lobby.

"Thanks, Steve," Ben said as he walked to the door.

When he walked in, he saw a young woman sitting at a reception desk. He approached her and introduced himself. The reception office was beautiful and well furnished. Ben noticed how clean everything was. The young woman invited him to take a seat, and she would let the committee know he was here. The clock on the wall read two fifty-nine. The young woman came out of the meeting room in a few seconds, with Mr. Fenton right behind her. Ben thought he looked a little older than he sounded on the phone. Mr. Fenton was immediately impressed by the fact that Mr. Nathan looked much younger than he expected. The two men shook hands and exchanged greetings. Paul turned toward the doorway he had come out of and gestured toward the room. “Come on in, Mr. Nathan. We’re looking forward to talking with you.”

Ben followed him into the room. There was a modest conference table with five chairs on each side and one at each end. Paul Fenton sat at one end of the table and to his right sat the other two men, to his left sat the three women. Each had a notebook in front of them. They invited Ben to sit at the other end. Paul Fenton opened the discussion by introducing all the committee members. He then looked around at the members and said, “Who would like to start?”

For a moment, there was no movement among them, then Claire Auwood spoke, “I’ll start, Paul.” She looked directly at Ben. “Tell me, Mr. Nathan, are you intending to make New York City your permanent residence?”

Ben looked directly back at her. “No, Mrs. Auwood, not at this time. I live in Great Britain at the present, and I own residences in several other countries. At this time my residence here would be for my occasional use. Of course, I wouldn’t rule out living here full time at some future date.” He smiled at her, and she smiled back.

There was another long moment of no activity as Paul looked from side to side. Finally Ron McGory spoke up, “Mr. Nathan, might you allow others to use this apartment in your absence?”

Ben wasn’t sure if he meant long or short-term. “I couldn’t rule out the possibility that among my few close associates there could occasionally be the need to use the apartment for a night or two, but if you mean would I let someone else move in and stay here for a longer period of time, the answer is no.”

Mr. Shapiro spoke up immediately, so if Ron McGory had a follow-up question, he wouldn’t have time to ask it.

“Mr. Nathan, this is a very quiet building. Even when a resident does occasionally have some social engagement, a party if you will, they tend to be very low key. Others in the building would not know there was a party going on unless they were invited. Do you feel that would be restrictive?”

“Not at all, Mr. Shapiro. I’m not one to be throwing parties. I am a very private person and I go out of my way to preserve my privacy.”

Francis Cantor raised her hand signaling she had a question. Paul called on her as if he were the teacher in a classroom.

"Mr. Nathan, do you have a family?"

"Not at the moment, Mrs. Cantor." By now they were impressed with his ability to remember everyone's name. "I do, however, have a lady friend and I hope we'll be getting married in the near future and starting a family." The answer brought a smile to her face.

Paul Fenton looked around at the members. No one made a further move to speak. "Any other questions from the committee?" he asked. The members simply shook their heads. Of course, financial qualifications had already been reviewed by the committee, and unless there was some question about an applicant being in a position to bear the expense, questions regarding finances were never asked. No doubt some of the committee members would like to have known where he accumulated almost a billion dollars, but they weren't going to ask.

Paul spoke up, "Well, I guess that's all the questions we have for you, Mr. Nathan. We would like to thank you for coming to see us. We'll let you know our decision in the near future."

Ben stood up. "It's been a pleasure meeting all of you. Thank you for your time." With that, he turned and left the room.

The committee sat quietly for a moment looking at each other. Paul finally spoke, "Any observations?"

Ann Vellone spoke first, "He's a lot younger than I expected. I'm not sure if he's in his thirties or forties."

Ron and Claire agreed.

Paul spoke again, "OK, OK, we agree he looks surprisingly young. Any observations that actually relate to our residency consideration?"

The members all shook their heads. Paul spoke again, "All right then, all in favor of accepting Mr. Nathan's application raise your hands." All six hands went up.

"It's unanimous," Paul said, stating the obvious.

Claire spoke, "Paul, why don't you stop up to Mr. Nathan's apartment and let him know of our decision. He's staying in the building, and it will save you having to write a letter."

Paul looked around. "You all feel it would be appropriate to do that?"

They all nodded their approval.

"OK, I will. I'll wait a little while though. I don't want it to be too obvious it only took us about one minute to decide."

Chapter 98

When Ben left the committee he walked out the front entrance where Steve opened the door for him. "Hello, Mr. Nathan, all done already?"

"It didn't take long, Steve. I don't know if that's a good sign or a bad one."

Steve looked at him. "Oh, that's a good one, don't worry."

"Say, there may be someone stopping by this evening asking for me."

"Oh, that General who was here a few days ago?"

"No, not him, it will be someone else. His name is Frank. If he comes by, call me and let me know will you? I want to see him."

"Sure, Mr. Nathan, no problem. I'm here until nine tonight. If you think he'll be here later than that, I'll be happy to stick around."

"Thanks, Steve, that's really nice of you. If he hasn't shown by nine, why don't you call me and we'll make a decision. Would that be all right?"

"Sure, no problem."

"Great. Thanks, Steve."

"You're welcome, Mr. Nathan."

Ben went back into the building and into the elevator. He wondered if Frank Saunders would stop by. He also wondered what he could do to help him. He had been sorry to hear their discussion had caused problems for Frank.

He let himself back into the apartment to find Gus and Barbara sitting in the living room talking. They each had a glass of wine. "Well, aren't you two looking pretty comfortable."

Gus looked up at Ben. "Hey, we're snuggled up in the lap of luxury, how could we not be comfortable?"

Ben laughed, "The lap of luxury, huh?"

Barbara looked up at him. "Pour yourself a glass of wine, and come sit down," she said, as she patted the couch next to her. Ben walked over to the little bar in the corner and poured himself a glass from the bottle that was open. He then walked over and sat down next to Barbara. She spoke, "How did it go?"

He shook his head. "Not good."

She seemed a little surprised. "Not good, what do you mean not good?" Gus looked at him with a similar look of surprise.

Ben looked at them both with a serious look. "They said my financial report raised questions as to whether or not I could afford to live here."

They both looked at him with disbelief.

Gus, saw a little twinkle in his eye, and started to laugh out loud. This made Ben laugh, which made Barbara realize he had been joking, and she also started to laugh.

Ben looked at his watch and saw that it was almost three-thirty. He wanted to be around for Frank if he showed up, but he had told him to come at night.

"How about going out for an early dinner?"

Barbara looked at him, appreciating his ability to laugh at himself, including his wealth. "Sure, I'm actually a little hungry anyway."

"Me, too," Gus added.

"Where should we go? Do we need a car?" Barbara asked.

Ben looked at Gus. "Gus, you know any place in the city?"

"Not really," Gus answered.

"Well, then, let's see if we can get Ken to help us out." Ben walked over to the phone on a table next to the chair Gus was sitting in and dialed a number off of a slip of paper.

"Hi, Ken, it's Ben Nathan. We'd like to go out and get an early dinner. Can you pick us up and recommend a place?" He listened for a minute or so. "That sounds great. Sure, we're ready any time. OK. Great, see you in a few minutes." He hung up the phone.

"He'll be here in less than ten minutes. He said he knows a great little place not far from here."

Barbara said, "I need a few minutes to freshen up." She jumped up, and headed into her room.

Ben and Gus sat looking at each other.

"Gus, listen, there's something I've been wanting to discuss with you."

Gus looked at him with a little smile on his face.

Ben looked at him. "What? What are you smiling about?"

Gus said, "I know what you want to talk about."

"Oh, you do, do you? And what is that exactly?"

"You think I'm some old fool? You think I don't see how you look at this girl? You think I don't think about the fact that she's along on this trip, and that you dropped a ton of money buying her clothes today? You think I don't know that you're in love with this girl?"

"I'm thinking I'm going to ask her to marry me."

"I think that's a good idea. She told me you told her everything, but what about children? You always said that was a big problem."

"If we have children, I'll just have to be careful to keep them out of the public view. They'll grow up having to be careful, like me. Besides, I don't think they're going to have to hide for six thousand years. I have a feeling something's going to happen way before then."

"Really? What do you think is going to happen?"

Ben looked at Gus with a very serious look on his face. "I don't really know, but it will be a major world event, I can tell you that."

Barbara came back out into the living room. "I'm ready to go." They all went out and found the limo waiting in front of the building for them.

Ken took them to a little restaurant just off of Times Square on 44th. It was small, and the service was excellent. They ate a leisurely dinner at a quiet table in a corner of the dining room. There was no one sitting near them. It was too early for the regular dinner crowd, and the lunch crowd had cleared out over an hour earlier. Ben ordered a bottle of champagne as the dishes were cleared. Barbara and Gus looked at him. Ben gave a quick wink to Gus and looked at Barbara. She looked back at him and said, "What are we celebrating?"

Ben smiled, "I'm not sure, but I think we'll find something to celebrate. After all, we're in New York City.

The waiter reappeared with the champagne, and opened it. He poured a little into Ben's glass and Ben tasted it. He nodded to the waiter, who then poured three glasses, and put the bottle in a bucket of ice.

Ben reached into his jacket pocket, and as he did so he said to Barbara, "I want to ask you something."

She looked at him also smiling. "Yes, darling, and just what is it you want to ask me?"

He put the little black box down on the table in front of her. She gasped when she saw it. She picked it up, and opened it. It was one of the rings she had tried on earlier in the day at Tiffany's. It was the one she liked most. It was a two and a quarter carat diamond in a platinum setting. She was speechless. She looked at Ben with her mouth open.

He loved her surprise. "Barbara, I would be honored if you would marry me."

She couldn't get any words out. Tears began to run down her cheeks. She took the ring out of the box, and slipped it onto her finger. She held her hand out and looked at it. Finally, she looked over at Gus. "What do you think, Gus? Should I marry him?"

Ben and Gus laughed.

Gus said, "I don't think it would be a bad decision, and I have to tell you I never thought I'd hear him ask that question of *an*y woman."

She looked at Ben with her tear-filled eyes, reached over and took his hands in hers, and kissed them. Ben felt a sense of love and tenderness beyond anything he had felt before.

She looked back up at him and said, "Yes, Benjamin Nathan, or whatever your name really is, I will marry you."

Ben picked up his glass of champagne, and held it up. "You see," he said, "I knew we'd find something to celebrate."

They drank the champagne, discussed preliminary wedding plans, and headed back to the apartment. They got back a little before six. Ben settled down to watch the news. It was the only time he ever watched television. He did like to know what was going on in the world, even though most of the information was discouraging. By seven o'clock, they were starting to feel the effects of the time loss from the flight over. As far as their bodies were concerned, it was midnight. Gus said he was turning in. He gave Ben a hug like a big brother. "Congratulations, boss. I think it's great."

"Thanks, Gus. Not only for your support in this, but for everything over the years."

They clapped each other on the back, and Gus headed toward his bedroom.

Ben sat down on the couch next to Barbara, and put his arm up on the back of the couch. She snuggled in against his shoulder, and closed her eyes. His arm dropped onto her shoulder. He leaned his head onto the top of her head. He loved the smell of her hair. He closed his eyes and they both drifted off into a light sleep.

The ringing phone woke them up. Ben looked at his watch. It was just after nine-thirty. He picked up the phone. "Hello?"

"Mr. Nathan, it's Steve at the door. I haven't seen your visitor. Do you want me to stay a little longer? Ben was surprised Frank hadn't come by. He was sure he was going to. He hated to keep Steve around for no reason, but he knew if Frank showed up after he left there would be no way for him to get through. "Would you be willing to stay until ten, Steve?"

"Sure, Mr. Nathan, no problem." He hung up. Ben made a note to tell Steve tomorrow how much he appreciated his cooperation.

Barbara looked at him and said, "I can't stay up, Ben, I'm going to call it a night." She kissed him, went to her room, and closed the door. Ben wanted to stay up a little longer to see if Frank showed up.

There was a knock on the door a few minutes later, and Ben jumped up thinking it was Frank. He walked to the door and looked through the peephole. He was surprised to see Paul Fenton standing there. He opened the door. "Mr. Fenton. What can I do for you?"

"I hope it's not too late, Mr. Nathan. May I come in for a moment?"

Ben stepped away from the door. "Certainly, please, come in."

Paul stepped in and looked around. "You know, this is one of my favorite apartments. The decorating done by the previous owner is truly delightful, don't you think?"

Ben looked around. "Yes, I certainly do."

"Well, Mr. Nathan, let me get right to the point. The committee unanimously approved your residency, and I just thought rather than make you wait a week to receive a letter in Great Britain, I would come up and give you the news in person." He extended his hand. "Welcome to the building."

Ben shook his hand. "Thank you, Mr. Fenton, and please thank the committee for me, as well."

Fenton reached for the door. "I certainly will. You have a safe trip home."

"Thank you." With that, he left.

Ben decided to get ready for bed. If the phone rang, he could always get up. He, too, was tired.

As he lay in bed contemplating the day, his proposal and impending marriage, the phone rang again. He reached over to the table next to the bed and picked up the phone. "Hello?"

It was Steve again. "It's me again, Mr. Nathan. Nobody yet."

"Let's call it a night, Steve. I don't think he's coming if he hasn't been here by now."

"OK, Mr. Nathan. Good night."

"Thanks, Steve, good night."

Ben closed his eyes and thought about the wedding. He thought they would get married at Balmoor. He would ask old Mr. MacRoiter, who was a Justice of the Peace in Winterton by the Sea, to come up and perform the ceremony.

He realized he knew nothing of Barbara's family. He had no idea whether her parents were alive, or if she had any sisters or brothers. He knew the ceremony would be private, but if she had family nearby he would expect her to want them there. That could be a problem years from now, but he would worry about it then. As he thought about these things, he drifted off to sleep.

In the morning they did a little sightseeing, and a little more shopping. At three in the afternoon their plane was in the air, heading back to Heathrow. It was eight p.m. at Balmoor. Stanley would be leaving Balmoor at nine, so that he would get to Heathrow by midnight. Their plane was due in at about one.

Chapter 99

Barbara thought about the wedding plans. She knew without having to discuss it with Ben, he would want to have a private civil ceremony. She understood him well enough to recognize the need for privacy, and she knew that he avoided any religious association.

But she didn't know how he would feel about her inviting her family or close friends, not that she had many. Her mother and father lived in Norwich, only about an hour from Balmoor. They were retired, living carefully on their pensions. She had a sister who was married and lived in Liverpool with her husband and one daughter. Her brother-in-law was a bus driver. He was a nice enough fellow, and on the few occasions she saw her sister, she seemed very happy.

Barbara had one close friend in Winterton. She also worked at the bank, and was a single girl, a few years younger than Barbara. Her name was Marie, and they often spent time together. Their personalities clicked, and they enjoyed each other's company.

Her thoughts drifted to the long-term prospects of this relationship. She realized that within ten years they were going to look the same age, and in twenty years she was going to look older than him. But what about thirty, or forty years from now? How was she going to feel when she looked like his mother, or his grandmother? Those prospects frightened her, but not enough to say no to marrying this man she had come to love.

Barbara had been in relationships before. Ben was not the first man she felt she loved, but now she realized how different it was when the love was genuine. Her other relationships had ended in typical fashion after months. She had never given either man a second thought. But now, contemplating marriage to this man who really loved her, she thought she needed to let him know about them. He had gone to great lengths to explain to her his view of sexual relationships being tied to marriage. He hadn't asked her about her past relationships, and she assumed her past didn't matter, but she told herself she needed to discuss it with him, to be sure.

She couldn't help be intrigued at the thought of their wedding night. Based on everything he told her, he was a virgin. Their sexual encounter that first night would be his first. She chuckled thinking about it. Then, she contemplated his being perfect. That was a term so loosely thrown around, but this was different. This was a man who was literally physically perfect. What would that mean in regards to their sexual relationship? Would he be the perfect size when he was aroused? Would he have perfect physical control?

She remembered her first real sexual experience with Willie, her second boyfriend. He had taken his clothes off, and was lying on her bed watching her undress. She saw arousal was certainly not a problem for him. She had teasingly taken off her dress. Then she reached behind her and unhooked her bra, allowing it to fall away. She had full, firm breasts and as soon as Willie laid eyes on them, he gave new meaning to the word "pre-mature." She wondered if being married to a physically perfect man would mean perfect lovemaking. She hoped it would be the case.

She knew this relationship was going to have unusual challenges, but she believed in her heart that whatever time she had to be with Ben, it was going to be worth it.

She was still contemplating her future, as the plane began its approach to Heathrow.

Chapter 100

Vinnie DeRoma had been the black sheep of the family ever since he decided to go to college, rather than go into the family construction business. His father, Frank DeRoma, started the business in the early fifties, and they were now one of the largest contractors in the five boroughs, grossing over four hundred million a year. Frank hoped his two sons would share the running of the business, but Vinnie insisted he wanted to go to college, study criminal justice, and become a cop. Frank had ranted and raved, but in the end, he paid for Vinnie's college education and set up a trust fund with two million dollars that became Vinnie's when he turned thirty. He had access to the interest from the trust each year, and it provided him with more than enough money to live comfortably.

His brother, Angelo, on the other hand, inherited the family business, paying his father five million dollars over ten years for a business that was worth fifty million.

Angelo and Vinnie were very close, and saw each other almost every week. Angelo and his wife Anna had a son who was born a year after Angelo became the owner of the business. They named him Frankie.

Vinnie received his degree in criminal justice, along with a minor in psychology, and went to work for the New York City Police Department. He was a street patrolman for two years, during which time his superior officers recognized his intelligence and street savvy, and invited him to work undercover. He accepted the challenge, and was very effective in undercover work for four years.

The one thing about undercover work he didn't like was the difficulty he had seeing his family. He could only get away to visit with Angelo and the kids once every few months. He would usually see his mother at the same time. When he was a regular street cop, he saw his mother several times a week. His father passed away during his first year as a patrolman. Toward the end of his third year, he became involved in an operation that kept him undercover for more than eight months. It was a huge operation that took them to the very top of one of the major drug-trafficking operations in New York City. Trying to visit his mother or brother would have jeopardized his life, and theirs. The investigation eventually led to the arrest of several top level New York drug dealers, and dozens of their underlings. Drugs with a street value of over a hundred million dollars were seized, along with seven million dollars in cash. Four undercover officers, including Vinnie, were given special citations and promoted to detectives. His mother and brother were very proud of him, and they were in the audience to watch him receive his citation and gold shield. After the ceremony, his mother told him she was still mad at him for not visiting her for eight months.

Vinnie had been a detective assigned to the Eighteenth Precinct, more commonly called the Midtown North Precinct, for two weeks, when he took the phone call that would change his life. It was a parking garage manager on West 62nd. There were two cars parked side-by-side in his garage. The owners hadn't shown up in several days. Both cars had dark tinted windows. When they shined a flashlight into the cars, there was obviously a body in each car.

"Did you open either car?" Vinnie asked, sure that the evidence had been tampered with.

"No, they're both locked," the manager replied.

"How do you know they're both locked?"

"My attendant tried the doors."

"So your attendant touched all the doors?"

"Well … I don't know if he touched them all or just the driver's door."

"OK, look, get the people away from the cars, and don't you or anyone else touch them, you understand?"

"Yes."

"What's your name?"

"James."

"OK, James, we'll be over in a few minutes. You stick around, and the attendant who first looked in the cars, keep him around too, OK?"

"OK."

Vinnie hung up, finished making some notes for himself from the conversation and closed his notebook. He picked up his phone and dialed a number. He identified himself and requested a crime scene team to meet him at the parking garage. He looked around the squad room for his partner. Louise Murphy had been a cop for nine years, and a detective for the past three. Her husband, Sean, was a Lieutenant in the Twelfth Precinct. Vinnie had been working with her for only two weeks, but he found her to be extremely qualified, and willing to teach him everything she knew.

She came into the room from the area of the rest rooms and coffee lounge. Their desks faced each other. As she approached her desk, he got up and told her about the call.

She looked at him and smiled, "Your first case as the primary, and it's a double. Way to go, DeRoma," as she said it she took her coat off the back of her chair. He did the same, and they walked out to the garage.

The car they used was a two-year-old Chevy Caprice. It was dark blue and unmarked, except for the several antennas. Which didn't mean much in New York.

Vinnie almost always drove. It wasn't a male versus female thing. It was Louise's preference. She hated driving in the city. She would do it if she had too, but she didn't like it.

They drove over to the garage and when they got to the entry gate, Vinnie pulled up and flashed his badge. The attendant opened the gate immediately and told them they wanted the third level. When they got to the third level, it didn't take any searching to find the cars. There were at least twenty people standing around.

Vinnie parked the car in the middle of the lane and he and Louise got out and walked over to the group of people. Vinnie took out his badge and showed it around. "Who's James?"

A middle-aged black man stepped over to him. "I'm James." He seemed nervous, but Vinnie knew dead bodies had a way of affecting people like that.

"James, I'm Detective DeRoma and this is Detective Murphy. Who finally looked in the cars?"

James pointed to a short, heavy-set young black man wearing a leather jacket. "That's him right there, his name is Jarvis."

"That's his first or last name?" Vinnie asked.

"That's his first name. Last name's Maclellan."

"OK, James, when did these cars come in?"

James had a clipboard in his hand, and on the clipboard was a computer sheet. Vinnie was impressed. James held up the clipboard and read off of it. "The Buick came in last Tuesday at around six o'clock in the evening. The Honda didn't come in until Thursday morning."

"Great work, James. How about asking Jarvis to come over here."

James turned toward the young man and barked his name. Jarvis walked over to them. James introduced him to the two detectives, and Vinnie spoke to him.

"Jarvis, James tells us you're the one who saw bodies in the cars."

Jarvis nodded his head. "That's right. I couldn't see in the cars because of the tinting, it's real dark tinting, so I went back to the office and got a flashlight. As soon as I looked in the first window with the flashlight, I saw a dead man in there. It scared the crap out of me, I'll tell you that."

"Jarvis, how did you know the man was dead?"

"His brains are all splattered on the window, man. You can be sure he's dead."

"How about the other car?"

"Well, I couldn't see a bullet hole or anything, but the way his head is back and he doesn't move, I'm pretty sure he's dead, too."

"What did you touch?"

"Oh, nothin', man, except the window. When I put my face up against it I had my hand on the side of my face like this." He demonstrated what he was describing.

"How about the door handles?"

"Hell no, I didn't touch the door handles."

"Then how did you know the cars are locked?"

Jarvis looked at him like he was crazy. "I got no idea if the cars are locked or not, I never touched the door handles. I don't want to open the door of a car that's got a dead man in it."

"OK, Jarvis, you've been real helpful. James has your phone number if we need to get in touch with you, right?

Jarvis nodded.

"OK, thanks. We'll be in touch if we need you."

Vinnie and Louise started to walk toward the cars, and as they did so the crime scene team pulled up behind them. They waited a minute and two crime scene specialists climbed out of a mini-van. They carried what looked like large plastic toolboxes with them.

The four of them talked for a minute, before walking over to the two automobiles.

They approached the Buick first. One of the technicians put on latex gloves while the other one took pictures from every angle and several different distances. After the pictures were taken, the one with the gloves tried the driver's door and found it locked. He tried all the doors, they were all locked. He opened his toolbox and pulled out a long, flat piece of metal with notches in it. He slipped it in between the window and the car door, moved it up and down a few times and pulled it out. He reached for the door handle and opened the door of the car, very slowly.

He recoiled from the smell that came from the car. Reaching back into his box, he pulled out a paper filter that he put over his nose and mouth. The other technician dug into his kit, and pulled out three of the same filters. He put one on, and gave one each to Vinnie and Louise.

They took pictures inside the car of the man lying on the front seat. The cash he had been counting was still in his hand, the glove box still open. It was obvious robbery was not a motive. They took note of the dried blood and tissue on the inside of the window and door. The bullet wound was on the right temple, and from the blood and tissue on the door they knew when they moved him, they would find little remaining of the left side of his head.

They moved over to the Honda. Here, too, they found all the doors locked. They had already taken pictures, and the technician used the same tool to unlock the door. The interior of the car was much cleaner.

Their initial analysis was this was a suicide. The weapon was still in his right hand. There was a hole the size of a half-dollar in the back of his head, just above the neck. They took pictures inside the car. They put the gun into a plastic bag without touching it. They suspected it was the same weapon that killed the other man, but a ballistics test would be done to verify.

Wallets were found on both bodies, along with Frank's CIA identification, and these were given to Vinnie. By the time the crime scene technicians were finished, the coroner's van was there. Two tow trucks waited out on the street to bring the cars to the police impound.

Vinnie and Louise spent about ten minutes discussing the scene with the technicians. When they were through, all agreed the man in the Buick, Clayton Edwards, had been shot by the man in the Honda, Frank Saunders, and that Saunders then killed himself. Vinnie and Louise had been surprised by the CIA identification. Looking through Edwards' wallet, they found a military ID that let them know he was a General.

They returned to the squad room, started to make some phone calls, and run some computer checks. Within thirty minutes they were sitting speechless with the information that Frank Saunders was the acting assistant deputy director of the CIA, and that Clayton Edwards up until just a few days ago had been a General on the Joint Chiefs of Staff. Two men in such high-level Washington positions involved in what seemed to be a murder-suicide in New York City!

Louise eventually broke the silence, "Well, DeRoma, I gotta hand it to you. You really know how to pick 'em. No simple homicide for you. No way. You start out with a spy and a member of the Joint Chiefs! Good goin', man." She was laughing quietly.

Vinnie sat there looking at her laughing, and he smiled too. He didn't want to seem overly sensitive, but he knew already he was going to have a big problem with this case.

His analysis at the scene was that Saunders killed Edwards. He was confident ballistics was going to prove that. Then, for some reason, Saunders waited until he could park right next to Edwards, then killed himself.

The coroner told him their guess was that Edwards had been dead about a day longer. Vinnie was worried that once the murder-suicide was confirmed by the Medical Examiner and ballistics, he was going to be told the investigation was over. One man killed another, then killed himself. End of story. But to Vinnie, it wasn't going to be the end of the story. Why did a high ranking CIA agent kill an Army General? And Vinnie thought he could understand why he would kill himself afterwards, but why did he feel a need to have his car parked next to the car of the man he killed? That just didn't make any sense, and Vinnie knew he was going to have to find out the answer.

He looked over at Louise, grateful he had a partner with a sense of humor. He knew all too often he lacked that.

They made phone calls to the CIA and to the Army to inform them of the situation. The responses were what they had expected. Both individuals asked for their names, and how they could be reached in New York. Both said they would be in touch soon.

Vinnie decided he should also try to notify the next of kin, so he called information in the Washington area. Both numbers were unpublished and Vinnie had to identify himself as a New York City Detective, and give the operator a particular code. He soon had the two phone numbers. He dialed Clayton Edwards' number first and got no answer, no machine.

He dialed the second number, and the phone was answered on the third ring. Vinnie was caught off guard. He wasn't sure if it was a woman or a young girl. She said hello a second time, and he knew he had to speak or she was going to hang up. "Hello, is this Mrs. Saunders?"

"No, this is her daughter. Can I help you?"

"Uh, no. Is Mrs. Saunders available?"

"Who's calling, please?"

"My name is Vincent DeRoma and I'm calling from New York City regarding an important matter."

There was a momentary hesitation. "Hold on, please."

Vinnie could hear her put the phone down and he heard her off in the distance, yelling for her mother. He heard her say, "It's someone from New York, and he says it's important."

A few seconds later, an extension was picked up and he heard a woman's voice. "Hello?"

Vinnie didn't want to say too much until he heard the other phone hang back up. "Is this Mrs. Saunders?'

"Yes, it is. Who is this please?"

"Mrs. Saunders are you married to a Frank Saunders?"

"Yes, I am. What's this about?"

"Mrs. Saunders, my name is Vincent DeRoma, and I'm with the New

York City Police Department. Could you do me a favor please and get a pencil and paper? I need you to write something down for me."

There was a brief hesitation on the other end. "OK, hold on." A few seconds later she was back. "All right, Mr. DeRoma, I have a pencil and paper."

"Good, write down my name, Vincent DeRoma." And he spelled it for her. He waited a few seconds and gave her his direct phone number into the squad room. "You got that down, Mrs. Saunders?"

"Yes I do, now what's this all about?"

"Well, Mrs. Saunders, I'm afraid I have some bad news for you. Are you sitting down ma'am?"

"Mr. DeRoma, you're starting to make me very nervous."

"Mrs. Saunders, I don't mean to do that. I'm sorry to have to tell you that your husband's body was found today in a parking garage here in the city. It appears to be a case of suicide." There was silence on the other end.

"Mrs. Saunders, I know this must be a terrible blow. We don't have to talk now. You have my name and number. Call me back when you can, and we'll discuss the disposition of your husband's body." He could hear quiet sobbing and the phone went dead.

Chapter 101

Tuesday morning's New York Post carried both their pictures on the front page. They were both older file photos. The headline read: "DC DUO — MURDER/SUICIDE — NYPD BAFFLED." The article stated that Frank Saunders had murdered General Clayton Edwards, and then killed himself. It went on to say there was no known motive, and the police were investigating. Anyone with information was asked to call the tip hot line.

Steve walked into Paul Fenton's office with the Post under his arm. Fenton's receptionist was at her desk. She smiled at him when he came in, but she saw right away that something was troubling him. He wasn't his usual, friendly self.

"Is he in?"

She nodded.

"Good." He walked into Paul's office. Paul looked up from his desk, a little surprised that Steve had simply walked in unannounced. Usually his receptionist would call in and let him know when someone, anyone, was there to see him.

Steve walked over to his desk. "Seen the morning paper?" and as he said the words he opened the paper and laid it on his desk in front of him.

Paul looked at the front page absorbing the information, and started to read the article.

"Holy …" his voice faded before the next word came out.

He looked up at Steve. "This is the person who showed up here last week looking for Benjamin Nathan."

"No kidding, Sherlock! Why do you think I came bustin' in here with this? What should we do?"

Paul thought for a minute. "I'm not sure we should do anything. Why?"

Steve looked at him like he was crazy. "Paul, this is a murder investigation. They're asking for anyone who knows anything to call them. If we don't call them and somehow their investigation leads to us, we could be in big trouble."

"How could it lead to us?" Paul asked.

"I don't know, but it could. I mean this guy Edwards comes here looking for Mr. Nathan. Mr. Nathan tells me a man named Frank is supposed to come to see him."

Paul interrupted him, "He did?"

"Yeah, the night he stayed here. He asked me to stay a little later because he was expecting someone named Frank to stop by to see him, and he was afraid he would show up and not be able to get in. I stayed until ten. Then he told me to forget it."

Paul couldn't believe that Mr. Nathan could some how be mixed up in this. "Did he actually say this man's last name, Saunders?"

"No, but come on, Paul. The General is definitely the one I talked to, and this other guy is named Frank. It's way too coincidental. It has to be the same man."

Paul shook his head. He wondered if telling Mr. Nathan that Clayton Edwards had come looking for him had anything to do with this. He suddenly remembered Mr. Nathan had asked him where the General was staying, and he had told him. Did that mean he could be an accessory? He put his head in his hands with his elbows on his desk. How in the world could he have ever thought something like this could come from his mentioning Edwards' inquiry to Mr. Nathan? After all, the man said he was an old friend.

He looked up at Steve. "OK, Steve. Here's what I think. You call the number and talk to the cops. Tell them that Edwards came here inquiring about a resident. Tell them you told him we don't give that information out. Tell them that a few days later, Mr. Nathan told you a man named Frank might stop by. The only thing I don't want you to tell them is that you discussed any of this with me, fair enough?"

Steve looked confused. "I guess so, but why do you care if they know I asked you what to do?"

Paul realized Steve had no idea he had spoken to Mr. Nathan about it a few days before he arrived.

"I don't have a problem with the cops knowing what we know, but I would rather not get involved, that's all."

Steve shrugged his shoulders. "OK, boss. No problem." He walked out of the office.

Chapter 102

It was not the lead story on the world news at noon on British television, but it was important enough to be discussed before the first commercial break.

Ben and Gus were sitting watching the news together, and were shocked to see the pictures of the two men and hear the story. Ben was deeply saddened by the death of both men. The General had started to become somewhat of a nemesis, but he hadn't thought Frank would take his life. He thought back to his conversation with Frank and remembered Frank saying he would "take care" of the General, and that he wouldn't be causing any problem. Ben tried to remember what he thought Frank meant when he said that. He certainly hadn't thought it meant he was going to kill him.

He was even more upset that Frank had taken his own life. Having called Frank to talk about Edwards, Ben felt responsible. The news had mentioned Frank left a wife and two daughters.

Chapter 103

The call came in to the hot line at eight-thirty Tuesday morning, and was immediately forwarded to Vinnie. Vinnie wrote down the name and address where Steve worked and said he would see him in a few minutes. It only took him and Louise a few minutes to get there.

Steve told them everything he knew, except the part about him getting Mr. Fenton involved with the General. Vinnie wrote everything down in his pad. They asked Steve for his home address and his phone number, and asked him not to leave town for the next week or so, just in case they needed to ask him a few more questions.

They went back to the station. There was a message waiting for Vinnie from someone whose name he did not recognize, but the phone number was from the DC area. He called the number and spoke with a woman who identified herself as Sarah Saunders' sister. She said her sister wanted to make arrangements to get Frank's body back for burial, and they had no idea where it was. Vinnie explained that the Medical Examiner had the body, and had not yet finished his autopsy, but he would call her back as soon as the body could be released. She thanked him and he asked her to again extend his sympathy to Mrs. Saunders. She said she would.

He put a call in to the Medical Examiner's office and asked them to let him know as soon as they were done with the body.

He and Louise reviewed the information they had. Ballistics had already confirmed that the weapon Frank used to kill himself had also killed Edwards. The autopsy on Edwards had been completed, and the report sent up to them an hour earlier. He had been shot twice. The first bullet hit him in the lower neck, glancing off his clavicle and severing his pulmonary artery. That wound alone would have killed him in about a minute and a half. The second shot entered just above the right temple and blew out the left side of his skull, along with a third of his brain. Vinnie thought that Saunders didn't want to take any chances. He wanted the General dead for some reason.

They had gotten a call from the clerk at the Mayflower hotel. He confirmed Clayton Edwards had checked into the hotel last Tuesday afternoon. According to their computerized system he had gone out once, come back to the hotel about thirty minutes later, then gone out again later in the evening. The clerk told Vinnie that another man had come in Wednesday afternoon and asked about the General. He had flashed a CIA badge and the clerk admitted he told the man that Edwards was staying in the hotel.

When housekeeping went in to clean up the room the next day, all of Edwards' things were there, but the General was nowhere to be found. They cleaned up the room assuming the General had gone out early. When they went into the room on Thursday morning, all the General's things were just as they had left them. They filed a report with the desk; something didn't seem right. They checked the computer, and it showed that someone had entered the room Wednesday night and had left very early Thursday morning. They also activated the message light on the phone in the room, expecting the General to call the desk when he got back. He never did come back, and on Friday they removed his belongings and put them into safekeeping.

They had not yet reviewed the security tape from the lobby area to see who came in at the time the computer indicated that someone returned to the room. Vinnie had requested the tape, and now had it in his possession. They were going to review it shortly.

The doorman on Central Park West told them that the General had come to the building inquiring about a Mr. Nathan, wanting to know if he lived there. He was told they don't give out such information. The doorman said he never saw him again. The next day Mr. Nathan showed up, and stayed in his apartment for one night. He asked the doorman to keep his eye out for a man named Frank, who was due to pay him a visit. Vinnie and Louise both agreed with the doorman that it was too much of a coincidence. Even though Mr. Nathan never mentioned a last name, it had to be Saunders.

They took the videotape and put it into one of the time-lapse recorders. Vinnie fast-forwarded the tape to six in the evening the day the coroner said Edwards was killed. He played the tape and watched. At ten thirty-five they saw Frank Saunders enter the lobby and go to the elevator. They watched an additional half hour, and he did not reappear. Vinnie fast-forwarded to five the next morning, and then played it back at the regular speed. Sure enough, at twenty after six in the morning the camera caught Frank Saunders coming out of the elevator and leaving the building. Now they knew Saunders spent the night in the General's room. The question was, why? Was it simply to save the cost of a room? Or was there something that Saunders was looking for in the room?

At one in the afternoon, Vinnie got another call from the desk clerk at the Mayflower. He wanted Vinnie to know that in checking their phone records they discovered the General had made a phone call from his room the night before he was murdered. The records also showed that about a half hour later, he received a phone call, but the computer system didn't register the number of an incoming call. They did, however, have the number he called. Vinnie wrote it down and thanked the clerk. He made a phone call and in two minutes he knew that the General had called the business office of the Central Park West apartment house where Mr. Nathan had an apartment.

Vinnie and Louise agreed the return call could have come from the same number. Vinnie made another call and requested the phone records of all incoming and outgoing calls for that number within the hour of those calls. Twenty minutes later, the fax machine produced the list he requested. The record showed a call from that number to the Mayflower at the same time the Mayflower's computer registered a call into the General's room. When they interviewed the doorman, he had given them Paul Fenton's name as the Building Manager, but they had been told he knew nothing of the conversation with the General.

Now, they had an added element. How did the General come to be talking with Fenton, and why didn't Fenton come forward with this information? They would have to talk with Mr. Fenton.

Chapter 104

It was almost six in the evening when Ben picked up the telephone and dialed a number. The call was answered by an automated system that asked him for a code which he dialed. The system then gave him another dial tone and he was now free to make a call that was virtually untraceable. He dialed the number that was a direct line to Tim Groff at IMA. The phone rang twice.

"Groff speaking."

"Good morning, Tim."

There was a hesitation. "Adam, is that you?"

"Yes, it's me. How are you?"

"I'm fine, how are you? I wasn't sure I would ever hear from you again."

"The truth of the matter is, under normal circumstances you wouldn't, but I have a situation I need your assistance with."

"Of course, Adam, anything. Just name it."

"Do you remember the Army officer visiting you about six months ago asking about me?"

"Sure."

"Well, he was sent by a General Clayton Edwards. Edwards had recently been trying to track me down. I put a call into the CIA agent who had come to see me, and the next thing I know the General and the CIA agent are front-page news in New York City. Seems the agent killed the General, and then killed himself."

"That's unbelievable!"

"I'll say. I feel terrible. I never thought the man would resort to something as drastic as that. But, listen, here's where you come in. I want you to check the story; supposedly, the CIA agent, his name was Frank Saunders, leaves a wife and two daughters. Confirm those details. I'm going to transfer a million dollars into IMA. It'll appear in a couple of days. I want you to cut an IMA check to the woman, and send it with the standard letter. If it turns out he didn't have a wife and children, consider it an extra million to the fund."

"No problem, Adam."

"So how's everything going? The new arrangement working out OK?"

"Great, everyone is on the same page. All dedicated to helping people out."

"That's good to hear. Thanks, Tim, I appreciate your help. Obviously, this conversation never took place."

"No problem."

"Take care, Tim."

"You too, Adam." They hung up. He hoped the money would help in some small way.

Chapter 105

When Vinnie and Louise went to see Mr. Fenton, he kept them waiting for ten minutes. Vinnie was sure it was a stall while he tried to figure out what he was going to tell them. When he finally came out they took note that there was no one else in his office with him.

He invited them into the office and closed the door behind them. He then came around and sat at his desk. He put his hands down on the desk with his fingertips touching. Vinnie recognized it from his psychology classes as a classic indicator of confidence. In this case he was sure it was for show. Fenton's eyes did not seem confident, but he smiled and said, "So, Detectives, what can I do for you?"

Vinnie was the lead cop, so he answered, "Well, Mr. Fenton, when we spoke to your doorman we got the distinct impression he hadn't talked to you about General Edwards or Frank Saunders. We thought we should get a clarification from you on this. Is it true he didn't discuss the General with you at all?"

They could see in his immediate body language he was extremely uncomfortable. He was going to lie to them.

"That's correct, I had no idea the man had come here looking for Mr. Nathan."

Vinnie kept his cool, and Louise was impressed. "Now, here's what I find confusing Mr. Fenton, I'm sure there's a logical explanation, and I'd appreciate your clearing it up for me. The records at the Mayflower show General Edwards making a call to the number here in your office the night before he was murdered. And the phone records we requested from the phone company today on your number here in the office, shows a phone call being made back to the Mayflower about a half hour later." He waited to let that sink in.

Any trace of confidence Fenton had been displaying was gone.

Vinnie continued, "Now, Mr. Fenton, we haven't questioned your doorman about this yet. We believe he was withholding information, although we don't know why. We thought we would give you first shot to set the record straight."

Now they sat back and waited. These types of interviews were very similar to high-stakes negotiating. Vinnie knew they had reached the place where the next person to blink loses. They were going to give Fenton all the time he needed to blink.

Fenton realized they were waiting for him to speak. Beads of perspiration were forming on his forehead. He finally held his hands up, with his palms facing out towards them. This was another classic sign, but one of surrender.

"All right, look, Steve told you he hadn't talked with me because I asked him to. He came in here the morning the paper carried the story and he showed it to me. He was adamant he had to call the police and tell him what he knew. I didn't think my knowing about it made any difference, so I asked him not to mention it."

Louise spoke, "Why, Mr. Fenton? Why did you care about our knowing you knew?"

Fenton buried his face in his hands for a moment and shook his head back and forth. Through his hands he muttered, "I can't believe something like this is happening."

Vinnie asked, "Something like what?"

Fenton put his hands down and looked at them. He looked like a whipped puppy, sorry for whatever it was that made its master angry. "OK, look, I'm really sorry that I haven't been completely honest with you. I've been in this community for a long time. I have a good reputation. I sit on several important boards, and I volunteer quite a bit of my time to some of the museums and art galleries. I'm not some sort of criminal."

Vinnie jumped in, "No one is implying you are."

Fenton was regaining a little of his confidence. Now he was going to tell the truth, and he felt better. "I appreciate that, Detective. The problem is, I guess I'm feeling a little like a criminal. You see, I think I might be partially responsible for what happened to those two men."

This surprised Vinnie and Louise. "Why do you feel that way?" Vinnie asked.

"Because when the General showed up here looking for someone, Steve called me and I told him to tell the man we don't give out that sort of information. Steve told me he didn't seem to be the type who took 'no' for an answer too easily. I told him to give him my name and number and tell him that he would have to call me.

"Well, a few hours later, he did call here asking for me, but I didn't take his call. I stalled him. He identified himself as a U.S. Army General, so I called a friend of mine who does a lot of work with the military. He confirmed there was a General Clayton Edwards, and that until very recently he had been on the Joint Chiefs, so I knew I was dealing with someone who wasn't going to give up too quickly. I called him back, and he told me he was an old friend of a Mr. Benjamin Nathan and he wanted to know if he was a resident of the building."

"Is he?" Vinnie asked.

Fenton wasn't going to create any new issues. "Yes he is, technically."

"What do you mean, 'technically'?"

"Well, he bought an apartment in the building from a former tenant. Before he could actually live here he had to come in for an interview with the Residency Committee. He actually lives somewhere in Great Britain, but he did come in last Wednesday for an interview."

"Last Wednesday, two days after the General was asking about him?"

"Yes, exactly."

"So, how do you figure you had anything to do with what happened?"

"Well, coincidentally, on Tuesday Mr. Nathan called me. He had a completely unrelated question for me regarding his visit. I happened to mention to him General Edwards had called. He seemed a little surprised, and he asked me if the General left any information about where he was staying. Because I had called the General back, I knew where he was staying and I figured they were old friends. So, what would be the harm in telling him?"

"So you did?" Louise asked.

Fenton nodded his head. "Yes, I did."

"How about Frank Saunders?" Vinnie asked.

"No, I really didn't know anything about him. Steve told me the morning he came in here with the paper that Mr. Nathan had mentioned that someone named Frank might stop by, and that it was all right to let him up."

They could tell he was now telling them the truth.

"What can you give me on this Mr. Nathan?"

"Nothing, really. We cater to very wealthy individuals, and we don't ask a lot of questions. I can tell you he's very wealthy."

Vinnie looked at him. "Multi-millions?"

Fenton gave him the same look back. "Almost a billion."

Vinnie whistled. "No address where he lives now?"

"You can look at the file if you want, there's no address asked for and none given."

"Who was the former owner of the apartment? Maybe he knows where this guy lives."

Fenton sighed a deep sigh, letting them know this was information he didn't really want to give them. "His name was Adam Adamson. His last address we had on file was in upstate New York, but that was about twenty years ago."

"Well, write it down for me. Maybe it will help us to track him down."

Fenton turned around and opened a file drawer in his credenza. He pulled out a file and wrote an address on a piece of paper and handed it to Vinnie.

Vinnie folded it and put it in his shirt pocket. "Thank you for coming clean with us, Mr. Fenton. We know sometimes when people are faced with having to talk to cops they get a little nervous, and they sometimes say things they don't mean to say or that they wish they hadn't said. So, we're going to just let the early denial slide by this time." As he said this, he and Louise stood up. There was an obvious look of relief on Paul's face.

"And as a side note, based on what you told us, there's no way you share in what went down."

They each shook hands with Paul and left.

When they got back there were several messages for Vinnie. One was from the Medical Examiner's office regarding the autopsy results. Saunders had died from the one self-inflicted gunshot wound. It had blown his brain stem out completely, and killed him instantly. In the opinion of the Examiner, the aim hadn't been luck. He knew exactly what he was doing. Neither man tested positive for any alcohol or drugs. The other message was from another person at the same department just to let Vinnie know that a funeral home had stopped and taken Frank Saunders' body. They had been sent by Mrs. Saunders. The General's body had also been claimed by his brother. The third message was from his Commanding Officer that said to come and see him as soon as he got back.

He walked to the C.O.'s office and the door was open. He approached and knocked on the door trim.

His C.O. was Lieutenant Sam Nelson. Nelson was in his late fifties, but he was in excellent physical condition. He had a reputation for being a fair, levelheaded Commander who stood behind his people when there was a need.

He looked up from what he was doing and smiled when he saw Vinnie. "Hey, Vincent! Come in." He motioned to a chair.

Vinnie came in and sat down. The Lieutenant got right to the point. "So, where do you see this case going?"

Vinnie thought for a moment, "I'm not sure, Lieutenant, why?"

"Well, I'vc rcad what you got so far and it seems like, from our point, the case is closed. Everything points to one guy whacking the other then killing himself. Am I right?"

"Well, yeah, I suppose you're right, Loo, but I'm not sure that should be the end of it."

"What do you mean?"

"Well, the one whacking the other and then himself seems right, but I don't have any motive. I'd like to know why he did it."

The Lieutenant sighed heavily, "Look, you're new at this, and I think you're going to be a terrific detective, but you have a lot to learn. Now, I admire your curiosity, but you have to remember that we're paid to solve crimes, not to figure out all the angles to them. If we figured Saunders whacked Edwards and Saunders was still alive, then motive would be important. There would be a trial and the D.A. would want us to come up with a plausible motive. There isn't going to be any criminal trial. We know how it happened, and we can close the case. We don't really care *wh*y it happened."

Vinnie sat in the chair in front of the Lieutenant's desk without saying anything.

The Lieutenant looked at him, and could see Vinnie wasn't necessarily on the same page. He sighed again, "What's on your mind, DeRoma?"

Vinnie sat back and stared up at the ceiling. He knew he should just let the case go, and he knew the Lieutenant was not going to like what he had to say.

"I hear what you're saying, Lieutenant, and in my mind I know you're right. The problem is, in my *hear*t I feel like we're overlooking something big."

"Like what?" The Lieutenant had just a slight tone of annoyance in his voice.

"Well, like this man who is one of the top in the CIA comes to New York and murders a General who was one of the Joint Chiefs. You don't think that's pretty weird?"

The Lieutenant thought for a moment. "Yeah, it's weird, but if we started paying more attention to every weird thing we dealt with, we'd never get anything done!"

"Lieutenant, look, there's something about this case that screams out to me to dig a little. Let me just spend another day or two checking some things out, OK? If I don't come up with something substantial in a few days, I'll drop it like a rock."

The Lieutenant looked at him like he just asked for the keys to his brand-new car. He liked Vinnie and he knew he was going to be a good detective. "OK, DeRoma. Two days, but that's it. Unless you come up with something amazing, the case closes out in two days, understood?"

Vinnie nodded. "Understood. Thanks, Lieutenant." He got up and out of his office before he could change his mind. The Lieutenant sat there shaking his head. He figured he must be getting old, giving in like that.

Vinnie called the CIA and identified himself as the Investigating Detective. He asked for the name of Frank Saunders' supervisor. He was told it was Deputy Director Harold Quinley. He asked for Quinley and was put through to his office. A woman answered. "Mr. Quinley's office."

She sounded young. Vinnie played a little game when he thought the woman on the other end of the phone was young. He tried to picture what she looked like, based on her voice. He guessed this one was tall and thin, with long dark hair. "Yes, hello, my name is Vincent DeRoma. I'm a homicide detective with the New York City Police Department. I would like to speak with Mr. Quinley, please."

"I'm sorry, Mr. Quinley is not in his office at the moment. Could I take a message?" She sounded sincere.

"Can you tell me when you expect him back?"

"I'm sorry I can't, but he is in the building, so I do expect him back at some point."

Vinnie didn't think she was trying to put him off. "Well, could I leave my number for him to return my call?"

"Certainly."

Vinnie thought she sounded very nice. He gave her his phone number. Then he decided to get a little bold. "Can I ask you something?"

"That depends on what it is." She was good.

"Is Mr. Quinley the type of man who will return my call?"

"Absolutely, Detective." Again, there was a ring of truth in her voice.

"Well, thank you very much. Uh … what did you say your name was?"

"I don't believe I did."

Vinnie wanted to drive down to Washington just to take her to dinner.

"You're right you didn't, but you've been so nice I wanted to thank you, and I thought it would be more personal if I knew your name. But, I don't mean to be forward, please forgive me."

"No problem, Detective, and it's Alissa."

Vinnie smiled, he still had the touch.

"Thank you very much, Alissa, you have great day."

"Thank you, you too, Detective." They hung up.

Vinnie wondered if she was married or if she had a boyfriend. He figured she dated some professional football player who would probably crush him into the sidewalk if he even looked at her funny.

Louise came into the room and sat down at her desk across from him. "You closing out the case?"

He shook his head. "No, the boss gave me a couple more days to play with it."

She looked a little surprised. "What exactly does that mean?"

He looked at her. She was a very attractive woman, and she had a reputation for being an excellent cop. She was also very patient with him and he didn't want to appear to be abusing her patience. "I told him there were some things about the case that made me uncomfortable, and I wanted a couple more days to see if I could clear them up."

"Like, what kind of things?"

"Like, why does a top CIA agent come to New York to murder a top Army officer? These aren't your run-of-the-mill drug dealers or pimps killing each other over turf or unpaid debts. These are people who don't get involved in this kind of stuff. What's the General doing in New York City? Why is he looking for this guy, Nathan? Does Nathan have a connection to Saunders? There's an awful lot of loose ends here, Louise, and I don't like it."

She thought about what he said, and she was about to say something when his phone rang. He looked at her, knowing she was going to say something. "Hold that thought." He picked up. "DeRoma."

The voice on the other end sounded like a professional radio announcer, very deep and smooth. "Detective DeRoma, this is Harold Quinley with the CIA. How can I help you?"

Vinnie reached for a pad and pencil on the desk. "Mr. Quinley, thank you very much for getting back to me. I'm the Investigating Officer on the case involving Frank Saunders, and it's my understanding that you were his direct supervisor."

"That is correct, Detective."

"Tell me, Mr. Quinley, was Mr. Saunders in New York City on official CIA business?"

"I'm sorry, Detective, I'm not free to comment on that."

Vinnie was a little surprised. "Mr. Quinley, I'm not asking you to reveal what the business might have been, I'm simply asking if it was official business that brought him here."

"I understood your question, Detective, but CIA policy prohibits me from commenting on any of Mr. Saunders activities before his death. I hope you understand."

"Well, to be honest, sir, I really don't understand. I hope you understand you're not being willing to answer my question is going to cause me to assume he was on official business. Because it seems to me, if he wasn't, under the circumstances you would want me to know that."

There was a long silence at the other end. Finally, Mr. Quinley spoke, "Well, Detective, you can assume that if you choose to. I won't comment on Mr. Saunders activities, but I have no problem commenting on your assumption. Your assumption would be incorrect."

Vinnie was stunned. He couldn't believe this top CIA honcho was giving in to him and telling him what he wanted to know.

"Mr. Quinley, one last question, sir."

"Yes."

"Your secretary, is she as beautiful as she sounds?"

There was a hesitation, and Vinnie thought he shouldn't have asked.

"Yes," was all he said, and he hung up.

Vinnie shared the information with Louise that Frank Saunders wasn't in New York City on official business. She contemplated that, and Vinnie asked her what she was going to say before the phone rang.

She smiled, "I was going to say that sometimes it can be dangerous to go after loose ends."

He looked at her with his best confused look. "Really, why would that be dangerous?"

"Because they're going to make you close the book on this case in a couple of days, no matter what. You go pulling on loose ends now and come up with something that interests you even more, and it's going to just make it tougher in a couple of days when they say that's it."

He smiled at her, "So you're worried about me, is that it?"

She laughed, "Yeah, that's it, I'm just worried about you. I don't want you going off on some wild-goose chase and putting me in a position where I either have to go with you, or I have to fight with you about it."

Vinnie held up his two hands. "Hey, I'm cool with it. I appreciate your concern and your position. I just want to dig a little, that's all. The Lieutenant is giving me two more days, and if I feel the need, I can devote the weekend to it. So I really have four days. If I had just one *mor*e day, I could tell you for sure who killed JFK."

She laughed again because he was funny, and because she enjoyed working with him. She figured it was his money that allowed him the luxury of not taking anything too seriously. He had never said a word about his money, but her husband mentioned it to her when she was partnered up with him. Her husband only mentioned it out of concern for her safety. Vinnie had gained a reputation for being a little too quick to take chances, and Louise's husband knew all too well that some risk taken by a partner can result in a dead cop. So far, Louise had not seen any sign of Vinnie acting that way.

Vinnie took out his notebook, opened it and dialed a phone number. Louise wondered what he was up to now. He looked at her while the phone rang. Someone picked up.

"Hello, is this Mrs. Saunders?" Vinnie paused. "Mrs. Saunders, it's

Detective DeRoma with the NYPD. I wanted to see how you were doing and if you were able to recover your husband's body?" He listened. "Good. Say, Mrs. Saunders, I was wondering if I came down to your area, could we talk for a few minutes?" Another pause. "No, not today, it's too late today, but I was thinking tomorrow." He listened to her. "OK, sure, yes, eleven in the morning would be fine. Yes, directions would be very helpful." He pulled out his notebook and started to write. "Yes, I have it down. Thank you, Mrs. Saunders, I'll see you tomorrow. Bye." He hung up, looked at Louise and smiled, "Guess what?"

She looked at him with a look that said she thought he was crazy. "Oh, let me guess, you're going to Washington tomorrow!"

He looked at her. "Wrong! *We're* going to Washington tomorrow."

She shook her head. "Not me, buster. You want to go to Washington, have a good time."

He stopped smiling. "Come on, Louise, I need you with me. I can't trust myself to remember everything she says, and besides, I need a woman with me to help her to trust me more. Please, I really need you with me."

She looked at him with his disappointed little boy look. "But you told her eleven in the morning. Do you know what time we have to leave to get there by eleven?"

He shrugged. "Sure, it's about four hours, so we have to be on the road by seven, that's not so bad."

"Try more like six, you have to figure rush-hour traffic, and time to find her house."

"OK, six then, that's still not so terrible. Please Louise, I can't do this without you."

Now she held up her hands. "OK, OK, but I know I'm going to regret it."

Chapter 106

It had taken very little time for the talk around Balmoor Castle to turn to wedding plans. It was the subject of discussion among the servants as they speculated about the ceremony. Who would officiate, and what would the honeymoon plans be?

Ben and Barbara, on the other hand, did not spend a lot of time discussing wedding plans. They had agreed the ceremony would be a quiet, private affair. They had agreed to get married in three weeks. Ben brought up the old Justice of the Peace, Mr. MacRoiter in Winterton, and Barbara thought he would do fine. Ben said he would talk to him.

Barbara expressed a desire to have her parents and her sister present, and Ben had agreed wholeheartedly. He told Barbara he would have Victor prepare some of the additional bedrooms for guests. Barbara would call her sister, and invite her and her husband. Ben asked her about Marie because she had mentioned her several times, and he knew she was her only close friend at work. Barbara was quite pleased Ben had brought her up, and she agreed to talk with her at work.

Ben brought up the issue of her job, and asked her how she felt about it. Barbara said that she enjoyed it and didn't think she would want to stop working right away. They talked about the distance she would have to drive each day, living at the castle. She told Ben she didn't mind because it was a beautiful drive. He told her he wanted to trade her car in for something a little newer.

"And exactly what did you have in mind?" she asked in a little joking tone.

Ben played along. "Oh, I don't know, hadn't really given it much thought. What would you like?"

She looked up at the ceiling, as if it somehow improved her thinking ability. "My, now that's an interesting question. What budget are we working with?"

Ben laughed at the thought of it. "Pounds, or U.S. dollars?"

"Pounds."

"Oh, let's say a hundred thousand."

Barbara frowned in a mock way, "Well, then, I'll just have to settle for second or third choice."

Ben laughed out loud, “Really, what was your first choice?”

“A nice big blue one like yours.”

This brought another laugh. “Well, you can just take that one.”

Now, she laughed, and they hugged. She had never known anyone so generous, but then she had never known anyone so wealthy. She told herself her feelings for him were not related to the amount of money he had, but she knew if it weren’t for his wealth they would never have met.

She assured him they would be able to find something within his restrictive budget.

They talked about a honeymoon. Ben explained he owned property in Spain and Switzerland, and he hadn’t seen either of them in a long time. He thought it might be nice if they spent a week at each location. He promised her they were both beautiful homes, and she told him that she had no doubt. She would be happy to go to Spain and Switzerland for a honeymoon.

Barbara called her parents and gave them the news. They were surprised, because she hadn’t said anything about Ben to them. Barbara explained she didn’t want them to get their hopes built up if it didn’t lead to anything. That was why she hadn’t mentioned it. Barbara’s mother said they would be delighted to attend the wedding, but they weren’t sure how they would get there. They were both older, and they didn’t drive. They were able to get everything they needed within walking distance of their apartment.

Barbara said she was going to call her sister and invite them as well. Perhaps they would be able to pick them up as they came through Norwich on their way out to Balmoor. Her mother was intrigued that they were going to live in a castle. She wanted to know if it was a real castle. “Yes,” Barbara assured her, “it is real.”

She called her sister Elizabeth. The first fifteen minutes of the conversation consisted of small talk. She wanted to know how her sister was, and how her husband and daughter were. After the small talk, she told her sister she was going to be getting married. Her sister didn’t believe her at first, but Barbara finally convinced her she wasn’t joking.

She talked to her sister as seldom as she talked to her mother, but her sister was still upset she hadn’t told her sooner. Elizabeth was also surprised to find out the wedding was going to be in three weeks. Yes, she and her husband would be delighted to attend, and they could pick their parents up on their way. Barbara told her there were only a few people being invited, and they were requesting there be no gifts.

Elizabeth started to question such a request, and Barbara explained her husband-to-be was wealthy beyond imagination, there was nothing they needed except family to share their special day.

She explained about the castle, gave her sister directions, and said there would be accommodations for overnight guests. If they wanted to come up the night before, or stay the night of the wedding, or both, it would be fine.

Elizabeth was curious about the wealthy part. "So, when you say wealthy, you mean as in millions?"

Barbara thought about how her sister had to struggle to make ends meet on her husbands earnings as a bus driver. She suddenly felt self-conscious.

"No, actually I was thinking more along the line of billion."

She heard her sister gasp, "Oh, Babs, you're not marrying some old geezer for his money, are you?"

Barbara laughed, "No, Liz, not at all. Ben is not that old (she thought about how weird that statement was), and I'm marrying him because we fell in love, not because of money."

"Billions, you say, do you think he might sport us a few pounds?" her sister said with a little laugh in her voice. Barbara couldn't help but feel she probably wasn't joking. She also knew if she said something to Ben, he would give her sister whatever she asked him to. That was the way he was.

"I didn't say billions, I said billion, and I know you're joking, but I'm sure if you need money, Ben would give you whatever you needed."

"Babs, we always need money, and I'm not sure what I would say if someone asked me how much money I needed. Does anyone *kno*w how much money they need?"

"Liz, you know what I meant. Ben isn't about to just freely give away fortunes, but he is a very generous man who would help anyone with a specific need."

Elizabeth realized she was getting herself into an embarrassing situation, "Babs, forget I even said anything. I was joking."

They discussed a few details, and went over the directions again. She asked her sister to call their parents and discuss whether they wanted to come on Friday or Saturday, and to let her know. She gave her sister the phone number.

Later in the evening she and Ben spoke about a variety of things including the conversation she had had with her sister. She told Ben about her sister's comment about the money.

Ben looked at her with a more serious look. "How much money does she need?"

Barbara looked at him, not sure if he was being serious. "My sister said she didn't know if anyone knew how much money they needed."

Ben laughed, "That's a good answer, she's probably right, but what I meant was if there was some particular pressing need."

Barbara thought about that. Her sister hadn't specified anything. "I don't think it's that kind of thing, Ben, it's more a case of her husband having a job that pays just enough to survive on. I'm sure it's difficult for them financially, but that's not really something that you should have to worry about." She leaned over and kissed him on the cheek.

"I'm not worried, darling. You know, being very wealthy allows me to do a lot of things others can't do, including help other people. Over the last fifty or so years, I've worked as the president of some large corporations in the U.S. and every penny of my salary went to charity. Over the fifty years it was over one hundred and seventy-five million dollars, and that went to help people I didn't know. Now, if there are people who are going to be related to me through my marriage to the woman I love, why wouldn't I help them? The biggest trick sometimes is helping people in a way that allows them to keep their dignity. Even someone in dire need might be too proud to simply take a hand out."

Barbara just looked at him. He was too much. She wanted to drag him upstairs, throw him into a bedroom, rip his clothes off and make love to him. Instead, a tear escaped the corner of an eye and ran down her cheek.

He looked surprised to see it. "Darling, why are you crying?"

She moved closer to him and put her arms around him and buried her face in his neck.

"Sometimes you just overwhelm me, that's all. You're too good and too kind and it's hard to believe you're mine."

Chapter 107

Vinnie and Louise pulled up in front of the address they had for Frank Saunders at twenty after eleven in the morning. It was much easier to find than they had anticipated. There were two cars in the driveway.

Vinnie looked over at Louise. "Any last minute thoughts?"

She gave him her best deadpan. "Yeah. What in the world are we doing here?"

He laughed lightly, "Come on, let's go pay our respects to the family."

They walked to the front door and Vinnie rang the doorbell. They could hear the bell ringing clearly. After a few moments, the door was opened by a woman who looked old enough to be Mrs. Saunders. She opened the storm door just enough to talk through it.

Vinnie spoke up first, "Mrs. Saunders?"

The woman shook her head no. "I'm her sister. Can I help you?"

Vinnie showed her his badge and ID through the storm window. "My name is Vincent DeRoma, and this is Louise Murphy. We're Detectives with the New York Police Department. Mrs. Saunders is expecting us."

The woman opened the door and asked them to come in, closing the door behind them. They were standing in a small foyer. Off to one side of the foyer was a dining room. The room off to the other side appeared to be a living room, although he could not see very much in the room.

The woman introduced herself to them, "I'm Deborah Marks, Sarah's sister. She's upstairs. Why don't you make yourselves comfortable in the living room, and I'll go get my sister." She motioned toward the living room, and Vinnie and Louise went in and sat down.

They both looked around and Vinnie said, "Nice house."

Louise's reply was simple, "Yes, it is."

In just a few minutes the two women came into the living room. Vinnie and Louise both expected to see a woman in mourning, disheveled with eyes all red and puffy, but Mrs. Saunders was neither. She was dressed in jeans and a sweater, and seemed unusually cheerful for the circumstances. Vinnie and Louise both stood up when entered. Vinnie and Louise both stood up when they entered.

"Mrs. Saunders, I'm Vincent DeRoma, and this is Louise Murphy."

Mrs. Saunders smiled, "It's nice to meet you both. Would either of you like something to drink, a cup of coffee, or anything?"

"No, thank you for asking. We were just hoping you could answer a few questions for us."

"What's this all about, Detectives? I was told my husband's death was a suicide."

"That's true, Mrs. Saunders, but I'm sure you understand from all the newspapers that your husband also killed someone, before he took his own life?"

She looked puzzled. "Yes, I know that and it's very strange. But then, Frank had been strange for a while."

Louise leaned forward in her chair. "Why do you think it's so strange, Mrs. Saunders?"

She looked at Louise, and then over at Vinnie. "My husband was with the CIA for a long time. Before that, he was with the Special Forces in Vietnam. He was a pretty tough guy in the Army and saw a lot in Vietnam. He came home from there a different person. He was much more peaceful, and easygoing. Some of the training a CIA agent goes through is a little unusual. When Frank was first with the agency, he would come home and we would talk about some of the things that bothered him. He was taught how to kill people with poison, with a knife, with a pen or pencil. That training made him uncomfortable. He didn't like killing anything. He was the kind of person who, if he found a spider in the house, would get a can, put the spider in the can, and take it outside. He used to talk all the time about how 'out of his element' he often felt at the agency. But, his father was an agent before him, and it just seemed like destiny to him that he would join the agency after the service."

"Mrs. Saunders, you said your husband had been acting strange for a while. Can you tell us a little about that? How was he acting strange?" Vinnie asked.

She took a moment to gather her thoughts. It was as if she had a story to tell, and wanted to start at the beginning. "It all started when he got a phone call from his father, about six months ago. His father is long retired from the CIA, and he lives in Arizona. Frank came home and told me about what he called a 'weird' phone call his father had gotten from someone he had done business with forty years ago. The man was in his eighties, and he actually called Frank's father from a hospital bed after he had a heart attack. He called him because he wanted Frank's father to know he had seen another man he had worked with forty years earlier, but he said the man still looked exactly like he did forty years earlier. He hadn't aged a day, and it freaked him out. So much that he had a heart attack right in the restaurant. He wanted

Frank to check him out."

"And did he?" Vinnie asked.

"Yes, he did. Even though he thought it was a wild-goose chase at first, out of respect for his father, he looked into it."

"And what did he come up with?"

"Well, I can't tell you much because before too long, Frank took a whole different attitude about it. He talked to me at first because he thought the whole thing was kind of funny. But then he stopped talking to me about it, which told me he no longer thought it was funny. I was married to him for a long time and I knew not to pry into any agency business, and for some reason he had decided this thing really was agency business."

"I'm guessing this isn't what you mean by 'acting strange'?"

She sighed, "No, not at all. Frank flew out to California as part of his investigation. He always told me where he was going even though he wouldn't say why, so I know he was in California. He was out there a couple of days and when he came back, he was different."

"How?" Vinnie asked.

Sarah looked up at the ceiling. "I'm not sure how to describe it. I guess I would say he seemed preoccupied, or mentally consumed by this person he met out there."

"Was it the person his father called about?" Louise asked.

"I believe it was, although he never mentioned a name from his father's conversation."

"Did he mention a name after the California trip?" Louise asked again.

"Oh yes, he mentioned the name. The name was Adam Adamson. He mentioned it about a thousand times in the next six months. It was all he talked about. But what made it really strange was he would mention his name and say something like 'he is an amazing person,' but then he would never explain what it was that made him so 'amazing.' He would just say something like: 'I can't tell you, because it could put him in danger.' Or 'you wouldn't be able to understand.' After a while it made me a little crazy. It started to have a real adverse affect on our relationship."

"How adverse?" Vinnie asked.

"Well, first I forced him to see a psychiatrist. He did, but it didn't seem to help. Of course he only went to see him once, and said he wasn't going back. Eventually, he and I went together to see a marriage counselor. That was a disaster. Shortly after that, I filed for a legal separation and served him with papers."

Vinnie and Louise both looked a little surprised. Vinnie spoke, "How long ago was that?"

"Only about a week ago."

Vinnie and Louise looked at each other as if they had learned something surprising. Sarah Saunders saw them exchange the look. "I loved my husband, Detectives, and I was simply trying to force him to get help. I never expected him to leave the house, let alone get involved in something like this."

"Mrs. Saunders, can you shed any light on how General Edwards was involved?"

"Well, I don't know much, but I did talk to my father-in-law over the phone. He's flying in tomorrow for the funeral. He told me he had talked to Edwards around the same time he talked to Frank. I guess the General was somehow involved in all of this. I know he was a member of the Joint Chiefs, and just a week ago, the final conclusion of an investigation resulted in his being removed and honorably discharged from the Army. It was in all the newspapers. I'm quite sure it had something to do with this whole mess."

"Mrs. Saunders, the CIA won't tell us anything. Can you give us any other information about your husband's trip out to the West Coast that could help us?"

She thought for a moment. "Not really. I know he worked with another agent out there named Dino Argento. Dino used to live here in the Washington area, and we socialized with him. When he came back from California he told me he had spent time with Dino, and that he said 'hello.'"

Vinnie didn't have any more questions. Louise had none either. She stood up and as she did so, Vinnie did the same. She extended her hand to Sarah Saunders. "Thank you, Mrs. Saunders, for taking the time to talk with us. We're sorry for your loss." They shook hands, and the sister let them out.

When they got back in the car Vinnie looked at her. "Well, what do you think?"

"What do you mean, what do I think? I think we did a lot of driving for very little information."

Vinnie looked surprised. "Very little information! Come on, we now know the person Saunders went out to see in California was the same guy that owned the apartment in New York before Nathan bought it, and that he freaked Saunders out for some reason."

Louise laughed, "Vinnie, what has any of that got to do with the case? It doesn't change a thing. Saunders killed Edwards, and then killed himself. What's really changed?"

"I'm not sure," Vinnie said. "We know Saunders was in contact with Nathan, right? Nathan was expecting Saunders the night the General was killed. The wife says Saunders was obsessed with Adamson. Suppose there's a connection between Adamson and Nathan?"

Louise was shaking her head. "No matter what you come up with, it isn't going to change the case. One guy kills another then himself, end of story."

"I suppose that's true, but come on, don't you have any curiosity as to why?"

She looked at him, a little irritated. "Vinnie, there's plenty of times I wonder about stuff we deal with. A man murders his wife, I wonder how things got that bad. One drug dealer kills another, I wonder why they couldn't have worked out their differences. There's plenty of things I wonder about, but the city doesn't pay me to wonder, they pay me to figure out who did what, and arrest the person who broke the law. They don't pay me to figure out motive when the victim and the perp are both dead."

"Hey, calm down. You're right, it's just my nature to want to know why something like this happened. I think I'm going to fly out to the West Coast and see if I can talk to this Argento. You want to go?"

"Are you nuts? I can see telling Sean I'm going to California with you. He'd cuff me to the radiator, and come over to your place and break you in half. Besides, you think the Department is going to foot the bill for you to fly out to the West Coast?"

"No, I'm going to pay for it myself. I've got a little money put aside. I'll pick up your cost, too." Vinnie never discussed his financial situation with anyone at work.

She shook her head again. "You're on your own on this wild-goose chase."

Vinnie started the car. "Suit yourself. If you don't want to visit sunny California, I can go by myself."

"What about the Lieutenant saying two days?"

"Hey, tomorrow is the second day, and it's Friday. I figure I've got until Monday morning to file a closing report."

Chapter 108

Ian MacRoiter was sweeping the walkway from his front door to the street when the Rolls Royce came slowly up the lane. He stopped to admire the beauty of it, and realized it had stopped in front of his house. MacRoiter was seventy-two years old, but had the physical health of someone much younger, and the spirit of a young man. It made him a very popular figure in the little town of Winterton by the Sea. He had performed many marriages as the Justice of the Peace. He watched as the chauffeur climbed out of the car and opened the back door. A man climbed out, walked around the car, and came toward him. He was a handsome man, young, from Ian's perspective. He guessed him to be in his mid-forties. The man walked up the walkway Ian was sweeping, and when he got close, he asked, "Mr. MacRoiter?"

Ian was a little surprised he knew his name. "Yes."

The man was now close enough to extend his hand. "My name is Ben Nathan."

They shook hands. MacRoiter had never met him, but recognized the name as the man who purchased the castle at Balmoor. He spent a lot of time at the town hall, and knew everything that went on in town.

"Mr. Nathan, how nice to meet you."

"Likewise. I was hoping to have a few moments of your time."

Ian gestured toward the porch with two rocking chairs on it. "Certainly, Mr. Nathan. Please, come sit down." The two men walked onto the porch and sat down.

"Can I offer you something to drink? Perhaps a cup of tea?"

"No thank you, I don't want to be any more trouble than I already am. I can see I'm keeping you from your chore."

MacRoiter waved at the broom. "Ah that, the walk will wait for me no matter what." They both chuckled. MacRoiter continued, "So, Mr. Nathan, I believe you're the new resident at Balmoor, am I correct?"

"That you are, sir. I've been living there for about six months."

MacRoiter rocked back in the chair. "I haven't been up to the castle in over thirty years. I believe I stopped in one day while they were making electrical changes for the previous owner. Never did meet him. How's the place look these days?"

"Well, Mr. MacRoiter," Ben paused for effect, "I'm hoping you'll do me the honor of coming to Balmoor in about three weeks to perform a wedding there."

MacRoiter's face lit up like he had won a wonderful prize. "You don't say, a wedding! My goodness, I think I've performed seventy or more weddings. I lost track. Who's getting married, if I may ask?"

Ben smiled, "I am."

MacRoiter seemed genuinely surprised. "You are? And you want me to perform the wedding, do you?"

"Yes, sir, I do. It is going to be a very private ceremony with just a few of the bride's family attending, along with the staff."

"Well, Mr. Nathan, I must let you know, my wedding service tends to be very simple and not the least bit religious. I always thought if people wanted a religious ceremony, they wouldn't come to a Justice of the Peace, they would go to a priest." He was very animated and expressive, and Ben found him to be an enjoyable character.

"That would be fine."

"Exactly when are you intending to get married, sir?"

"We'd like to get married in three weeks on Saturday."

MacRoiter raised his eyebrows. "Have you and the prospective bride-to-be had blood tests?"

It was something Ben hadn't even thought about. MacRoiter could tell from the expression on his face that the answer was no. He spoke up, "Well, it's not a great matter. There's a clinic just behind the grocery store in town. You and your bride can go in there and tell them you need a blood test for a marriage license, and it's a rush. They'll have the results in a couple of days. Just stop here with the results, and I'll have all the forms. We can fill them out and I could spend a few minutes talking with you and your future wife. You could help me with anything you might particularly like me to say, or for that matter, anything you might like me to avoid saying." He chuckled at himself, and it made Ben laugh, too.

The old man suddenly had a serious look on his face. "Say, Mr. Nathan, one thing though. I haven't driven in eight years. Here everything is within walking distance. My reflexes aren't what they used to be. I had a little scare about eight years ago, and haven't driven since. I still have my car in the garage, and every once in a while I'll start it and back it out into the driveway for a few minutes, but I would be afraid to drive it, especially all the way to Balmoor."

Ben appreciated what a kindly old man MacRoiter was. "Mr. MacRoiter, I would be happy to send my car around to pick you up."

MacRoiter looked over at the shiny blue Rolls parked in front of his house. “That’s one fine automobile, Mr. Nathan. I’ve never had occasion to ride in one.”

“Well, consider that one to be at your disposal any time.” He took out a pen and some paper from his vest pocket. As he wrote he spoke, “Here’s my number should you ever need the car. I’ll visit the clinic with my fiancée tomorrow, and we’ll stop over as soon as we have the results. In the meantime, may I assume that you will be available for the third Saturday coming?”

“You certainly may, Mr. Nathan,” and the old man got up as he said this. They shook hands and Ben went back to the car while Ian went back to sweeping his walk.

Chapter 109

Vinnie took the earliest flight he could get on Friday morning. The flight left JFK at nine-fifteen in the morning. With the time zone changes being three hours difference and the flight taking a little over five hours, he arrived in L.A. at 11:15. He knew the CIA wasn't going to list their address in the phone book, so he went directly to the Los Angeles Police Department, identified himself as a New York City Detective working a case, and asked them to direct him to the CIA office.

He pulled into their parking lot at exactly noon. He walked into the office where a receptionist greeted him with a smile. He approached her, showed her his badge, explained briefly he was on business from New York City, and needed to see Dino Argento. The receptionist told Vinnie she hadn't seen Dino yet this morning, and she couldn't be sure he was coming in at all. She picked up the phone and tried his office. After a few rings, she determined he wasn't there. She dialed another number, and as it started to ring she explained to Vinnie it was Dino's supervisor.

Someone answered the phone and she spoke, "Hi, Bob, this is Marcia. Do you know if Dino is coming in this morning?" She paused, listening to the other person. "OK, thanks."

She smiled back up at Vinnie, "He said Dino had some problem with his car yesterday and he was supposed to stop and take care of it this morning on his way in, so he is going to be a little late, but he will be here."

Vinnie smiled, "Great, I'll wait." He sat down in the obviously designated waiting area. He noticed there was no reading material, which probably meant that people were never expected to wait long. He had been sitting there for fifteen minutes when a man walked into the office with a sport jacket over his shoulder. He had thinning blond hair brushed straight back. He was wearing light linen pants and penny loafers. He stopped at the reception desk, and Vinnie heard the receptionist talk to him in a hushed voice. He couldn't hear what she was saying. The man turned and looked at him, and walked over. Vinnie stood up as the man approached. He looked friendly enough, and as he got close he held out his hand. "Hi, I'm Dino Argento."

Vinnie shook his hand. He noticed that Argento had a strong grip. "Hi, Dino, Vinnie DeRoma, New York City Police Department."

Dino scrunched his eyes. "New York City, aren't you just a little outside your territory?" He was smiling as he said this, and it was what Vinnie expected.

"I guess I am," Vinnie admitted, "but I want to talk with you for a few minutes if I could about Frank Saunders."

The smile disappeared from Dino's face instantly. "Then I shouldn't be joking with you, because nothing about that situation is funny. Come on back to my office."

He walked back over to the receptionist. "Marcia, can I have a pass for Mr. DeRoma?" She handed him a plastic visitors pass on a thin chain. He handed it to Vinnie, and Vinnie put it around his neck. They walked back through a maze of cubicles and offices to Dino's office. It was a good-sized office, which told Vinnie he had some seniority.

There were two chairs in front of the desk. Vinnie sat in one of them and Dino sat in the other. Dino turned his chair so that it faced Vinnie. "So, what can I help you with?"

"Frank's wife told me you were involved with Frank when he came out here about six months ago."

"Well, it was closer to seven months ago, but yes, I did see Frank."

"Were you involved in whatever it was he was doing out here?"

Dino looked at Vinnie for a moment, as if sizing him up. "You know, Detective — "

Vinnie interrupted him, "Please, call me Vinnie."

Dino nodded. "You know, Vinnie, it's strictly against agency policy to discuss any agency matter with non-agency personnel."

"I respect that, and I'm certainly not asking you to breach any policy. But I'm hoping you'll be more concerned about keeping the *spiri*t of the policy than the *lette*r of the policy."

Dino looked at him for a moment. "What the hell does that even mean?"

Vinnie laughed, "It means I think the agency doesn't want you revealing any agency secrets, and I'm not looking for any. I hope you'll help me out by answering questions that don't reveal anything I shouldn't know."

Dino nodded again. "Fair enough. Yes, I was involved with him in an investigation he was conducting."

"His wife said when he came home he was different, and he started acting strange. Could you shed any light on why that might have been?"

Dino shifted in his chair. "Vinnie, let me ask you something."

"Sure, anything."

"I saw a copy of a preliminary agency report on this incident with Saunders and General Edwards. Their report was based on the findings of your Medical Examiner. It said Frank Saunders killed General Edwards, and then, probably the next day, killed himself. Do you believe that is true?"

Vinnie nodded. "I do, yes."

"Then, with all due respect, what possible reason could you have for being out here? Why the questions? What are you looking for, Vinnie?"

Vinnie noticed Dino had green eyes. He noticed it because those green eyes were now boring into him. This man was not afraid to ask the hard questions, and then stare at you until you answered.

Vinnie took a deep breath. "Well, sir, that's an excellent question. The short and simple answer is I want to understand why a responsible, professional man like Frank Saunders drives to New York City and kills a U.S. Army General who, until a week earlier, had been a member of the Joint Chiefs, and then kills himself. I would also like to know what the General was doing in New York City."

Dino smiled, "Again, with all due respect, Detective, I don't see how that has anything to do with your case."

Vinnie looked into those green eyes. "It doesn't, but I'm the kind of guy that likes to understand the dynamics of a situation like this."

"So, the city of New York flies you out here so you can satisfy your curiosity?"

"No, I flew out here on my own. The only thing the city did was float me the day as part of the investigation."

"You spent your own money to come all the way out here and talk to me?"

Vinnie smiled, as if the silliness of it was starting to sink in. "I guess you could say that."

Dino looked at his watch. "You know it's twelve-thirty. You had lunch?" Vinnie shook his head no. Dino got up from the chair. "Come on, money bags, you can afford to come out here on your own, you can buy me lunch."

He started to walk out of the office and Vinnie followed him. They got into Dino's car and pulled out of the parking lot and headed down the street.

Dino made small talk, "How long you been with the NYPD?"

"About four years."

Dino seemed surprised. "Only four years and you're a detective? You must be some wonder boy or something?"

"Nah, nothing that good. I was undercover for a couple years, and we made a huge bust. All the primaries got commendations and gold shields. I guess I was just lucky. This is actually my first homicide."

Dino looked over at him for a long time, which made Vinnie a little nervous because he was driving pretty fast. "Your first homicide, this case?"

Vinnie nodded.

"Man, that's a piece of bad luck."

"Why, you said yourself it's open and shut. Saunders kills Edwards, then kills himself. Strictly on a 'who-done-it?' basis, the case is cleared already."

"Yeah, but you said you're not the kind of guy who can clear it and then forget it. You have to know why. That could make this case very tough."

Vinnie looked over at him. "Really?"

Dino nodded, and Vinnie was thankful he didn't look back over at him. "Yes, really."

They pulled into a parking lot and Vinnie looked out and saw a diner. It was called the "Sun Spot." He looked over at Dino, and Dino shrugged. "Hey, it's only the best food in L.A."

They walked in and the waitress greeted Dino by name. She flirted with him a little, and Vinnie knew that Dino was a regular. They walked to one end of the place and sat in a booth. The booth next to them was empty. The waitress walked over, pad and pencil in hand. "What'll it be, men?"

Dino looked up at her. "Honey, we're going to need a little privacy this afternoon while we eat."

The waitress put her pad and pencil back in her apron and walked away. Vinnie watched her walk behind the counter and into the kitchen. In just a few moments she came back out with two large flat racks of glasses, one on top of the other. It looked to Vinnie like something out of the dishwasher. She put them down right in the middle of the table of the booth next to them. No one would come in and sit in that booth. She then walked back over to them, and took the pad and pencil back out.

Dino looked at her. "You're way too good to me, sweetheart."

She was very attractive and she smiled at Dino. "I'm only nice to the big tippers, honey, and don't you forget it."

They ordered lunch and made small talk until it came. After the waitress brought the food and walked away, Dino got serious. "OK, Vinnie, here's the deal. You and I are going to have a conversation we never had. The reason we're going to have this conversation is because it's information the agency doesn't have. Frank came out here on business, and he filed a report with his superiors in Washington. It wasn't a truthful report, but I don't think that matters now. What does matter is you can't quote me, you can't quote an 'unnamed CIA source' you can't even quote a source at all. Do you want answers that bad?"

Vinnie nodded.

"OK, one other condition. You don't listen to what I'm going to tell you and then tell me I'm crazy, OK? I've kept this to myself ever since Frank was out here, and it's *makin*g me crazy. I'm going to tell you because it might make me feel a little better, but be warned, it's probably going to make you crazy, too."

Vinnie thought this was amusing, but he noticed that Dino wasn't smiling. He actually seemed a little upset. "OK." was all he said.

Dino sighed heavily, "Frank's father was a retired CIA agent. Did you know that?"

Vinnie nodded he did.

"One day about seven months ago, Frank gets a call from his father out in Arizona. His father tells him about a phone call he got from some doctor out here on the Coast who called and left a message for him at the CIA that he should call an old business associate, and that it was very important. The old man was in the hospital, had just had a heart attack, and was asking for him specifically. Frank's old man calls him. He tells him a fantastic story about going to a restaurant with his family, and sitting in a nearby booth is a man the old man worked with forty-some years ago. The problem was, the old man was in his eighties and this other guy should have been as well, but there he was sitting in the restaurant looking exactly the same as he did forty years ago. It freaked the old man out, and that's what caused him to have a heart attack.

"How did this old man come to have a CIA contact like Frank's father?"

"He was involved in the development of airplane interiors and they did a lot of work for the CIA. The old man and Frank's father did a lot of work together. As a courtesy to his father, Frank came out to check out the story."

"Who was the man he was checking out?"

"His name was Adam Adamson."

That was the name Vinnie had expected to hear. He knew Dino was being honest with him. "And what was the result of the investigation?"

Dino looked at him, those green eyes burning in. "This is the crazy part. Frank had done some research and determined that if he hadn't aged in forty years, it was possible he hadn't aged in thousands of years."

"What?" Vinnie looked at Dino like he was crazy.

"See? I told you," Dino said, and then he took a bite of food. He let what he had just said sink in. "Frank didn't want to discuss any of this with me when he came out here. I more or less forced him to tell me what was going on. He told me he wanted to meet with Adamson so he could size him up for himself. He told me he had reason to believe that he could possibly be thousands of years old. That through some genetic fluke, he didn't age."

"That's the craziest thing I ever heard," Vinnie muttered.

"I know, I felt the same way."

Vinnie looked up at him suddenly. "Felt, as in past tense?"

"You got it."

"Are you saying you now believe the same thing Frank believed?"

"Well," Dino took a deep breath, "we went to see Adamson. I waited downstairs while Frank went upstairs. When he came down, I would have to go along with his wife, he *was* weird. We got in the car to head back to the office and Frank didn't talk at all, at first. I pressed him, and basically he told me his suspicions were right."

Vinnie was having a hard time believing what he was hearing, "You're telling me that Frank Saunders told you that this guy was, in fact, thousands of years old?"

"Six thousand to be exact."

Vinnie laughed.

Dino looked at him. "Go ahead and laugh, I don't blame you. But Frank told me he wasn't going to put any of this information in his report. He knew it would be useless, that the agency would consider him nuts, or even worse, they would believe him and arrest Adamson, and interrogate him. He figured if he was thousands of years old, the government would immediately see that as some type of threat, and they wouldn't be happy until he was dead. When he got back to Washington, he found out General Edwards had already dispatched some local National Guard General to arrest Adamson and ship him back to Washington."

"How did he know anything about it?"

"Saunders' father was impatient. He called the General, another one of his old buddies, and he laid the story on him. The General was one of the old school paranoid types who believed everything was a threat, one way or another. Frank calls me and asks me to go to Adamson's apartment and warn him, because we knew where he lived, but it was a private number, so we couldn't call him."

"Did you go?"

Dino nodded. "Yup, the same day. Spoke with the man myself."

"And?"

"He told me he appreciated my going out of my way to warn him."

"Anything else?"

"We didn't talk about how old he was, if that's what you're asking."

"So what is it that made you a believer?"

Dino thought about it. "I'm not really sure. I think it's a combination of my respect for Frank and the impression I got when I met the man. I mean, I stop to tell him that the Army is out looking for him and he doesn't get excited, he doesn't even seem nervous, and he doesn't ask why. It was obvious he knew why. I just came out of there with a feeling this man was someone unique. I think I have always felt Frank was sure, and it made me feel it was possible. When I heard about what happened in New York, it cemented my conviction that Frank was probably on the money."

Vinnie had eaten half of his sandwich and he knew he wouldn't be eating any more of it. His mind was spinning with this information. "What happened to Adamson?"

"He disappeared the same morning I talked with him. Got on a plane and disappeared into the horizon. No doubt he changed his name. He could be anywhere. Oh, did I forget to mention that the guy's net worth was in the billions? It's much easier to vanish when you're fabulously wealthy."

Vinnie scratched his head, confused. "You know, all this somehow involves a man named Benjamin Nathan who recently bought a multi-million dollar apartment in New York City. This happened right around the time he was coming in to meet with a committee that approves all new residents. Frank Saunders was expected as a visitor, but he never showed."

Dino thought about this for a minute. "Chances are, Nathan is Adamson. Somehow the General must have found out he was coming to New York."

Vinnie was thinking too. He had several big pieces to a complicated puzzle he didn't have before. "Maybe," he said. But he was thinking that the General probably had no idea Nathan was coming to New York. He was probably just following up on the property. Somehow he knew Nathan was who he was looking for.

Dino looked at his watch. "Well, I'd love to stay and talk, but I have to get back to work."

Vinnie paid the bill and they drove to the office. Vinnie was deep in thought. When they got back, he thanked Dino for talking with him. He assured him the information would not be made public in any way. Dino went in, and Vinnie headed to the airport. He bought a ticket back to New York, and within an hour he was on the plane. He thought about the story he just heard. What could he do with this information? Could he even tell any of this to Louise? He had no idea how she would react, but then he wasn't really sure how *he* was reacting. He didn't know what he thought. He couldn't say he believed it, but he didn't think it was totally off the wall either. He tried to sort it all out. Somehow, the General must have found out the property in New York had changed hands, and Adamson, under a different name, bought the apartment. Maybe it was really a transfer from his old name to a new name. Maybe he had been the owner all the time. Maybe the General searched a real estate transfer database and came up with this transaction. He wondered how uncommon the name Adamson was. He knew the last name Nathan was common. He figured there would be hundreds of transaction with those names. Then it dawned on him. If Adamson was a billionaire, he probably owned all kinds of properties. Maybe the General found Adamson by isolating transactions from the one name to the other. Searching through transaction under the seller "Adamson" could take a long time, and so could transactions under the buyer "Nathan." But, pull out transactions from Adamson to Nathan and you narrow the field. Vinnie figured someone who was a member of the Joint Chiefs would likely have access to that type of database. He looked at his watch. It was almost five o'clock. He would be back in New York in five hours, but it would be after midnight with the time zones. Tomorrow morning he would have a much better understanding of jet lag.

Chapter 110

A week after Frank Saunders' funeral, there was an envelope in the mail addressed to Sarah Saunders. The return address was not anything Sarah recognized. It said IMA with a California street address. She was going to rip it in half and throw it away, which was what she did with junk mail, but she noticed the stamp was full postage and that stopped her. It had been her observation that junk mail was always mailed bulk, and the postage was considerably less. She opened the envelope. There was a letter on stationary that had the same IMA on the top. Under those letters in smaller print were the words International Multicultural Assistance. She read the letter.

Dear Mrs. Saunders:

We were very sorry to hear about the loss of your husband. It is our understanding he served in the armed services and completed two tours of duty in Vietnam. He also served for many years as a member of the Central Intelligence Agency, most recently serving as an assistant deputy director.

The International Multicultural Assistance agency has, for many years, provided financial aid to individuals, as well as entire communities, where there has been a sudden and financially devastating loss.

Please accept the enclosed check as a token of our understanding of your loss.

The letter was signed with a stamp of the organization. It was not signed personally by anyone. Attached to the letter with a paper clip was a check. Sarah looked at it for a long time, trying to fully comprehend what she was looking at. It was a check made out to her in the amount of one million dollars.

There had been some money in the bank, and Frank did have a life insurance policy for two hundred thousand dollars. His CIA benefits included a life insurance policy equal to his salary, so all in all, Sarah had a little over three hundred thousand dollars in the bank. She thought she would be able to get by, but she also thought about her children's college education, and knew easily half of her money could go for that.

She sat stunned, trying to justify that some organization, completely unknown to her, was sending her a million dollars.

Chapter 111

The night before the wedding, Barbara's sister and brother-in-law arrived at Balmoor, with Barbara's parents. Barbara's sister Elizabeth was six years older than Barbara, but she looked very young. Ben could see a definite resemblance.

Elizabeth's husband's name was Weldon, and Ben found him likable. He was a big man, a little taller than Ben, and a good forty pounds heavier. He seemed to be in good shape with no excess fat. He was outgoing and intelligent, and Ben realized he had drawn some pre-conclusions based on his employment as a bus driver. Barbara's parents were interesting, as well. Barbara's mother's name was Frances and her father's name was Archie. Archie was a retired banker, and had been instrumental in getting Barbara her first job in a bank.

Victor did an outstanding job of preparing for these guests, and there was a sumptuous meal served a little later to accommodate the arrivals.

After dinner everyone sat around and talked. Barbara and her mother and sister talked in a corner of the library. Victor had a fire in the fireplace. Ben and Weldon sat in another corner and talked, while Archie looked at the books on the shelves. Certain books Ben did not want anyone to see had been relocated to the top shelves, which could not be reached without a ladder. The ladder had been removed from the room.

Ben and Weldon talked about Weldon's work. He worked for a private bus company. They would hire out to tour groups and other organizations for day trips. Weldon knew a lot about the business, and it was clear to Ben he was capable of being much more than a bus driver. Ben questioned him on the quality of the buses. Weldon told him most of them were new. Even the ones that were older were in excellent condition. He asked about business. Weldon told him they were booked months in advance, all year long. Their biggest problem was finding dependable drivers. Weldon's one complaint was the owner's son had recently started working for the company. Weldon felt he was incompetent. He saw him as a spoiled kid who could only get a management job because his father owned the company. He was sure if the old man ever turned the business over to him entirely, he would ruin it within a year.

Ben asked him what he thought the business was worth. Weldon said he hadn't given it any thought, but it was probably worth two or three hundred thousand pounds. They were busy and had a good reputation, but they weren't a large company. They only had seven buses. Ben asked Weldon if he thought he would be capable of running such a bus company himself, and Weldon said he was sure he could. Ben next asked what Weldon thought he could do if he were running the company and had unlimited funds to improve the company. Weldon thought he would increase the size of the company by purchasing more buses, but, of course he would only buy three or four more, because there was only so much business to go around in the area. He would solve the driver problem by paying a little more than other companies, thereby attracting the quality drivers. He explained to Ben the increased number of buses would allow them to do some two and three day trips, and that was where the real profit was.

Ben told Weldon he would look into buying the bus company, and if he was able to do so, he would put Weldon in charge. He told Weldon not to say a word to the owner or anyone else at the company. He didn't want anyone to know who it was that was offering to buy the company. Weldon asked if he was joking, and he assured him he was not. He said he would put out feelers as soon as he got back from his honeymoon, and likely Weldon could be running the bus company by the end of the month, at a substantial increase in pay and a share of the profits.

Weldon asked what he would do if they didn't want to sell. Ben smiled and explained he would simply have to buy new buses, and start his own bus company. Weldon realized he wasn't joking, and he was able to do anything he wanted to when it came to finances.

Barbara had taken her mother and sister on a tour of the castle. They were amazed at the number of rooms there were, and by the modern conveniences that had been added. Barbara showed them the master bathroom with a stone tub big enough for six people. She took them up to the tower room, where they could clearly see the North Sea even at night. They thought the castle was extraordinary.

They asked Barbara about Ben. What did he do? How old was he? Had he ever been married before? Did he have any children? Were they going to have children? Barbara answered the questions as best she could. Ben did whatever he wanted to do. He had many investments, and he didn't have to do anything. No, he had never been married and he had no children. Yes, they talked about having children, and probably would. They talked about the honeymoon. Barbara told them they were going to Spain and Switzerland, because Ben owned homes in both places and he thought it would be a good opportunity to check on them.

The women talked well into the evening. Barbara hadn't seen her mother or her sister in over six months, and she hadn't been together with both of them in over a year. She told them she thought she would continue to work. She enjoyed her job at the bank, and they were willing to be flexible with her hours.

Her mother and sister asked her if she was happy at the prospect of marrying Ben, and she told them she was. The question surprised her, and she asked her sister why she asked it. Her sister said she just thought it was important to be happy and she wanted to be sure that Ben made her feel that way. Barbara assured them both he did. She told them she and Ben had no secrets, and she thought to herself they could never comprehend the depth of that statement.

Chapter 112

The envelope Vinnie had been waiting for finally arrived. He sat in his living room and opened it eagerly, anticipating the contents. He took out the copy of the document. It was bound with a black plastic binding ring, and it was almost four inches thick. It was a copy of the entire transcript of the inquiry regarding General Clayton Edwards that led to his removal from the Joint Chiefs and his discharge.

Vinnie requested the document through the Freedom of Information Act, the Tuesday after he got back from the West Coast. He filed his final papers on the case and handed them in on the Monday before. The Lieutenant was relieved he presented it as a simple "open and shut" case. One man killing another, then himself. All the forensic evidence supported that conclusion, and Vinnie knew any further digging would have to be done on his own.

He opened the cover and was surprised to see that much of the printed material was blacked out. He held the document up to the light with one page sticking out, to see if he could read the blacked out information, but he could not. The document had been blacked out and then copied.

As he read, he found it was mostly names blacked out. He didn't really care about names because he thought he knew who was involved. What he was looking for was any collaboration to the story he got from Dino Argento. He found what he was looking for about a third of the way into the information.

Testimony, from someone who he assumed was the General, was that he received a phone call from someone whose name was also blacked out regarding a person whose name was blacked out who supposedly had not gotten any older in almost fifty years. The individual testifying stated he "viewed such a person as someone the government needed to talk to, at the very least."

Vinnie was amazed to read of the General's flight to New York on a military helicopter, including the landing at JFK, with nothing more than a warning to the air traffic controllers they were going to be entering the airspace and landing. By the time he finished reading through the testimony he was convinced of two things. One was the General should have been relieved of all responsibilities, and the other was, as misdirected as he might have been, he was thoroughly convinced there was a threat to national security. Why else would a seasoned military man with a position on the Joint Chiefs risk everything?

Could there really be something to this story of a person living for hundreds of years, or longer? He had not been able to put his conversation with Dino Argento out of his mind. Now this information supported what Argento told him, and he couldn't help but wonder how it was the members of the Board of Inquiry didn't give more consideration to what the General told them. It seemed they accepted Frank Saunders' report with no question, and discounted everything the General said.

When Vinnie and Louise were investigating the double homicide and it became known that Benjamin Nathan might have been involved in some way, they attempted to determine where he was. Paul Fenton did not have any address for him. All of his correspondence with Mr. Nathan had been through a real estate agency in California. Louise spoke to them on the phone and they were emphatic about not giving out any confidential information.

Louise questioned whether anything to do with real estate transactions was confidential, and they told her she would have to get a court order before they would discuss anything more with her. They also made it clear it would have to be a court order from a California court, not a New York court.

In checking with the airlines, they did find that Benjamin Nathan and two other people with him left JFK on Thursday, the day after Saunders killed himself. The flights were to Heathrow, which they agreed didn't narrow the search down quite enough. The tickets were purchased through an account connected to a Swiss bank, and a phone call to them was an immediate dead end. They explained they only dealt with account numbers, and their records did not contain the name of the customer. Yes, they acknowledged the account number used to purchase the tickets did exist in their system, but who the account belonged to was unknown to them. One of the other tickets was issued to a woman named Barbara Grady, and Vinnie filed a search request with Scotland Yard on the assumption that Barbara Grady was from Great Britain.

The case was officially closed and Vinnie and Louise had several other cases they were working on, but Vinnie was still waiting for the report back from Scotland Yard. They were notorious for taking a long time to get back with anything. Since they were asking for a search on a person who simply was a passenger on a plane with someone possibly involved in a homicide, the request was low on their priority.

A week after the transcript of General Edwards' inquiry arrived, the response from Scotland Yard showed up on Vinnie's desk. It was three pages with general information on eleven women named Barbara Grady. Vinnie knew from talking with the doorman and the building manager that the Barbara Grady they were looking for was in her early to mid-thirties, so he was able to eliminate five of the listed women who were too old, or too young. That left six women to follow up on. Vinnie knew he would have to do this on his own time.

Chapter 113

It was a bright sunny Saturday morning when the Rolls pulled up in front of Ian MacRoiter's home. Stanley went to the front door and knocked lightly. The door opened and Ian MacRoiter stepped out onto the porch dressed in his finest suit. They exchanged greetings and walked back to the car. Stanley opened the door for Mr. MacRoiter, and he slid into the luxurious back seat. He couldn't help but admire the beauty of the interior.

At Balmoor, the household staff was busy with all the final preparations. There were only seven guests including the Justice of the Peace, but fresh flowers had just been delivered and needed to be set in vases and placed throughout the castle. Victor was overseeing the kitchen staff in the preparation of food that would be served after the ceremony. He was also supervising the packing for the honeymoon.

Sitting on the front lawn of the castle was a four-passenger Bell helicopter. It went with the one hundred and sixty-foot yacht that was anchored one thousand feet off shore in the North Sea behind the castle. Ben had rented the boat with a crew of six for the next three weeks. It would be their transportation to Spain. The yacht would take them south through the Strait of Dover, into the English Channel, out into the Atlantic, then down around Spain and into the Mediterranean Sea. There, the yacht would anchor and the helicopter would take them to Ben's home.

The yacht would sit for four or five days, and then take the couple across the Mediterranean nearer to Switzerland, where it would again anchor while Ben and Barbara spent several days at Ben's home in Switzerland. Eventually, they would yacht back around to Balmoor.

Right now, the helicopter was waiting for the luggage so all would be set when the couple was ready to go. The staffs at the houses in Spain and Switzerland had been alerted to the visit, and they eagerly anticipated meeting the new owner. No staff member at either house had been there more than ten years, so no one would have any idea who Ben was.

Ben was having coffee in the library contemplating the day, and the impact that this day was going to have on his future. He found himself wondering if he was being unfair to Barbara, knowing eventually she would grow old while he remained unchanged. He also questioned whether or not he was allowing himself to be lulled by his own desire into telling himself that marrying was acceptable. He loved Barbara. He loved being with her and talking with her. He had a physical attraction to her, as well. He desired her, and he had been telling himself he hadn't felt that for a woman before.

But in the last several weeks he thought more and more about this point, and he had come to the realization there had been other women in his life he had desired, but his inner sense told him that he couldn't marry, so he forced himself to put those desires aside. Now he had this relationship with Barbara, and again he was dealing with physical desire, but this time he was allowing himself to think that marriage wasn't so out of the question. He had decided that it could work. They could avoid relatives after a while. If they had children he would be able to teach them how to survive and provide for them monetarily, so they would not have to work and mingle unnecessarily with other people. By keeping to themselves, and moving every so often, they would not draw attention to themselves. He reconsidered everything from several different angles, and he felt sure his reasoning was sound.

He had not seen Barbara this morning because she said that she didn't want him to see her until the wedding. He was surprised when she said this to him, and he asked her if she was superstitious. She laughed and told him she wasn't at all, but she simply preferred to wait until the wedding. He told her it was her special day as well as his, and if she wanted to not see him until the wedding, that was all right with him.

There was a light knock on the library door and Barbara's father peeked in. Ben looked up and saw him. "Archie, come on in."

Archie had a cup of coffee in his hand. He shuffled into the library, and sat down in the chair directly across from Ben. He had a serious look on his face.

"What's on your mind, Archie?" Ben asked quietly.

Archie looked a little uneasy. "Nothing really, Ben. I just thought we should have a father and son talk, now that you're going to be my son-in-law."

Ben found that amusing and he smiled, "Sounds good to me, what would you like to talk about?"

"Well," Archie said, "I just want to make sure you love my daughter, and you're going to take good care of her." His eyes looked a little red as he spoke and Ben understood the man's emotions. From conversations with Barbara, he knew Archie had been a good father to his daughters and he loved them dearly. Ben admired the old man for being a parent loved by his adult children. Ben thought that young children tended to love their parents no matter what, almost automatically. But when adult children still loved their parents, it said something for the parents.

Ben looked at Archie. "I love her very much, Archie. And I will do everything I can to take the best care of her for the rest of her life."

Archie smiled, "That's what I wanted to hear, Ben. I'm sure you'll take good care of her." With that, he got up from the chair and exited the library. Ben wondered if that was a typical father and son-in-law talk before a wedding.

A few minutes later, there was another knock at the door, this time it was Gus. Ben was glad to see him. "Hey, Gus, come on in and sit down." Gus came in and sat in the same chair Archie had just left.

They stared at each other for a moment, and then Gus spoke, "So how you feeling?"

"Great."

"You're ready to do this?"

"Absolutely."

"Ben, I have to ask you something, and I want you to feel you can be completely straight with me."

Ben looked a little confused. "OK."

"Where do you think this marriage should leave me? I mean, really, Ben, now that you're going to have a wife, would it be better for you if I was out of the picture? I suppose I could go back to the States."

Ben thought for a minute. "Do you want to go back to the States, Gus?"

"No, not really, but I don't want to get in your way either. Things are going to be different now."

"That's true, but I really don't see why marrying Barbara would have any affect on your presence here. In all the months we've been seeing each other, and in the last couple of months when we have talked seriously of marriage, your being here has never come up as an issue. Barbara recognizes you're my closest friend and part of my family, wherever I go. I can tell you, Gus, I would really prefer you stay with me, but if you want to go back to the States or anywhere else, you know you can go."

"But you're saying that you really rather I stay?"

"That's what I'm saying."

Gus smiled, "Then, you know I'm staying."

The two men stood up and embraced, and as they did Gus said, "Congratulations, Ben, I'm really happy for you."

They separated and Ben said, "Thanks, Gus, and thanks for sticking with me all these years."

Gus said, "I'll leave you alone for a few minutes." And left the library.

At ten o'clock Stanley returned to Balmoor with Mr. MacRoiter. He took a few minutes to have a cup of coffee and look around the first floor of the castle.

At eleven everyone gathered in the large drawing room on the first floor. It was the most formal room in the castle and for this occasion it had been filled with fresh flowers.

Present in the room were Ben, Gus, Ian MacRoiter, Barbara's mother, sister and brother-in-law, and her friend Marie from the bank, Victor, Stanley and two other household staff. All stood quietly as Barbara entered the room with her father. She was dressed in a simple white dress. Around her neck was a diamond necklace. She carried a beautiful bouquet of flowers. She looked stunning, and Archie had a smile that stretched from ear to ear. They walked through the room to where Ben and Gus stood. When they got to Ben, Barbara removed her arm from around her father's, and put it around Ben's. Archie and Ben shook hands and Archie walked over to his wife and stood with her.

Ian MacRoiter started to speak, and it was immediately obvious he had done this many times before. He had no notes, but he spoke clearly, fluently, and kindly about marriage and what a wonderful institution it was when entered into by two people who really loved each other. He spoke for about ten minutes, and the entire ceremony lasted a total of fifteen minutes.

Following the ceremony, everyone enjoyed a wonderful meal, and at two o'clock Ben and Barbara said good-bye and walked to the helicopter, which was now parked on the south lawn having already shuttled all the luggage over to the yacht.

The ride to the yacht took only a few minutes, and by two-twenty the helicopter had been secured on its pad, and the boat was under way heading south. Ben and Barbara stood on the back deck, each holding a glass of champagne as the boat eased through the water.

Barbara finished her champagne and said, "I'm going down to change."

Ben kissed her on the cheek. "Go ahead, I'll be down in a minute. Don't change too quickly." He smiled with a little twinkle in his eye.

Barbara put on a mock look of surprise, "But, darling, it's the middle of the day!"

Ben laughed, "You're right, Mrs. Nathan, I suppose we should wait until dark just to be respectable."

She put her arms around him. "Not on your life, Mr. Nathan. If you're not down in five minutes, I'll be up here naked as a jay bird looking for you." She kissed him lightly.

He looked into her eyes and saw the same desire he felt himself. "That won't be necessary," he said softly. She turned, and walked away.

Ben looked back over at the castle in the distance. He thought about how difficult it had become after so many years to experience anything that was truly *ne*w. But today was one of those days. He had a wife he loved, and who would now be his partner for what he hoped would be a long time. He knew in a few minutes they would be making love, and he was already basking in the pleasure of thinking about it. He put his glass down next to Barbara's on a small table, and walked into the main cabin of the boat. He knew he was about to start a new chapter in his life.

Chapter 114

Vinnie DeRoma poured over the information several times. He could not ignore the conclusion the information drew him to. Somewhere out there was a man who possibly has been alive for thousands of years. It was impossible for him to just forget it, but he didn't feel it was something that he wanted to bring to everyone else's attention. He had deliberated within himself for days, and he finally decided on a course of action.

His trust fund had been producing almost two hundred thousand dollars a year in earnings for the last seven years, so Vinnie was already financially independent. He loved his work as a detective, but this was too big to forget. He could always come back to his work later.

It was late at night and there was no one in the squad room at the moment. He left a letter on the Lieutenant's desk explaining his need to take some time away from the job. He asked the Lieutenant to consider it as a sabbatical, although he couldn't say when he would be back. If that wasn't possible, he realized it would have to be considered his resignation from the force. He left the letter with his badge and service weapon on the desk.

On Louise's desk he also left a letter. In it, he apologized for leaving in the middle of the night without talking to her. He thanked her for her help, and told her how much he enjoyed working with her.

As he reached the exit, he turned back and looked at the squad room that had been his home for barely two months. He had no idea what he was going to find, or what he was going to do once he found it. He had purchased a one-way ticket to England, and his flight departed tomorrow morning. He didn't know when he would be back, or even if he would be back.

He looked at it as a new chapter in his life.

***